EVERYBODY
Loves Flashman!

SIGNET Books You'll Want to Read

FLASHMAN

From the Flashman Papers
1839-1842

Edited and Arranged by
GEORGE MACDONALD FRASER

A SIGNET BOOK from
NEW AMERICAN LIBRARY
TIMES MIRROR

for Kath

Explanatory Note

The great mass of manuscript known as the Flashman Papers was discovered during a sale of household furniture at Ashby, Leicestershire, in 1965. The papers were subsequently claimed by Mr Paget Morrison, of Durban, South Africa, the nearest known living relative of their author.

A point of major literary interest about the papers is that they clearly identify Flashman, the school bully of Thomas Hughes' *Tom Brown's Schooldays,* with the celebrated Victorian soldier of the same name. The papers are, in fact, Harry Flashman's personal memoirs from the day of his expulsion from Rugby School in the late 1830's to the early years of the present century. He appears to have written them some time between 1900 and 1905, when he must have been over eighty. It is possible that he dictated them.

The papers, which had apparently lain untouched for fifty years, in a tea chest, until they were found in the Ashby sale-room, were carefully wrapped in oilskin covers. From correspondence found in the first packet, it is evident that their original discovery by his relatives in 1915 after the great soldier's death caused considerable consternation; they seem to have been unanimously against publication of their kinsman's autobiography— one can readily understand why—and the only wonder is that the manuscript was not destroyed.

Fortunately, it was preserved, and what follows is the

content of the first packet, covering Flashman's early adventures. I have no reason to doubt that it is a completely truthful account; where Flashman touches on historical fact he is almost invariably accurate, and readers can judge whether he is to be believed or not on more personal matters.

Mr Paget Morrison, knowing of my interest in this and related subjects, asked me to edit the papers. Beyond correcting some minor spelling errors, however, there has been no editing to do. Flashman had a better sense of narrative than I have, and I have confined myself to the addition of a few historical notes.

The quotation from *Tom Brown's Schooldays* was pasted to the top page of the first packet; it had evidently been cut from the original edition of 1856.

G.M.F.

FLASHMAN, Harry Paget. Brigadier-general, V.C., K.C.B., K.C.I.E.; Chevalier, Legion of Honour; U.S. Medal of Honor; San Serafino Order of Purity and Truth, 4th Class. b. 1822, s. H. Flashman, Esq., Ashby, and Hon. Alicia Paget; educ. Rugby School. m. Elspeth Rennie Morrison, d. Lord Paisley; one s., one d. Served Afghanistan, 1841-42 (medals, thanks of Parliament); Crimea (staff); Indian Mutiny (Lucknow, etc., V.C.); China, Taiping Rebellion. Served U.S. Army (major, Union forces, 1862; colonel [staff] Army of the Confederacy, 1863). Travelled extensively in military and civilian capacities; a.d.c., Emperor Maximilian of Mexico; milit. adviser, H.M. Queen Ranavalona of Madagascar; chief of staff to Rajah of Sarawak; dep. marshal, U.S. Chmn, Flashman and Bottomley, Ltd.; dir. British Opium Trading Co.; governor, Rugby School; hon. pres. Mission for Reclamation of Reduced Females. Publications: Dawns and Departures of a Soldier's Life; Twixt Cossack and Cannon; The Case Against Army Reform. Clubs: White's, United Service, Blackjack (Batavia). Recreation: oriental studies, angling. Add.: Gandamack Lodge, Ashby, Leics.

One fine summer evening Flashman had been regaling himself on gin-punch, at Brownsover; and, having exceeded his usual limits, started home uproarious. He fell in with a friend or two coming back from bathing, proposed a glass of beer, to which they assented, the weather being hot, and they thirsty souls, and unaware of the quantity of drink which Flashman had already on board. The short result was, that Flashy became beastly drunk. They tried to get him along, but couldn't; so they chartered a hurdle and two men to carry him. One of the masters came upon them, and they naturally enough fled. The flight of the rest excited the master's suspicions, and the good angel of the fags incited him to examine the freight, and, after examination, to convoy the hurdle himself up to the School-house; and the Doctor, who had long had his eye on Flashman, arranged for his withdrawal next morning.

—THOMAS HUGHES, *Tom Brown's Schooldays.*

Hughes got it wrong, in one important detail. You will have read, in *Tom Brown*, how I was expelled from Rugby School for drunkenness, which is true enough, but when Hughes alleges that this was the result of my deliberately pouring beer on top of gin-punch, he is in error. I knew better than to mix my drinks, even at seventeen.

I mention this, not in self-defence, but in the interests of strict truth. This story will be completely truthful; I am breaking the habit of eighty years. Why shouldn't I? When a man is as old as I am, and knows himself thoroughly for what he was and is, he doesn't care much. I'm not ashamed, you see; never was—and I have enough on what Society would consider the credit side of the ledger—a knighthood, a Victoria Cross, high rank, and some popular fame. So I can look at the picture above my desk, of the young officer in Cardigan's Hussars; tall, masterful, and roughly handsome I was in those days (even Hughes allowed that I was big and strong, and had considerable powers of being pleasant), and say that it is the portrait of a scoundrel, a liar, a cheat, a thief, a coward—and, oh yes, a toady. Hughes said more or less all these things, and his description was pretty fair, except in matters of detail such as the one I've mentioned. But he was more concerned to preach a sermon than to give facts.

But I am concerned with facts, and since many of them are discreditable to me, you can rest assured they are true.

At all events, Hughes was wrong in saying I suggested beer. It was Speedicut who ordered it up, and I had drunk it (on top of all those gin-punches) before I knew what I was properly doing. That finished me; I was really drunk then—"beastly drunk," says Hughes, and he's right—and when they got me out of the "Grapes" I could hardly see, let alone walk. They bundled me into a sedan, and then a beak hove in sight and Speedicut lived up to his name and

11

bolted. I was left sprawling in the chair, and up came the master and saw me. It was old Rufton, one of Arnold's housemasters.

"Good God!" he said. "It's one of our boys—drunk!"

I can still see him goggling at me, with his great pale gooseberry eyes and white whiskers. He tried to rouse me, but he might as well have tried to wake a corpse. I just lay and giggled at him. Finally he lost his temper, and banged the top of the chair with his cane and shouted:

"Take him up, chairmen! Take him to the School! He shall go before the Doctor for this!"

So they bore me off in procession, with old Rufton raging behind about disgusting excesses and the wages of sin, and old Thomas and the chairmen took me to the hospital, which was appropriate, and left me on a bed to sober up. It didn't take me long, I can tell you, as soon as my mind was clear enough to think what would come of it. You know what Arnold was like, if you have read Hughes, and he had no use for me at the best of times. The least I could expect was a flogging before the school.

That was enough to set me in a blue funk, at the very thought, but what I was really afraid of was Arnold himself.

They left me in the hospital perhaps two hours, and then old Thomas came to say the Doctor wanted to see me. I followed him downstairs and across to the School-house, with the fags peeping round corners and telling each other that the brute Flashy had fallen at last, and old Thomas knocked at the Doctor's door, and the voice crying "Come in!" sounded like the crack of doom to me.

He was standing before the fireplace, with his hands behind looping up his coat-tails, and a face like a Turk at a christening. He had eyes like sabre-points, and his face was pale and carried that disgusted look that he kept for these occasions. Even with the liquor still working on me a little I was as scared in that minute as I've ever been in my life—and when you have ridden into a Russian battery at Balaclava and been chained in an Afghan dungeon waiting for the torturers, as I have, you know what fear means. I still feel uneasy when I think of him, and he's been dead sixty years.

He was live enough then. He stood silent a moment, to let me stew a little. Then:

"Flashman," says he, "there are many moments in a schoolmaster's life when he must make a decision, and afterwards wonder whether he was right or not. I have made a decision, and for once I am in no doubt that I *am* right. I have observed you for several years now, with increasing concern. You have been an evil influence in the school. That you are a bully, I know; that you are untruthful, I have long suspected; that you are deceitful and mean, I have feared; but that you had fallen so low as to be a drunkard—that, at least, I never imagined. I have looked in the past for some signs of improvement in you, some spark of grace, some ray of hope that my work here had not, in your case, been unsuccessful. It has not come, and this is the final infamy. Have you anything to say?"

He had me blubbering by this time; I mumbled something about being sorry.

"If I thought for one moment," says he, "that you *were* sorry, that you had it in you to show *true* repentance, I might hesitate from the step that I am about to take. But I know you too well, Flashman. You must leave Rugby to-morrow."

If I had had my wits about me I suppose I should have thought this was no bad news, but with Arnold thundering I lost my head.

"But, sir," I said, still blubbering, "it will break my mother's heart!"

He went pale as a ghost, and I fell back. I thought he was going to hit me.

"Blasphemous wretch!" he cried—he had a great pulpit trick with phrases like those—"your mother has been dead these many years, and do you dare to plead her name—a name that should be sacred to you—in defence of your abominations? You have killed any spark of pity I had for you!"

"My father—"

"Your father," says he, "will know how to deal with you. I hardly think," he added, with a look, "that his heart will be broken." He knew something of my father, you see, and probably thought we were a pretty pair.

He stood there drumming his fingers behind him a moment, and then he said, in a different voice:

"You are a sorry creature, Flashman. I have failed in you. But even to you I must say, this is not the end. You cannot continue here, but you are young, Flashman, and there is time yet. Though your sins be as red as crimson, yet shall they be as white as snow. You have fallen very low, but you can be raised up again. . . ."

14 GEORGE MACDONALD FRASER

I haven't a good memory for sermons, and he went on like this for some time, like the pious old hypocrite that he was. For he was a hypocrite, I think, like most of his generation. Either that or he was more foolish than he looked, for he was wasting his piety on me. But he never realised it.

Anyway, he gave me a fine holy harangue, about how through repentance I might be saved—which I've never believed, by the way. I've repented a good deal in my time, and had good cause, but I was never ass enough to suppose it mended anything. But I've learned to swim with the tide when I have to, so I let him pray over me, and when he had finished I left his study a good deal happier than when I went in. I had escaped flogging, which was the main thing; leaving Rugby I didn't mind a button. I never much cared for the place, and the supposed disgrace of expulsion I didn't even think about. (They had me back a few years ago to present prizes; nothing was said about expulsion *then*, which shows that they are just as big hypocrites now as they were in Arnold's day. I made a speech, too; on Courage, of all things.)

I left the school next morning, in the gig, with my box on top, and they were damned glad to see me go, I expect. Certainly the fags were; I'd given them toco in my time. And who should be at the gate (to gloat, I thought at first, but it turned out otherwise) but the bold Scud East. He even offered me his hand.

"I'm sorry, Flashman," he said.

I asked him what he had to be sorry for, and damned his impudence.

"Sorry you're being expelled," says he.

"You're a liar," says I. "And damn your sorrow, too."

He looked at me, and then turned on his heel and walked off. But I know now that I misjudged him then; he *was* sorry, heaven knows why. He'd no cause to love me, and if I had been him I'd have been throwing my cap in the air and hurrahing. But he was soft: one of Arnold's sturdy fools, manly little chaps, of course, and full of virtue, the kind that schoolmasters love. Yes, he was a fool then, and a fool twenty years later, when he died in the dust at Cawnpore with a Sepoy's bayonet in his back. Honest Scud East; that was all that his gallant goodness did for *him*.

I didn't linger on the way home. I knew my father was in London, and I wanted to get over as soon as I could the painful business of telling him I had been kicked out of Rugby. So I decided to ride to town, letting my bags follow, and hired a horse accordingly at the "George". I am one of those who rode as soon as he walked—indeed, horsemanship and my trick of picking up foreign tongues have been the only things in which you could say I was born gifted, and very useful they have been.

So I rode to town, puzzling over how my father would take the good news. He was an odd fish, the guv'nor, and he and I had always been wary of each other. He was a nabob's grandson, you see, old Jack Flashman having made a fortune in America out of slaves and rum, and piracy, too, I shouldn't wonder, and buying the place in Leicestershire where we have lived ever since. But for all their moneybags, the Flashmans were never the thing— "the coarse streak showed through, generation after generation, like dung beneath a rosebush," as Greville said. In other words, while other nabob families tried to make themselves pass for quality, ours didn't, because we couldn't. My own father was the first to marry well, for my mother was related to the Pagets, who as everyone knows sit on the right hand of God. As a consequence he kept an eye on me to see if I gave myself airs; before mother died he never saw much of me, being too busy at the clubs or in the House or hunting—foxes sometimes, but women mostly—but after that he had to take some interest in his heir, and we grew to know and mistrust each other.

He was a decent enough fellow in his way, I suppose, pretty rough and with the devil's own temper, but well enough liked in his set, which was country-squire with enough money to pass in the West End. He enjoyed some lingering fame through having gone a number of rounds with Cribb, in his youth, though it's my belief that Champion Tom went easy with him because of his cash. He lived half in town, half in country now, and kept an expensive house, but he was out of politics, having been sent to the knacker's yard at Reform. He was still occupied, though, what with brandy and the tables, and hunting—both kinds.

I was feeling pretty uneasy, then, when I ran up the steps and hammered on the front door. Oswald, the butler, raised a great cry when he saw who it was, because it was nowhere near the end of the half, and this brought other servants: they scented scandal, no doubt.

"My father's home?" I asked, giving Oswald my coat and straightening my neck-cloth.

"Your father, to be sure, Mr Harry," cried Oswald, all smiles. "In the saloon this minute!" He threw open the door, and cried out: "Mr Harry's home, sir!"

My father had been sprawled on a settee, but he jumped up when he saw me. He had a glass in his hand and his face was flushed, but since both those things were usual it was hard to say whether he was drunk or not. He stared at me, and then greeted the prodigal with:

"What the hell are you doing here?"

At most times this kind of welcome would have taken me aback, but not now. There was a woman in the room, and she distracted my attention. She was a tall, handsome, hussy-looking piece, with brown hair piled up on her head and a come-and-catch-me look in her eye. "This is the new one," I thought, for you got used to his string of madames; they changed as fast as the sentries at St James'.

She was looking at me with a lazy, half-amused smile that sent a shiver up my back at the same time as it made me conscious of the schoolboy cut of my clothes. But it stiffened me, too, all in an instant, so that I answered his question pat:

"I've been expelled," I said, as cool as I could.

"Expelled? D'ye mean thrown out? What the devil for, sir?"

"Drunkenness, mainly."

"Mainly? Good God!" He was going purple. He looked from the woman back to me, as though seeking enlightenment. She seemed much amused by it, but seeing the old fellow in danger of explosion I made haste to explain what had happened. I was truthful enough, except that I made rather more of my interview with Arnold than was the case; to hear me you would suppose I had given as good as I got. Seeing the female eyeing me I acted pretty offhand, which was risky, perhaps, with the guv'nor in his present mood. But to my surprise he took it pretty well; he had never liked Arnold, of course.

"Well, I'm damned!" he said, when I had finished, and poured himself another glass. He wasn't grinning, but his brow had cleared. "You young dog! A pretty state of things, indeed. Expelled in disgrace, by gad! Did he flog you? No? I'd have had the hide off your back—perhaps I will, damme!" But he was smiling now, a bit sour, though. "What d'you make of this, Judy?" he said to the woman.

"I take it this is a relative?" she says, letting her fan droop towards me. She had a deep husky voice, and I shivered again.

"Relative? Eh? Oh, dammit, it's my son Harry, girl! Harry, this is Judy. . . . er, Miss Parsons."

She smiled at me now, still with that half-amused look, and I preened myself—I was seventeen, remember—and sized up her points while the father got himself another glass and damned Arnold for a puritan hedge-priest. She was what is called junoesque, broad-shouldered and full-breasted, which was less common then than it is now, and it seemed to me she liked the look of Harry Flashman.

"Well," said my father at last, when he had finished fulminating against the folly of putting prigs and scholars in charge of public schools. "Well, what's to be done with you, eh? What'll you do, sir? Now that you've disgraced the home with your beastliness, eh?"

I had been thinking this over on my way home, and said straight out that I fancied the army.

"The army?" he growled. "You mean I'm to buy you colours so that you can live like a king and ruin me with bills at the Guards' Club, I suppose?"

"Not the Guards," I said. "I've a notion for the 11th Light Dragoons."

He stared at this. "You've chosen a regiment already? By gad, here's a cool hand!"

I knew the 11th were at Canterbury, after long service in India, and unlikely for that reason to be posted abroad. I had my own notions of soldiering. But this was too fast for the guv'nor; he went on about the expense of buying in, and the cost of army life, and worked back to my expulsion and my character generally, and so back to the army again. The port was making him quarrelsome, I could see, so I judged it best not to press him. He growled on:

"Dragoons, damme! D'ye know what a cornet's commission costs? Damned nonsense. Never heard the like. Impudence, eh, Judy?"

Miss Judy observed that I might look very well as a dashing dragoon.

"Eh?" said my father, and gave her a queer look. "Aye, like enough he would. We'll see." He looked moodily at me. "In the meantime, you can get to your bed," he said. "We'll talk of this tomorrow. For the moment you're still in disgrace." But as I left them I could hear him blackguarding Arnold again, so I went to bed well pleased, and relieved into the bargain. He was an odd fish, all right; you could never tell how he would take anything.

In the morning, though, when I met my father at breakfast, there was no talk of the army. He was too busy damning Brougham—who had, I gathered, made a violent attack on the Queen in the House[1]—and goggling over some scandal about Lady Flora Hastings[2] in the *Post*, to give me much attention, and left presently for his club. Anyway, I was content to let the matter rest just now; I have always believed in one thing at a time, and the thing that was occupying my mind was Miss Judy Parsons.

Let me say that while there have been hundreds of women in my life, I have never been one of those who are forever boasting about their conquests. I've raked and ridden harder than most, no doubt, and there are probably a number of middle-aged men and women who could answer to the name of Flashman if only they knew it. That's by the way; unless you are the kind who falls in love—which I've never been—you take your tumbles when you've the chance, and the more the better. But Judy has a close bearing on my story.

I was not inexperienced with women; there had been maids at home and a country girl or two, but Judy was a woman of the world, and that I hadn't attempted. Not that I was concerned on that account, for I fancied myself (and rightly) pretty well. I was big and handsome enough for any of them, but being my father's mistress she might think it too risky to frolic with the son. As it turned out, she wasn't frightened of the guv'nor or anyone else.

She lived in the house—the young Queen was newly on the throne then, and people still behaved as they had under the Prince Regent and King Billy; not like later on, when mistresses had to stay out of sight. I went up to her room before noon to spy out the land, and found her still in bed, reading the papers. She was glad to see me, and we talked, and from the way she looked and laughed and let me toy with her hand I knew it was only a question of finding the time. There was an abigail fussing about the room, or I'd have gone for her then and there.

However, it seemed my father would be at the club that night, and playing late, as he often did, so I agreed to come back and play écarte with her in the evening. Both of us knew it wouldn't be cards we would be playing. Sure enough, when I did come back, she was sitting prettying herself before her glass, wearing a bedgown that would have made me a small handkerchief. I came straight up behind her, took her big breasts out in either hand, stopped her gasp with my mouth, and pushed her on to the bed. She was as eager as I was, and we bounced about in rare style, first one on top and then the other. Which reminds me of something which has stayed in my head, as these things will: when it was over, she was sitting astride me, naked and splendid, tossing the hair out of her eyes —suddenly she laughed, loud and clearly, the way one does at a good joke. I believed then she was laughing with pleasure, and thought myself a hell of a fellow, but I feel sure now she was laughing *at* me. I was seventeen, you remember, and doubtless she found it amusing to know how pleased with myself I was.

Later we played cards, for form's sake, and she won, and then I had to sneak off because my father came home early. Next day I tried her again, but this time, to my surprise, she slapped my hands and said: "No, no, my boy; once for fun, but not twice. I've a position to keep up here." Meaning my father, and the chance of servants gossiping, I supposed.

I was annoyed at this, and got ugly, but she laughed at me again. I lost my temper, and tried to blackmail her by threatening to let my father find out about the night before, but she just curled her lip.

"You wouldn't dare," she said. "And if you did, I wouldn't care."

"Wouldn't you?" I said. "If he threw you out, you slut?"

"My, the brave little man," she mocked me. "I misjudged you. At first sight I thought you were just another noisy brute like your father, but I see you've a strong streak of the cur in you as well. Let me tell you he's twice the man you are—in bed or out of it."

"I was good enough for you, you bitch," I said.

"Once," she said, and dropped me a mock curtsey. "That was enough. Now get out, and stick to servant girls after this."

I went in a black rage, slamming the door, and spent the next hour striding about the Park, planning what I would do to her if ever I had the chance. After a while my anger passed, and I just put Miss Judy away in a corner of my mind, as one to be paid off when the chance came.

Oddly enough, the affair worked to my advantage. Whether some wind of what had happened on the first night got to my father's ears, or whether he just caught something in the air, I don't know, but I suspect it was the second; he was shrewd, and had my own gift of sniffing the wind. Whatever it was, his manner towards me changed abruptly; from harking back to my expulsion and treating me fairly offhand, he suddenly seemed sulky at me, and I caught him giving me odd looks, which he would hurriedly shift away, as though he were embarrassed.

Anyway, within four days of my coming home, he suddenly announced that he had been thinking about my notion of the army, and had decided to buy me a pair of colours. I was to go over to the Horse Guards to see my Uncle Bindley, my mother's brother, who would arrange matters. Obviously, my father wanted me out of the house, and quickly, so I pinned him then and there, while the iron was hot, on the matter of an allowance. I asked for £500 a year to add to my pay, and to my astonishment he agreed without discussion. I cursed myself for not asking £750, but £500 was twice what I'd expected, and far more than enough, so I was pretty pleased, and set off for Horse Guards in a good humour.

A lot has been said about the purchase of commissions —how the rich and incompetent can buy ahead of better men, how the poor and efficient are passed over—and most of it, in my experience, is rubbish. Even with purchase abolished, the rich rise faster in the Service than the poor, and they're both inefficient anyway, as a rule. I've seen ten men's share of service, through no fault of my own, and can say that most officers are bad, and the higher you go, the worse they get, myself included. We were supposed to be rotten with incompetence in the Crimea, for example, when purchase was at its height, but the bloody mess they made in South Africa recently seems to have been just as bad—and they didn't buy their commissions.

However, at this time I'd no thought beyond being a humble cornet, and living high in a crack regiment, which was one of the reasons I had fixed on the 11th Dragoons. Also, that they were close to town.

I said nothing of this to Uncle Bindley, but acted very keen, as though I was on fire to win my spurs against the Mahrattas or the Sikhs. He sniffed, and looked down his nose, which was very high and thin, and said he had never suspected martial ardour in me.

"However, a fine leg in pantaloons and a penchant for folly seem to be all that is required today," he went on. "And you can ride, as I collect?"

"Anything on legs, uncle," says I.

"That is of little consequence, anyway. What concerns me is that you cannot, by report, hold your liquor. You'll agree that being dragged from a Rugby pothouse, reeling, I believe, is no recommendation to an officers' mess?"

I hastened to tell him that the report was exaggerated.

"I doubt it," he said. "The point is, were you silent in your drunken state, or did you rave? A noisy drunkard is intolerable; a passive one may do at a pinch. At least, if he has money; money will excuse virtually any conduct in the army nowadays, it seems."

This was a favourite sneer of his; I may say that my mother's family, while quality, were not over-rich. However, I took it all meekly.

"Yes," he went on, "I've no doubt that with your allowance you will be able either to kill or ruin yourself in a short space of time. At that, you will be no worse than half the subalterns in the service, if no better. Ah, but wait. It was the 11th Light Dragoons, wasn't it?"

"Oh, yes, uncle."

"And you are determined on that regiment?"

"Why, yes," I said, wondering a little.

"Then you may have a little diversion before you go the way of all flesh," said he, with a knowing smile. "Have you, by any chance, heard of the Earl of Cardigan?"

I said I had not, which shows how little I had taken notice of military affairs.

"Extraordinary. He commands the 11th, you know. He

succeeded to the title only a year or so ago, while he was in India with the regiment. A remarkable man. I understand he makes no secret of his intention to turn the 11th into the finest cavalry regiment in the army."

"He sounds like the very man for me," I said, all eagerness.

"Indeed, indeed. Well, we mustn't deny him the service of so ardent a subaltern, must we? Certainly the matter of your colours must be pushed through without delay. I commend your choice, my boy. I'm sure you will find service under Lord Cardigan—ah—both stimulating and interesting. Yes, as I think of it, the combination of his lordship and yourself will be rewarding for you both."

I was too busy fawning on the old fool to pay much heed to what he was saying, otherwise I should have realised that anything that pleased him would probably be bad for me. He prided himself on being above my family, whom he considered boors, with some reason, and had never shown much but distaste for me personally. Helping me to my colours was different, of course; he owed that as a duty to a blood relation, but he paid it without enthusiasm. Still, I had to be civil as butter to him, and pretend respect.

It paid me, for I got my colours in the 11th with surprising speed. I put it down entirely to influence, for I was not to know then that over the past few months there had been a steady departure of officers from the regiment, sold out, transferred, and posted—and all because of Lord Cardigan, whom my uncle had spoken of. If I had been a little older, and moved in the right circles, I should have heard all about him, but in the few weeks of waiting for my commission my father sent me up to Leicestershire, and the little time I had in town I spent either by myself or in the company of such of my relatives as could catch me. My mother had had sisters, and although they disliked me heartily they felt it was their duty to look after the poor motherless boy. So they said; in fact they suspected that if I were left to myself I would take to low company, and they were right.

However, I was to find out about Lord Cardigan soon enough.

In the last few days of buying my uniforms, assembling the huge paraphernalia that an officer needed in those days —far more than now—choosing a couple of horses, and arranging for my allowance, I still found time on my hands, and Mistress Judy in my thoughts. My tumble with her had only whetted my appetite for more of her, I discovered; I tried to get rid of it with a farm girl in Leicestershire and a young whore in Covent Garden, but the one stank and the other picked my pocket afterwards, and neither was any substitute anyway. I wanted Judy, at the same time as I felt spite for her, but she had avoided me since our quarrel and if we met in the house she simply ignored me.

In the end it got too much, and the night before I left I went to her room again, having made sure the guv'nor was out. She was reading, and looking damned desirable in a pale green negligée; I was a little drunk, and the sight of her white shoulders and red mouth sent the old tingle down my spine again.

"What do you want?" she said, very icy, but I was expecting that, and had my speech ready.

"I've come to beg pardon," I said, looking a bit hangdog. "Tomorrow I go away, and before I went I had to apologise for the way I spoke to you. I'm sorry, Judy; I truly am; I acted like a cad and . . . and a ruffian, and, well . . . I want to make what amends I can. That's all."

She put down her book and turned on her stool to face me, still looking mighty cold, but saying nothing. I shuffled like a sheepish schoolboy—I could see my reflection in the mirror behind her, and judge how the performance was going—and said again that I was sorry.

"Very well, then," she said at last. "You're sorry. You have cause to be."

I kept quiet, not looking at her.

"Well, then," she said, after a pause. "Goodnight."

"Please, Judy," I said, looking distraught. "You make it very hard. If I behaved like a boor—"

"You did."

"—it was because I was angry and hurt and didn't understand why . . . why you wouldn't let me . . ." I let it trail off and then burst out that I had never known a woman like her before, and that I had fallen in love with her, and only came to ask her pardon because I couldn't bear the thought of her detesting me, and a good deal more in the same strain—simple enough rubbish, you may think, but I was still learning. At that, the mirror told me I was doing well. I finished by drawing myself up straight, and looking solemn, and saying:

"And that is why I had to see you again . . . to tell you. And to ask your pardon."

I gave her a little bow, and turned to the door, rehearsing how I would stop and look back if she didn't stop me. But she took me at face value, for as I put my hand to the latch she said:

"Harry." I turned round, and she was smiling a little, and looking sad. Then she smiled properly, and shook her head and said:

"Very well, Harry, if you want my pardon, for what it's worth you have it. We'll say no. . . ."

"Judy!" I came striding back, smiling like soul's awakening. "Oh, Judy, thank you!" And I held out my hand, frank and manly.

She got up and took it, smiling still, but there was none of the old wanton glint about her eye. She was being stately and forgiving, like an aunt to a naughty nephew. The nephew, had she known it, was intent on incest.

"Judy," I said, still holding her hand, "we're parting friends?"

"If you like," she said, trying to take it away. "Goodbye, Harry, and good luck."

I stepped closer and kissed her hand, and she didn't seem to mind. I decided, like the fool I was, that the game was won.

"Judy," I said again, "you're adorable. I love you, Judy. If only you knew, you're all I want in a woman. Oh, Judy, you're the most beautiful thing, all bum, belly and bust, I love you."

And I grabbed her to me, and she pulled free and got away from me.

"No!" she said, in a voice like steel.

"Why the hell not?" I shouted.

"Go away!" she said, pale and with eyes like daggers. "Goodnight!"

"Goodnight be damned," says I. "I thought you said we were parting friends? This ain't very friendly, is it?"

She stood glaring at me, but if they had seen Judy agitated in a negligée they would think of some other way of describing feminine distress.

"I was a fool to listen to you for a moment," she says. "Leave this room at once!"

"All in good time," says I, and with a quick dart I caught her round the waist. She struck at me, but I ducked it, and we fell on the bed together. I had hold of the softness of her, and it maddened me. I caught her wrist as she struck at me again, like a tigress, and got my mouth on hers, and she bit me on the lip for all she was worth.

I yelped and broke away, holding my mouth, and she, raging and panting, grabbed up some china dish and let fly at me. It missed by a long chalk, but it helped my temper over the edge completely. I lost control of myself altogether.

"You bitch!" I shouted, and hit her across the face as hard as I could. She staggered, and I hit her again, and she went clean over the bed and on to the floor on the other side. I looked round for something to go after her with, a cane or a whip, for I was in a frenzy and would have cut her to bits if I could. But there wasn't one handy, and by the time I had got round the bed to her it had flashed across my mind that the house was full of servants and my full reckoning with Miss Judy had better be postponed to another time.

I stood over her, glaring and swearing, and she pulled herself up by a chair, holding her face. But she was game enough.

"You coward!" was all she would say. "You coward!"

"It's not cowardly to punish an insolent whore!" says I. "D'you want some more?"

She was crying—not sobbing, but with tears on her cheeks. She went over to her chair by the mirror, pretty unsteady, and sat down and looked at herself. I cursed her again, calling her the choicest names I could think of, but she worked at her cheek, which was red and bruised, with a hare's foot, and paid no heed. She did not speak at all.

"Well, be damned to you!" says I, at length, and with that I slammed out of the room. I was shaking with rage, and the pain in my lip, which was bleeding badly, reminded me that she had paid for my blows in advance. But she had got something in return, at all events; she would not forget Harry Flashman in a hurry.

The 11th Light Dragoons at this time were newly back from India, where they had been serving since before I was born. They were a fighting regiment, and—I say it without regimental pride, for I never had any, but as a plain matter of fact—probably the finest mounted troops in England, if not in the world. Yet they had been losing officers, since coming home, hand over fist. The reason was James Brudenell, Earl of Cardigan.

You have heard all about him, no doubt. The regimental scandals, the Charge of the Light Brigade, the vanity, stupidity, and extravagance of the man—these things are history. Like most history, they have a fair basis of fact. But I knew him, probably as few other officers knew him, and in turn I found him amusing, frightening, vindictive, charming, and downright dangerous. He was God's own original fool, there's no doubt of that—although he was not to blame for the fiasco at Balaclava; that was Raglan and Airey between them. And he was arrogant as no other man I've ever met, and as sure of his own unshakable rightness as any man could be—even when his wrong-headedness was there for all to see. That was his great point, the key to his character: he could never be wrong.

They say that at least he was brave. He was not. He was just stupid, too stupid ever to be afraid. Fear is an emotion, and his emotions were all between his knees and his breast-bone; they never touched his reason, and he had little enough of that.

For all that, he could never be called a bad soldier. Some human faults are military virtues, like stupidity, and arrogance, and narrow-mindedness. Cardigan blended all three with a passion for detail and accuracy; he was a perfectionist, and the manual of cavalry drill was his Bible. Whatever rested between the covers of that book he could perform, or cause to be performed, with marvellous efficiency, and God help anyone who marred that per-

formance. He would have made a first-class drill sergeant
—only a man with a mind capable of such depths of folly
could have led six regiments into the Valley at Balaclava.

However, I devote some space to him because he played
a not unimportant part in the career of Harry Flashman,
and since it is my purpose to show how the Flashman of
Tom Brown became the glorious Flashman with four
inches in *Who's Who* and grew markedly worse in the
process, I must say that he was a good friend to me. He
never understood me, of course, which is not surprising. I
took good care not to let him.

When I met him in Canterbury I had already given a
good deal of thought to how I should conduct myself in
the army. I was bent on as much fun and vicious amusement as I could get—my contemporaries, who praise God
on Sundays and sneak off to child-brothels during the week,
would denounce it piously as vicious, anyway—but I have
always known how to behave to my superiors and shine in
their eyes, a trait of mine which Hughes pointed out, bless
him. This I had determined on, and since the little I knew
of Cardigan told me that he prized smartness and show
above all things, I took some pains over my arrival in
Canterbury.

I rolled up to regimental headquarters in a coach, resplendent in my new uniform, and with my horses led behind and a wagon-load of gear. Cardigan didn't see me ar-
rive, unfortunately, but word must have been carried to
him, for when I was introduced to him in his orderly
room he was in good humour.

"Haw-haw," said he, as we shook hands. "It is Mr
Fwashman. How-de-do, sir. Welcome to the wegiment. A
good turn-out, Jones," he went on to the officer at his
elbow. "I delight to see a smart officer. Mr Fwashman,
how tall are you?"

"Six feet, sir," I said, which was near enough right.

"Haw-haw. And how heavy do you wide, sir?"

I didn't know, but I guessed at twelve and a half stone.

"Heavy for a light dwagoon," said he, shaking his head.
"But there are compensations. You have a pwoper figure,
Mr Fwashman, and bear yourself well. Be attentive to
your duties and we shall deal very well together. Where
have you hunted?"

"In Leicestershire, my lord," I said.

"Couldn't be better," says he. "Eh, Jones? Very good,
Mr Fwashman—hope to see more of you. Haw-haw."

Now, no one in my life that I could remember had ever been so damned civil to me, except toad-eaters like Speedicut, who didn't count. I found myself liking his lordship, and did not realise that I was seeing him at his best. In this mood, he was a charming man enough, and looked well. He was taller than I, straight as a lance, and very slender, even to his hands. Although he was barely forty, he was already bald, with a bush of hair above either ear and magnificent whiskers. His nose was beaky and his eyes blue and prominent and unwinking—they looked out on the world with that serenity which marks the nobleman whose uttermost ancestor was born a nobleman, too. It is the look that your *parvenu* would give half his fortune for, that unrufflable gaze of the spoiled child of fortune who knows with unshakeable certainty that he is right and that the world is exactly ordered for his satisfaction and pleasure. It is the look that makes underlings writhe and causes revolutions. I saw it then, and it remained changeless as long as I knew him, even through the roll-call beneath Causeway Heights when the grim silence as the names were shouted out testified to the loss of five hundred of his command. "It was no fault of mine," he said then, and he didn't just believe it; he knew it.

I was to see him in a different mood before the day was out, but fortunately I was not the object of his wrath; quite the reverse, in fact.

I was shown about the camp by the officer of the day, a fair young captain, named Reynolds,[3] with a brick-red face from service in India. Professionally, he was a good soldier, but quiet and no blood at all. I was fairly offhand with him, and no doubt insolent, but he took it without comment, confining himself to telling me what was what, finding me a servant, and ending at the stables where my mare—whom I had christened Judy, by the way—and charger were being housed.

The grooms had Judy trimmed up with her best leather-work—and it was the best that the smartest saddler in London could show—and Reynolds was admiring her, when who should ride up but my lord in the devil of a temper. He reined in beside us, and pointed with a hand that shook with fury to a troop that had just come in, under their sergeant, to the stable yard.

"Captain Weynolds!" he bawled, and his face was scarlet. "Is this your twoop?"

Reynolds said it was.

"And do you see their sheepskins?" bawled Cardigan. These were the saddle sheepskins. "Do you see them, sir? What colour are they, I should like to know? Will you tell me, sir?"

"White, my lord."

"White, you say? Are you a fool, sir? Are you colour-blind? They are not white, they are yellow—with inattention and slovenliness and neglect! They are filthy, I tell you."

Reynolds stood silent, and Cardigan raged on.

"This was no doubt very well in India, where you learned what you probably call your duty. I will not have it here, do you understand, sir?" His eye rolled round the stable and rested on Judy. "Whose horse is this?" he demanded.

I told him, and he turned in triumph on Reynolds.

"You see, sir, an officer new joined, and he can show you and your other precious fellows from India their duty. Mr Fwashman's sheepskin is white, sir, as yours should be —would be, if you knew anything of discipline and good order. But you don't, sir, I tell you."

"Mr Flashman's sheepskin is new, sir," said Reynolds, which was true enough. "They discolour with age."

"So you make excuses now!" snapped Cardigan. "Haw-haw! I tell you, sir, if you knew your duty they would be cleaned, or if they are too old, wenewed. But you know nothing of this, of course. Your slovenly Indian ways are good enough, I suppose. Well, they will not do, let me tell you! These skins will be cwean tomorrow, d'you hear, sir? Cwean, or I'll hold you wesponsible, Captain Weynolds!"

And with that he rode off, head in the air, and I heard his "Haw-haw" as he greeted someone outside the stable yard.

I felt quite pleased to have been singled out for what was, in effect, praise, and I fancy I said something of this to Reynolds. He looked me up and down, as though seeing me for the first time, and said, in that odd, Welsh-sounding voice that comes with long service in India:

"Ye-es, I can see you will do very well, Mr Flashman. Lord Haw Haw may not like us Indian officers, but he likes plungers, and I've no doubt you'll plunger very prettily."

I asked him what he meant by plunging.

"Oh," says he, "a plunger is a fellow who makes a great turnout, don't you know, and leaves cards at the best houses, and is sought by the mamas, and strolls in the Park very languid, and is just a hell of a swell generally. Sometimes they even condescend to soldier a little—when it doesn't interfere with their social life. Good-day, Mr Flashman."

I could see that Reynolds was jealous, and in my conceit I was well pleased. What he had said, though, was true enough: the regiment was fairly divided between Indian officers—those who had not left since returning home —and the plungers, to whom I naturally attached myself. They hailed me among them, even the noblest, and I knew how to make myself pleasant. I was not as quick with my tongue as I was to become later, but they knew me for a sporting fellow before I had been there long—good on a horse, good with the bottle (for I took some care at first), and ready for mischief. I toadied as seemed best—not openly, of course, but effectively just the same; there is a way of toadying which is better than fawning, and it consists of acting bluff and hearty and knowing to an inch how far to go. And I had money, and showed it.

The Indian officers had a bad time. Cardigan hated them. Reynolds and Forrest were his chief butts, and he was forever pestering them to leave the regiment and make way for gentlemen, as he put it. Why he was so down on those who had served in India, I was never entirely sure; some said it was because they were not of the smart set, or well connected, and this was true up to a point. He was the damnedest snob, but I think his hatred of the Indian officers ran deeper. They were, after all, real soldiers with service experience, and Cardigan had never heard a shot outside the shooting range in his twenty years' service.[4]

Whatever the cause, he made their lives miserable, and there were several resignations in my first six months' service. Even for us plungers it was bad enough, for he was a devil for discipline, and not all the plungers were competent officers. I saw how the wind set, and studied harder than ever I had at Rugby, mastering my drill, which wasn't difficult, and perfecting myself in the rules of camp life. I had got an excellent servant, named Basset, a square-headed oaf who knew everything a soldier ought to know and nothing more, and with a genius for boot-polish. I thrashed him early in our acquaintance, and he seemed to think the better of me for it, and treated me as a dog does its master.

Fortunately, I cut a good figure on parade and at exercise, which was where it counted with Cardigan. Probably only the regimental sergeant major and one or two of the troop-sergeants were my equals on horseback, and his lordship congratulated me once or twice on my riding.

"Haw-haw!" he would say. "Fwashman sits well, I tell you. He will make an aide yet."

I agreed with him. Flashman was sitting very well.

In the mess things went well enough. They were a fast crowd, and the money ran pretty free, for apart from parties and the high state which Cardigan demanded we should keep, there was some heavy gaming. All this expense discouraged the Indian men, which delighted Cardigan, who was forever sneering at them that if they could not keep up with gentlemen they had better return to farming or set themselves up in trade—"selling shoes and pots and pans," he would say, and laugh heartily, as though this were the funniest thing imaginable.

Strangely enough, or perhaps not strangely, his Indian prejudice did not extend to the men. They were a tough lot, and excellent soldiers so far as I could see; he was a tyrant to them, and never a week passed without a court-martial for neglect of duty or desertion or drunkenness. The last offence was common, but not seriously regarded, but for the other two he punished hard. There were frequent floggings at the rings in the side of the riding school, when we all had to attend. Some of the older officers—the Indian ones—grumbled a good deal and pretended to be shocked, but I guessed they would not have missed it. Myself, I liked a good flogging, and used to have bets with Bryant, my particular crony, on whether the man would cry out before the tenth stroke, or when he would faint. It was better sport than most, anyway.

Bryant was a queer little creature who attached himself to me early in my career and clung like a leech. He was your open toady, with little money of his own, but a gift of pleasing and being on hand. He was smart enough, and contrived to cut a decent figure, although never splendid, and he had all the gossip, and knew everybody, and was something of a wit. He shone at the parties and mess nights which we gave for the local society in Canterbury, where he was very forward. He was first with all the news, and could recount it in a fashion that amused Cardigan—not that this was too difficult. I found him useful, and tolerated him accordingly, and used him as a court jester when it suited—he was adept in this role, too. As Forrest said, if you kicked Bryant's arse, he always bounced most obligingly.

He had a considerable gift of spite against the Indian officers, which also endeared him to Cardigan—oh, we were a happy little mess, I can tell you—and earned him their hatred. Most of them despised me, too, along with the other plungers, but we despised them for different reasons, so we were square there.

But to only one officer did I take an active dislike, which was prophetic, and I guessed that he returned it from the first. His name was Bernier, a tall, hard hawk of a man with a big nose and black whiskers and dark eyes set very close. He was the best blade and shot in the regiment, and until I came on the scene the best rider as well. He didn't love me for that, I suppose, but our real hatred dated from the night when he made some reference to nabob families of no breeding, and seemed to me to look in my direction.

I was fairly wine-flown, or I'd have kept my mouth shut, for he looked like what the Americans call a "killing gentleman"—indeed, he was very like an American whom I knew later, the celebrated James Hickok, who was also a deadly shot. But being part tipsy, I said I would rather be a nabob Briton, and take my chance on breeding, than be half-caste foreign. Bryant crowed, as he always did at my jokes, and said: "Bravo, Flash! Old England forever!" and there was general laughter, for my usual heartiness and general bluffness had earned me the name of being something of a John Bull. Bernier only half-caught what I said, for I had kept my voice low so that only those nearest heard, but someone must have told him later, for he never gave me anything but an icy stare from then on, and never spoke to me. He was sensitive about his foreign name—actually, he was a French Jew, if you went back far enough, which accounts for it.

But it was a few months after this incident that I really ran foul of Bernier, and began to make my reputation—the reputation which I still enjoy today. I pass over a good deal of what happened in that first year—Cardigan's quarrel with the *Morning Post,*[5] for example, which had the regiment, and the public generally, in a fine uproar, but in which I had no part—and come to the famous Bernier-Flashman duel, which you will still hear talked about. I think of it only with pride and delight, even now. Only two men ever knew the truth of it, and I was one.

It was a year almost to the day after I left Rugby that I was taking the air in Canterbury, in the Park, and on my way to some mama's house or other to make a call. I was in full fig, and feeling generally pleased with myself, when I spied an officer walking under the trees with a lady, arm in arm. It was Bernier, and I looked to see what heifer he was ploughing with. In fact, she was no heifer, but a wicked-looking little black-haired piece with a turned-up nose and a saucy smile. I studied her, and the great thought formed in my head.

I had had two or three mistresses in Canterbury, off and on, but nothing in particular. Most of the younger officers maintained a paramour in the town or in London, but I had never set up any establishment like that. I guessed that this was Bernier's mare of the moment, and the more I looked at her the more she intrigued me. She looked the kind of plump little puss who would be very knowing in bed, and the fact that she was Bernier's—who fancied himself irresistible to women—would make the tumbling all the sweeter.

I wasted no time, but found out her direction by inquiry, chose my time when Bernier was on duty, and called on the lady. She had a pleasant little retreat, very tastefully furnished, but in no great style: Bernier's purse was less fat than mine, which was an advantage. I pursued it.

She was French herself, it turned out, so I could be more direct than with an English girl. I told her straight out that I had taken a fancy to her, and invited her to consider me as a friend—a close friend. I hinted that I had money—she was only a whore, after all, for all her fashionable airs.

At first she made a show of being shocked, and la-la'd a good deal, but when I made to leave she changed her tune. My money aside, I think she found me to her fancy; she toyed with a fan and looked at me over it with big, almond-shaped eyes, playing the sly minx.

"You have poor opeenion of French girls, then?" says she.

"Not I," says I, charming again. "I've the highest opinion of you, for example. What's your name?"

"Josette." She said it very pretty.

"Well, Josette, let's drink to our future acquaintance—at my expense"—and I dropped my purse on the table, at which her eyes widened. It was not a small purse.

You may think me crude. I was. But I saved time and trouble, and perhaps money, too—the money that fools waste in paying court with presents before the fun begins. She had wine in the house, and we drank to each other and talked a good five minutes before I began to tease her into undressing. She played it very prettily, with much pouting and provocative looks, but when she had stripped she was all fire and wickedness, and I was so impatient I had her without getting out of my chair.

Whether I found her unusually delectable because she was Bernier's mistress or because of her French tricks, I can't say, but I took to visiting her often, and in spite of my respect for Bernier, I was careless. It was within a week, certainly, that we were engaged heavily one evening when there were footsteps on the stair, the door flew open, and there was the man himself. He stood glaring for a moment, while Josette squeaked and dived beneath the covers, and I scrambled to get under the bed in my shirt-tail —the sight of him filled me with panic. But he said nothing; a moment passed, the door slammed, and I came out scrabbling for my breeches. At that moment I wanted only to put as much distance between myself and him as I could, and I dressed in some haste.

Josette began to laugh, and I asked her what the devil amused her.

"It is so fonnee," she giggled. "You . . . you half beneath de bed, and Charles glaring so fierce at your derrière." And she shrieked with laughter.

I told her to hold her tongue, and she stopped laughing and tried to coax me back to bed again, saying that Bernier had undoubtedly gone, and sitting up and shaking her tits at me. I hesitated, between lust and fright, until she hopped out and bolted the door, and then I decided I might as well have my sport while I could, and pulled off my clothes again. But I confess it was not the most joyous pleasuring I have taken part in, although Josette was at her most spirited; I suspect she was thrilled by the situation.

I was in two minds whether to go back to the mess afterwards, for I was sure Bernier must call me out. But, to my surprise, when I pulled my courage together and went in to dinner, he paid me not the slightest notice. I couldn't make it out, and when next day and the next he was still silent, I took heart again, and even paid Josette another visit. She had not seen him, so it seemed to me that he intended to do nothing at all. I decided that he was a poor-spirited thing after all, and had resigned his mistress to me—not, I was sure, out of fear of me, but because he could not bear to have a trollop who cheated him. Of course the truth was that he couldn't call me out without exposing the cause, and making himself look ridiculous; and knowing more of regimental custom than I did, he hesitated to provoke an affair of honour over a mistress. But he was holding himself in with difficulty.

Not knowing this, I took to throwing my chest out again, and let Bryant into the secret. The toady was delighted, and soon all the plungers knew. It was then only a matter of time before the explosion came, as I should have known it would.

It was after dinner one night, and we were playing cards, while Bernier and one or two of the Indian men were talking near by. The game was vingt-et-un, and it happened that at that game I had a small joke concerning the Queen of Diamonds, which I maintained was my lucky card. Forrest had the bank, and when he set down my five-card hand with an ace and the Queen of Diamonds, Bryant, the spiteful ass, sang out:

"Hullo! He's got your queen, Flashy! That the biter bit, bigod!"

"How d'ye mean?" said Forrest, taking up the cards and stakes.

"With Flashy it's t'other way, you know," says Bryant. "He makes off with other chaps' queens."

"Aha," says Forrest, grinning. "But the Queen of Diamonds is a good Englishwoman, ain't she, Flash? Mounting French fillies is your style, I hear."

There was a good deal of laughter, and glances in Bernier's direction. I should have kept them quiet, but I was fool enough to join in.

"Nothing wrong in a French filly," I said, "so long as

the jockey's an English one. A French trainer is well enough, of course, but they don't last in a serious race."

It was feeble enough stuff, no doubt, even allowing for the port we had drunk, but it snapped the straw. The next I knew my chair had been dragged away, and Bernier was standing over me as I sprawled on the floor, his face livid and his mouth working.

"What the devil—" began Forrest, as I scrambled up, and the others jumped up also. I was half on my feet when Bernier struck me, and I lost my balance and went down again.

"For God's sake, Bernier!" shouts Forrest, "are you mad?" and they had to hold him back, or he would have savaged me on the ground, I think. Seeing him held, I came up with an oath, and made to go for him, but Bryant grabbed me, crying "No, no, Flash! Hold off, Flashy!," and they clustered round me as well.

Truth is, I was nearly sick with fear, for the murder was out now. The best shot in the regiment had hit me, but with provocation—fearful or not, I have always been quick and clear enough in my thinking in a crisis—and there couldn't be any way out except a meeting. Unless I took the blow, which meant an end to my career in the army and in society. But to fight him was a quick road to the grave.

It was a horrible dilemma, and in that moment, as they held us apart, I saw I must have time to think, to plan, to find a way out. I shook them off, and without a word stalked out of the mess, like a man who must remove himself before he does someone a mischief.

It took me five minutes of hard thinking, and then I was striding back into the mess again. My heart was hammering, and no doubt I looked pretty furious, and if I shook they thought it was anger.

The chatter died away as I came in; I can feel that silence now, sixty years after, and see the elegant blue figures, and the silver gleaming on the table, and Bernier, alone and very pale, by the fireplace. I went straight up to him. I had my speech ready.

"Captain Bernier," I said, "you have struck me with your hand. That was rash, for I could take you to pieces with mine if I chose." This was blunt, English Flashman, of course. "But I prefer to fight like a gentleman, even if you do not." I swung round on my heel. "Lieutenant Forrest, will you act for me?"

Forrest said yes, like a shot, and Bryant looked piqued. He expected I would have named him, but I had another part for him to play.

"And who acts for you?" I asked Bernier, very cool. He named Tracy, one of the Indian men, and I gave Tracy a bow and then went over to the card table as though nothing had happened.

"Mr Forrest will have the details to attend to," I said to the others. "Shall we cut for the bank?"

They stared at me. "By gad, Flash, you're a cool one!" cries Bryant.

I shrugged, and took up the cards, and we started playing again, the others all very excited—too excited to notice that my thoughts were not on my cards. Luckily, vingt-et-un calls for little concentration.

After a moment Forrest, who had been conferring with Tracy, came over to tell me that, with Lord Cardigan's permission, which he was sure must be forthcoming, we should meet behind the riding school at six in the morning. It was assumed I would choose pistols—as the injured party I had the choice.[6] I nodded, very offhand, and told Bryant to hurry with the deal. We played a few more hands, and then I said I was for bed, lit my cheroot and strolled out with an airy goodnight to the others, as though the thought of the pistols at dawn troubled me no more than what I should have for breakfast. Whatever happened, I had grown in popular esteem for this night at least.

I stopped under the trees on the way to my quarters, and after a moment, as I had expected, Bryant came hurrying after me, full of excitement and concern. He began to babble about what a devil of a fellow I was, and what a fighting Turk Bernier was, but I cut him off short.

"Tommy," says I. "You're not a rich man."

"Eh?" says he. "What the—"

"Tommy," says I. "Would you like ten thousand pounds?"

"In God's name," says he. "What for?"

"For seeing that Bernier stands up at our meeting tomorrow with an unloaded pistol," says I, straight out. I knew my man.

He goggled at me, and then began to babble again. "Christ, Flash, are you crazy? Unloaded . . . why . . ."

"Yes or no," says I. "Ten thousand pounds."

"But it's murder!" he squealed. "We'd swing for it!" No thought of honour, you see, or any of that rot.

"Nobody's going to swing," I told him. "And keep your voice down, d'ye hear? Now, then, Tommy, you're a sharp man with the sleight of hand at parties—I've seen you. You can do it in your sleep. For ten thousand?"

"My God, Flash," says he, "I don't dare." And he began babbling again, but in a whisper this time.

I let him ramble for a moment, for I knew he would come round. He was a greedy little bastard, and the thought of ten thousand was like Aladdin's cave to him. I explained how safe and simple it would be; I had thought it out when first I left the mess.

"Go and borrow Reynolds's duelling pistols, first off. Take 'em to Forrest and Tracy and offer to act as loader —you're always into everything, and they'll be glad to accept, and never think twice."

"Won't they, by God?" cried he. "They know I'm hellish thick with you, Flashy."

"You're an officer and a gentleman," I reminded him. "Now who will imagine for a moment that you would stoop to such a treacherous act, eh? No, no Tommy, it's cut and dried. And in the morning, with the surgeon and seconds standing by, you'll load up—carefully. Don't tell me you can't palm a pistol ball."

"Oh, aye," says he, "like enough. But—"

"Ten thousand pounds," I said, and he licked his lips.

"Jesus," he said at length. "Ten thousand. Phew! On your word of honour, Flash?"

"Word of honour," I said, and lit another cheroot.

"I'll do it!" says he. "My God! You're a devil, Flash! You won't kill him, though? I'll have no part in murder."

"Captain Bernier will be as safe from me as I'll be from him," I told him. "Now, cut along and see Reynolds."

He cut on the word. He was an active little rat, that I'll say for him. Once committed he went in heart and soul.

I went to my quarters, got rid of Basset who was waiting up for me, and lay down on my cot. My throat was dry and my hands were sweating as I thought of what I had done. For all the bluff front I had shown to Bryant, I was in a deathly funk. Suppose something went wrong and Bryant muffed it? It had seemed so easy in that moment of panicky thought outside the mess—fear stimulates thought, perhaps, but it may not be clear thought, because one sees the way out that one *wants* to see, and makes headlong for it. I thought of Bryant fumbling, or being too closely overseen, and Bernier standing up in front of me with a loaded pistol in a hand like a rock, and the muzzle pointing dead at my breast, and felt the ball tearing into me, and myself falling down screaming, and dying on the ground.

I almost shouted out at the horror of it, and lay there blubbering in the dark room; I would have got up and run, but my legs would not let me. So I began to pray, which I had not done, I should say, since I was about eight years old. But I kept thinking of Arnold and hell—which is no doubt significant—and in the end there was nothing for it but brandy, but it might as well have been water.

I did no sleeping that night, but listened to the clock chiming away the quarters, until dawn came, and I heard Basset approaching. I had just sense enough left to see that it wouldn't do for him to find me red-eyed and shivering, so I made believe to sleep, snoring like an organ, and I heard him say:

"If that don't beat! Listen to 'im, sound as a babby. Isn't he the game-cock, though?"

And another voice, another servant's, I suppose, replied:

"They's all alike, bloody fools. 'E won't be snorin' tomorrow mornin', after Bernier's done with 'im. 'E'll be sleepin' too sound for that."

Right, my lad, whoever you are, I thought, if I come through this it'll be strange if I can't bring you to the rings at the riding school, and we'll see your backbone when the farrier-sergeant takes the cat to you. We'll hear how loud you can snore yourself. And with that surge of anger I suddenly felt confidence replacing fear—Bryant would see it through, all right—and when they came for me I was at least composed, if not cheerful.

When I am frightened, I go red in the face, not pale, as most men do, so that in me fear can pass for anger, which has been convenient more than once. Bryant tells me that I went out to the riding school that morning wattled like a turkey cock; he said the fellows made sure I was in a fury to kill Bernier. Not that they thought I had a chance, and they were quiet for once as we walked across the parade just as the trumpeter was sounding reveille.

They had told Cardigan of the affair, of course, and some had thought he might intervene to prevent it. But when he had heard of the blow, he had simply said:

"Where do they meet?"

and gone back to sleep again, with instruction to be called at five. He did not approve of duelling—although he duelled himself in famous circumstances—but he saw that in this case the credit of the regiment would only be hurt if the affair were patched up.

Bernier and Tracy were already there, with the surgeon, and the mist was hanging a little under the trees. Our feet thumped on the turf, which was still wet with dew, as we strode across to them, Forrest at my side, and Bryant with the pistol case beneath his arm following on with the others. About fifty yards away, under the trees by the fence, was a little knot of officers, and I saw Cardigan's bald head above his great caped coat. He was smoking a cigar.

Bryant and the surgeon called Bernier and me together, and Bryant asked us if we would not resolve our quarrel. Neither of us said a word; Bernier was pale, and looked fixedly over my shoulder, and in that moment I came as near to turning and running as ever I did in my life. I felt that my bowels would squirt at any moment, and my hands were shuddering beneath my cloak.

"Very good, then," says Bryant, and went with the surgeon to a little table they had set up. He took out the pistols, and from the corner of my eye I saw him spark the flints, pour in the charges, and rummage in the shot-case. I daren't watch him closely, and anyway Forrest came just then and led me back to my place. When I turned round again the surgeon was stooping to pick up a fallen powder flask, and Bryant was ramming home a wad in one of the barkers.

They conferred a moment, and then Bryant paced over to Bernier and presented a pistol to him; then he came to me with the other. There was no one behind me, and as my hand closed on the butt, Bryant winked quickly. My heart came up into my mouth, and I can never hope to describe the relief that flooded through my body, tingling every limb. I was going to live.

"Gentlemen, you are both determined to continue with this meeting?" Bryant looked at each of us in turn. Bernier said: "Yes," hard and clear. I nodded.

Bryant stepped back to be well out of the line of fire; the

seconds and the surgeon took post beside him, leaving Bernier and me looking at each other about twenty paces apart. He stood sideways to me, the pistol at his side, staring straight at my face, as though choosing his spot—he could clip the pips from a card at this distance.

"The pistols fire on one pressure," called Bryant. "When I drop my handkerchief you may level your pistols and fire. I shall drop it in a few seconds from now." And he held up the white kerchief in one hand.

I heard the click of Bernier cocking his pistol. His eyes were steady on mine. Sold again, Bernier, I thought; you're all in a stew about nothing. The handkerchief fell.

Bernier's right arm came up like a railway signal, and before I had even cocked my pistol I was looking into his barrel—a split second and it shot smoke at me and the crack of the charge was followed by something rasping across my cheek and grazing it—it was the wad. I fell back a step. Bernier was glaring at me, aghast that I was still on my feet, I suppose, and someone shouted: "Missed, by Jesus!" and another cried angrily for silence.

It was my turn, and for a moment the lust was on me to shoot the swine down where he stood. But Bryant might have lost his head, and it was no part of my design, anyway. I had it in my power now to make a name that would run through the army in a week—good old Flashy, who stole another man's girl and took a blow from him, but was too decent to take advantage of him, even in a duel.

They stood like statues, every eye on Bernier, waiting for me to shoot him down. I cocked my pistol, watching him.

"Come on, damn you!" he shouted suddenly, his face white with rage and fear.

I looked at him for a moment, then brought my pistol up no higher than hip level, but with the barrel pointing well away to the side. I held it negligently almost, just for a moment, so that everyone might see I was firing deliberately wide. I squeezed the trigger.

What happened to that shot is now regimental history; I had meant it for the ground, but it chanced that the surgeon had set his bag and bottle of spirits down on the turf in that direction, maybe thirty yards off, and by sheer good luck the shot whipped the neck off the bottle clean as a whistle.

"Deloped, by God!" roared Forrest. "He's deloped!"

They hurried forward, shouting, the surgeon exclaiming in blasphemous amazement over his shattered bottle. Bryant slapped me on the back, Forrest wrung my hand, Tracy stood staring in astonishment—it seemed to him, as it did to everyone, that I had spared Bernier and at the same time given proof of astounding marksmanship. As for Bernier, he looked murder if ever a man did, but I marched straight up to him with my hand held out, and he was forced to take it. He was struggling to keep from dashing his pistol into my face, and when I said:

"No hard feelings, then, old fellow?"

he gave an incoherent snarl, and turning on his heel, strode off.

This was not lost on Cardigan, who was still watching from a distance, and presently I was summoned from a boozy breakfast—for the plungers celebrated the affair in style, and waxed fulsome over the way I had stood up to him, and then deloped. Cardigan had me to his office, and there was the adjutant and Jones, and Bernier looking like thunder.

"I won't have it, I tell you!" Cardigan was saying. "Ha, Fwashman, come here! Haw-haw. Now then, shake hands directly, I say, Captain Bernier, and let me hear that the affair is done and honour satisfied."

I spoke up. "It's done for me, and indeed I'm sorry it ever happened. But the blow was Captain Bernier's, not mine. But here's my hand, again."

Bernier said, in a voice that shook: "Why did you delope? You have made a mock of me. Why didn't you take your shot at me like a man?"

"My good sir," I said. "I didn't presume to tell you where to aim your shot; don't tell me where I should have aimed mine."

That remark, I am told, has found its way since into some dictionary of quotations; it was in *The Times* within the week, and I was told that when the Duke of Wellington heard it, he observed:

"Damned good. And damned right, too."

So that morning's work made a name for Harry Flashman—a name that enjoyed more immediate celebrity than if I had stormed a battery alone. Such is fame, especially in peacetime. The whole story went the rounds, and for a time I even found myself pointed out in the street, and a clergyman wrote to me from Birmingham, saying that as I had shown mercy, I would surely obtain mercy, and Parkin, the Oxford Street gunmaker, sent me a brace of barkers in silver mountings, with my initials engraved—good for trade, I imagine. There was also a question in the House, on the vicious practice of duelling, and Macaulay replied that since one of the participants in the recent affair had shown such good sense and humanity, the Government, while deploring such meetings, hoped this might prove a good example. ("Hear, hear," and cheers.) My Uncle Bindley was heard to say that his nephew had more to him than he supposed, and even Basset went about throwing a chest at being servant to such a cool blade.

The only person who was critical was my own father, who said in one of his rare letters:

"Don't be such an infernal fool another time. You don't fight duels in order to delope, but to kill your adversary."

So, with Josette mine by right of conquest—and she was in some awe of me, I may say—and a reputation for courage, marksmanship, and downright decency established, I was pretty well satisfied. The only snag was Bryant, but I dealt with that easily.

When he had finished toadying me on the day of the duel, he got round to asking about his ten thousand—he knew I had great funds, or at least that my father did, but I knew perfectly well I could never have pried ten thousand out of my guv'nor. I told Bryant so, and he gaped as though I had kicked him in the stomach.

"But you promised me ten thousand," he began to bleat.

"Silly promise, ain't it?—when you think hard about it," says I. "Ten thousand quid, I mean—who'd pay out that much?"

"You lying swine!" shouts he, almost crying with rage. "You swore you'd pay me!"

"More fool you for believing me," I said.

"Right, by God!" he snarled. "We'll see about this! You won't cheat me, Flashman, I'll—"

"You'll what?" says I. "Tell everyone all about it? Confess that you sent a man into a duel with an unloaded gun? It'll make an interesting story. You'd be confessing to a capital offence—had you thought of that? Not that anyone'd believe you—but they'd certainly kick you out of the service for conduct unbecoming, wouldn't they?"

He saw then how it lay, and there was nothing he could

do about it. He actually stamped and tore his hair, and then he tried pleading with me, but I laughed at him, and he finished up swearing to be even yet.

"You'll live to regret this!" he cried. "By God, I'll get you yet!"

"More chance of that than you have of getting ten thousand, anyway," I told him, and he slunk off.

He didn't worry me; what I'd said was gospel true. He daren't breathe a word, for his own safety's sake. Of course if he had thought at all he would have sniffed something fishy about a ten thousand bribe in the first place. But he was greedy, and I've lived long enough to discover that there isn't any folly a man won't contemplate if there's money or a woman at stake.

However, if I could congratulate myself on how the matter had turned out, and can look back now and say it was one of the most important and helpful incidents of my life, there was trouble in store for me very quickly as a result of it. It came a few weeks afterwards, and it ended in my having to leave the regiment for a while.

It had happened not long before that the regiment had been honoured (as they say) by being chosen to escort to London the Queen's husband-to-be, Albert, when he arrived in this country. He had become Colonel of the Regiment, and among other things we had been given a new-designed uniform and had our name changed to the Eleventh Hussars. That by the way; what mattered was that he took a close interest in us, and the tale of the duel made such a stir that he took special notice of it, and being a prying German busybody, found out the cause of it.

That almost cooked my goose for good. His lovely new regiment, he found, contained officers who consorted with French whores and even fought duels over them. He played the devil about this, and the upshot was that Cardigan had to summon me and tell me that for my own good I would have to go away for a while.

"It has been demanded," said he, "that you weave the wegiment—I take it the official intention is that that should be permanent, but I intend to interpwet it as tempowawy. I have no desire to lose the services of a pwomising officer—not for His Woyal Highness or anyone, let me tell you. You might go on weave, of course, but I think it best you should be detached. I shall have you posted, Fwashman, to another unit, until the fuss has died down."

I didn't much like the idea, and when he announced

that the regiment he had chosen to post me to was stationed in Scotland, I almost rebelled. But I realised it
would only be for a few months, and I was relieved to find
Cardigan still on my side—if it had been Reynolds who
had fought the duel it would have been a very different
kettle of fish, but I was one of his favourites. And one
must say it of old Lord Haw Haw, if you were his favourite he would stand by you, right, reason or none. Old fool.

I have soldiered in too many countries and known too many peoples to fall into the folly of laying down the law about any of them. I tell you what I have seen, and you may draw your own conclusions. I disliked Scotland and the Scots; the place I found wet and the people rude. They had the fine qualities which bore me—thrift and industry and long-faced holiness, and the young women are mostly great genteel boisterous things who are no doubt bedworthy enough if your taste runs that way. (One acquaintance of mine who had a Scotch clergyman's daughter described it as like wrestling with a sergeant of dragoons.) The men I found solemn, hostile, and greedy, and they found me insolent, arrogant, and smart.

This for the most part; there were exceptions, as you shall see. The best things I found, however, were the port and the claret, in which the Scotch have a nice taste, although I never took to whisky.

The place I was posted to was Paisley, which is near Glasgow, and when I heard of the posting I as near as a toucher sold out. But I told myself I should be back with the 11th in a few months, and must take my medicine, even if it meant being away from all decent living for a while. My forebodings were realised, and more, but at least life did not turn out to be boring, which was what I had feared most. Very far from it.

At this time there was a great unrest throughout Britain, in the industrial areas, which meant very little to me, and indeed I've never troubled to read up the particulars of it. The working people were in a state of agitation, and one heard of riots in the mill towns, and of weavers smashing looms, and Chartists[7] being arrested, but we younger fellows paid it no heed. If you were country-bred or lived in London these things were nothing to you, and all I gathered was that the poor folk were mutinous and wanted to do less work for more money, and the factory owners were damned if they'd let them. There may have been more to it than this, but I doubt it, and no one has ever convinced me that it was anything but a war between the two. It always has been, and always will be, as long as one man has what the other has not, and devil take the hindmost.

The devil seemed to be taking the workers, by and large, with government helping him, and we soldiers were the government's sword. Troops were called out to subdue the agitators, and the Riot Act was read, and here and there would be clashes between the two, and a few killed. I am fairly neutral now, with my money in the bank, but at that time everyone I knew was damning the workers up and down, and saying they should be hung and flogged and transported, and I was all for it, as the Duke would say. You have no notion, today, how high feeling ran; the mill-folk were the enemy then, as though they had been Frenchmen or Afghans. They were to be put down whenever they rose up, and we were to do it.

I was hazy enough, as you see, on the causes of it all, but I saw further than most in some ways, and what I saw was this: it's one thing leading British soldiers against foreigners, but would they fight their own folk? For most of the troopers of the 11th, for example, were of the class and kind of the working people, and I couldn't see them fighting their fellows. I said so, but all I was told was that discipline would do the trick. Well, thought I, maybe it will and maybe it won't, but whoever is going to be caught between a mob on one side and a file of red coats on the other, it isn't going to be old Flashy.

Paisley had been quiet enough when I was sent there, but the authorities had a suspicious eye on the whole area, which was regarded as being a hotbed of sedition. They were training up the militia, just in case, and this was the task I was given—an officer from a crack cavalry regiment instructing irregular infantry, which is what you might expect. They turned out to be good material, luckily; many of the older ones were Peninsular men, and the sergeant had been in the 42nd Regiment at Waterloo. So there was little enough for me to do at first.

I was billeted on one of the principal mill-owners of the area, a brass-bound old moneybags with a long nose and a hard eye who lived in some style in a house at Renfrew, and who made me welcome after his fashion when I arrived.

"We've no high opeenion o' the military, sir," said he,

"and could well be doing without ye. But since, thanks to slack government and that damnable Reform nonsense, we're in this sorry plight, we must bear with having soldiers aboot us. A scandal! D'ye see these wretches at my mill, sir? I would have the half of them in Australia this meenit, if it was left to me! And let the rest feel their bellies pinched for a week or two—we'd hear less of their caterwaulin' then."

"You need have no fear, sir," I told him. "We shall protect you."

"Fear?" he snorted. "I'm not feart, sir. John Morrison doesnae tremble at the whine o' his ain workers, let me tell you. As for protecting, we'll see." And he gave me a look and a sniff.

I was to live with the family—he could hardly do less, in view of what brought me there—and presently he took me from his study through the gloomy hall of his mansion to the family's sitting-room. The whole house was hellish gloomy and cold and smelled of must and righteousness, but when he threw open the sitting-room door and ushered me in, I forgot my surroundings.

"Mr Flashman," says he, "this is Mistress Morrison and my four daughters." He rapped out their names like a roll-call. "Agnes, Mary, Elspeth, and Grizel."

I snapped my heels and bowed with a great flourish—I was in uniform, and the gold-trimmed blue cape and pink pants of the 11th Hussars were already famous, and looked extremely well on me. Four heads inclined in reply, and one nodded—this was Mistress Morrison, a tall, beaknosed female in whom one could detect all the fading beauty of a vulture. I made a hasty inventory of the daughters: Agnes, buxom and darkly handsome—she would do. Mary, buxom and plain—she would not. Grizel, thin and mousy and still a schoolgirl—no. Elspeth was like none of the others. She was beautiful, fair-haired, blue-eyed, and pink-cheeked, and she alone smiled at me with the open, simple smile of the truly stupid. I marked her down at once, and gave all my attention to Mistress Morrison.

It was grim work, I may tell you, for she was a sour tyrant of a woman and looked on me as she looked on all soldiers, Englishmen, and men under fifty years of age—as frivolous, Godless, feckless, and unworthy. In this, it seemed, her husband supported her, and the daughters said not a word to me all evening. I could have damned the lot of them (except Elspeth), but instead I set myself to be pleasant, modest, and even meek where the old woman was concerned, and when we went into dinner—which was served in great state—she had thawed to the extent of a sour smile or two.

Well, I thought, that is something, and I went up in her estimation by saying "Amen" loudly when Morrison said grace, and struck while the iron was hot by asking presently—it was a Saturday—what time divine service was next morning. Morrison went so far as to be civil once or twice, after this, but I was still glad to escape at last to my room—dark brown tomb though it was.

You may wonder why I took pains to ingratiate myself with these puritan boors, and the answer is that I have always made a point of being civil to anyone who might ever be of use to me. Also, I had half an eye to Miss Elspeth, and there was no hope there without the mother's good opinion.

So I attended family prayers with them, and escorted them to church, and listened to Miss Agnes sing in the evening, and helped Miss Grizel with her lessons, and pretended an interest in Mistress Morrison's conversation—which was spiteful and censorious and limited to the doings of her acquaintances in Paisley—and was entertained by Miss Mary on the subject of her garden flowers, and bore with old Morrison's droning about the state of trade and the incompetence of government. And among these riotous pleasures of a soldier's life I talked occasionally with Miss Elspeth, and found her brainless beyond description. But she was undeniably desirable, and for all the piety and fear of hell-fire that had been drummed into her, I thought there was sometimes a wanton look about her eye and lower lip, and after a week I had her as infatuated with me as any young woman could be. It was not so difficult; dashing young cavalrymen with broad shoulders were rare in Paisley, and I was setting myself to charm.

However, there's many a slip 'twixt the crouch and the leap, as the cavalry used to say, and my difficulty was to get Miss Elspeth in the right place at the right time. I was kept pretty hard at it with the militia during the day, and in the evenings her parents chaperoned her like shadows. It was more for form's sake than anything else, I think, for they seemed to trust me well enough by this time, but it made things damnably awkward, and I was beginning to itch for her considerably. But eventually it was her father

himself who brought matters to a successful conclusion—
and changed my whole life, and hers. And it was because
he, John Morrison, who had boasted of his fearlessness,
turned out to be as timid as a mouse.

It was on a Monday, nine days after I had arrived, that
a fracas broke out in one of the mills; a young worker had
his arm crushed in one of the machines, and his mates
made a great outcry, and a meeting of workmen was held
in the streets beyond the mill gates. That was all, but some
fool of a magistrate lost his head and demanded that the
troops be called "to quell the seditious rioters." I sent his
messenger about his business, in the first place because
there seemed no danger from the meeting—although there
was plenty of fist-shaking and threat-shouting, by all accounts—and in the second because I do not make a practice of seeking sorrow.

Sure enough, the meeting dispersed, but not before the
magistrate had spread panic and alarm, ordering the shops
to close and windows in the town to be shuttered and God
knows what other folly. I told him to his face he was a
fool, ordered my sergeant to let the militia go home (but
to have them ready on recall), and trotted over to Renfrew.

There Morrison was in a state of despair. He peeped at
me round the front door, his face ashen, and demanded:

"Are they comin', in Goad's name?" and then "Why are
ye not at the head of your troops, sir? Are we tae be murdered for your neglect?"

I told him, pretty sharp, that there was no danger, but
that if there had been, his place was surely at his mill, to
keep his rascals in order. He whinnied at me—I've seldom
seen a man in such fright, and being a true-bred poltroon
myself, I speak with authority.

"My place is here," he yelped, "defendin' my hame and
bairns!"

"I thought they were in Glasgow today," I said, as I
came into the hall.

"My wee Elspeth's here," said he, groaning. "If the mob
was tae break in. . . ."

"Oh, for God's sake," says I, for I was well out of sorts,
what with the idiot magistrate and now Morrison, "there
isn't a mob. They've gone home."

"Will they stay hame?" he bawled. "Oh, they hate me,
Mr Flashman, damn them a'! What if they were to come
here? O, wae's me—and my poor wee Elspeth!"

Poor wee Elspeth was sitting in the window-seat, admiring her reflection in the panes, and perfectly unconcerned. Catching sight of her, I had an excellent thought.

"If you're nervous for her, why not send her to Glasgow, too?" I asked him, very unconcerned.

"Are ye mad, sir? Alone on the road, a lassie?"

I reassured him: I would escort her safely to her Mama.

"And leave me here?" he cried, so I suggested he come as well. But he wouldn't have that; I realised later he probably had his strongbox in the house.

He hummed and hawed a great deal, but eventually fear for his daughter—which was entirely groundless, as far as mobs were concerned—overcame him, and we were packed off together in the gig, I driving, she humming gaily at the thought of a jaunt, and her devoted parent crying instruction and consternation after us as we rattled off.

"Tak' care o' my poor wee lamb, Mr Flashman," he wailed.

"To be sure I will, sir," I replied. And I did.

The banks of the Clyde in those days were very pretty; not like the grimy slums that cover them now. There was a gentle evening haze, I remember, and a warm sun setting on a glorious day, and after a mile or two I suggested we stop and ramble among the thickets by the waterside. Miss Elspeth was eager, so we left the pony grazing and went into a little copse. I suggested we sit down, and Miss Elspeth was eager again—that glorious vacant smile informed me. I believe I murmured a few pleasantries, played with her hair, and then kissed her. Miss Elspeth was more eager still. Then I got to work in earnest, and Miss Elspeth's eagerness knew no bounds. I had great red claw-marks on my back for a fortnight after.

When we had finished, she lay in the grass, drowsy, like a contented kitten, and after a few pleased sighs she said:

"Was that what the minister means when he talks of fornication?"

Astonished, I said, yes, it was.

"Um-hm," said she. "Why has he such a down on it?"

It seemed to me time to be pressing on towards Glasgow. Ignorant women I have met, and I knew that Miss Elspeth must rank high among them, but I had not supposed until now that she had no earthly idea of elementary human relations. (Yet there were even married women in my time who did not connect their husbands' antics in bed with the conception of children.) She simply did not understand what had taken place between us. She liked it, certainly, but she had no thought of anything beyond the act—no notion of consequences, or guilt, or the need for secrecy. In her, ignorance and stupidity formed a perfect shield against the world: this, I suppose, is innocence.

It startled me, I can tell you. I had a vision of her remarking happily: "Mama, you'll never guess what Mr Flashman and I have been doing this evening. . . ." Not that I minded too much, for when all was said I didn't care a button for the Morrisons' opinion, and if they could not look after their daughter it was their own fault. But the less trouble the better: for her own sake I hoped she might keep her mouth shut.

I took her back to the gig and helped her in, and I thought what a beautiful fool she was. Oddly enough, I felt a sudden affection for her in that moment, such as I hadn't felt for any of my other women—even though some of them had been better tumbles than she. It had nothing to do with rolling her in the grass; looking at the gold hair that had fallen loose on her cheek, and seeing the happy smile in her eyes, I felt a great desire to keep her, not only for bed, but to have her near me. I wanted to watch her face, and the way she pushed her hair into place, and the steady, serene look that she turned on me. Hullo, Flashy, I remember thinking; careful, old son. But it stayed with me, that queer empty feeling in my inside, and of all the recollections of my life there isn't one that is clearer than of that warm evening by the Clyde, with Elspeth smiling at me beneath the trees.

Almost equally distinct, however, but less pleasant, is my memory of Morrison, a few days later, shaking his fist in my face and scarlet with rage as he shouted:

"Ye damned blackguard! Ye thieving, licentious, raping devil! I'll have ye hanged for this, as Goad's my witness! My ain daughter, in my ain hoose! Jesus Lord! Ye come sneaking here, like the damned viper that ye are. . . ."

And much more of the same, until I thought he would have apoplexy. Miss Elspeth had almost lived up to my expectation—only it had not been Mama she had told, but Agnes. The result was the same, of course, and the house was in uproar. The only calm person was Elspeth herself, which was no help. For of course I denied old Morrison's accusation, but when he dragged her in to confront me with my infamy, as he called it, she said quite matter-of-fact, yes, it had happened by the river on the way to Glasgow. I wondered, was she simple? It is a point on which I have never made up my mind.

At that, I couldn't deny it any longer. So I took the other course and damned Morrison's eyes, asking him what did he expect if he left a handsome daughter within a man's reach? I told him we were not monks in the army, and he fairly screamed with rage and threw an inkstand at me, which fortunately missed. By this time others were on the scene, and his daughters had the vapours—except Elspeth—and Mrs Morrison came at me with such murder in her face that I turned tail and ran for dear life.

I decamped without even having time to collect my effects—which were not sent on to me, by the way—and decided that I had best set up my base in Glasgow. Paisley was likely to be fairly hot, and I resolved to have a word with the local commandant and explain, as between gentlemen, that it might be best if other duties were found for me that would not take me back there. It would be somewhat embarrassing, of course, for he was another of these damned Presbyterians, so I put off seeing him for a day or two. As a result I never called on him at all. Instead I had a caller myself.

He was a stiff-shouldered, brisk-mannered fellow of about fifty; rather dapper in an almost military way, with a brown face and hard grey eyes. He looked as though he might be a sporting sort, but when he came to see me he was all business.

"Mr Flashman, I believe?" says he. "My name is Abercrombie."

"Good luck to you, then," says I. "I'm not buying anything today, so close the door as you leave."

He looked at me sharp, head on one side. "Good," says he. "This makes it easier. I had thought you might be a smooth one, but I see you're what they call a plunger."

I asked him what the devil he meant.

"Quite simple," says he, taking a seat as cool as you please. "We have a mutual acquaintance. Mrs Morrison of Renfrew is my sister. Elspeth Morrison is my niece."

This was an uneasy piece of news, for I didn't like the look of him. He was too sure of himself by half. But I gave him a stare and told him he had a damned handsome niece.

"I'm relieved that you think so," said he. "I'd be distressed to think that the Hussars were not discriminating."

He sat looking at me, so I took a turn round the room.

"The point is," he said, "that we have to make arrangements for the wedding. You'll not want to lose time."

I had picked up a bottle and glass, but I set them down sharp at this. He had taken my breath away.

"What the hell d'you mean?" says I. Then I laughed. "You don't think I'll marry her, do you? Good God, you must be a lunatic."

"And why?" says he.

"Because I'm not such a fool," I told him. Suddenly I was angry, at this damned little snip, and his tone with me. "If every girl who's ready to play in the hay was to get married, we'd have damned few spinsters left, wouldn't we? And d'you suppose I'd be pushed into a wedding over a trifle like this?"

"My niece's honour."

"Your niece's honour! A mill-owner's daughter's honour! I'm to mend that at the altar, am I? Oh, I see the game! You see an excellent chance of a match, eh? A chance to marry your niece to a gentleman? You smell a fortune, do you? Well, let me tell you—"

"As to the excellence of the match," said he, "I'd sooner see her marry a Barbary ape. I take it, however, that you decline the honour of my niece's hand?"

"Damn your impudence! You take it right. Now, get out!"

"Excellent," says he, very bright-eyed. "It's what I hoped for." And he stood up, straightening his coat.

"What's that meant to mean, curse you?"

He smiled at me. "I'll send a friend to talk to you. He will arrange matters. I don't approve of meetings, myself, but I'll be delighted, in this case, to put either a bullet or a blade into you." He clapped his hat on his head. "You know, I don't suppose there has been a duel in Glasgow these fifty years or more. It will cause quite a stir."

I gaped at the man, but gathered my wits soon enough. "Lord," says I, with a sneer, "you don't suppose I would fight you?"

"No?"

"Gentlemen fight gentlemen," I told him, and ran a scornful eye over him. "They don't fight shop-keepers."

"Wrong again," says he, cheerily. "I'm a lawyer."

"Then stick to your law. We don't fight lawyers, either."

"Not if you can help it, I imagine. But you'll be hard put to it to refuse a brother officer, Mr Flashman. You see, although I've no more than a militia commission now, I was formerly of the 93rd Foot—you have heard of the Sutherlands, I take it?—and had the honour to hold the rank of captain. I even achieved some little service in the field." He was smiling almost benignly now. "If you doubt my bona fides, may I refer you to my former chief, Colonel Colin Campbell?[8] Good day, Mr Flashman."

He was at the door before I found my voice.

"To hell with you, and him! I'll not fight you!"

He turned. "Then I'll enjoy taking a whip to you in the street. I really shall. Your own chief—my Lord Cardigan, isn't it?—will find that happy reading in *The Times*, I don't doubt."

He had me in a cleft stick, as I saw at once. It would mean professional ruin—and at the hands of a damned provincial infantryman, and a retired one at that. I stood there, overcome with rage and panic, damning the day I ever set eyes on his infernal niece, with my wits working for a way out. I tried another tack.

"You may not realise who you're dealing with," I told him, and asked if he had not heard of the Bernier affair: it seemed to me that it must be known about, even in the wilds of Glasgow, and I said so.

"I think I recollect a paragraph," says he. "Dear me, Mr Flashman, should I be overcome? Should I quail? I'll just have to try to hold my pistol steady, won't I?"

"Damn you," I shouted, "wait a moment."

He stood attentive, watching me.

"All right, blast you," I said. "How much do you want?"

"I thought it might come to that," he said. "Your kind of rat generally reaches for its purse when cornered. You're wasting time, Flashman. I'll take your promise to marry Elspeth—or your life. I'd prefer the latter. But it's one or the other. Make up your mind."

And from that I could not budge him. I pleaded and swore and promised any kind of reparation short of marriage; I was almost in tears, but I might as well have tried to move a rock. Marry or die—that was what it amounted to, for I'd no doubt he would be damnably efficient with the barkers. There was nothing for it: in the end I had to give in and say I would marry the girl.

"You're sure you wouldn't rather fight?" says he, regretfully. "A great pity. I fear the conventions are going to burden Elspeth with a rotten man, but there." And he passed on to discussion of the wedding arrangements—he had it all pat.

When at last I was rid of him I applied myself to the brandy, and things seemed less bleak. At least I could think of no one I would rather be wedded and bedded with, and if you have money a wife need be no great encumbrance. And presently we should be out of Scotland, so I need not see her damnable family. But it was an infernal nuisance, all the same—what was I to tell my father? I couldn't for the life of me think how he would take it—he wouldn't cut me off, but he might be damned uncivil about it.

I didn't write to him until after the business was over. It took place in the Abbey at Paisley, which was appropriately gloomy, and the sight of the pious long faces of my bride's relations would have turned your stomach. The Morrisons had begun speaking to me again, and were very civil in public—it was represented as being a sudden love-match, of course, between the dashing hussar and the beautiful provincial, so they had to pretend I was their beau ideal of a son-in-law. But the brute Abercrombie was never far away, to see I came up to scratch, and all in all it was an unpleasant business.

When it was done, and the guests had begun to drink themselves blind, as is the Scottish custom, Elspeth and I were seen off in a carriage by her parents. Old Morrison was crying drunk, and made a disgusting spectacle.

"My wee lamb!" he kept snuffling. "My bonny wee lamb!"

His wee lamb, I may say, looked entrancing, and no more moved than if she had just been out choosing a pair of gloves, rather than getting a husband—she had taken the whole thing without a murmur, neither happy nor sorry, apparently, which piqued me a little.

Anyway, her father slobbered over her, but when he turned to me he just let out a great hollow groan, and gave place to his wife. At that I whipped up the horses, and away we went.

For the life of me I cannot remember where the honeymoon was spent—at some rented cottage on the coast, I remember, but the name has gone—and it was lively enough. Elspeth knew nothing, but it seemed that the only thing that brought her out of her usual serene lethargy was a man in bed with her. She was a more than willing playmate, and I taught her a few of Josette's tricks, which she picked up so readily that by the time we came back to Paisley I was worn out.

And there the shock was waiting: it hit me harder, I think, than anything had in my life. When I opened the letter and read it, I couldn't speak at first; I had to read it again and again before it made sense.

> "Lord Cardigan [it read] has learned of the marriage contracted lately by Mr Flashman, of this regiment, and Miss Morrison, of Glasgow. In view of this marriage, his lordship feels that Mr Flashman will not wish to continue to serve with the 11th Hussars (Prince Albert's), but that he will wish either to resign or to transfer to another regiment."

That was all. It was signed "Jones"—Cardigan's toady.

What I said I don't recall, but it brought Elspeth to my side. She slid her arms round my waist and asked what was the matter.

"All hell's the matter," I said. "I must go to London at once."

At this she raised a cry of delight, and babbled with excitement about seeing the great sights, and society, and having a place in town, and meeting my father—God help us—and a great deal more drivel. I was too sick to heed her, and she never seemed to notice me as I sat down among the boxes and trunks that had been brought in from the coach to our bedroom. I remember I damned her at one point for a fool and told her to hold her tongue, which silenced her for a minute; but then she started off again, and was debating whether she should have a French maid or an English one.

I was in a furious rage all the way south, and impatient to get to Cardigan. I knew what it was all about—the bloody fool had read of the marriage and decided that Elspeth was not "suitable" for one of his officers. It will sound ridiculous to you, perhaps, but it was so in those days in a regiment like the 11th. Society daughters were all very well, but anything that smacked of trade or the middle classes was anathema to his lofty lordship. Well, I was not going to have his nose turned up at me, as he would find. So I thought, in my youthful folly.

I took Elspeth home first. I had written to my father while we were on honeymoon, and had had a letter back saying: "Who is the unfortunate chit, for God's sake?

Does she know what she has got?" So all was well enough in its way on that front. And when we arrived there who should be the first person we met in the hall but Judy, dressed for riding. She gave me a tongue-in-the-cheek smile as soon as she saw Elspeth—the clever bitch probably guessed what lay behind the marriage—but I got some of my own back by my introduction.

"Elspeth," I said, "this is Judy, my father's tart."

That brought the colour into her face, and I left them to get acquainted while I looked for the guv'nor. He was out, as usual, so I went straight off in search of Cardigan, and found him at his town house. At first he wouldn't see me, when I sent up my card, but I pushed his footman out of the way and went up anyway.

It should have been a stormy interview, with high words flying, but it wasn't. Just the sight of him, in his morning coat, looking as though he had just been inspecting God on parade, took the wind out of me. When he had demanded to know, in his coldest way, why I intruded on him, I stuttered out my question: why was he sending me out of the regiment?

"Because of your marriage, Fwashman," says he. "You must have known very well what the consequences would be. It is quite unacceptable, you know. The lady, I have no doubt, is an excellent young woman, but she is—nobody. In these circumstances your resignation is imperative."

"But she is respectable, my lord," I said. "I assure you she is from an excellent family; her father—"

"Owns a factory," he cut in. "Haw-haw. It will not do. My dear sir, did you not think of your position? Of the wegiment? Could I answer, sir, if I were asked: 'And who is Mr Fwashman's wife?' 'Oh, her father is a Gwasgow weaver, don't you know?'"

"But it will ruin me!" I could have wept at the pure, block-headed snobbery of the man. "Where can I go? What regiment will take me if I'm kicked out of the 11th?"

"You are not being kicked out, Fwashman," he said, and he was being positively kindly. "You are wesigning. A very different thing. Haw-haw. You are twansferring. There is no difficulty. I wike you, Fwashman; indeed, I had hopes of you, but you have destwoyed them with your foolishness. Indeed, I should be extwemely angwy. But I shall help in your awwangements: I have infwuence at the Horse Guards, you know."

"Where am I to go?" I demanded miserably.

"I have given thought to it, let me tell you. It would be impwoper to twansfer to another wegiment at home; it will be best if you go overseas, I think. To India. Yes—"

"India?" I stared at him in horror.

"Yes, indeed. There are caweers to be made there, don't you know? A few years' service there, and the matter of your wesigning fwom my wegiment will be forgotten. You can come home and be gazetted to some other command."

He was so bland, so sure, that there was nothing to say. I knew what he thought of me now: I had shown myself in his eyes no better than the Indian officers whom he despised. Oh, he was being kind enough, in his way; there were "caweers" in India, all right, for the soldier who could get nothing better—and who survived the fevers and the heat and the plague and the hostile natives. At that moment I was at my lowest; the pale, haughty face and the soft voice seemed to fade away before me; all I was conscious of was a sullen anger, and a deep resolve that wherever I went, it would not be India—not for a thousand Cardigans.

"So you won't, hey?" said my father, when I told him.

"I'm damned if I do," I said.

"You're damned if you don't," chuckled he, very amused. "What else will you do, d'you suppose?"

"Sell out," says I.

"Not a bit of it," says he. "I've bought your .colours, and by God, you'll wear 'em."

"You can't make me."

"True enough. But the day you hand them back, on that day the devil a penny you'll get out of me. How will you live, eh? And with a wife to support, bigad? No, no, Harry; you've called the tune, and you can pay the piper."

"You mean I'm to go?"

"Of course you'll go. Look you, my son, and possibly my heir, I'll tell you how it is. You're a wastrel and a bad lot—oh, I daresay it's my fault, among others, but that's by the way. *My* father was a bad lot, too, but I grew up some kind of man. You might, too, for all I know. But I'm certain sure you won't do it here. You might do it by reaping the consequences of your own lunacy—and that means India. D'you follow me?"

"But Elspeth," I said. "You know it's no country for a woman."

"Then don't take her. Not for the first year, in any event, until you've settled down a bit. Nice chit, she is. And don't make piteous eyes at me, sir; you can do without her a while—by all accounts there are women in India, and you can be as beastly as you please."

"It's not fair!" I shouted.

"Not fair! Well, well, this is one lesson you're learning. Nothing's fair, you young fool. And don't blubber about not wanting to go and leave her—she'll be safe enough here."

"With you and Judy, I suppose?"

"With me and Judy," says he, very softly. "And I'm not sure that the company of a rake and a harlot won't be better for her than yours."

That was how I came to leave for India; how the foundation was laid of a splendid military career. I felt myself damnably ill-used, and if I had had the courage I would have told my father to go to the devil. But he had me, and he knew it. Even if it hadn't been for the money part of it, I couldn't have stood up to him, as I hadn't been able to stand up to Cardigan. I hated them both, then. I came to think better of Cardigan, later, for in his arrogant, pigheaded, snobbish way he was trying to be decent to me, but my father I never forgave. He was playing the swine, and he knew it, and found it amusing at my expense. But what really poisoned me against him was that he didn't believe I cared a button for Elspeth.

There may be better countries for a soldier to serve in than India, but I haven't seen them. You may hear the greenhorns talk about heat and flies and filth and the natives and the diseases; the first three you must get accustomed to, the fifth you must avoid—which you can do, with a little common sense—and as for the natives, well, where else will you get such a docile, humble set of slaves? I liked them better than the Scots, anyhow; their language was easier to understand.

And if these things were meant to be drawbacks, there was the other side. In India there was power—the power of the white man over the black—and power is a fine thing to have. Then there was ease, and time for any amount of sport, and good company, and none of the restrictions of home. You could live as you pleased, and lord it among the niggers, and if you were well-off and properly connected, as I was, there was the social life among the best folk who clustered round the Governor-General. And there were as many women as you could wish for.

There was money to be had, too, if you were lucky in your campaigns and knew how to look for it. In my whole service I never made half as much in pay as I got from India in loot—but that is another story.

I knew nothing of this when we dropped anchor in the Hooghly, off Calcutta, and I looked at the red river banks and sweated in the boiling sun, and smelt the stink, and wished I was in hell rather than here. It had been a damnable four-months voyage on board the crowded and sweltering Indiaman, with no amusement of any kind, and I was prepared to find India no better.

I was to join one of the Company's native lancer regiments[9] in the Benares District, but I never did. Army inefficiency kept me kicking my heels in Calcutta for several weeks before the appropriate orders came through, and by that time I had taken fortune by the foreskin, in my own way.

In the first place, I messed at the Fort with the artillery officers in the native service, who were a poor lot, and whose messing would have sickened a pig. The food was bad to begin with, and by the time the black cooks had finished with it you would hardly have fed it to a jackal.

I said so at our first dinner, and provoked a storm among these gentlemen, who considered me a Johnny Newcome.

"Not good enough for the plungers, eh?" says one. "Sorry we have no *foi gras* for your lordship, and we must apologise for the absence of silver plate."

"Is it always like this?" I asked. "What is it?"

"What is the dish, your grace?" asked the wit. "Why, it's called curry, don't you know? Kills the taste of old meat."

"If that's all it kills, I'm surprised," says I, disgusted. "No decent human being could stomach this filth."

"We stomach it," said another. "Ain't we human beings?"

"You know best about that," I said. "If you take my advice you'll hang your cook." And with that I stalked out, leaving them growling after me. Yet their mess, I discovered, was no worse than any other in India, and better than some. The men's messes were indescribable, and I wondered how they survived such dreadful food in such a climate. The answer was, of course, that many of them didn't.

However, it was obvious to me that I would be better shifting for myself, so I called up Basset, whom I had brought with me from England—the little bastard had blubbered at the thought of losing me when I left the 11th, God knows why—gave him a fistful of money, and told him to find a cook, a butler, a groom, and half a dozen other servants. These people were to be hired for virtually nothing. Then I went myself to the guard room, found a native who could speak English passably well, and went out to find a house.[10]

I found one not far from the Fort, a pleasant place with a little garden of shrubs, and a verandah with screens, and my nigger fetched the owner, who was a great fat rogue with a red turban; we haggled in the middle of a crowd of jabbering blacks, and I gave him half what he asked for and settled into the place with my establishment.

First of all I sent for the cook, and told him through my nigger: "You will cook, and cook cleanly. You'll wash your hands, d'ye see, and buy nothing but the finest meat and vegetables. If you don't, I'll have the cat taken to you until there isn't a strip of hide left on your back."

He jabbered away, nodding and grinning and bowing, so I took him by the neck and threw him down and lashed him with my riding whip until he rolled off the verandah, screaming.

"Tell him he'll get that night and morning if his food's not fit to eat," I told my nigger. "And the rest of them may take notice."

They all howled with fear, but they paid heed, the cook most of all. I took the opportunity to flog one of them every day, for their good and my own amusement, and to these precautions I attribute the fact that in all my service in India I was hardly ever laid low with anything worse than fever, and that you can't avoid. The cook was a good cook, as it turned out, and Basset kept the others at it with his tongue and his boot, so we did very well.

My nigger, whose name was Timbu-something-or-other, was of great use at first, since he spoke English, but after a few weeks I got rid of him. I've said that I have a gift of language, but it was only when I came to India that I realised this. My Latin and Greek had been weak at school, for I paid little attention to them, but a tongue that you hear spoken about you is a different thing. Each language has a rhythm for me, and my ear catches and holds the sounds; I seem to know what a man is saying even when I don't understand the words, and my own tongue slips easily into any new accent. In any event, after a fortnight listening to Timbu and asking him questions, I was speaking Hindustani well enough to be understood, and I paid him off. For one thing, I had found a more interesting teacher.

Her name was Fetnab, and I bought her (not officially, of course, although it amounted to the same thing) from a merchant whose livestock consisted of wenches for the British officers and civilian residents in Calcutta. She cost me 500 rupees, which was about 50 guineas, and she was a thief's bargain. I suppose she was about sixteen, with a handsome enough face and a gold stud fixed in her nostril, and great slanting brown eyes. Like most other Indian dancing girls, she was shaped like an hour-glass, with a waist that I could span with my two hands, fat breasts like melons, and a wobbling backside.

If anything she was a shade too plump, but she knew the ninety-seven ways of making love that the Hindus are supposed to set much store by—though mind you, it is all nonsense, for the seventy-fourth position turns out to be the same as the seventy-third, but with your fingers crossed. But she taught me them all in time, for she was devoted to her work, and would spend hours oiling herself with perfume all over her body and practising Hindu exercises to keep herself supple for night-time. After my first two days with her I thought less and less about Elspeth, and even Josette paled by comparison.

However, I put her to other good uses. In between bouts we would talk, for she was a great chatterbox, and I learned more of the refinements of Hindi from her than I would have done from any munshi. I give the advice for what it is worth: if you wish to learn a foreign tongue properly, study it in bed with a native girl—I'd have got more of the classics from an hour's wrestling with a Greek wench than I did in four years from Arnold.

So this was how I passed my time in Calcutta—my nights with Fetnab, my evenings in one of the messes, or someone's house, and my days riding or shooting or hunting, or simply wandering about the town itself. I became quite a well-known figure to the niggers, because I could speak to them in their own tongue, unlike the vast majority of officers at that time—even those who had served in India for years were usually too bored to try to learn Hindi, or thought it beneath them.

Another thing I learned, because of the regiment to which I was due to be posted, was how to manage a lance. I had been useful at sword exercise in the Hussars, but a lance is something else again. Any fool can couch it and ride straight, but if you are to be any use at all you must be able to handle all nine feet of it so that you can pick a playing card off the ground with the point, or pink a running rabbit. I was determined to shine among the Company men, so I hired a native rissalder of the Bengal Cavalry to teach me; I had no thought then of anything beyond tilting at dummies or wild pig sticking, and the thought of couching a lance against enemy cavalry was not one that I dwelt on much. But those lessons were to save my life once at least—so that was more well-spent money. They also settled the question of my immediate future, in an odd way.

I was out on the maidan one morning with my rissalder, a big, lean, ugly devil of the Pathan people of the frontier, named Muhammed Iqbal. He was a splendid horseman and managed a lance perfectly, and under his guidance I was learning quickly. That morning he had me tilting at pegs, and I speared so many that he said, grinning, that he must charge me more for my lessons.

We were trotting off the maidan, which was fairly empty that morning, except for a palankeen escorted by a couple of officers, which excited my curiosity a little, when Iqbal suddenly shouted:

"See, huzoor, a better target than little pegs!" and pointed towards a pariah dog which was snuffling about some fifty yards away. Iqbal couched his lance and went for it, but it darted out of his way, so I roared "Tally-ho!" and set off in pursuit. Iqbal was still ahead of me, but I was only a couple of lengths behind when he made another thrust at the pi-dog, which was racing ahead of him, swerving and yelping. He missed again, and yelled a curse, and the pi-dog suddenly turned almost beneath his hooves and leaped up at his foot. I dropped my point and by great good luck spitted the beast through the body.

With a shout of triumph I heaved him, twisting and still yelping, high into the air, and he fell behind me. Iqbal cried: "Shabash!" and I was beginning to crow over him when a voice shouted:

"You there! You, sir! Come here, if you please, this moment."

It came from the palankeen, towards which our run had taken us. The curtains were drawn, and the caller was revealed as a portly, fierce-looking gentleman in a frock coat, with a sun-browned face and a fine bald head. He had taken off his hat, and was waving insistently, so I rode across.

"Good morning," says he, very civil. "May I inquire your name?"

It did not need the presence of the two mounted dandies by the palankeen to tell me that this was a highly senior officer. Wondering, I introduced myself.

"Well, congratulations, Mr Flashman," says he. "Smart a piece of work as I've seen this year: if we had a regiment who could all manage a lance as well as you we'd have no trouble with damned Sikhs and Afghans, eh, Bennet?"

"Indeed not, sir," said one of the exquisite aides, eyeing me. "Mr Flashman; I seem to know the name. Are you not lately of the 11th Hussars, at home?"

"Eh, what's that?" said his chief, giving me a bright grey eye. "Bigod, so he is; see his Cherrypicker pants"—I was still wearing the pink breeches of the Hussars, which strictly I had no right to do, but they set off my figure admirably—"so he is, Bennet. Now, dammit, Flashman, Flashman—of course, the affair last year! You're the de-loper! Well I'm damned! What are you doing here, sir, in God's name?"

I explained, cautiously, trying to hint without actually saying so, that my arrival in India had followed directly from my meeting with Bernier (which was almost true, anyway), and my questioner whistled and exclaimed in excitement. I suppose I was enough of a novelty to rouse his interest, and he asked me a good deal about myself, which I answered fairly truthfully; in my turn I learned as he questioned me that he was General Crawford, on the staff of the Governor-General, and as such a commander of influence and importance.

"Bigad, you've had bad luck, Flashman," says he. "Banished from the lofty Cherrypickers, eh? Damned nonsense, but these blasted militia colonels like Cardigan have no sense. Eh, Bennet? And you're bound for Company service, are you? Well, the pay's good, but it's a damned shame. Waste your life teaching the sowars how to perform on galloping field days. Damned dusty work. Well, well, Flashman, I wish you success. Good day to you, sir."

And that would have settled that, no doubt, but for a queer chance. I had been sitting with my lance at rest, the point six feet above my head, and some of the pi-dog's blood dribbled down onto my hands; I gave an exclamation of disgust, and turning to Iqbal, who was sitting silently behind, I said:

"Khabadar, rissaldar! Larnce sarf karo, juldi!" which is to say, "Look out, sergeant-major. Take this lance and get it clean, quickly." And with that I tossed it to him. He caught it, and I turned back to take my leave of Crawford. He had stopped in the act of pulling his palankeen curtains.

"Here, Flashman," says he. "How long have you been

in India? What, three weeks, you say? But you speak the lingo, dammit!"

"Only a word or two, sir."

"Don't tell me, sir; I heard several words. Damned sight more than I learned in thirty years. Eh, Bennet? Too many 'ee's' and 'um's' for me. But that's damned extraordinary, young man. How'd you pick it up?"

I did more explaining, about my gift for languages, and he shook his bald head and said he'd never heard the like. "A born linguist and a born lancer, bigod. Rare combination—too dam' good for Company cavalry—all ride like pigs, anyway. Look here, young Flashman, I can't think at this time in the morning. You call on me tonight, d'ye hear? We'll go into this further. Hey, Bennet?"

And presently away he went, but I did call on him that evening, resplendent in my Cherrypicker togs, as he called them, and he looked at me and said:

"By God, Emily Eden mustn't miss this! She'd never forgive me!"

To my surprise, this was his way of indicating that I should go with him to the Governor-General's palace, where he was due for dinner, so of course I went, and had the privilege of drinking lemonade with their excellencies on their great marble verandah, while a splendid company stood about, like a small court, and I saw more quality in three seconds than in my three weeks in Calcutta. Which was very pleasant, but Crawford almost spoiled it by telling Lord Auckland about my duel with Bernier, at which he and Lady Emily, who was his sister, looked rather stiff —they were a stuffy pair, I thought—until I said fairly coolly to Crawford that I would have avoided the whole business if I could, but it had been forced upon me. At this Auckland nodded approval, and when it came out that I had been under Arnold at Rugby, the old bastard became downright civil. Lady Emily was even more so— thank God for Cherrypicker pants—and when she discovered I was only nineteen years old she nodded sadly, and spoke of the fair young shoots on the tree of empire.

She asked about my family, and when she learned I had a wife in England, she said:

"So young to be parted. How *hard* the service is."

Her brother observed, fairly drily, that there was nothing to prevent an officer having his wife in India with him, but I muttered something about winning my spurs, an inspired piece of nonsense which pleased Lady E. Her brother remarked that an astonishing number of young officers somehow survived the absence of a wife's consolation, and Crawford chortled, but Lady E. was on my side by now, and giving them her shoulder, asked where I was to be stationed.

I told her, and since it seemed to me that if I played my cards right I might get a more comfortable posting through her interest—Governor-General's aide was actually in my mind—I indicated that I had no great enthusiasm for Company service.

"Don't blame him, either," said Crawford. "Man's a positive Pole on horseback; shouldn't be wasted, eh, Flashman? Speaks Hindustani, too. Heard him."

"Really?" says Auckland. "That shows a remarkable zeal in study, Mr Flashman. But perhaps Dr Arnold may be to thank for that."

"Why must you take Mr Flashman's credit away from him?" says Lady E. "I think it is *quite* unusual. I think he should be found a post where his talents can be *properly* employed. Do you not agree, General?"

"Own views exactly, ma'am," says Crawford. "Should've heard him. 'Hey, rissaldar', says he, 'um-tiddly-o-karo', and the fellow understood every word."

Now you can imagine that this was heady stuff to me; this morning I had been any old subaltern, and here I was hearing compliments from a Governor-General, and General, and the First Lady of India—foolish old trot though she was. You're made, Flashy, I thought; it's the staff for you, and Auckland's next words seemed to bear out my hopes.

"Why not find something for him, then?" says he to Crawford. "General Elphinstone was saying only yesterday that he would need a few good gallopers."

Well, it wasn't the top of the tree, but galloper to a General was good enough for the time being.

"Bigod," says Crawford, "your excellency's right. What d'you say, Flashman? Care to ride aide to an army commander, hey? Better than Company work at the back of beyond, what?"

I naturally said I would be deeply honoured, and was starting to thank him, but he cut me off.

"You'll be more thankful yet when you know where Elphinstone's service'll take you," says he, grinning. "By gad, I wish I was your age and had the same chance. It's a Company army mostly, of course, and a damned good

one, but it took 'em a few years of service—as it would
have taken you—to get where they wanted to be."

I looked all eagerness, and Lady E. sighed and smiled
together.

"Poor boy," she said. "You must not tease him."

"Well, it will be out by tomorrow, anyway," says Crawford. "You don't know Elphinstone, of course, Flashman
—commands the Benares Division, or will do until midnight tonight. And then he takes over the Army of the Indus—what about that, eh?"

It sounded all right, and I made enthusiastic noises.

"Aye, you're a lucky dog," says Crawford, beaming.
"How many young blades would give their right leg for the
chance of service with him? In the very place for a dashing lancer to win his spurs, bigad!"

A nasty feeling tickled my spine, and I asked where that
might be.

"Why, Kabul, of course," says he. "Where else but Afghanistan?"

The old fool actually thought I must be delighted at this
news, and of course I had to pretend to be. I suppose any
young officer in India would have jumped at the opportunity, and I did my best to look gratified and eager, but I
could have knocked the grinning idiot down, I was so
angry. I had thought I was doing so well, what with my
sudden introduction to the exalted of the land, and all it
had won me was a posting to the hottest, hardest, most
dangerous place in the world, to judge by all accounts.
There was talk of nothing but Afghanistan in Calcutta at
that time, and of the Kabul expedition, and most of it
touched on the barbarity of the natives, and the unpleas-
antness of the country. I could have been sensible, I told
myself, and had myself quietly posted to Benares—but no,
I had had to angle round Lady Emily, and now looked
like getting my throat cut for my pains.

Thinking quickly, I kept my eager smile in place but
wondered whether General Elphinstone might not have
preferences of his own when it came to choosing an aide;
there might be others, I thought, who had a better
claim. . . .

Nonsense, says Crawford, he would go bail Elphinstone
would be delighted to have a man who could talk the language *and* handle a lance like a Cossack, and Lady Emily
said she was sure he would find a place for me. So there

was no way out; I was going to have to take it and pretend that I liked it.

That night I gave Fetnab the soundest thrashing of her pampered life and broke a pot over the sweeper's head.

I was not even given a decent time to prepare myself. General Elphinstone (or Elphy Bey, as the wags called him) received me next day, and turned out to be an elderly, fussy man with a brown wrinkled face and heavy white whiskers; he was kind enough, in a doddering way, and as unlikely a commander of armies as you could imagine, being nearly sixty, and none too well either.

"It is a great honour to me," says he, speaking of his new command, "but I could wish it had fallen on younger shoulders—indeed, I am sure it should." He shook his head, and looked gloomy, and I thought, well, here's a fine one to take the field with.

However, he welcomed me to his staff, damn him, and said it was most opportune; he could use me at once. Since his present aides were used to his service, he would keep them with him just now, to prepare for the journey; he would send me in advance to Kabul—which meant, I supposed, that I was to herald his coming, and see that his quarters were swept out for his arrival. So I had to gather up my establishment, hire camels and mules for their transport, lay in stores for the journey, and generally go to a deal of expense and bother. My servants kept well out of my way in those days, I can tell you, and Fetnab went about whimpering and rolling her eyes. I told her to shut up or I would give her to the Afghans when we got to Kabul, and she was so terrified that she actually kept quiet.

However, after my first disappointment I realised there was no sense crying over spilt milk, and looked on the bright side. I was, after all, to be aide to a general, which would be helpful in years to come, and gave one great distinction. Afghanistan was at least quiet for the moment, and Elphy Bey's term of command could hardly last long, at his age. I could take Fetnab and my household with me, including Basset, and with Elphy Bey's influence I was allowed to enlist Muhammed Iqbal in my party. He spoke Pushtu, of course, which is the language of the Afghans, and could instruct me as we went. Also, he was an excellent fellow to have beside you, and would be an invaluable companion and guide.

Before we started out, I got hold of as much information as I could about matters in Afghanistan. They seemed to stand damned riskily to me, and there were others in Calcutta—but not Auckland, who was an ass—who shared this view. The reason we had sent an expedition to Kabul, which is in the very heart of some of the worst country in the world, was that we were afraid of Russia. Afghanistan was a buffer, if you like, between India and the Turkestan territory which Russia largely influenced, and the Russians were forever meddling in Afghan affairs, in the hope of expanding southwards and perhaps seizing India itself. So Afghanistan mattered very much to us, and thanks to that conceited Scotch buffoon Burnes the British Government had invaded the country, if you please, and put our puppet king, Shah Sujah, on the throne in Kabul, in place of old Dost Mohammed, who was suspected of Russian sympathies.

I believe, from all I saw and heard, that if he had Russian sympathies it was because we drove him to them by our stupid policy; at any rate, the Kabul expedition succeeded in setting Sujah on the throne, and old Dost was politely locked up in India. So far, so good, but the Afghans didn't like Sujah at all, and we had to leave an army in Kabul to keep him on his throne. This was the army that Elphy Bey was to command. It was a good enough army, part Queen's troops, part Company's, with British regiments as well as native ones, but it was having its work cut out trying to keep the tribes in order, for apart from Dost's supporters there were scores of little petty chiefs and tyrants who lost no opportunity of causing trouble in the unsettled times, and the usual Afghan pastimes of blood-feud, robbery, and murder-for-fun were going ahead full steam. Our army prevented any big rising —for the moment, anyway—but it was forever patrolling and manning little forts, and trying to pacify and buy off the robber chiefs, and people were wondering how long this could go on. The wise ones said there was an explosion coming, and as we started out on our journey from Calcutta my foremost thought was that whoever got blown up, it should not be me. It was just my luck that I was going to end up on top of the bonfire.

Travelling, I think, is the greatest bore in life, so I'll not weary you with an account of the journey from Calcutta to Kabul. It was long and hot and damnably dull; if Basset and I had not taken Muhammed Iqbal's advice and shed our uniforms for native dress, I doubt whether we would have survived. In desert, on scrubby plain, through rocky hills, in the forests, in the little mud villages and camps and towns—the heat was horrible and ceaseless; your skin scorched, your eyes burned, and you felt that your body was turning into a dry bag of bones. But in the loose robes and pyjamy trousers one felt cooler—that is, one fried without burning quite black.

Basset, Iqbal and I rode horses, the servants tramped behind with Fetnab in a litter, but our pace was so slow that after a week we got rid of them all but the cook. The servants we turned off, amid great lamentations, and Fetnab I sold to a major in the artillery, whose camp we passed through. I regretted that, for she had become a habit, but she was peevish on the journey and too tired and mopish at night to be much fun. Still, I can't recall a wench I enjoyed more.

We pushed on faster after that, west and then northwest, over the plains and great rivers of the Punjab, through the Sikh country, and up to Peshawar, which is where India ends. There was nothing to remind you of Calcutta now; here the heat was dry and glaring, and so were the people—lean, ugly, Jewish-looking creatures, armed and ready for mischief by the look of them. But none was uglier or looked readier for mischief than the governor of the place, a great, grey-bearded ox of a man in a dirty old uniform coat, baggy trousers, and gold-tasselled forage cap. He was an Italian, of all things, with the spiky waxed moustache that you see on organ-grinders nowadays, and he spoke English with a dreadful dago American accent. His name was Avitabile,[11] and the Sikhs

72

and Afghans were more scared of him than of the devil himself; he had drifted to India as a soldier of fortune, commanded Shah Sujah's army, and now had the job of keeping the passes open to our people in Kabul.

He did it admirably, in the only way those brutes understood—by fear and force. There were five dead Afghans swinging in the sunlight from his gateway arch when we rode through, which was both reassuring and unnerving at once. No one minded them more than if they had been swatted flies, least of all Avitabile, who had strung them up.

"Goddam, boy," says he, "how you think I keep the peace if I don' keep killing these bastards? These are Gilzais, you know that? *Good* Gilzais, now I've 'tended to them. The bad Gilzais are up in the hills, between here and Kabul, watchin' the passes and lickin' their lips and thinkin'—but thinkin's all they do just now, 'cos of Avitabile. Sure, we pay 'em to be quiet; you think that would stop them? No, sir, fear of Avitabile"—and he jerked a huge thumb at his chest—"fear's what stops 'em. But if I stopped hangin' 'em now and then, they'd stop bein' afraid. See?"

He had me to dinner that night, and we ate an excellent stew of chicken and fruit on a terrace looking over the dirty rooftops of Peshawar, with the sounds and smells of the bazaar floating up to us. Avitabile was a good host, and talked all night of Naples and women and drink; he seemed to take a fancy to me, and we got very drunk together. He was one of your noisy, bellowing drunkards, and we sang uproariously, I remember, but at dawn, as we were staggering to our beds, he stopped outside my room, with his great dirty hand on my shoulder, and looked at me with his bright grey eyes, and said in a very sober, quiet voice:

"Boy, I think you are another like me, at heart: a condottieri, a rascal. Maybe with a little honour, a little courage. I don't know. But, see now, you are going beyond the Khyber, and some day soon the Gilzais and others will be afraid no longer. Against that day, get a swift horse and some Afghans you can trust—there are some, like the Kuzzilbashis—and if the day comes, don't wait to die on the field of honour." He said it without a sneer. "Heroes draw no higher wages than the others, boy. Sleep well."

And he nodded and stumped off down the passage, with his gold cap still firmly on his head. In my drunken state I took little heed of what he had said, but it came back to me later.

In the morning we rode north into one of the world's awful places—the great pass of the Khyber, where the track twists among the sun-scorched cliffs and the peaks seem to crouch in ambush for the traveller. There was some traffic on the road, and we passed a commissary train on its way to Kabul, but most of those we saw were Afghan hillmen, rangy warriors in skull caps or turbans and long coats, with immensely long rifles, called jezzails, at their shoulders, and the Khyber knife (which is like a pointed cleaver) in their belts. Muhammed Iqbal was gay at returning to his own place, and had me airing my halting Pushtu on those we spoke to; they seemed taken aback to find an English officer who had their own tongue, however crudely, and were friendly enough. But I didn't like the look of them; you could see treachery in their dark eyes—besides, there is something odd about men who look like Satan and yet wear ringlets and love-locks hanging out beneath their turbans.

We were three nights on the road beyond the Khyber, and the country got more hellish all the way—it beat me how a British army, with all its thousands of followers and carts and wagons and guns had ever got over those flinty paths. But at last we came to Kabul, and I saw the great fortress of Bala Hissar lowering over the city, and beyond it to the right the neat lines of the cantonment beside the water's edge, where the red tunics showed like tiny dolls in the distance and the sound of a bugle came faintly over the river. It was very pretty in the summer's evening, with the orchards and gardens before us, and the squalor of Kabul Town hidden behind the Bala Hissar. Aye, it was pretty then.

We crossed the Kabul River bridge and when I had reported myself and bathed and changed into my regimentals I was directed to the general commanding, to whom I was to deliver despatches from Elphy Bey. His name was Sir Willoughby Cotton, and he looked it, for he was round and fat and red-faced. When I found him he was being hectored by a tall, fine-looking officer in faded uniform, and I at once learned two things—in the Kabul garrison there was no sense of privacy or restraint, and the most senior officers never thought twice about discussing their affairs before their juniors.

". . . the biggest damned fool this side of the Indus,"

the tall officer was saying when I presented myself. "I tell you, Cotton, this army is like a bear in a trap. If there's a rising, where are you? Stuck helpless in the middle of a people who hate your innards, a week from the nearest friendly garrison, with a bloody fool like McNaghten writing letters to that even bloodier fool Auckland in Calcutta that everything's all right. God help us! And they're relieving you—"

"God be thanked," said Cotton.

"—and sending us Elphy Bey, who'll be under McNaghten's thumb and isn't fit to command an escort anyway. The worst of it is, McNaghten and the other political asses think we are safe as on Salisbury Plain! Burnes is as bad as the rest—not that he thinks of anything but Afghan women—but they're all so sure they're right! That's what upsets me. And who the devil are you?"

This was to me. I bowed and presented my letters to Cotton, who seemed glad of the interruption.

"Glad to see you, sir," says he, dropping the letters on the desk. "Elphy's herald, eh? Well, well. Flashman, did you say? Now that's odd. There was a Flashman with me at Rugby, oh, oh, forty years ago. Any relation?"

"My father, sir."

"Ye don't say? Well, I'm damned. Flashy's boy." And he beamed all over his red face. "Why, it *must* be forty years. . . . He's well I trust? Excellent, excellent. What'll you have, sir? Glass of wine? Here, bearer. Of course, your father will have spoke of me, eh? I was quite a card at school. Got expelled, d'ye know."

This was too good a chance to miss, so I said: "I was expelled from Rugby, too, sir."

"Good God! You don't say! What for, sir?"

"Drunkenness, sir."

"No! Well, damme! Who'd have believed they would kick you out for that? They'll be expellin' for rape next. Wouldn't have done in my time. I was expelled for mutiny, sir—yes, mutiny! Led the whole school in revolt! [12] Splendid! Well, here's your health, sir!"

The officer in the faded coat, who had been looking pretty sour, remarked that expulsion from school was all very well, but what concerned him was expulsion from Afghanistan.

"Pardon me," said Cotton, wiping his lips. "Forgot my manners. Mr Flashman, General Nott. General Nott is up from Kandahar, where he commands. We were discussing the state of the army in Afghanistan. No, no, Flashman, sit down. This ain't Calcutta. On active service the more you know the better. Pray proceed, Nott."

So I sat, a little bewildered and flattered, for generals don't usually talk before subalterns, while Nott resumed his tirade. It seemed that he had been offended by some communication from McNaghten—Sir William McNaghten, Envoy to Kabul, and head British civilian in the country. Nott was appealing to Cotton to support him in protest, but Cotton didn't seem to care for the idea.

"It is a simple question of policy," said Nott. "The country, whatever McNaghten may think, is hostile, and we have to treat it as such. We do this in three ways—through the influence which Sujah exerts on his unwilling subjects, which is little enough; through the force of our army here, which with respect is not as all-powerful as McNaghten imagines, since you're outnumbered fifty to one by one of the fiercest warrior nations in the world; and thirdly, by buying the good will of important chiefs with money. Am I right?"

"Talking like a book," said Cotton. "Fill your glass, Mr Flashman."

"If one of those three instruments of policy fails—Sujah, our strength, or our money—we're done for. Oh, I know I'm a 'croaker', as McNaghten would say; he thinks we are as secure here as on Horse Guards. He's wrong, you know. We exist on sufferance, and there won't be much of that if he takes up this idea of cutting the subsidy to the Gilzai chiefs."

"It would save money," said Cotton. "Anyway, it's no more than a thought, as I understand."

"It would save money if you didn't buy a bandage when you were bleeding to death," said Nott, at which Cotton guffawed. "Aye, laugh, Sir Willoughby, but this is a serious matter. Cutting the subsidy is no more than a thought, you say. Very good, it may never happen. But if the Gilzais so much as suspect it *might,* how long will they continue to keep the passes open? They sit above the Khyber —your lifeline, remember—and let our convoys come and go, but if they think their subsidy is in danger they'll look for another source of revenue. And that will mean convoys ambushed and looted, and a very pretty business on your hands. That is why McNaghten's a fool even to *think* of cutting the subsidy, let alone *talk* about it."

"What do you want me to do?" says Cotton, frowning.

"Tell him to drop the notion at all costs. He won't listen to me. And send someone to talk to the Gilzais, take a few gifts to old what's-his-name at Mogala—Sher Afzul. He has the other Gilzai khans under his thumb, I'm told."

"You know a lot about this country," said Cotton, wagging his head. "Considering this ain't your territory."

"Someone's got to," said Nott. "Thirty years in the Company's service teaches you a thing or two. I wish I thought McNaghten had learned as much. But he goes his way happily, seeing no farther than the end of his nose. Well, well, Cotton, you're one of the lucky ones. You'll be getting out in time."

Cotton protested at this that he was a 'croaker' after all —I soon discovered that the word was applied to everyone who ventured to criticise McNaghten or express doubts about the safety of the British force in Kabul. They talked on for a while, and Cotton was very civil to me and seemed intent on making me feel at home. We dined in his headquarters, with his staff, and there for the first time I met some of the men, many of them fairly junior officers, whose names were to be household words in England within the next year—"Sekundar" Burnes, with his mincing Scotch voice and pretty little moustache; George Broadfoot, another Scotsman, who sat next to me; Vincent Eyre, "Gentleman Jim" Skinner, Colonel Oliver, and various others. They talked with a freedom that was astonishing, criticising or defending their superiors in the presence of general officers, condemning this policy and praising that, and Cotton and Nott joined in. There was not much good said about McNaghten, and a general gloom about the army's situation; it seemed to me they scared rather easily, and I told Broadfoot so.

"Wait till ye've been here a month or two, and ye'll be as bad as the rest," he said brusquely. "It's a bad place, and a bad people, and if we don't have war on our hands inside a year I'll be surprised. Have you heard of Akbar Khan? No? He's the son of the old king, Dost Mohammed, that we deposed for this clown Sujah, and he's in the hills now, going from this chief to that, gathering support for the day when he'll raise the country against us. McNaghten won't believe it, of course, but he's a gommeril."

"Could we not hold Kabul?" I asked. "Surely with a force of five thousand it should be possible, against undisciplined savages."

"These savages are good men," says he. "Better shots than we are, for one thing. And we're badly placed here, with no proper fortifications for the cantonment—even the stores are outside the perimeter—and an army that's going downhill with soft living and bad discipline. Forbye, we have our families with us, and that's a bad thing when the bullets are flying—who thinks of his duty when he has his wife and weans to care for? And Elphy Bey is to command us when Cotton goes." He shook his head. "You'll know him better than I, but I'd give my next year's pay to hear he wasn't coming and we had Nott instead. I'd sleep at nights, anyway."

This was depressing enough, but in the next few weeks I heard this kind of talk on all hands—there was obviously no confidence in the military or political chiefs, and the Afghans seemed to sense this, for they were an insolent crowd and had no great respect for us. As an aide to Elphy Bey, who was still on his road north, I had time on my hands to look about Kabul, which was a great, filthy sprawling place full of narrow lanes and smelling abominably. But we seldom went there, for the folk hardly made us welcome, and it was pleasant out by the cantonment, where there was little attention to soldiering but a great deal of horse-racing and lounging in the orchards and gossiping on the verandahs over cool drinks. There were even cricket matches, and I played myself—I had been a great bowler at Rugby, and my new friends made more of the wickets I took than of the fact that I was beginning to speak Pushtu better than any of them except Burnes and the politicals.

It was at one of these matches that I first saw Shah Sujah, the king, who had come down as the guest of McNaghten. He was a portly, brown-bearded man who stood gravely contemplating the game, and when McNaghten asked him how he liked it, said:

"Strange and manifold are the ways of God."

As for McNaghten himself, I despised him on sight. He had a clerk's face, with a pointed nose and chin, and peered through his spectacles suspiciously, sniffing at you. He was vain as a peacock, though, and would strut about in his tall hat and frock-coat, lording it greatly, with his nose turned up. It was evident, as someone said, that he saw only what he wanted to see. Anyone else would have realised that his army was in a mess, for one thing, but not McNaghten. He even seemed to think that Sujah was popular with the people, and that we were honoured guests in the country; if he had heard the men in the bazaar calling us "kaffirs" he might have realised his mistake. But he was too lofty to hear.

However, I passed the time pleasantly enough. Burnes, the political agent, when he heard about my Pushtu, took some interest in me, and as he kept a splendid table, and was an influential fellow, I kept in with him. He was a pompous fool, of course, but he knew a good deal about the Afghans, and would go about from time to time in native dress, mixing with the crowds in the bazaar, listening to gossip and keeping his nose to the wind generally. He had another reason for this, of course, which was that he was forever in pursuit of some Afghan woman or other, and had to go to the city to find them. I went with him on these expeditions frequently, and very rewarding they were.

Afghan women are handsome rather than pretty, but they have this great advantage to them, that their own men don't care for them overmuch. Afghan men would as soon be perverts as not, and have a great taste for young boys; it would sicken you to see them mooning over these painted youths as though they were girls, and our troops thought it a tremendous joke. However, it meant that the Afghan women were always hungry for men, and you could have your pick of them—tall, graceful creatures they were, with long straight noses and proud mouths, running more to muscle than fat, and very active in bed.

Of course, the Afghans didn't care for this, which was another score against us where they were concerned.

The first weeks passed, as I say, pleasantly, and I was beginning to like Kabul, in spite of the pessimists, when I was shaken out of my pleasant rut, thanks to my friend Burnes and the anxieties of General Nott, who had gone back to Kandahar but left his warnings ringing in Sir Willoughby Cotton's ears. They must have rung an alarm, for when he sent for me to his office in the cantonment he was looking pretty glum, with Burnes at his elbow.

"Flashman," says Cotton, "Sir Alexander here tells me you get along famously with the Afghans."

Thinking of the women, I agreed.

"Hm, well. And you talk their frightful lingo?"

"Passably well, sir."

"That means a dam' sight better than most of us. Well, I daresay I shouldn't do it, but on Sir Alexander's suggestion"—here Burnes gave me a smile, which I felt somehow boded no good—"and since you're the son of an old friend, I'm going to give you some work to do—work which'll help your advancement, let me say, if you do it well, d'you see?" He stared at me a moment, and growled to Burnes: "Dammit, Sandy, he's devilish young, y'know."

"No younger than I was," says Burnes.

"Umph. Oh, well, I suppose it's all right. Now, look here, Flashman—you know about the Gilzais, I suppose? They control the passes between here and India, and are devilish tricky fellows. You were with me when Nott was talking about their subsidy, and how there were rumours that the politicals would cut it, dam' fools, with all respect, Sandy. Well, it will be cut—in time—but for the present it's imperative they should be told that all's well, d'you see? Sir William McNaghten has agreed to this—fact is, he's written letters to Sher Afzul, at Mogala, and he's the leader of the pack, so to speak."

This seemed to me a pretty piece of duplicity on Mc-Naghten's part, but it was typical of our dealings with the Afghans, as I was to discover.

"You're going to be our postman, like Mr Rowland Hill's fellows at home. You'll take the messages of good will to Sher Afzul, hand 'em over, say how splendid everything is, be polite to the old devil—he's half-mad, by the way—set his mind at rest if he's still worried about the subsidy, and so forth."

"It will all be in the letters," says Burnes. "You must just give any added reassurance that may be needed."

"All right, Flashman?" says Cotton. "Good experience for you. Diplomatic mission, what?"

"It's very important," says Burnes. "You see, if they thought there was anything wrong, or grew suspicious, it could be bad for us."

It could be a damned sight worse for me, I thought. I didn't like this idea above half—all I knew of the Gilzais was that they were murderous brutes, like all country Afghans, and the thought of walking into their nests, up in the hills, with not the slightest hope of help if there was trouble—well, Kabul might not be Hyde Park, but at least it was safe for the present. And what the Afghan women did to prisoners was enough to start my stomach turning at the thought—I'd heard the stories.

Some of this must have showed in my face, for Cotton

asked fairly sharply what was the matter. Didn't I want to go?

"Of course, sir," I lied. "But—well, I'm pretty raw, I know. A more experienced officer. . . ."

"Don't fret yourself," says Burnes, smiling. "You're more at home with these folk than some men with twenty years in the service." He winked. "I've seen you, Flashman, remember. Hah-ha! And you've got what they call 'a fool's face.' No disrespect: it means you look honest. Besides, the fact that you have some Pushtu will win their confidence."

"But as General Elphinstone's aide, should I not be here. . . ."

"Elphy ain't due for a week," snapped Cotton. "Dammit, man, this is an opportunity. Any young feller in your shoes would be bursting to go."

I saw it would be bad to try to make further excuses, so I said I was all eagerness, of course, and had only wanted to be sure I was the right man, and so forth. That settled it: Burnes took me to the great wall map, and showed me where Mogala was—needless to say, it was at the back of nowhere, about fifty miles from Kabul, in hellish hill country south of the Jugdulluk Pass. He pointed out the road we should take, assuring me I should have a good guide, and produced the sealed packet I was to deliver to the half-mad (and doubtless half-human) Sher Afzul.

"Make sure they go into his own hands," he told me. "He's a good friend to us—just now—but I don't trust his nephew, Gul Shah. He was too thick with Akbar Khan in the old days. If there's ever trouble among the Gilzais, it will come from Gul, so watch out for him. And I don't have to tell you to be careful of old Azful—he's sharp when he's sane, which is most of the time. He's lord of life and death in his own parish, and that includes you. Not that he's likely to offer you harm, but keep on his good side."

I began to wonder if I could manage to fall ill in the next hour or two—jaundice, possibly, or something infectious. Cotton set the final seal on it.

"If there's trouble," says he, "you must just ride for it."

To this fatherly advice he and Burnes added a few words about how I should conduct myself if the matter of subsidy was discussed with me, bidding me be reassuring at all costs—no thought of who should reassure *me*, I may say—and dismissed me. Burnes said they had high hopes of me, a sentiment I found it difficult to share.

However, there was nothing for it, and next morning found me on the road east, with Iqbal and an Afghan guide on either side and five troopers of the 16th Lancers for escort. It was a tiny enough guard to be useless against anything but a stray robber—and Afghanistan never lacked for those—but it gave me some heart, and what with the fresh morning air, and the thought that all would probably be well and the mission another small stepping stone in the career of Lieutenant Flashman, I felt rather more cheerful.

The sergeant in charge of the Lancers was called Hudson, and he had already shown himself a steady and capable man. Before setting out he had suggested I leave behind my sabre—they were poor weapons, the Army swords, and turned in your grip [13]—and take instead one of the Persian scimitars that some of the Afghans used. They were light and strong, and damned sharp. He had been very business-like about it, and about such matters as rations for the men and fodder for the horses. He was one of those quiet, middle-sized, square-set men who seem to know exactly what they are doing, and it was good to have him and Iqbal at my back.

Our first day's march took us as far as Khoord-Kabul, and on the second we left the track at Tezeen and went south-east into the hills. The going had been rough enough on the path, but now it was frightful—the land was all sun-scorched rock and jagged peaks, with stony defiles that were like ovens, where the ponies stumbled over the loose stones. We hardly saw a living creature for twenty miles after we left Tezeen, and when night came we were camped on a high pass, in the lee of a cliff that might have been the wall of hell. It was bitter cold, and the wind howled up the pass; far away a wolf wailed, and we had barely enough wood to keep our fire going. I lay in my blanket cursing the day I got drunk at Rugby, and wishing I were snug in a warm bed with Elspeth or Fetnab or Josette.

Next day we were picking our way up a long stony slope when Iqbal muttered and pointed, and far ahead on a rocky shoulder I made out a figure which vanished almost as soon as I saw it.

"Gilzai scout," said Iqbal, and in the next hour we saw a dozen more of them; as we rode upwards we were aware of them in the hills on either side, behind boulders or on the ledges, and in the last few miles there were horsemen shadowing us on either side and behind. Then we came out of a defile, and the guide pointed ahead to a height crowned with a great grey fortress, with a round tower behind its outer wall, and a cluster of huts outside its embattled gate. This was Mogala, stronghold of the Gilzai chieftain, Sher Afzul. I seldom saw a place I liked less at first sight.

We went forward at a canter, and the horsemen who had been following us galloped into the open on either side, keeping pace to the fort, but not approaching too close to us. They rode Afghan ponies, carried long jezzails and lances, and were a tough-looking crowd; some wore mail over their robes, and a few had spiked helmets; they looked like warriors from an Eastern fairy tale, with their outlandish clothes and fierce bearded faces—and of course, they were.

Close by the gate was a row of four wooden crosses, and to my horror I realised that the blackened, twisted things nailed to them were human bodies. Sher Afzul obviously had his own notions of discipline. One or two of the troopers muttered at the sight, and there were anxious glances at our shadowers, who had lined up on either side of the gateway. I was feeling a trifle wobbly myself, but I thought, to hell with these blackamoors, we are Englishmen, and so I said, "Come on, lads, ride to attention," and we clattered under the frowning gateway.

I suppose Mogala is about a quarter of a mile from wall to wall, but inside its battlements, in addition to its huge keep, there were barracks and stables for Sher Afzul's warriors, storehouses and armouries, and the house of the Khan himself. In fact, it was more of a little palace than a house, for it stood in a pretty garden under the shadow of the outer wall, shaded by cypress trees, and it was furnished inside like something from Burton's *Arabian Nights*. There were tapestries on the walls, carpets on the paved floor, intricately carved wood screens in the archways, and a general air of luxury—he did himself well, I thought, but he took no chances. There were sentries all over the place, big men and well armed.

Sher Afzul turned out to be a man about sixty, with a beard dyed jet black, and a lined, ugly face whose main features were two fierce, burning eyes that looked straight through you. He received me civilly enough in his fine

presence chamber, where he sat on a small throne with his
court about him, but I couldn't doubt Burnes's assertion
that he was half-mad. His hands twitched continuously,
and he had a habit of jerking his turbanned head in a
most violent fashion as he spoke. But he listened atten-
tively as one of his ministers read aloud McNaghten's letter, and seemed satisfied, and he and his people exclaimed
with delight over the present that Cotton had sent—a pair
of very handsome pistols by Manton, in a velvet case, with
a matching shot pouch and powder flask. Nothing would
do but we must go straight into the garden for the Khan
to try them out; he was a rotten shot, but at the fourth
attempt he managed to blow the head off a very handsome
parrot which sat chained on a perch, screeching at the ex-
plosions until the lucky shot put an end to it.

There was loud applause, and Sher Afzul wagged his
head and seemed well pleased.

"A splendid gift," he told me, and I was pleased to find
that my Pushtu was quite good enough for me to follow
him. "You are the more welcome, Flashman bahadur, in
that your guns are true. By God, it is a soldier's weapon!"

I said I was delighted, and had the happy idea of presenting one of my own pistols on the spot to the Khan's
son, a bright, handsome lad of about sixteen, called Ilderim. He shouted with delight, and his eyes shone as he
handled the weapon—I was off to a good start.

Then one of the courtiers came forward, and I felt a
prickle up my spine as I looked at him. He was a tall man
—as tall as I was—with those big shoulders and the slim
waist of an athlete. His coat was black and well fitting, he
wore long boots, and there was a silk sash round his waist
to carry his sabre. On his head he had one of those polished steel casques with vertical prongs, and the face
under it was strikingly handsome in the rather pretty Eastern way which I personally don't like. You have seen them
—straight nose, very full lips, woman's cheeks and jaw.
He had a forked beard and two of the coldest eyes I ever
saw. I put him down as a nasty customer, and I was right.

"I can kill parrots with a sling," he said. "Are the feringhee pistols good for anything else?"

Sher Afzul damned his eyes, more or less, for casting
doubt on his fine new weapons, and thrusting one into the
fellow's hand, told him to try his luck. And to my amazement, the brute turned straight about, drew a bead on one

of the slaves working in the garden, and shot him on the spot.

I was shaken, I can tell you. I stared at the twitching body on the grass, and the Khan wagging his head, and at the murderer handing back the pistol with a shrug. Of course, it was only a nigger he had killed, and I knew that among Afghans life is dirt cheap; they think no more of killing a human being than you and I do of shooting a pheasant or catching a fish. But it's a trifle unsettling to a man of my temperament to know that he is in the power —for, guest or no, I was in their power—of blackguards who kill as wantonly and readily as that. That thought, more than the killing itself, rattled me.

Young Ilderim noticed this, and rebuked the black-coated man—not for murder, mark you, but for discourtesy to a guest!

"One does not bite the coin of the honoured stranger, Gul Shah," was what he said, meaning you don't look a gift horse in the mouth. For the moment I was too fascinated at what I had seen to pay much heed, but as the Khan, talking rapidly, escorted me inside again, I remembered that this Gul Shah was the customer Burnes had warned me about—the friend of the arch-rebel, Akbar Khan. I kept an eye on him as I talked with Sher Afzul, and it seemed to me he kept an eye on me in return.

Sher Afzul talked sanely enough, mostly about hunting and blood-letting of a sterner kind, but you couldn't miss the wild gleam in his eye, or the fact that his evil temper was never far from the surface. He was used to playing the tyrant, and only to young Ilderim, whom he adored, was he more than civil. He snarled at Gul from time to time, but the big man looked him in the eye and didn't seem put out.

That evening we dined in the Khan's presence chamber, sitting about on cushions forking with our fingers into the bowls of stew and rice and fruit, and drinking a pleasant Afghan liquor which had no great body to it. There would be about a dozen there, including Gul Shah, and after we had eaten and belched accordingly, Sher Afzul called for entertainment. This consisted of a good conjurer, and a few weedy youths with native flutes and tom-toms, and three or four dancing girls. I had pretended to be amused by the conjurer and musicians, but one of the dancing girls struck me as being worth more than a polite look: she was a glorious creature, very tall and long-legged, with a sulky, cold face and hair that had been dyed bright red and hung down in a tail to her backside. It was about all the covering she had; for the rest she wore satin trousers clasped low on her hips, and two brass breastplates which she removed at Sher Afzul's insistence.

He beckoned her to dance close in front of him, and the sight of the golden, near-naked body writhing and quivering made me forget where I was for the moment. By the time she had finished her dance, with the tom-toms throbbing and the sweat glistening on her painted face, I must have been eating her alive with my eyes; as she salaamed to Sher Afzul he suddenly grabbed her by the arm and pulled her towards him, and I noticed Gul Shah lean forward suddenly on his cushion.

Sher Afzul saw it too, for he looked one way and the other, grinning wickedly, and with his free hand began to fondle the girl's body. She took it with a face like stone, but Gul was glowering like thunder. Sher Afzul cackled and said to me:

"You like her, Flashman bahadur? Is she the kind of she-cat you delight to scratch with? Here, then, she is yours!"

And he shoved her so hard towards me that she fell headlong into my lap. I caught her, and with an oath Gul Shah was on his feet, his hand dropping to his hilt.

"She is not for any Frank dog," he shouted.

"By God, is she not?" roared Sher Afzul. "Who says so?"

Gul Shah told him who said so, and there was a pretty little exchange which ended with Sher Afzul ordering him from the room—and it seemed to me that the girl's eyes followed him with disappointment as he stamped off. Sher Afzul apologised for the disturbance, and said I must not mind Gul Shah, who was an impudent bastard, and very greedy where women were concerned. Did I like the girl? Her name was Narreeman, and if she did not please me I was not to hesitate to flog her to my heart's content.

All this, I saw, was deliberately aimed at Gul Shah, who presumably lusted after this female himself, thus giving Sher Afzul a chance to torment him. It was a dilemma for me: I had no desire to antagonise Gul Shah, but I could not afford to refuse Sher Afzul's hospitality, so to speak— also the hospitality was very warm and naked, and was lying across my lap, gasping still from the exertion of her dance, and causing me considerable excitement.

So I accepted at once, and waited impatiently while the time wore on with Sher Afzul talking interminably about his horses and his dogs and his falcons. At last it was over, and with Narreeman following I was conducted to the private room that had been allotted me—it was a beautiful, balmy evening with the scents wafting in from the garden, and I was looking forward to a sleepless night. As it turned out, it was a tremendous sell, for she simply lay like a side of beef, staring at the roof as though I weren't there. I coaxed at first, and then threatened, and then taking Sher Afzul's advice I pulled her across my knees and smartened her up with my riding switch. At this she suddenly rounded on me like a panther, snarling and clawing, and narrowly missed raking my eyes. I was so enraged that I laid into her for all I was worth, but she fought like fury, naked as she was, and only when I got home a few good cuts did she try to run for it. I hauled her away from the door, and after a vicious struggle I managed to rape her—the only time in my life I have found it necessary, by the way. It has its points, but I shouldn't care to do it regularly. I prefer willing women.

Afterwards I shoved her out—I'd no wish to get a thumbnail in my eye during the night—and the guards took her away. She had not uttered a word the whole time.

Sher Afzul, seeing my scratched face in the morning, demanded details, and he and his toadies crowed with delight when I told them. Gul Shah was not present, but I had no doubt willing tongues would bear the tale to him.

Not that I cared, and there I made a mistake. Gul was only a nephew of Sher Afzul, and a bastard at that, but he was a power among the Gilzais for his fighting skill, and was itching to topple old Sher Afzul and steal his throne. It would have been a poor look-out for the Kabul garrison if he had succeeded, for the Gilzais were trembling in the balance all the time about us, and Gul would have tipped the scale. He hated the British, and in Afzul's place would have closed the passes, even if it had meant losing the lakhs that were paid from India to keep them open. But Afzul, although ageing, was too tough and clever to be deposed just yet, and Ilderim, though only a boy, was well liked and regarded as certain to succeed him. And both of them were friendly, and could sway the other Gilzai chieftains.

A good deal of this I learned in the next two days, in

which I and my party were the honoured guests of Mogala. I kept my eyes and ears open, and the Gilzais were most hospitable, from Afzul down to the villagers whose huts crouched outside the wall. This I will say for the Afghan—he is a treacherous, evil brute when he wants to be, but while he is your friend he is a first-rate fellow. The point is, you must judge to a second when he is going to cease to be friendly. There is seldom any warning.

Looking back, though, I can say that I probably got on better with the Afghans than most Britons do. I imagine Thomas Hughes would have said that in many respects of character I resembled them, and I wouldn't deny it. However it may be, I enjoyed those first two days: we had horse races and other riding competitions, and I earned a good deal of credit by showing them how a Persian pony can be put over the jumps. Then there was hawking, in which Sher Afzul was an adept, and tremendous feasting at nights, and Sher Afzul gave me another dancing girl, with much cackling and advice on how to manage her, which advice proved to be unnecessary.

But while it was pleasant enough, you could never forget that in Afghanistan you are walking a knife-edge the whole time, and that these were cruel and blood-thirsty savages. Four men were executed on the second day, for armed robbery, in front of a delighted crowd in the courtyard, and a fifth, a petty chieftain, was blinded by Sher Afzul's physician. This is a common punishment among the Afghans: if a man is too important to be slaughtered like an ordinary felon, they take away his sight so that he can do no more harm. It was a sickening business, and one of my troopers got into a fight with a Gilzai over it, calling them filthy foreigners, which they could not understand. "A blind man is a dead man," was how they put it, and I had to make excuses to Sher Afzul and instruct Sergeant Hudson to give the trooper a punishment drill.

In all this I had nearly forgotten Gul Shah and the Narreeman affair, which was careless. I had my reminder on the third morning, when I was least expecting it.

Sher Afzul had said we must go boar-hunting, and we had a good hour's sport in the thicketed gullies of the Mogala valley, where the wild pigs bred. There were about twenty of us, including Hudson, Muhammed Iqbal and myself, with Sher Afzul directing operations. It was exciting work, but difficult in that close country, and we were frequently separated. Muhammed Iqbal and I made one sortie which took us well away from the main body, into a narrow defile where the forest ended, and there they were waiting for us—four horsemen, with spears couched, who made not a sound but thundered straight down on us. Instinctively I knew they were Gul's people, bent on murdering me—and no doubt compromising Sher Afzul with the British at the same time.

Iqbal, being a Pathan and loving a fight, gave a yell of delight, "Come on, huzoor!" and went for them. I didn't hesitate; if he wanted to take on odds it was his affair; I wheeled my pony and went hell-for-leather for the forest, with one eye cocked over my shoulder for safety.

Whether he realised I was leaving him alone, I don't know; it wouldn't have made any difference to him. Like me, he had a lance, but in addition he had a sword and pistol in his belt, so he got rid of the lance at once, hurling it into the chest of the leading Gilzai, and driving into the other three with his sabre swinging. He cut one down, but the other two swerved past him—it was me they wanted.

I dug my spurs in as they came tearing after me, with Iqbal wheeling after them in turn. He was bawling at me to turn and fight, the fool, but I had no thought but to get away from those hellish lance-points and the wolf-like bearded faces behind them. I rode like fury—and then the pony stumbled and I went over his head, crashing into the bushes and finishing up on a pile of stones with all the breath knocked out of me.

The bushes saved me, for the Gilzais couldn't come at me easily. They had to swerve round the clump, and I scrambled behind a tree. One of the ponies reared up and nearly knocked the other off balance; the rider yelled and had to drop his lance to save being thrown, and then Iqbal was on them, howling his war-cry. The Gilzai who was clutching his pony's mane was glaring at me and cursing, and suddenly the snarling face was literally split down the middle as Iqbal's sabre came whistling down on his head, shearing through cap and skull as if they had been putty. The other rider, who had been trying to get in a thrust at me round the tree-trunk, wheeled as Iqbal wrenched his sword free, and the pair of them closed as their ponies crashed into each other.

For one cursing, frantic moment they were locked together, Iqbal trying to get his point into the other's side, and the Gilzai with his dagger out, thrusting at Iqbal's body. I heard the thuds as the blows struck, and Iqbal shouting: "Huzoor! huzoor!" and then the ponies parted and the struggling men crashed into the dust.

From behind my tree I suddenly noticed that my lance was lying within a yard of me, where it had dropped in my fall. Why I didn't follow the instinct of a lifetime and simply run for it and leave them to fight it out, I don't know—probably I had some thought of possible disgrace. Anyway, I darted out and grabbed the lance, and as the Gilzai struggled uppermost and raised his bloody knife, I jammed the lance-point squarely into his back. He screamed and dropped the knife, and then lurched into the dust, kicking and clutching, and died.

Iqbal tried to struggle up, but he was done for. His face was grey, and there was a great crimson stain welling through his shirt. He was glaring at me, and as I ran to him he managed to rear up on one elbow.

"Soor kabaj," he gasped. "Ya, huzoor! Soor kabaj!"

Then he groaned and fell back, but as I knelt over him his eyes opened for a moment, and he gave a little moan and spat in my face, as best he could. So he died, calling me "son of a swine" in Hindi, which is the Muslim's crowning insult. I saw his point of view, of course.

So there I was, and there also were five dead men—at least, four were dead and the one whom Iqbal had sabred first was lying a little way up the defile, groaning with the side of his skull split. I was shaken by my fall and the scuffle, but it came to me swiftly that the quicker that one breathed his last, the better, so I hurried up with my lance, took a rather unsteady aim, and drove it into his throat. And I had just jerked it out, and was surveying the shambles, when there was a cry and a clatter of hooves, and Sergeant Hudson came galloping out of the wood.

He took it in at a glance—the corpses, the blood-stained ground, and the gallant Flashy standing in the middle, the sole survivor. But like the competent soldier he was, as soon as he realized that I was all right, he went round the bodies, to make sure no one was playing possum. He whistled sadly over Iqbal, and then said quietly: "Orders, sir?"

I was getting my wind and my senses back, and wondering what to do next. This was Gul's work, I was sure, but what would Sher Afzul do about it? He might argue that here was his credit destroyed with the British anyway, and make the best of a bad job by cutting all our throats. This was a happy thought, but before I had time to digest it there was a crashing and hallooing in the woods, and out came the rest of the hunting party, with Afzul at their head.

Perhaps my fear sharpened my wits—it often does. But I saw in a flash that the best course was to take a damned high hand. So before they had done more than shout their astonishment and call on the name of God and come piling off their ponies, I had strode forward to where Afzul was sitting his horse, and I shook the bloody lance point under his nose.

"Gilzai hospitality!" I roared. "Look on it! My servant murdered, myself escaped by a miracle! Is this Gilzai honour?"

He glared at me like someone demented, his mouth working horribly, and for a minute I thought we were done for. Then he covered his face with his hands, and began bawling about shame and disgrace and the guests who had eaten his salt. He was mad enough at the moment, I think, and probably a good thing too, for he kept wailing on in the same strain, and tearing at his beard, and finally he rolled out of the saddle and began beating at the ground. His creatures hurried round him, lamenting and calling on Allah—all except young Ilderim, who simply gazed at the carnage and said:

"This is Gul Shah's doing, my father!"

This brought old Afzul up short, and he set off on a new tack, raving about how he would tear out Gul's eyes and entrails and hang him on hooks to die by inches, and more excellent ideas. I turned my back on him, and mounted the pony which Hudson had brought, and at this Afzul came hurrying up to me, and grabbed my boot, and swore, with froth on his lips, that this assault on my person and his honour would be most horribly avenged.

"My person is my affair," says I, very British-officer-like, "and your honour is yours. I accept your apology."

He raved some more at this, and then began imploring me to tell him what he could do to put things right. He was in a rare taking for his honour—and no doubt his subsidy—and swore that anything I named should be done: only let him and his be forgiven.

"My life! My son's life! tribute, treasure, Flashman bahadur! Hostages! I will go to McNaghten huzoor, and humble myself! I will pay!"

He went babbling on, until I cut him short by saying that we did not accept such things as payment for debts of honour. But I saw that I had better go a little easier while his mood lasted, so I ended by saying that, but for the death of my servant, it was a small matter, and we would put it from our minds.

"But you shall have pledges of my honour!" cries he. "Aye, you shall see that the Gilzai pay the debt! In God's name! My son, my son Ilderim, I will give as a hostage to you! Carry him to McNaghten huzoor, as a sign of his father's faith! Let me not be shamed, Flashman Huzoor, in my old age!"

Now this business of hostages was a common one with the Afghans, and it seemed to me that it had great advantages in this case. With Ilderim in my keeping, it wasn't likely that this hysterical old lunatic, when his madness took a new turn, would try any mischief. And young Ilderim looked pleased enough at the idea; he was probably thinking of the excitement of going to Kabul, and seeing the great Queen's army, and riding with it, too, as my protégé.

So there and then I took Sher Afzul at his word, and swore that the dishonour would be wiped out, and Ilderim would ride with me until I released him. At this the old Khan grew maudlin, and hauled out his Khyber knife and made Ilderim swear on it that he would be my man, which he did, and there was general rejoicing, and Sher Afzul went round and kicked all the corpses of the Gilzais and called on God to damn them good and proper. After which we rode back to Mogala, and I resisted the old Khan's entreaties to stay longer in proof of friendship: I had orders, I said, and must go back to Kabul. It would not do, I added, for me to linger when I had so important a hostage as the son of the khan of Mogala to take back.

He took this most seriously, and swore that his son would go as befitted a prince (which was stretching it a bit), and gave him a dozen Gilzai riders as escort, to stay with him and me. So there was more oath-swearing, and Sher Afzul finished up in excellent humour, vowing it was an honour to the Gilzais to serve such a splendid warrior as Flashman huzoor, who had accounted for four enemies single-handed (Iqbal being conveniently forgotten), and who would forever be dear to the Gilzais for his courage and magnanimity. As proof of which he would send me Gul Shah's ears, nose. eyes, and other essential organs as soon as he could lay hold of them.

So we left Mogala, and I had collected a personal following of Afghan tribesmen, and a reputation, as a result of the morning's work. The twelve Gilzais and Ilderim were the best things I found in Afghanistan, and the nickname "Bloody Lance," which Sher Afzul conferred, did me no harm either. Incidentally, as a result of all this Sher Afzul was keener than ever to maintain his alliance with the British, so my mission was a success as well. I was pretty pleased with myself as we set off for Kabul.

Of course, I had not forgotten that I had also made an outstanding enemy in Gul Shah. How bitter an enemy I was to find out in time.

Any excitement that the affair at Mogala might have caused in Kabul when we got back and told our tale was overshadowed by the arrival on the same day of the new army commander, General Elphinstone, my chief and sponsor. I was piqued at the time, for I thought I had done pretty well, and was annoyed to find that no one thought my skirmish with the Gilzais and securing of hostages worth more than a cocked eyebrow and an "Oh, really?"

But looking back I can say that, all unwittingly, Kabul and the army were right to regard Elphy's arrival as an incident of the greatest significance. It opened a new chapter: it was a prelude to events that rang round the world. Elphy, ably assisted by McNaghten, was about to reach the peak of his career; he was going to produce the most shameful, ridiculous disaster in British military history.

No doubt Thomas Hughes would find it significant that in such a disaster I would emerge with fame, honour, and distinction—all quite unworthily acquired. But you, having followed my progress so far, won't be surprised at all.

Let me say that when I talk of disasters I speak with authority. I have served at Balaclava, Cawnpore, and Little Big Horn. Name the biggest born fools who wore uniform in the nineteenth century—Cardigan, Sale, Custer, Raglan, Lucan—I knew them all. Think of all the conceivable misfortunes that can arise from combinations of folly, cowardice, and sheer bad luck, and I'll give you chapter and verse. But I still state unhesitatingly, that for pure, vacillating stupidity, for superb incompetence to command, for ignorance combined with bad judgement—in short, for the true talent for catastrophe—Elphy Bey stood alone. Others abide our question, but Elphy outshines them all as the greatest military idiot of our own or any other day.

Only he could have permitted the First Afghan War and

let it develop to such a ruinous defeat. It was not easy: he started with a good army, a secure position, some excellent officers, a disorganised enemy, and repeated opportunities to save the situation. But Elphy, with the touch of true genius, swept aside these obstacles with unerring precision, and out of order wrought complete chaos. We shall not, with luck, look upon his like again.

However, I tell you this not as a preface to a history of the war, but because if you are to judge my career properly, and understand how the bully expelled from Rugby became a hero, you have to know how things were in that extraordinary year of 1841. The story of the war and its beginnings is the background of the picture, although dashing Harry Flashman is the main figure in the foreground.

Elphy came to Kabul, then, and was met with great junketings and packed streets. Sujah welcomed him at the Bala Hissar, the army in the cantonment two miles outside the city paraded for him, the ladies of the garrison made much of him, McNaghten breathed a sigh of relief at seeing Willoughby Cotton's back, and there was some satisfaction that we had got such a benevolent and popular commander. Only Burnes, it seemed to me on that first day, when I reported in to him, did not share the gaiety.

"I suppose it is right to rejoice," he told me, stroking in his conceited way at his little back moustache. "But, you know, Elphy's arrival changes nothing. Sujah is no firmer on his throne, and the defences of the cantonment are no better, simply because Elphy turns the light of his countenance on us. Oh, I daresay it will be all right, but it might have been better if Calcutta had sent us a stronger, brisker man."

I suppose I should have resented this patronising view of my chief a little, but when I saw Elphy Bey later in the day there was no doubt that Burnes was right. In the weeks since I had parted from him in Calcutta—and he had not been in the best of health then—he had gone downhill. There was this wasted, shaky look about him, and he preferred not to walk much; his hand trembled as he shook mine, and the feel of it was of a bundle of dry sticks in a bag. However, he was pleased to see me.

"You have been distinguishing yourself among the Gilzais, Flashman," he said. "Sir Alexander Burnes tells me you have won hostages of importance; that is excellent news, especially to our friend the Envoy," and he turned to McNaghten, who was sitting by drinking tea and holding his cup like an old maid.

McNaghten sniffed. "The Gilzais need not concern us very much, I think," says he. "They are great brigands, of course, but only brigands. I would rather have hostages for the good behaviour of Akbar Khan."

"Shall we send Mr Flashman to bring some?" says Elphy, smiling at me to show I shouldn't mind McNaghten's snub. "He seems to have gifts in that direction." And he went on to ask for details of my mission, and told me that I must bring young Ilderim Khan to meet him, and generally behaved very civilly to me.

But it was an effort to remember that this frail old gentleman, with his pleasant small talk, was the commander of the army. He was too polite and vague, even in those few minutes, and deferred too much to McNaghten, to inspire confidence as a military leader.

"How would he do, do you think, if there was any trouble with the Afghans?" says Burnes later. "Well, let's hope we don't have to find out."

In the next few weeks, while I was in fairly constant attendance on Elphy, I found myself sharing his hope. It was not just that Elphy was too old and feeble to be much use as an active leader: he was under McNaghten's thumb from the start, and since McNaghten was determined to believe that all was well, Elphy had to believe it, too. And neither of them got on with Shelton, a rude boor of a man who was Elphy's second-in-command, and this dissension at the top made for uneasiness and mistrust farther down.

If that was not bad enough, the situation of the army made it worse. The cantonment was a poor place for a garrison to be, without proper defences, with its principal stores outside its walls, and some of the principal officers —Burnes himself, for example—quartered two miles away in Kabul City. But if protests were made to McNaghten —and they were, especially by active men like Broadfoot —they were dismissed as "croaking", and it was pointed out sharply that the army was unlikely to be called on to fight anyway. When this kind of talk gets abroad, there is no confidence, and the soldiers get slack. Which is dangerous anywhere, but especially in a strange country where the natives are unpredictable.

Of course, Elphy pottering about the cantonment and McNaghten with his nose deep in correspondence with Calcutta, saw nothing to indicate that the peaceful situation was an uneasy one. Nor did most of the army, who were ignorantly contemptuous of the Afghans, and had treated the Kabul expedition as a holiday from the first. But some of us did.

A few weeks after Elphy's arrival Burnes obtained my detachment from the staff because he wanted to make use of my Pushtu and my interest in the country. "Oh dear," Elphy complained, "Sir Alexander is so busy about everything. He takes my aides away, even, as though I could readily spare them. But there is so much to do, and I am not well enough to be up to it." But I was not sorry to go; being about Elphy was like being an orderly in a medical ward.

Burnes was keen that I should get about and see as much of the country as I could, improve my command of the language, and become known to as many influential Afghans as possible. He gave me a number of little tasks like the Mogala one—it was carrying messages, really, but it was valuable experience—and I travelled to towns and villages about Kabul, meeting Douranis and Kohistanis and Baruzkis and so on, and "getting the feel of the place," as Burnes put it.

"Soldiering's all very well," he told me, "but the men who make or break the army in a foreign country are we politicals. We meet the men who count, and get to know 'em, and sniff the wind; we're the eyes and ears—aye, and the tongues. Without us the military are blind, deaf, and dumb."

So although boors like Shelton sneered at "young pups gadding about the hills playing at niggers," I listened to Burnes and sniffed the wind. I took Ilderim with me a good deal, and sometimes his Gilzais, too, and they taught me some of the lore of the hills, and the ways of the people—who mattered, and what tribes were better to deal with, and why, and how the Kohistanis were more friendly disposed to us than the Abizai were, and which families were at feud with each other, and how the feeling ran about the Persians and the Russians, and where the best horses could be obtained, and how millet was grown and harvested: all the trivial information which is the small change of a country's life. I don't pretend that I became an expert in a few weeks, or that I ever "knew" Afghanistan, but I picked up a little here and there, and began to realise that those who studied the country only from the cantonment at Kabul knew no more about it than you would learn about a strange house if you stayed in one room of it all the time.

But for anyone with eyes to look beyond Kabul the signs were plain to see. There was mischief brewing in the hills, among the wild tribes who didn't want Shah Sujah for their king, and hated the British bayonets that protected him in his isolation in the Bala Hissar fortress. Rumours grew that Akbar Khan, son of old Dost Mohammed whom we had deposed, had come down out of the Hindu Kush at last and was gathering support among the chiefs; he was the darling of the warrior clans, they said, and presently he would sweep down on Kabul with his hordes, fling Sujah from his throne, and either drive the feringhees back to India or slaughter them all in their cantonment.

It was easy, if you were McNaghten, to scoff at such rumours from your pleasantly furnished office in Kabul; it was something else again to be up on the ridges beyond Jugdulluk or down towards Ghuznee and hear of councils called and messengers riding, of armed assemblies harangued by holy men and signal fires lit along the passes. The covert smiles, the ready assurances, the sight of swaggering Ghazis, armed to the teeth and with nothing apparent to do, the growing sense of unease—it used to make the hairs crawl on my neck.

For don't mistake me, I did not like this work. Riding with my Gilzais and young Ilderim, I was made welcome enough, and they were infallible eyes and ears—for having eaten the Queen's salt they were ready to serve her against their own folk if need be—but it was dangerous for all that. Even in native dress, I would meet black looks and veiled threats in some places and hear the British mocked and Akbar's name acclaimed. As a friend of the Gilzais and a slight celebrity—Ilderim lost no opportunity of announcing me as "Bloody Lance"—I was tolerated, but I knew the toleration might snap at any moment. At first I went about in a continual funk, but after a while one became fatalistic; possibly it came from dealing with people who believe that every man's fortune is unchangeably written on his forehead.

So the clouds began to gather on the mountains, and in Kabul the British army played cricket and Elphinstone and McNaghten wrote letters to each other remarking how tranquil everything was. The summer wore on, the sentries drowsed in the stifling heat of the cantonment, Burnes yawned and listened idly to my reports, dined me royally and took me off whoring in the bazaar—and one bright day McNaghten got a letter from Calcutta complaining at the cost of keeping our army in Kabul, and looked about for economies to make.

It was unfortunate that he happened, about this time, to be awaiting his promotion and transfer to the Governorship of Bombay; I think the knowledge that he was leaving may have made him careless. At any rate, seeking means of reducing expenditure, he recalled the idea which had appalled General Nott, and decided to cut the Gilzais' subsidy.

I had just come back to Kabul from a visit to Kandahar garrison, and learned that the Gilzai chiefs had been summoned and told that instead of 8,000 rupees a year for keeping the passes open, they were now to receive 5,000. Ilderim's fine young face fell when he heard it, and he said:

"There will be trouble, Flashman huzoor. He would have been better offering pork to a Ghazi than cheat the Gilzais of their money."

He was right, of course: he knew his own people. The Gilzai chiefs smiled cheerfully when McNaghten delivered his decision, bade him good afternoon, and rode quietly out of Kabul—and three days later the munitions convoy from Peshawar was cut to ribbons in the Khoord–Kabul pass by a force of yelling Gilzais and Ghazis who looted the caravan, butchered the drivers, and made off with a couple of tons of powder and ball.

McNaghten was most irritated, but not concerned. With Bombay beckoning he was not going to alarm Calcutta over a skirmish, as he called it.

"The Gilzais must be given a drubbing for kicking up this kind of row," said he, and hit on another bright idea: he would cut down expense by sending a couple of battalions back to India, and they could take a swipe at the Gilzais on their way home. Two birds with one stone. The only trouble was that his two battalions had to fight damned nearly every inch of the way as far as Gandamack, with the Gilzais potting at them from behind rocks and sweeping down in sudden cavalry charges. This was bad enough, but what made it worse was that our troops fought badly. Even under the command of General Sale —the tall, handsome "Fighting Bob" who used to invite his men to shoot him when they felt mutinous—clearing the passes was a slow, costly process.

I saw some of it, for Burnes sent me on two occasions with messages to Sale from McNaghten, telling him to get on with it.

It was a shocking experience the first time. I set off thinking it was something of a joy-ride, which it was until the last half-mile into Sale's rearguard, which was George Broadfoot's camp beyond Jugdulluk. Everything had been peaceful as you please, and I was just thinking how greatly exaggerated had been the reports arriving in Kabul from Sale, when out of a side-nullah came a mounted party of Ghazis, howling like wolves and brandishing their knives.

I just clapped in my spurs, put my head down, and cut along the track as if all the fiends in hell were behind me —which they were. I tumbled into Broadfoot's camp half-dead with terror, which he fortunately mistook for exhaustion. George had the bad taste to find it all rather funny; he was one of those nerveless clods, and was in the habit of strolling about under the snipers' fire polishing his spectacles, although his red coat and even redder beard made him a marked man.

He seemed to think everyone else was as unconcerned as he was, too, for he sent me back to Kabul that same night with another note, in which he told Burnes flatly that there wasn't a hope of keeping the passes open by force; they would have to negotiate with the Gilzais. I backed this up vehemently to Burnes, for although I had had a clear run back to Kabul, it was obvious to me that the Gilzais meant business, and at all the way stations there had been reports of other tribesmen massing in the hills above the passes.

Burnes gave me some rather odd looks as I made my report; he thought I was scared and probably exaggerating. At any rate, he made no protest when McNaghten said Broadfoot was an ass and Sale an incompetent, and that they had better get a move on if they were to have cleared a way to Jallalabad—which was about two-thirds of the way from Kabul to Peshawar—before winter set in. So Sale's brigade was left to struggle on, and Burnes (who was much preoccupied with the thought of getting McNaghten's job as Envoy when McNaghten went to Bombay) wrote that the country was "in the main very tranquil". Well, he paid for his folly.

A week or two later—it was now well into October—he

sent me off again with a letter to Sale. Little progress was being made in clearing the passes, the Gilzais were as active as ever and out-shooting our troops all the time, and there were growing rumours of trouble brewing in Kabul itself. Burnes had sense enough to show a little concern, although McNaghten was still as placidly blind as ever, while Elphy Bey simply looked from one to the other, nodding agreement to whatever was said. But even Burnes showed no real urgency about it all; he just wanted to nag at Sale for not keeping the Gilzais quiet.

This time I went with a good escort of my Gilzais, under young Ilderim, on the theory that while they were technically sworn to fight their own kinsfolk, they would be unlikely in practice to get into any shooting scrapes with them. However, I never put this to the test, for it became evident as we rode eastward through the passes that the situation was worse than anyone in Kabul had realised, and I decided that I, at any rate, would not try to get through to Sale. The whole country beyond Jugdulluk was up, and the hills were swarming with hostile Afghans, all either on their way to help beat up Sale's force, or else preparing for something bigger—there was talk among the villagers of a great *jehad* or holy war, in which the feringhees would be wiped out; it was on the eve of breaking out, they said. Sale was now hopelessly cut off; there was no chance of relief from Jallalabad, or even from Kabul—oh, Kabul was going to be busy enough looking after itself.

I heard this shivering round a camp-fire on the Soorkab road, and Ilderim shook his head in the shadows and said:

"It is not safe for you to go on, Flashman huzoor. You must return to Kabul. Give me the letter for Sale; although I have eaten the Queen's salt my own people will let me through."

This was such obvious common sense that I gave him the letter without argument and started back for Kabul that same night, with four of the Gilzai hostages for company. At that hour I wanted to get as many miles as possible between me and the gathering Afghan tribes, but if I had known what was waiting for me in Kabul I would have gone on to Sale and thought myself lucky.

Riding hard through the next day, we came to Kabul at nightfall, and I never saw the place so quiet. Bala Hissar loomed over the deserted streets; the few folk who were about were grouped in little knots in doorways and at street corners; there was an air of doom over the whole place. No British soldiers were to be seen in the city itself, and I was glad to get to the Residency, where Burnes lived in the heart of the town, and hear the courtyard gates grind to behind me. The armed men of Burnes's personal guard were standing to in the yard, while others were posted on the Residency walls; the torches shone on belt-plates and bayonets, and the place looked as though it was getting ready to withstand a siege.

But Burnes himself was sitting reading in his study as cool as a minnow, until he saw me. At the sight of my evident haste and disorder—I was in Afghan dress, and pretty filthy after days in the saddle—he started up.

"What the deuce are you doing here?" says he.

I told him, and added that there would probably be an Afghan army coming to support my story.

"My message to Sale," he snapped. "Where is it? Have you not delivered it?"

I told him about Ilderim, and for once the dapper little dandy forgot his carefully cultivated calm.

"Good God!" says he. "You've given it to a *Gilzai* to deliver?"

"A friendly Gilzai," I assured him. "A hostage, you remember."

"Are you mad?" says he, his little moustache all a-quiver. "Don't you know that you can't trust an Afghan, hostage or not?"

"Ilderim is a khan's son and a gentleman in his own way," I told him. "In any event, it was that or nothing. I couldn't have got through."

"And why not? You speak Pushtu; you're in native dress—God knows you're dirty enough to pass. It was your duty to see that message into Sale's own hand—and bring an answer. My God, Flashman, this is a pretty business, when a British officer cannot be trusted . . ."

"Now, look you here, Sekundar," says I, but he came up straight like a little bantam and cut me off.

"Sir Alexander, if you please," says he icily, as though I'd never seen him with his breeches down, chasing after some big Afghan bint. He stared at me and took a pace or two round the table.

"I think I understand," says he. "I have wondered about you lately, Flashman—whether you were to be fully relied on, or . . . Well, it shall be for a court-martial to decide—"

"Court-martial? What the devil!"

"For wilful disobedience of orders," says he. "There may

be other charges. In any event, you may consider yourself under arrest, and confined to this house. We are all confined anyway—the Afghans are allowing no one to pass between here and the cantonment."

"Well, in God's name. doesn't that bear out what I've been telling you?" I said. "The country's all up to the eastward, man, and now here in Kabul . . ."

"There is no rising in Kabul," says he. "Merely a little unrest which I propose to deal with in the morning." He stood there, cock-sure little ass, in his carefully pressed linen suit, with a flower in his button-hole, talking as though he was a schoolmaster promising to reprimand some unruly fags. "It may interest you to know -you who turn tail at rumours—that I have twice this evening received direct threats to my life. I shall not be alive by morning, it is said. Well, well, we shall see about that."

"Aye, maybe you will," says I. "And as to your fine talk that I turn tail at rumours, you may see about that, too. Maybe Akbar Khan will come to show you himself."

He smiled at me, not pleasantly. "He is in Kabul; I have even had a message from him. And I am confident that he intends no harm to us. A few dissidents there are, of course, and it may be necessary to read them a lesson. However, I trust myself for that."

There was no arguing with his complacency, but I pitched into him hard on his threat of a court-martial for me. You might have thought that any sensible man would have understood my case, but he simply waved my protests aside, and finished by ordering me to my room. So I went, in a rare rage at the self-sufficient folly of the man, and heartily hoping that he would trip over his own conceit. Always so clever, always so sure—that was Burnes. I would have given a pension to see him at a loss for once.

But I was to see it for nothing.

It came suddenly, just before breakfast-time, when I was rubbing my eyes after a pretty sleepless night which had dragged itself away very slowly, and very silently for Kabul. It was a grey morning, and the cocks were crowing; suddenly I became aware of a distant murmur, growing to a rumble, and hurried to the window. The town lay still, with a little haze over the houses; the guards were still on the wall of the Residency compound, and in the distance, coming closer, the noise was identifiable as the tramping of feet and the growing clamour of a mob.

There was a shouted order in the courtyard, a clatter of

feet on the stairs, and Burnes's voice calling for his
brother, young Charlie, who lived in the Residency with
him. I snatched my robe from its peg and hurried down,
winding my puggaree on to my head as I went. As I
reached the courtyard there was the crack of a musket
shot, and a wild yell from beyond the wall; a volley of
blows hammered on the gate, and across the top of the
wall I saw the vanguard of a charging horde streaming out
from between the nearest houses. Bearded faces, flashing
knives, they surged up to the wall and fell back, yelling
and cursing, while the guards thrust at them with their
musket butts. For a moment I thought they would charge
again and sweep irresistibly over the wall, but they hung
back, a jostling, shrieking crowd, shaking their fists and
weapons, while the guardsmen lining the wall looked anx-
iously back for orders and kept their thumbs poised on
their musket-locks.

Burnes strolled out of the front door and stood in full
view at the top of the steps. He was as fresh and calm as a
squire taking his first sniff of the morning, but at the sight
of him the mob redoubled its clamour and rolled up to the
wall, yelling threats and insults while he looked right and
left at them, smiling and shaking his head.

"No shooting, havildar," says he to the guard commander. "It will all quieten down in a moment."

"Death to Sekundar!" yelled the mob. "Death to the
feringhee pig!"

Jim Broadfoot, who was George's younger brother, and
little Charlie Burnes, were at Sekundar's elbow, both looking mighty anxious, but Burnes himself never lost his
poise. Suddenly he raised his hand, and the mob beyond
the wall fell quiet; he grinned at that, and touched his
moustache in that little, confident gesture he had, and then
he began to talk to them in Pushtu. His voice was quiet,
and must have carried only faintly to them, but they listened for a little as he coolly told them to go home, and
stop this folly, and reminded them that he had always
been their friend and had done them no harm.

It might have succeeded, for he had the gift of the gab,
but show-off that he was, he carried it just too far, and
patronised them, and first there were murmurs, and then
the clamour swelled up again, more savage than before.
Suddenly one Afghan started forward and hurled himself
on to the wall, knocking down a sentry; the nearest guard
drove at the Afghan with his bayonet, someone in the

crowd fired his jezzail, and with one hellish roar the whole mob swept forward, scrambling up the wall.

The havildar yelled an order, there was the ragged crash of a volley, and the courtyard was full of struggling men, crazy Afghans with their knives hacking and the guard falling back, stabbing with their bayonets and going down beneath the rush. There was no holding them; I saw Broadfoot grab Burnes and hustle him inside the house, and a moment later I was inside myself, slamming the side door in the face of a yelling Ghazi with a dozen of his fellows bounding at his heels.

It was a stout door, thank God, like the others in the Residency; otherwise we should all have been butchered within five minutes. Blows shattered on the far side of it as I slipped the bar home, and as I hurried along the passage to the main hallway I could hear above the shrieking and shooting outside the crash and thud of countless fists and hilts on panels and shutters—it was like being inside a box with demented demons pounding on the lid. Suddenly above the din there was the crash of an ordered volley from the courtyard, and then another, and as the yelling subsided momentarily the havildar's voice could be heard urging the remnant of the guard into the house. Little bloody odds it would make, I thought; they had us cornered, and it was a case of having our throats cut now or later.

Burnes and the others were in the hallway, and Sekundar as usual was showing off, affecting carelessness in a tight spot.

"Wake Duncan with thy knocking," he quoted, cocking his head on one side at the pounding of the mob. "How many of the guard are inside, Jim?"

Broadfoot said about a dozen, and Burnes said: "That's splendid. That makes, let's see, twelve, and the servants, and us three—hullo, here's Flashman! Mornin' Flash; sleep well? Apologise for this rude awakening—about twenty-five, I'd say; twenty fighting men, anyway."

"Few enough," says Broadfoot, examining his pistols. "The niggers'll be inside before long—we can't cover every door and window, Sekundar."

A musket ball crashed through a shutter and knocked a cloud of plaster off the opposite wall. Everyone ducked, except Burnes.

"Nonsense!" says he. "Can't cover 'em from down here, I grant you, but we don't have to. Now Jim, take the guard, all of 'em, upstairs, and have 'em shoot down from the balconies. That'll clear these mad fellows away from the sides of the house. There ain't many guns among them, I fancy, so you can get a good sight of them without fear of being hit—much. Up you go, laddie, look sharp!"

Broadfoot clattered away, and a moment later the red-coated jawans were mounting the stairs, with Burnes shouting "Shabash!" to encourage them while he belted his sword over his suit and stuck a pistol in his belt. He seemed positively to be enjoying himself, the bloody ass. He clapped me on the shoulder and asked didn't I just wish I'd galloped on to Sale after all—but never a word of acknowledgement that my warning had proved correct. I reminded him of it, and pointed out that if he had listened then, we shouldn't be going to get our throats cut now, but he just laughed and straightened his button-hole.

"Don't croak so, Flashy," says he. "I could hold this house with two men and a whore's protector." There was a sound of ragged firing over our heads. "You see? Jim's setting about 'em already. Come on, Charlie, let's see the fun!" And he and his brother hurried upstairs, leaving me alone in the hall.

"What about my bloody court-martial?" I shouted after him, but he never heard.

Well, his plan worked, at first. Broadfoot's men did clear away the rascals from round the walls, shooting down from the upper windows and balcony, and when I joined them on the upper floor there were about twenty Ghazi corpses in the courtyard. A few shots came the other way, and one of the jawans was wounded in the thigh, but the main mob had now retreated to the street, and contented themselves with howling curses from the cover of the wall.

"Excellent! Bahut achha!" said Burnes, puffing a cheroot and peering out of the window. "You see, Charlie, they've drawn off, and presently Elphy will be wondering down in the cantonment what all the row's about, and send someone to see."

"Won't he send troops, then?" says little Charlie.

"Of course. A battalion, probably—that's what I'd send. Since it's Elphy, though, he's as likely to send a brigade, eh, Jim?"

Broadfoot, squatting at the other window, peered along his pistol barrel, fired, swore, and said: "So long as he sends someone."

"Don't you fret," says Burnes. "Here, Flashy, have a cheroot. Then you can try your hand at potting off some of these chaps beyond the wall. I'd say Elphy'll be on the move inside two hours, and we'll be out of here in three. Good shot, Jim! That's the style!"

Burnes was wrong, of course. Elphy didn't send troops; indeed, so far as I've been able to learn, he did nothing at all. If even a platoon had arrived in that first hour, I believe the mob would have melted before them; as it was, they began to pluck up courage, and started clambering the wall again, and sneaking round to the rear, where the stables gave them cover. We kept up a good fire from the windows—I shot three myself, including an enormously fat man, at which Burnes said: "Choose the thin ones, Flashy; that chap couldn't have got in the front door anyway." But as two hours passed he joked rather less, and actually made another attempt to talk to our attackers from the balcony, but they drove him inside with a shot or two and a volley of missiles.

Meanwhile, some of the Ghazis had set fire to the stables, and the smoke began to drift into the house. Burnes swore, and we all strained our eyes peering across the rooftops towards the cantonment, but still no sign of help appeared, and I felt the pumping of fear again in my throat. The howling of the mob had risen again, louder than ever, some of the jawans were looking scared, and even Burnes was frowning.

"Blast Elphy Bey," says he. "He's cutting it dooced fine. And I believe these brutes have got muskets from somewhere at last—listen." He was right; there were as many shots coming from outside as from inside the house. They were smacking into the walls and knocking splinters from the shutters, and presently another jawan gave a yelp and staggered back into the room with his shoulder smashed and blood pouring down his shirt.

"Hm," says Burnes, "this is gettin' warm. Like Montrose at the Fair, eh, Charlie?" Charlie gave him the ghost of a smile; he was scared stiff and trying not to show it.

"How many rounds have you got, Flashy?" says Burnes. I had only six left, and Charlie had none; the ten jawans had barely forty among them.

"How about you, Jim?" shouts Burnes to Broadfoot, who was at the far window. Broadfoot shouted something back, but in the din I didn't catch it, and then Broadfoot stood slowly up, and turned towards us, looking down at his shirt-front. I saw a red spot there, and suddenly it grew to a great red stain, and Broadfoot took two steps back and went head first over the window sill. There was a sickening crash as he hit the courtyard, and a tremendous shriek from the mob; the firing seemed to redouble, and from the rear, where the smoke of the burning stables was pouring in on us, came the measured smashing of a ram at the back door.

Burnes fired from his window, and ducked away. He squatted down near me, spun his pistol by the guard, whistled for a second or two through his teeth, and then said: "Charlie, Flashy, I think it's time to go."

"Where the hell to?" says I.

"Out of here," says he. "Charlie, cut along to my room; you'll find native robes in the wardrobe. Bring 'em along. Lively, now." When Charlie had gone, he said to me "It's not much of a chance, but it's all we have, I think. We'll try it at the back door; the smoke looks pretty thick, don't you know, and with all the confusion we might get clear away. Ah, good boy, Charlie. Now send the havildar across to me."

While Burnes and Charlie struggled into their gowns and puggarees, Burnes talked to the havildar, who agreed that the mob probably wouldn't hurt him and his men, not being feringhees, but would concentrate on looting the place.

"But you, sahib, they will surely kill," he said. "Go while ye can, and God go with you."

"And remain with you and yours," says Burnes, shaking his hand. "Shabash and salaam, havildar. All ready, Flash? Come on, Charlie."

And with Burnes in the lead and myself last, we cut out down the staircase, across the hall, and through the passage towards the kitchen. From the back door, out of sight to our right, there came a crackling of breaking timber; I took a quick glance through a loophole, and saw the garden almost alive with Ghazis.

"Just about in time," says Burnes, as we reached the kitchen door. I knew it led into a little fenced-off pen, where the swill-tubs were kept; once we got into that, and provided we weren't actually seen leaving the house, we stood a fair chance of getting away.

Burnes slipped the bar quietly from the door, and opened it a crack.

"Luck of the devil!" says he. "Come on, juldi!"

We slipped out after him; the pen was empty. It consisted of two high screen walls running from either side of the door; there was no one in sight through the opening at the other end, and the smoke was billowing down in great clouds now, with the mob kicking up the most hellish din on either side of us.

"Pull her to, Flashy!" snapped Burnes, and I shut the door behind us. "That's it—now, try to batter the damned thing down!" And he jumped at the closed door, hammering with his fists. "Open, unbelieving swine!" he bawled. "Feringhee pigs, your hour has come! This way, brothers! Death to the bastard Sekundar!"

Seeing his plan, we hammered along with him, and presently round the end of the pen came a handful of Ghazis to see what was what. All they saw, of course, was three of the Faithful trying to break down a door, so they joined in, and after a moment we left off, Burnes cursing like blazes, and went out of the pen, ostensibly to seek another entrance to hammer at.

There were Afghans all over the garden and round the burning stables; most of them, it seemed to me, were just berserk and running about and yelling for no particular reason, waving their knives and spears, and presently there was a tremendous howl and a crash as the back door caved in, and a general move in that direction. The three of us kept going for the stable gate, past the burning building; it was a creepy feeling, hurrying through the confused crowd of our enemies, and I was in dread that little Charlie, who was new to native dress, and not nearly as dark as Burnes and I, would do something to be spotted. But he kept his hood well forward over his face, and we got outside the gate in safety, where the hangers-on were congregated, yelling and laughing as they watched the Residency, hoping no doubt to see the bodies of the hated feringhees launched from the upper windows.

"May dogs defile the grave of the swine Burnes!" roared Sekundar, spitting towards the Residency, and the bystanders gave him a cheer. "So far, so good," he added to me. "Now shall we stroll down to the cantonments and have a word with Elphy? Ready, Charlie? Best foot forward, then, and try to swagger like a regular badmash. Take your cue from Flashy here; ain't he the ugliest-lookin' Bashie-Bazouk you ever saw?"

With Burnes in the lead we pushed out boldly into the street, Sekundar thrusting aside the stragglers who got in the way like any Yusufzai bully; I wanted to tell him to go easy, for it seemed to me he must attract attention, and his face was all too familiar to the Kabulis. But they gave way before him, with a curse or two, and we won clear to the end of the street without being spotted; now, thought I, we're home in a canter. The crowd was still fairly thick, but not so noisy, and every stride was taking us nearer the point where, at worst, we could cut and run for it towards the cantonment.

And then Burnes, the over-confident fool, ruined the whole thing.

We had reached the end of the street, and he must pause to yell another curse against the feringhees, by way of a final brag: I could imagine him showing off later to the garrison wives, telling them how he'd fooled the Afghans by roaring threats against himself. But he overdid it; having called himself the grandson of seventy pariah dogs at the top of his voice, he muttered something in an undertone to Charlie, and laughed at his own witticism.

The trouble is, an Afghan doesn't laugh like an Englishman. He giggles high-pitched, but Burnes guffawed. I saw a head turn to stare at us, and grabbing Burnes by one arm and Charlie by the other I was starting to hurry them down the street when I was pushed aside and a big brute of a Ghazi swung Burnes round by the shoulder and peered at him.

"Jao, hubshi!" snarled Burnes, and hit his hand aside, but the fellow still stared, and then suddenly shouted:

"Mashallah! Brothers, it is Sekundar Burnes!"

There was an instant's quiet, and then an almighty yell. The big Ghazi whipped out his Khyber knife, Burnes locked his arm and snapped it before he could strike, but then about a dozen others were rushing in on us. One jumped at me, and I hit him so hard with my fist that I overbalanced; I jumped up, clawing for my own sword, and saw Burnes throwing off the wounded Ghazi and shouting:

"Run, Charlie, run!"

There was a side-alley into which Charlie, who was nearest, might have escaped, but he hesitated, standing white-faced, while Burnes jumped between him and the charging Afghans. Sekundar had his Khyber knife out now; he parried a blow from the leader, closed with him, and shouted again:

"Get out, Charlie! Cut, man!"

And then, as Charlie still hesitated, petrified, Burnes yelled in an agonised voice:

"Run, baby, please! Run!"

They were the last words he spoke. A Khyber knife swept down on his shoulder and he reeled back, blood spouting; then the mob was on top of him, hacking and striking. He must have taken half a dozen mortal cuts before he even hit the ground. Charlie gave a frenzied cry, and ran towards him; they cut him down before he had gone three steps.

I saw all this, because it happened in seconds; then I had my own hands full. I jumped over the man I had hit and dived for the alley, but a Ghazi was there first, screaming and slashing at me. I had my own sword out, and turned his cut, but the way was blocked and the mob was howling at my heels. I turned, slashing frantically, and they gave back an instant; I got my back to the nearest wall as they surged in again, the knives flashed before my eyes, I thrust at the snarling faces and heard the screams and curses. And then something hit me a dreadful blow in the stomach and I went down before the rush of bodies; a foot stamped on my hip, and even as I thought, oh, sweet Jesus, this is death, I had one fleeting memory of being trampled in the scrimmage in the Schoolhouse match. Something smashed against my head, and I waited for the horrible bite of sharp steel. And then I remember nothing more.[14]

When I came to my senses I was lying on a wooden floor, my cheek against the boards. My head seemed to be opening and shutting with pain, and when I tried to raise it I found that my face was stuck to the boards with my own dried blood, so that I cried out with the pain as it pulled free.

The first thing I noticed was a pair of boots, of fine yellow leather, on the floor about two yards away; above them were pyjamy trousers and the skirt of a black coat, and then a green sash and two lean hands hooked into it by the thumbs, and above all, a dark, grinning face with pale grey eyes under a spiked helmet. I knew the face, from my visit to Mogala, and even in my confused state I thought: this is bad news. It was my old enemy, Gul Shah.

He sauntered over and kicked me in the ribs. I tried to speak, and the first words that came out, in a hoarse whisper, were: "I'm alive."

"For the moment," said Gul Shah. He squatted down beside me, smiling his wolf's smile. "Tell me, Flashman: what does it feel like to die?"

"What d'ye mean?" I managed to croak.

He jerked his thumb. "Out in the street yonder: you were down, with the knives at your neck, and only my timely intervention saved you from the same fate as Sekundar Burnes. They cut him to pieces, by the way. Eighty-five pieces, to be exact: they have been counted, you see. But you, Flashman, must have known what it was like to die in that moment. Tell me: I am curious."

I guessed there was no good coming from these questions; the evil look of the brute made my skin crawl. But I thought it best to answer.

"It was bloody horrible," says I.

He laughed with his head back, rocking on his heels, and others laughed with him. I realised there were perhaps half a dozen others—Ghazis, mostly—in the room with us. They came crowding round to leer at me, and if anything they looked even nastier than Gul Shah.

When he had finished laughing he leaned over me. "It can be more horrible," says he, and spat in my face. He reeked of garlic.

I tried to struggle up, demanding to know why he had saved me, and he stood up and kicked me again. "Yes, why?" he mocked me. I couldn't fathom it; I didn't want to. But I thought I'd pretend to act as though it were all for the best.

"I'm grateful to you, sir," says I, "for your timely assistance. You shall be rewarded—all of you—and. . . ."

"Indeed we will," says Gul Shah. "Stand him up."

They dragged me to my feet, twisting my arms behind me. I told them loudly that if they took me back to the cantonment they would be handsomely paid, and they roared with laughter.

"Any paying the British do will be in blood," says Gul Shah. "Yours first of all."

"What for, damn you?" I shouted.

"Why do you suppose I stopped the Ghazis from quartering you?" says he. "To preserve your precious skin, perhaps? To hand you as a peace offering to your people?" He stuck his face into mine. "Have you forgotten a dancing girl called Narreeman, you pig's bastard? Just another slut, to the likes of you, to be defiled as you chose, and then forgotten. You are all the same, you feringhee swine; you think you can take our women, our country, and our honour and trample them all under foot. We do not matter, do we? And when all is done, when our women are raped and our treasure stolen, you can laugh and shrug your shoulders, you misbegotten pariah curs!" He was screaming at me, with froth on his lips.

"I meant her no harm," I was beginning, and he struck me across the face. He stood there, glaring at me and panting. He made an effort and mastered himself.

"She is not here," he said at last, "or I would give you to her and she would give you an eternity of suffering before you died. As it is, we shall do our poor best to accommodate you."

"Look," says I. "Whatever I've done, I beg your pardon for it. I didn't know you cared for the wench, I swear. I'll make amends any way you like. I'm a rich man, a really rich man." I went on to offer him whatever he wanted in ransom and as compensation to the girl, and it seemed to quiet him for a minute.

"Go on," says he, when I paused. "This is good to listen to."

I would have done, but just the cruel sneer told me he was mocking me, and I fell silent.

"So, we are where we began," says he. "Believe me, Flashman, I would make you die a hundred deaths, but time is short. There are other throats besides yours, and we are impatient people. But we shall make your passing as memorable as possible, and you shall tell me again what it is like to die. Bring him along."

They dragged me from the room, along a passage, and I roared for help and called Gul Shah every filthy name I could lay tongue to. He strode on ahead, heedless, and presently threw open a door; they ran me across the threshold and I found I was in a low, vaulted chamber, perhaps twenty yards long. I had half-expected racks and thumbscrews or some such horrors, but the room was entirely bare. The one curious feature of it was that half way it was cut in two by a deep culvert, perhaps ten feet wide and six deep. It was dry, and where it ran into the walls on either side the openings were stopped up with rubble. This had obviously been done only recently, but I could not imagine why.

Gul Shah turned to me. "Are you strong, Flashman?"

"Damn you!" I shouted. "You'll pay for this, you dirty nigger!"

"Are you strong?" he repeated. "Answer, or I'll have your tongue cut out."

One of the ruffians grabbed my jaw in his hairy paw and brought his knife up to my mouth. It was a convincing argument. "Strong enough, damn you."

"I doubt that," smiled Gul Shah. "We have executed two rascals here of late, neither of them weaklings. But we shall see." To one of his crew he said: "Bring Mansur. I should explain this new entertainment of mine," he went on, gloating at me. "It was inspired partly by the unusual shape of this chamber, with its great trench in the middle, and partly by a foolish game which your British soldiers play. Doubtless you have played it yourself, which will add interest for you, and us. Yah, Mansur, come here."

As he spoke a grotesque figure waddled into the room. For a moment I could not believe it was a man, for he was no more than four feet high. But he was terrific. He was literally as broad as he was long, with huge knotted arms and a chest like an ape's. His enormous torso was carried on massive legs. He had no neck that I could see, and his yellow face was as flat as a plate, with a hideous nose spread across it, a slit of a mouth, and two black button eyes. His body was covered in dark hair, but his skull was as smooth as an egg. He wore only a dirty loincloth, and as he shuffled across to Gul Shah the torchlight in that windowless room gave him the appearance of some hideous Nibelung dragging itself through dark burrows beneath the earth.

"A fine manikin, is he not?" said Gul Shah, regarding the hideous imp. "Your soul must be as handsome, Flashman. Which is fitting, for he is your executioner."

He snapped an order, and the dwarf, with a glance at me and a contortion of his revolting mouth which I took to be a grin, suddenly bounded into the culvert, and with a tremendous spring leaped up the other side, catching the edge and flipping up, like an acrobat. That done he turned and faced us, arms outstretched, a disgusting yellow giant-in-miniature.

The men who held me now dragged my arms in front of me, and bound my wrists tightly with a stout rope. One of them then took the coil and carried it across to the dwarf's side of the culvert; the manikin made a hideous bubbling noise and held his wrists up eagerly, and they were bound as mine had been. So we stood, on opposite edges of the culvert, bound to ends of the same rope, with the slack of it lying in the great trench between us.

There had been no further word of explanation, and in the hellish uncertainty of what was to come, my nerve broke. I tried to run, but they hauled me back, laughing, and the dwarf Mansur capered on his side of the culvert and snapped his fingers in delight at my terror.

"Let me go, you bastards!" I roared, and Gul Shah smiled and clapped his hands.

"You start at shadows," he sneered. "Behold the substance. Yah, Asaf."

One of his ruffians came to the edge of the trench, bearing a leather sack tied at the neck. Cautiously undoing it, and holding it by the bottom, he suddenly up-ended it into the culvert. To my horror, half a dozen slim, silver shapes that glittered evilly in the torchlight, fell writhing into the gap; they plopped gently to the floor of the culvert and then slithered with frightening speed towards the sides.

But they could not climb up at us. So they glided about their strange prison in deadly silence. You could sense the vicious anger in them as they slid about beneath us.

"Their bite is death," said Gul Shah. "Is all now plain, Flashman? It is what you call a tug-of-war—you against Mansur. One of you must succeed in tugging the other into the trench, and then—it takes a few moments for the venom to kill. Believe me, the snakes will be kinder than Narreeman would have been."

"Help!" I roared, although God knows I expected none. But the sight of those loathsome things, the thought of their slimy touch, of the stab of their fangs—I thought I should go mad. I raged and pleaded, and that Afghan swine clapped his hands and yelled with laughter. The dwarf Mansur hopped in eagerness to begin, and presently Gul Shah stepped back, snapped an order to him, and said to me:

"Pull for your life, Flashman. And present my salaams to Shaitan."

I had retreated as far as I could go from the culvert's edge, and was standing, half-paralysed, when the dwarf snapped his wrists impatiently at the rope. The jerk brought me to my senses; as I have said before, terror is a wonderful stimulant. I braced my boot-heels on the rough stone floor, and prepared to resist with all my strength.

Grinning, the dwarf scuttled backwards until the rope stretched taut between us; I guessed what his first move would be, and was ready for the sudden jerk when it came. It nearly lifted me off my feet, but I turned with the rope across my shoulder and gave him heave for heave. The rope drummed like a bowstring, and then relaxed; he leered across at me and made a dribbling, piping noise. Then he bunched his enormous shoulder muscles, and leaning back, began to pull steadily.

By God, he was strong. I strained until my shoulders cracked and my arms shuddered, but slowly, inch by inch, my heels slithered across the rough surface towards the edge of the trench. The Ghazis urged him on with cries of delight, Gul Shah came to the brink so that he could watch me as I was drawn inexorably to the limit, I felt one of my heels slip into space, my head seemed to be bursting with the effort and my ears roared—and then the tearing pain in my wrists relaxed, and I was sprawled on the very edge, exhausted, with the dwarf prancing and laughing on the other side and the rope slack between us.

The Ghazis were delighted, and urged him to give me a quick final jerk into the culvert, but he shook his head and backed away again, snapping the rope at me. I glanced down; the snakes seemed almost to know what was afoot, for they had concentrated in a writhing, hissing mass just below me. I scrambled back, wet with fear and rage, and hurled my weight on the rope to try to heave him off balance. But for all the impression I made it might have been anchored to a tree.

He was playing with me; there was no question he was far the stronger of us two, and twice he hauled me to the lip and let me go again. Gul Shah clapped his hands and the Ghazis cheered; then he snapped some order to the dwarf, and I realised with sick horror that they were going to make an end. In despair I rolled back again from the edge and got to my feet; my wrists were torn and bloody and my shoulder joints were on fire, and when the dwarf pulled on the rope I staggered forward and in doing so I nearly got him, for he had expected a stronger resistance, and almost overbalanced. I hauled for dear life, but he recovered in time, glaring and piping angrily at me as he stamped his feet for a hold.

When he had finally settled himself he started to draw again on the rope, but not with his full strength, for he pulled me in only an inch at a time. This, I supposed, was the final hideous refinement; I struggled like a fish on a line, but there was no resisting that steady, dreadful pull. I was perhaps ten feet from the lip when he turned away from me, as a tug-of-war team will when it has its opponents on the run, and I realised that if I was to make any last desperate bid it must be now, while I had a little space to play with. I had almost unbalanced him by an accidental yielding; could I do it deliberately? With the last of my strength I dug my heels in and heaved tremendously; it checked him and he glanced over his shoulder, surprise on the hideous face. Then he grinned and exerted his strength, lunging away on the rope. My feet slipped.

"Go with God, Flashman," said Gul Shah ironically.

I scrabbled for a foothold, found it only six feet from the edge, and then bounded forward. The leap took me to the very lip of the culvert, and the dwarf Mansur plunged forward on his face as the rope slackened. But he was up like a jack-in-the-box, gibbering with rage, in an instant; planting his feet, he gave a savage heave on the rope that almost dislocated my shoulders and flung me face down.

Then he began to pull steadily, so that I was dragged forward over the floor, closer and closer to the edge, while the Ghazis cheered and roared and I screamed with horror.

"No! No!" I shrieked. "Stop him! Wait! Anything—I'll do anything! Stop him!"

My hands were over the edge now, and then my elbows; suddenly there was nothing beneath my face, and through my streaming tears I saw the bottom of the culvert with the filthy worms gliding across it. My chest and shoulders were clear, in an instant I should overbalance; I tried to twist my head up to appeal to the dwarf, and saw him standing on the far edge, grinning evilly and coiling the slack rope round his right hand and elbow like a washerwoman with a clothes line. He glanced at Gul Shah, preparing to give the final pull that would launch me over, and then above my own frantic babbling and the roaring in my ears I heard the crash of a door flung open behind me, and a stir among the watchers, and a voice upraised in Pushtu.

The dwarf was standing stock-still, staring beyond me towards the door. What he saw I didn't know, and I didn't care; half-dead with fear and exhaustion as I was, I recognised that his attention was diverted, that the rope was momentarily slack between us, and that he was on the very lip of the trench. It was my last chance.

I had only the purchase of my body and legs on the stone; my arms were stretched out ahead of me. I jerked them suddenly back, sobbing, with all my strength. It was not much of a pull, but it took Mansur completely unawares. He was watching the doorway, his eyes round in his gargoyle face; too late he realised that he had let his attention wander too soon. The jerk, slight as it was, unbalanced him, and one leg slipped over the edge; he shrieked and tried to throw himself clear, but his grotesque body landed on the very edge, and he hung for a moment like a see-saw. Then with a horrible piping squeal he crashed sprawling into the culvert.

He was up again with a bound, and springing for the rim, but by the grace of God he had landed almost on top of one of those hellish snakes, and even as he came upright it struck at his bare leg. He screamed and kicked at it, and the delay gave a second brute the chance to fix itself in his hand. He lashed out blindly, making a most ghastly din, and staggered about with at least two of the things hang-

ing from him. He ran in his dreadful waddling way in a
little circle, and fell forward on his face. Again and again
the serpents struck at him; he tried feebly to rise, and then
collapsed, his misshapen body twitching.

I was dead beat, with exertion and shock; I could only
lie heaving like a bellows. Gul Shah strode to the edge of
the culvert and screamed curses at his dead creature; then
he turned, pointing to me, and shouted:

"Fling that bastard in beside him!"

They grabbed me and ran me to the pit's edge, for I
could make no resistance. But I remember I protested that
it wasn't fair, that I had won, and deserved to be let go.
They held me on the edge, hanging over the pit, and
waited for the final word from my enemy. I closed my
eyes to blot out the sight of the snarling faces and those
dreadful reptiles, and then I was pulled back, and the
hands fell away from me. Wondering, I turned wearily;
they had all fallen silent, Gul Shah with the rest of them.

A man stood in the doorway. He was slightly under
middle height, with the chest and shoulders of a wrestler,
and a small, neat head that he turned from side to side,
taking in the scene. He was simply dressed in a grey coat,
clasped about with a belt of chain mail, and his head was
bare. He was plainly an Afghan, with something of the
pretty look that was so repulsive in Gul Shah, but here the
features were stronger and plumper; he carried an air of
command, but very easily, without any of the strutting arrogance that so many of his race affected.

He came forward, nodding to Gul Shah and eyeing me
with polite interest. I noticed with astonishment that his
eyes, oriental though they were in shape, were of vivid
blue. That and the slightly curly dark hair gave him a European look, which suited his bluff, sturdy figure. He sauntered to the edge of the culvert, clicked his tongue ruefully
at the dead dwarf, and asked conversationally:

"What has happened here?"

He sounded like a vicar in a drawing-room, he was so
mild, but Gul Shah kept mum, so I burst out:

"These swine have been trying to murder me!"

He gave me a brilliant smile. "But without success,"
cried he. "I felicitate you. Plainly you have been in terrible danger, but have escaped by your skill and bravery. A
notable feat, and what a tale for your children's children!"

It was really too much. Twice in hours I had been on
the brink of violent death, I was battered, exhausted, and

smeared with my own blood, and here I was conversing with a lunatic. I almost broke down in tears, and I certainly groaned: "Oh, Jesus."

The stout man raised an eyebrow. "The Christian prophet? Why, who are you then?"

"I'm a British officer!" I cried. "I have been captured and tortured by these ruffians, and they'd have killed me, too, with their hellish snakes! Whoever you are, you must—"

"In the hundred names of God!" he broke in. "A feringhee officer? Plainly there has almost been a very serious accident. Why did you not tell them who you were?"

I gaped at him, my head spinning. One of us must be mad. "They knew," I croaked. "Gul Shah knew."

"Impossible," says the stout fellow, shaking his head. "It could not be. My friend Gul Shah would be incapable of such a thing; there has been an unfortunate error."

"Look," I said, reaching out towards him, "you must believe me: I am Lieutenant Flashman, on the staff of Lord Elphinstone, and this man has tried to do me to death—not for the first time. Ask him," I shouted, "how I came here! Ask the lying, treacherous bastard!"

"Never try to flatter Gul Shah," said the stout man cheerfully. "He'll believe every word of it. No, there has been a mistake, regrettably, but it has not been irreparable. For which God be thanked—and my timely arrival, to be sure." And he smiled at me again. "But you must not blame Gul Shah, or his people: they did not know you for what you were."

Now, as he said those words, he ceased to be a waggish madman; his voice was as gentle as ever, but there was no mistaking the steel underneath. Suddenly things became real again, and I understood that the kindly smiling man before me was strong in a way that folk like Gul Shah could never be: strong and dangerous. And with a great surge of relief I realised too that with him by I was safe: Gul Shah must have sensed it also, for he roused himself and growled that I was his prisoner, feringhee officer or not, and he would deal with me.

"No, he is my guest," said the stout man reprovingly. "He has met with a mishap on his way here, and needs refreshment and care for his wounds. You have mistaken again, Gul Shah. Now, we shall have his wrists unbound, and I shall take him to such entertainment as befits a guest of his importance."

My bonds were cut off in a moment, and two of the Ghazis—the same evil-smelling brutes that a few moments ago had been preparing to hurl me to the snakes—supported me from that hellish place. I could feel Gul Shah's eyes boring into my back, but he said not a word; it seemed to me that the only explanation was that this must be the stout man's house, and under the strict rules of Musselman hospitality his word was law. But in my exhausted state I couldn't attempt to make sense of it all, and was only glad to stagger after my benefactor.

They took me to a well-furnished apartment, and under the stout man's supervision the crack in my head was bathed, the blood washed from my torn wrists and oiled bandages applied, and then I was given strong mint tea and a dish of bread and fruit. Although my head ached damnably I was famishing, not having eaten all day, and while I ate the stout man talked.

"You must not mind Gul Shah," he said, sitting opposite me and toying with his small beard. "He is a savage—what Gilzai isn't?—and now that I think on your name I connect you with the incident at Mogala some time ago. 'Bloody Lance', is it not?" And he gave me that tooth-flashing smile again. "I imagine you had given him cause for resentment—"

"There was a woman," I said. "I didn't know she was his woman." Which wasn't true, but that was by the way.

"There is so often a woman," he agreed. "But I imagine there was more to it than that. The death of a British officer at Mogala would have been convenient politically for Gul—yes, yes, I see how it may have been. But that is past." He paused, and looked at me reflectively. "And so is the unfortunate incident in the cellar today. It is best, believe me, that it should be so. Not only for you personally, but for all your people here."

"What about Sekundar Burnes and his brother?" said I. "Your soft words won't bring them back."

"A terrible tragedy," he agreed. "I admired Sekundar. Let us hope that the ruffians who slew him will be apprehended, and meet with a deserved judgement."

"Ruffians?" says I. "Good God, man, those were Akbar Khan's warriors, not a gang of robbers. I don't know who you are, or what your influence may be, but you're behind the times where news is concerned. When they murdered Burnes and sacked his Residency, that was the beginning of a war. If the British haven't marched from their cantonment into Kabul yet, they soon will, and you can bet on that!"

"I think you exaggerate," he said mildly. "This talk of Akbar Khan's warriors, for example—"

"Look you," I said, "don't try to tell me. I rode in from the east last night: the tribes are up along the passes from here to Jugdulluk and beyond, thousands of 'em. They're trying to wipe out Sale's force, they'll be here as soon as Akbar has a mind to take Kabul and slit Shah Sujah's throat and seize his throne. And God help the British garrison and loyalists like yourself who help them as you've helped me. I tried to tell Burnes this, and he laughed and wouldn't heed me. Well, there you are." I stopped; all that talk had made me thirsty. When I had taken some tea I added: "Believe it or not as you like."

He sat quiet for a moment, and then remarked that it was an alarming story, but that I must be mistaken. "If it were as you say, the British would have moved by now— either out of Kabul, or into the Bala Hissar fort, where they would be safe. They are not fools, after all."

"You don't know Elphy Bey, that's plain," says I. "Or that ass McNaghten. They don't want to believe it, you see; they want to think all's well. They think Akbar Khan is still skulking away in the Hindu Kush; they refuse to believe the tribes are rallying to him, ready to sweep the British out of Afghanistan."

He sighed. "It may be as you say: such delusions are common. Or they may be right, and the danger smaller than you think." He stood up. "But I am a thoughtless host. Your wound is paining you, and you need rest, Flashman huzoor. I shall weary you no longer Here you can have peace, and in the morning we can talk again; among other things, of how to return you safely to your people." He smiled, and the blue eyes twinkled. "We want no more 'mistakes' from hotheads like Gul Shah. Now, God be with you."

I struggled up, but I was so weak and weary that he insisted I be seated again. I told him I was deeply grateful for all his kindness, that I would wish to reward him, but he laughed and turned to go. I mumbled some more thanks to him, and it occurred to me that I still didn't know who he was, or how he had the power to save me from Gul Shah. I asked him, and he paused in the curtained doorway.

"As to that," he said, "I am the master of this house.

My close friends call me Bakbook, because I incline to talk. Others call me by various names, as they choose." He bowed. "You may call me by my given name, which is Akbar Khan. Good night, Flashman huzoor, and a pleasant rest. There are servants within call if you need them."

And with that he was gone, leaving me gaping at the doorway, and feeling no end of a fool.

In fact, Akbar Khan did not return next day, or for a week afterwards, so I had plenty of time to speculate. I was kept under close guard in the room, but comfortably enough; they fed me well and allowed me to exercise on a little closed verandah with a couple of armed Barukzis to keep an eye on me. But not a word would anyone say in answer to my questions and demands for release. I couldn't even discover what was going on in Kabul, or what our troops were doing—or what Akbar Khan himself might be up to. Or, most important of all, why he was keeping me prisoner.

Then, on the eighth day, Akbar returned, looking very spruce and satisfied. When he had dismissed the guards he inquired after my wounds, which were almost better, asked if I was well cared for and so forth, and then said that if there was anything I wished to know he would do his best to inform me.

Well, I lost no time in making my wishes known, and he listened smiling and stroking his short black beard. At last he cut me off with a raised hand.

"Stop, stop, Flashman huzoor. I see you are like a thirsty man; we must quench you a little at a time. Sit down now, and drink a little tea, and listen."

I sat, and he paced slowly about the room, a burly, springy figure in his green tunic and pyjamys which were tucked into short riding boots. He was something of a dandy, I noticed; there was gold lace on the tunic, and silver edging to the shirt beneath it. But again I was impressed by the obvious latent strength of the man; you could see it even in his stance, with his broad chest that looked always as though he was holding a deep breath, and his long, powerful hands.

"First," he said, "I keep you here because I need you. How, you shall see later—not today. Second, all is well in Kabul. The British keep to their cantonment, and the Afghans snipe at them from time to time and make loud noises. The King of Afghanistan, Shah Sujah"—here he curled his lip in amusement—"sits doing nothing among his women in the Bala Hissar, and calls to the British to help him against his unruly people. The mobs rule Kabul itself, each mob under its leader imagining that it alone has frightened the British off. They do a little looting, and a little raping, and a little killing—their own people, mark you—and are content for the moment. There you have the situation, which is most satisfactory. Oh, yes, and the hill tribes, hearing of the death of Sekundar Burnes, and of the rumoured presence in Kabul of one Akbar Khan, son of the true king Dost Mohammed, are converging on the capital. They smell war and plunder. Now, Flashman huzoor, you are answered."

Well, of course, in answering half a dozen questions he had posed a hundred others. But one above all I had to be satisfied about.

"You say the British keep to their cantonment," I cried. "But what about Burnes's murder? D'you mean they've done nothing?"

"In effect, nothing," says he. "They are unwise, for their inaction is taken as cowardice. You and I know they are not cowards, but the Kabuli mobs don't, and I fear this may encourage them to greater excesses than they have committed already. But we shall see. However, all this leads me to my purpose in visiting you today—apart from my desire to inquire into your welfare." And he grinned again, that infectious smile which seemed to mock but which I couldn't dislike. "You understand that if I satisfy your curiosity here and there, I also have questions which I would wish answered."

"Ask away," says I, rather cautious.

"You said, at our first meeting—or at least you implied —that Elfistan Sahib and McLoten Sahib were . . . how shall I put it? . . . sometimes less than intelligent. Was that a considered judgement?"

"Elphinstone Sahib and McNaghten Sahib," says I, "are a pair of born bloody fools, as anyone in the bazaar will tell you."

"The people in the bazaar have not the advantage of serving on Elfistan Sahib's staff," says he drily. "That is why I attach importance to your opinion. Now, are they trustworthy?"

This was a deuced odd question, from an Afghan, I

thought, and for a moment I nearly replied that they were English officers, blast his eyes. But you would have been wasting your time talking that way to Akbar Khan.

"Yes, they're trustworthy," I said.

"One more than the other? Which would you trust with your horse, or your wife—I take it you have no children?"

I didn't think long about this. "I'd trust Elphy Bey to do his best like a gentleman," I said. "But it probably wouldn't be much of a best."

"Thank you, Flashman," says he, "that is all I need to know. Now, I regret that I must cut short our most interesting little discussion, but I have many affairs to attend to. I shall come again, and we shall speak further."

"Now, hold on," I began, for I wanted to know how long he intended to keep me locked up, and a good deal more, but he turned me aside most politely, and left. And there I was, for another two weeks, damn him, with no one but the silent Barukzis for company.

I didn't doubt what he had told me about the situation in Kabul was true, but I couldn't understand it. It made no sense—a prominent British official murdered, and nothing done to avenge him. As it proved, this was exactly what had happened. When the mob looted the Residency and Sekundar was hacked to bits, old Elphy and McNaghten had gone into the vapours, but they'd done virtually nothing. They had written notes to each other, wondering whether to march into the city, or move into the Bala Hissar fort, or bring Sale—who was still bogged down by the Gilzais at Gandamack—back to Kabul. In the end they did nothing, and the Kabuli mobs roamed the city, as Akbar said, doing what they pleased, and virtually besieging our people in the cantonment.

Elphy could, of course, have crushed the mobs by firm action, but he didn't; he just wrung his hands and took to his bed, and McNaghten wrote him stiff little suggestions about the provisioning of the cantonment for the winter. Meanwhile the Kabulis, who at first had been scared stiff when they realised what they had done in murdering Burnes, got damned uppish, and started attacking the outposts near the cantonment, and shooting up our quarters at night.

One attempt, and only one, was made to squash them, and that foul-tempered idiot, Brigadier Shelton, bungled it handsomely. He took a strong force out to Beymaroo, and the Kabulis—just a damned drove of shopkeepers and sta-

blehands, mark you, not real Afghan warriors—chased
him and his troops back to the cantonment. After that,
there was nothing to be done; morale in the cantonment
went to rock-bottom, and the countryside Afghans, who
had been watching to see what would happen, decided
they were on a good thing, and came rampaging into the
city. The signs were that if the mobs and the tribesmen
really settled down to business, they could swarm over the
cantonment whenever they felt like it.

All this I learned later, of course. Colin Mackenzie,
who was through it all, said it was pathetic to see how old
Elphy shilly-shallied and changed his mind, and Mc-
Naghten still refused to believe that disaster was approaching. What had begun as mob violence was rapidly develop-
ing into a general uprising, and all that was wanting on
the Afghan side was a leader who would take charge of
events. And, of course, unknown to Elphy and Mc-
Naghten and the rest of them, there was such a leader,
watching events from a house in Kabul, biding his time
and every now and then asking me questions. For after a
fortnight's lapse Akbar Khan came to me again, polite and
bland as ever, and talked about it and about, speculating
on such various matters as British policy in India and the
rate of march of British troops in cold weather. He came
ostensibly to gossip, but he pumped me for all he was
worth, and I let him pump. There was nothing else I could
do.

He began visiting me daily, and I got tired of demanding my release and having my questions deftly ignored.
But there was no help for it; I could only be patient and
see what this jovial, clever gentleman had in mind for me.
Of what he had in mind for himself I was getting a pretty
fair idea, and events proved me right.

Finally, more than a month after Burnes's murder,
Akbar came and told me I was to be released. I could
have kissed him, almost, for I was fed up with being
jailed, and not even an Afghan bint to keep me amused.
He looked mighty serious, however, and asked me to be
seated while he spoke to me "on behalf of the leaders of
the Faithful." He had three of his pals with him, and I
wondered if he meant them.

One of them, his cousin, Sultan Jan, he had brought before, a leery-looking cove with a fork beard. The others
were called Muhammed Din, a fine-looking old lad with a
silver beard, and Khan Hamet, a one-eyed thug with the

face of a horse-thief. They sat and looked at me, and Akbar talked.

"First, my dear friend Flashman," says he, all charm, "I must tell you that you have been kept here not only for your own good but for your people's. Their situation is now bad. Why, I do not know, but Elfistan Sahib has behaved like a weak old woman. He has allowed the mobs to rage where they will, he has left the deaths of his servants unavenged, he has exposed his soldiers to the worst fate of all—humiliation—by keeping them shut up in cantonments while the Afghan rabble mock at them. Now his own troops are sick at heart; they have no fight in them."

He paused, picking his words.

"The British cannot stay here now," he went on. "They have lost their power, and we Afghans wish to be rid of them. There are those who say we should slaughter them all—needless to say, I do not agree." And he smiled. "For one thing, it might not be so easy—"

"It is never easy," said old Muhammed Din. "These same feringhees took Ghuznee Fort; I saw them, by God."

"—and for another, what would the harvest be?" went on Akbar. "The White Queen avenges her children. No, there must be a peaceful withdrawal to India; this is what I would prefer myself. I am no enemy of the British, but they have been guests in my country too long."

"One of 'em a month too long," says I, and he laughed.

"You are one feringhee, Flashman, who is welcome to stay as long as he chooses," says he. "But for the rest, they have to go."

"They came to put Sujah on the throne," says I. "They won't leave him in the lurch."

"They have already agreed to do so," said Akbar smoothly. "Myself, I have arranged the terms of withdrawal with McLoten Sahib."

"You've seen McNaghten?"

"Indeed. The British have agreed with me and the chiefs to march out to Peshawar as soon as they have gathered provisions for the journey and struck their camp. Sujah, it is agreed, remains on the throne, and the British are guaranteed safe conduct through the passes."

So we were quitting Kabul; I didn't mind, but I wondered how Elphy and McNaghten were going to explain this away to Calcutta. Inglorious retreat, the bit about Sujah staying on the throne was all my eye; once we were out of the way they'd blind him quietly and pop him in a fortress and forget about him. And the man who would take his place was sitting watching how I took the news.

"Well," says I at last, "there it is, but what have I to do with it? I mean, I'll just toddle off with the rest, won't I?"

Akbar leaned forward. "I have made it sound too simple, perhaps. There are problems. For example, McLoten has made his treaty to withdraw not only with myself, but with the Douranis, the Gilzais, the Kuzzilbashies, and so on—all as equals. Now, when the British have gone, all these factions will be left behind, and who will be the master?"

"Shah Sujah, according to you."

"He can rule only if he has a united majority of the tribes supporting him. As things stand, that would be difficult, for they eye each other askance. Oh, McLoten Sahib is not the fool you think him; he has been at work to divide us."

"Well, can't you unite them? You're Dost Mohammed's son, ain't you—and all through the passes a month ago I heard nothing but Akbar Khan and what a hell of a fellow he was."

He laughed and clapped his hands. "How gratifying! Oh, I have a following, it is true—"

"You have all Afghanistan," growls Sultan Jan. "As for Sujah—"

"I have what I have," Akbar interrupted him, suddenly chilly. "It is not enough, if I am to support Sujah as he must be supported."

There was a moment of silence, not very comfortable, and Akbar went on:

"The Douranis dislike me, and they are powerful. It would be better if their wings were clipped—theirs and a few others. This cannot be done after the British have left. With British help it can be done in time."

Oho, I thought, now we have it.

"What I propose is this," says Akbar, looking me in the eye. "McLoten must break his treaty so far as the Douranis are concerned; he must assist me in their overthrow. In return for this, I will allow him—for with the Douranis and their allies gone I shall have the power—to stay in Kabul another eight months. In that time I shall become Sujah's Vizier, the power at his elbow. The country will be so quiet then—so quiet, that the cheep of a Kandahar mouse will be heard in Kabul—that the British will be able to withdraw in honour. Is not this fair? The alternative now is a hurried withdrawal, which no one here can guarantee in safety, for none has the power to restrain the wilder tribes. And Afghanistan will be left to warring factions."

I have observed, in the course of a dishonest life, that when a rogue is outlining a treacherous plan, he works harder to convince himself than to move his hearers. Akbar wanted to cook his Afghan enemies' goose, that was all, and perfectly understandable, but he wanted to look like a gentleman still—to himself.

"Will you carry my proposal secretly to McLoten Sahib, Flashman?" he asked.

If he'd asked me to carry his proposal of marriage to Queen Victoria I'd have agreed, so of course I said "Aye" at once.

"You may add that as part of the bargain I shall expect a down payment of twenty lakhs of rupees," he added, "and four thousand a year for life. I think McLoten Sahib will find this reasonable, since I am probably preserving his political career."

And your own, too, thinks I. Sujah's Vizier, indeed. Once the Douranis were out of the way it would be farewell Sujah, and long live King Akbar. Not that I minded; after all, I would be able to say I was on nodding terms with a king—even if he was only a king of Afghanistan.

"Now," went on Akbar, "you must deliver my proposals to McLoten Sahib personally, and in the presence of Muhammed Din and Khan Hamet here, who will accompany you. If it seems"—he flashed his smile—"that I don't trust you, my friend, let me say that I trust no one. The reflection is not personal."

"The wise son," croaked Khan Hamet, opening his mouth for the first time, "mistrusts his mother." Doubtless he knew his own family best.

I pointed out that the plan might appear to McNaghten to be a betrayal of the other chiefs, and his own part in it dishonourable; Akbar nodded, and said gently:

"I have spoken with McLoten Sahib, remember. He is a politician."

He seemed to think that was answer enough, so I let it be. Then Akbar said:

"You will tell McLoten that if he agrees, as I think he

will, he must come to meet me at Mohammed's Fort, beyond the cantonment walls, the day after tomorrow. He must have a strong force at hand within the cantonment, ready to emerge at the word and seize the Douranis and their allies, who will be with me. Thereafter we will dispose matters as seems best to us. Is this agreed?" And he looked at his three fellows, who nodded agreement.

"Tell McLoten Sahib," said Sultan Jan, with a nasty grin, "that if he wills he may have the head of Amenoolah Khan, who led the attack on Sekundar Burnes's Residency. Also, that in this whole matter we of the Barukzis have the friendship of the Gilzais."

If both Gilzais and Barukzis were in the plot, it seemed to me that Akbar was on solid ground; McNaghten would think so too. But to me, sitting looking at those four faces, bland Akbar and his trio of villains, the whole thing stank like a dead camel. I would have trusted the parcel of them as much as Gul Shah's snakes.

However, I kept a straight face, and that afternoon the guard at the cantonment's main gate was amazed by the sight of Lieutenant Flashman, clad in the mail of a Barukzi warrior, and accompanied by Muhammed Din and Khan Hamet,[15] riding down in state from Kabul City. They had thought me dead a month ago, chopped to bits with Burnes, but here I was larger than life. The word spread like fire, and when we reached the gates there was a crowd waiting for us, with tall Colin Mackenzie[16] at their head.

"Where the devil have you come from?" he demanded, his blue eyes wide open.

I leaned down so that no one else should hear and said, "Akbar Khan;" he stared at me hard, to see if I was mad or joking, and then said: "Come to the Envoy at once," and cleared a way through the crowd for us. There was a great hubbub and shouting of questions, but Mackenzie shepherded us all three straight to the Envoy's quarters and into McNaghten's presence.

"Can't it wait, Mackenzie?" says he peevishly. "I'm just about to dine." But a dozen words from Mackenzie changed his tune. He stared at me through his spectacles, perched as always on the very tip of his nose. "My God, Flashman! Alive! And from Akbar Khan, you say? And who are these?" And he indicated my companions.

"Once you suggested I should bring you hostages from

Akbar, Sir William," says I. "Well, here they are, if you like."

He didn't take it well, but snapped to me to come in directly to dinner with him. The two Afghans, of course, wouldn't eat at an unbeliever's table, so they waited in his office, where food was brought to them. Muhammed Din reminded me that Akbar's message must be delivered only in their presence, so I contented myself by telling Mc-Naghten that I felt as though I was loaded with explosives, but that it must wait till after dinner.

However, as we ate I was able to give him an account of Burnes's murder and my own adventures with Gul Shah; I told it very plain and offhand, but McNaghten kept exclaiming "Good God!" all the way through, and at the tale of my tug-of-war his glasses fell into his curry. Mackenzie sat watching me narrowly, pulling at his fair moustache, and when I was done and McNaghten was spluttering his astonishment, Mackenzie just said: "Good work, Flash." This was praise, from him, for he was a tough, cold ramrod of a man, and reckoned the bravest in the Kabul garrison, except maybe for George Broadfoot. If he told my tale—and he would—Flashy's stock would rise to new heights, which was all to the good.

Over the port McNaghten tried to draw me about Akbar, but I said it must wait until we joined the two Afghans; not that I minded, much, but it made McNaghten sniffy, which was always excuse enough for me. He said sarcastically that I seemed to have gone native altogether, and that I did not need to be so nice, but Mackenzie said shortly that I was right, which put His Excellency into the sulks. He muttered that it was a fine thing when important officials could be bearded by military whipper-snappers, and the sooner we got to business the better it would be.

So we adjourned to his study, and presently Muhammed and Hamet came in, greeted the Envoy courteously, and received his cool nod in reply. He was a conceited prig, sure enough. Then I launched into Akbar's proposal.

I can see them still: McNaghten sitting back in his cane chair, legs crossed, finger-tips together, staring at the ceiling; the two silent Afghans, their eyes fixed on him; and the tall, fair Mackenzie, leaning against the wall, puffing a cheroot, watching the Afghans. No one said a word as I talked, and no one moved. I wondered if McNaghten understood what I was saying; he never twitched a muscle.

When I was finished he waited a full minute, slowly took off his glasses and polished them, and said quietly:

"Most interesting. We must consider what the Sirdar Akbar has said. His message is of the greatest weight and importance. But of course it is not to be answered in haste. Only one thing will I say now: the Queen's Envoy cannot consider the suggestion of bloodshed contained in the offer of the head of Amenoolah Khan. That is repugnant to me." He turned to the two Afghans. "You will be tired, sirs, so we will detain you no longer. Tomorrow we will talk again."

It was still only early evening, so he was talking rot, but the two Afghans seemed to understand diplomatic language; they bowed gravely and withdrew. McNaghten watched the door close on them; then he sprang to his feet.

"Saved at the eleventh hour!" cried he. "Divide and conquer! Mackenzie, I had dreamed of something precisely like this." His pale, worn face was all smiles now. "I knew, I knew, that these people were incapable of keeping faith with one another. Behold me proved right!"

Mackenzie studied his cigar. "You mean you'll accept?"

"Accept? Of course I shall accept. This is a heaven-sent opportunity. Eight months, eh? Much can happen in that time: we may never leave Afghanistan at all, but if we do it will be with credit." He rubbed his hands and set to among the papers on his desk. "This should revive even our friend Elphinstone, eh, Mackenzie?"

"I don't like it," says Mackenzie. "I think it's a plot."

McNaghten stopped to stare at him. "A plot?" Then he laughed, short and sharp. "Oho, a plot! Let me alone for that—trust me for that!"

"I don't like it a bit," says Mackenzie.

"And why not, pray? Tell me why not. Isn't it logical? Akbar must be cock o' the walk, so out must go his enemies, the Douranis. He'll use us, to be sure, but it is to our own advantage."

"There's a hole in it," says Mac. "He'll never serve as Vizier to Sujah. He's lying in that, at least."

"What of it? I tell you, Mackenzie, it doesn't matter one per cent whether he or Sujah rules in Kabul, we shall be secured by this. Let them fight among themselves as they will; it makes us all the stronger."

"Akbar isn't to be trusted," Mac was beginning, but McNaghten pooh-poohed him.

"You don't know one of the first rules of politics: that a man can be trusted to follow his own interest. I see perfectly well that Akbar is after undisputed power among his own people; well, who's to blame him? And I tell you, I believe you wrong Akbar Khan; in our meetings he has impressed me more than any other Afghan I have met. I judge him to be a man of his word."

"The Douranis are probably saying that, too," says I, and had the icy spectacles turned on me for my pains. But Mackenzie took me up fast enough, and asked me what I thought.

"I don't trust Akbar either," says I. "Mind you, I like the chap, but he ain't straight."

"Flashman probably knows him better than we do," says Mac, and McNaghten exploded.

"Now, really, Captain Mackenzie! I believe I can trust my own judgement, do you know? Against even that of such a distinguished diplomatist as Mr Flashman here." He snorted and sat down at his desk. "I should be interested to hear precisely what Akbar Khan has to gain by treachery towards us? What purpose his proposal can have other than that which is apparent? Well, can you tell me?"

Mac just stubbed out his cheroot. "If I could tell you, sir,—if I *could* see a definite trick in all this—I'd be a happier man. Dealing with Afghans, it's what I don't see and don't understand that worries me."

"Lunatic philosophy!" says McNaghten, and wouldn't listen to another word. He was sold on Akbar's plan, plain enough, and so determined that next morning he had Muhammed and Hamet in and signified his acceptance in writing, which they were to take back to Akbar Khan. I thought that downright foolish, for it was concrete evidence of McNaghten's part in what was, after all, a betrayal. One or two of his advisers tried to dissuade him from putting pen to paper, at least, but he wouldn't budge.

"Trouble is the man's desperate," Mackenzie told me. "Akbar's proposal came at just the right moment, when McNaghten felt the last ray of hope was gone, and he was going to have to skulk out of Kabul with his tail between his legs. He wants to believe Akbar's offer is above board. Well, young Flash, I don't know about you, but when we go out to see Akbar tomorrow I'm taking my guns along."

I was feeling pretty nervous about it myself, and I

wasn't cheered by the sight of Elphy Bey, when Mc-
Naghten took me along to see him that afternoon. The old
fellow was lying on a daybed on his verandah, while one
of the garrison ladies—I forget who—was reading the
Scriptures to him. He couldn't have been more pleased to
see me, and was full of praise for my exploits, but he
looked so old and wasted, in his night-cap and gown, that
I thought, my God, what chance have we with this to
command us?

McNaghten was pretty short with him, for when Elphy
heard of Akbar's plan he looked down in the mouth, and
asked if McNaghten wasn't afraid of some treachery.

"None at all," says McNaghten. "I wish you to have
two regiments and two guns got ready, quickly and
quietly, for the capture of Mohammed Khan's fort, where
we shall meet Sirdar Akbar tomorrow morning. The rest
you can leave to me."

Elphy looked unhappy about this. "It is all very uncer-
tain," says he, fretting. "I fear they are not to be trusted,
you know. It is a very strange plot, to be sure."

"Oh, my God!" says McNaghten. "If you think so, then
let us march out and fight them, and I am sure we shall
beat them."

"I can't, my dear Sir William," says old Elphy, and it
was pathetic to hear his quavering voice. "The troops
aren't to be counted on, you see."

"Well, then, we must accept the Sirdar's proposals."

Elphy fretted some more, and McNaghten was nearly
beside himself with impatience. Finally he snapped out: "I
understand these things better than you!" and turned on
his heel, and stamped off the verandah.

Elphy was much distressed, and lamented on about the
sad state of affairs, and the lack of agreement. "I suppose
he is right, and he does understand better than I. At least I
hope so. But you must take care, Flashman; all of you
must take care."

Between him and McNaghten I felt pretty down, but
evening brought my spirits up, for I went to Lady Sale's
house, where there was quite a gathering of the garrison
and wives, and found I was something of a lion. Mackenzie had told my story, and they were all over me. Even
Lady Sale, a vinegary old dragon with a tongue like a
carving knife, was civil.

"Captain Mackenzie has given us a remarkable account

of your adventures," says she. "You must be very tired; come and sit here, by me."

I pooh-poohed the adventures, of course, but was told to hold my tongue. "We have little enough to our *credit*," says Lady Sale, "so we must make the most of what we have. You, at least, have behaved with *courage* and common sense, which is more than can be said for some *older* heads among us."

She meant poor old Elphy, of course, and she and the other ladies lost no time in taking his character to pieces. They did not think much of McNaghten, either, and I was surprised at the viciousness of their opinions. It was only later that I understood that they were really frightened women; they had cause to be.

However, everyone seemed to enjoy slanging Elphy and the Envoy, and it was quite a jolly party. I left about midnight; it was snowing, and bright moonlight, and as I walked to my billet I found myself thinking of Christmastime in England, and the coach-ride back from Rugby when the half ended, and warm brandy-punch in the hall, and the roaring fire in the dining-room grate with Father and his cronies talking and laughing and warming their backsides. I wished I was there, with my young wife, and at the thought of her my innards tightened. By God, I hadn't had a woman in weeks, and there was nothing to be had in the cantonments. That was something I would speedily put right after we had finished our business with Akbar in the morning, and things were back to normal. Perhaps it was reaction from listening to those whining females, but it seemed to me as I went to sleep that McNaghten was probably right, and our plot with Akbar was all for the best.

I was up before dawn, and dressed in my Afghan clothes; it was easier to hide a brace of pistols beneath them than in a uniform. I buckled on my sword, and rode over to the gate where McNaghten and Mackenzie were already waiting, with a few native troopers; McNaghten, in his frock coat and top hat, was sitting a mule and damning the eyes of a Bombay Cavalry cornet; it seemed the escort was not ready, and Brigadier Shelton had not yet assembled the troops who were to overpower the Douranis.

"You may tell the Brigadier there is never anything ready or right where he is concerned!" McNaghten was saying. "It is all of a piece; we are surrounded by military

incompetents; well, it won't do. I shall go out to the meeting, and Shelton must have his troops ready to advance
within the half hour. Must, I say! Is that understood?"

The cornet scuttled off, and McNaghten blew his nose
and swore to Mackenzie he would wait no longer. Mac
urged him to hold on at least till there was some sign that
Shelton was moving, but McNaghten said:

"Oh, he is probably in his bed still. But I've sent word
to Le Geyt; he will see the thing attended to. Ah, here are
Trevor and Lawrence; now gentlemen, there has been time
enough wasted. Forward!"

I didn't like this. The plan had been that Akbar and the
chiefs, including the Douranis, should be assembled near
Mohammed's Fort, which was less than a quarter of a
mile from the cantonment gates. Once McNaghten and
Akbar had greeted each other, Shelton was to emerge
from the cantonment at speed, and the Douranis would be
surrounded and overcome between our troops and the
other chiefs. But Shelton wasn't ready, we didn't even
have an escort, and it seemed to me that the five of us and
the native troopers—who were only half a dozen or so
strong—might have an uncomfortable time before Shelton
came on the scene.

Young Lawrence thought so, too, for he asked Mc-
Naghten as we trotted through the gate if it would not be
better to wait; McNaghten snapped his head off and said
we could simply talk to Akbar until Shelton emerged,
when the thing would be done.

"Suppose there's treachery?" says Lawrence. "We'd be
better to have the troops ready to move at the signal."

"I can't wait any longer!" cries McNaghten, and he was
shaking, but whether with fear or cold or excitement I
didn't know. And I heard him mutter to Lawrence that he
knew there might be treachery, but what could he do? We
must just hope Akbar would keep faith with us. Anyway,
McNaghten would rather risk his own life than be disgraced by scuttling hangdog out of Kabul.

"Success will save our honour," says he, "and make up
for all the rest."

We rode out across the snowy meadow towards the
canal. It was a sparkling clear morning, bitterly cold;
Kabul City lay straight ahead, grey and silent; to our left
Kabul River wound its oily way beneath the low banks,
and beyond it the great Bala Hissar fort seemed to crouch
like a watchdog over the white fields. We rode in silence

now, our hooves crunching the snow; from the four in front of me the white trails of breath rose over their shoulders. Everything was very quiet.

We came to the canal bridge, and just beyond it was the slope running down from Mohammed's Fort beside the river. The slope was dotted with Afghans; in the centre, where a blue Bokhara carpet was spread on the snow, was a knot of chieftains with Akbar in the midst. Their followers waited at a distance, but I reckoned there must be fifty men in view—Barukzis, Gilzais, Douranis, yes, by God, and Ghazis.[17] That was a nasty sight. We're mad, I thought, riding into this; why, even if Shelton advances at the double, we could have our throats cut before he's half way here.

I looked back over my shoulder to the cantonment, but there was no sign of Shelton's soldiers. Mind you, at this stage that was just as well.

We rode to the foot of the slope, and what I was shivering with was not the cold.

Akbar rode down to meet us, on a black charger, and himself very spruce in a steel back-and-breast like a cuirassier, with his spiked helmet wrapped about with a green turban. He was all smiles and called out greetings to McNaghten; Sultan Jan and the chiefs behind were all looking as jovial as Father Christmas, and nodding and bowing towards us.

"This looks damned unhealthy," muttered Mackenzie. The chiefs were advancing straight to us, but the other Afghans, on the slopes on either side, seemed to me to be edging forward. I gulped down my fear, but there was nothing for it but to go on now; Akbar and McNaghten had met, and were shaking hands in the saddle.

One of the native troopers had been leading a lovely little white mare, which he now took forward, and McNaghten presented it to Akbar, who received it with delight. Seeing him so cheerful, I tried to tell myself it was all right—the plot was laid, McNaghten knew what he was doing, I really had nothing to fear. The Afghans were round us now, anyway, but they seemed friendly enough still; only Mackenzie showed, by the cock of his head and his cold eye, that he was ready to drop his hand on his pistol butt at the first sign of a false move.

"Well, well," cries Akbar. "Shall we dismount?"

We did, and Akbar led McNaghten on to the carpet. Lawrence was right at their heels, and looking pretty wary; he must have said something, for Akbar laughed and called out:

"Lawrence Sahib need not be nervous. We're all friends here."

I found myself with old Muhammed Din beside me, bowing and greeting me, and I noticed that Mackenzie and Trevor, too, were being engaged in friendly conversation. It was all so pally that I could have sworn there was something up, but McNaghten seemed to have regained his confidence and was chatting away smoothly to Akbar. Something told me not to stand still, but to keep on the move; I walked towards McNaghten, to hear what was passing between him and Akbar, and the ring of Afghans seemed to draw closer to the carpet.

"You'll observe also that I'm wearing the gift of pistols received from Lawrence Sahib," Akbar was saying. "Ah, there is Flashman. Come up, old friend, and let me see you. McLoten Sahib, let me tell you that Flashman is my favourite guest."

"When he comes from you, prince," says McNaghten, "he is my favourite messenger."

"Ah, yes," says Akbar, flashing his smile. "He is a prince of messengers." Then he turned to look McNaghten in the eye, and said: "I understand that the message he bore found favour in your excellency's sight?"

The buzz of voices around us died away, and it seemed that everyone was suddenly watching McNaghten. He seemed to sense it, but he nodded in reply to Akbar.

"It is agreed, then?" says Akbar.

"It is agreed," says McNaghten, and Akbar stared him full in the face for a few seconds, and then suddenly threw himself forward, clapping his arms round McNaghten's body and pinning his hands to his sides.

"Take them!" he shouted, and I saw Lawrence, who had been just behind McNaghten, seized by two Afghans at his elbows. Mackenzie's cry of surprise sounded beside me, and he started forward towards McNaghten, but one of the Barukzis jumped between, waving a pistol. Trevor ran at Akbar, but they wrestled him down before he had gone a yard.

I take some pride when I think back to that moment; while the others started forward instinctively to aid McNaghten, I alone kept my head. This was no place for Flashman, and I saw only one way out. I had been walking towards Akbar and McNaghten, remember, and as soon as I saw the Sirdar move I bounded ahead, not at him, but past him, and so close that my sleeve brushed his back. Just beyond him, on the edge of the carpet, stood the little white mare which McNaghten had brought as a gift; there was a groom at her head, but I was too fast for him.

I mounted in one flying leap, and the little beast reared in astonishment, sending the groom flying and causing the others to give back from her flashing fore-hooves. She curvetted sideways before I got her under control with a hand in her mane; one wild glance round for a way out was all I had time for, but it showed me the way.

On all sides Afghans were running in towards the group on the carpet; the knives were out and the Ghazis were yelling blue murder. Straight downhill, ahead of me, they seemed thinnest; I jammed my heels into the mare's sides and she leaped forward, striking aside a ruffian in a skull-cap who was snatching at her head. The impact caused her to swerve, and before I could check her she was plunging towards the struggling crowd in the centre of the carpet.

She was one of your pure-bred, mettlesome bitches, all nerves and speed, and all I could do was clamp my knees to her flanks and hang on. One split second I had to survey the scene before she was in the middle of it; Mc-Naghten, with two Afghans holding his arms, was being pushed headlong down the hill, his tall hat falling from his head, his glasses gone, and his mouth open in horror. Mackenzie I saw being thrown like a bolster over the flanks of a horse with a big Barukzi in the saddle, and Lawrence was being served the same way; he was fighting like a mad thing. Trevor I didn't see, but I think I heard him; as my little mare drove into the press like a thunderbolt there was a horrid, bubbling scream, and an exultant yell of Ghazi voices.

I had no time for anything but clinging to the mare, yet even in my terror I noticed Akbar, sabre in hand, thrusting back a Ghazi who was trying to come at Lawrence with a knife. Mackenzie was shouting and another Ghazi thrust at him with a lance, but Akbar, cool as you please, struck the lance aside with his sword and shouted with laughter.

"Lords of my country, are you?" he yelled. "You'll protect me, will you, Mackenzie Sahib?"

Then my mare had bounded past them, I had a few

yards to steady her and to move in, and I set her head downhill.

"Seize him!" shouted Akbar. "Take him alive!"

Hands grabbed at the mare's head and at my legs, but we had the speed, thank God, and burst through them. Straight downhill, across the canal bridge, there was the level stretch beside the river, and beyond lay the cantonment. Once over the bridge, on this mare, there wasn't a mounted Afghan who could come near me. Gasping with fear, I clung to the mane and urged her forward.

It must have taken longer to seize my mount, burst through the press, and take flight than I had imagined, for I was suddenly aware that McNaghten and the two Afghans who were carrying him off were twenty yards down the hill, and almost right in my path. As they saw me bearing down on them one of them sprang back, grasping a pistol from his belt. There was no way of avoiding the fellow, and I lugged out my sword with one hand, holding on grimly with the other. But instead of shooting at me, he levelled his piece at the Envoy.

"For God's sake!" McNaghten cried, and then the pistol banged and he staggered back, clutching at his face. I rode full tilt into the man who had shot him, and the mare reared back on her haunches; there was a mob around us now, slashing at McNaghten as he fell, and bounding over the snow at me. I yelled in rage and panic, and swung my sword blindly; it whistled through the empty air; and I nearly overbalanced, but the mare righted me, and I slashed again and this time struck something that crunched and fell away. The air was full of howls and threats; I lunged furiously and managed to shake off a hand that was clutching at my left leg; something cracked into the saddle beside my thigh, and the mare shrieked and bounded forward.

Another leap, another blind slash of my sword and we were clear, with the mob cursing and streaming at our heels. I put my head down and my heels in, and we went like a Derby winner in the last furlong.

We were down the slope and across the bridge when I saw ahead of me a little party of horsemen trotting slowly in our direction. In front I recognised Le Geyt—this was the escort that was to have guarded McNaghten, but of Shelton and his troops there was no sign. Well, they might just be in time to convoy his corpse, if the Ghazis left any of it; I stood up in the stirrups, glancing behind to make sure the pursuit was distanced, and hallooed.

But the only effect was that the cowardly brutes turned straight round and made for the cantonment at full pelt; Le Geyt did make some effort to rally them, but they paid no heed. Well, I am a poltroon myself, but this was ridiculous; it costs nothing to make a show, when all is said. Acting on the thought, I wheeled my mare; sure enough, the nearest Afghans were a hundred yards in my rear, and had given up chasing me. As far again beyond them a crowd was milling round the spot where McNaghten had fallen; even as I watched they began to yell and dance, and I saw a spear upthrust with something grey stuck on the end of it. Just for an instant I thought: "Well, Burnes will get the job now," and then I remembered, Burnes was dead. Say what you like, the political service is a chancy business.

I could make out Akbar in his glittering steel breastplate, surrounded by an excited crowd, but there was no sign of Mackenzie or Lawrence. By God, I thought, I'm the only survivor, and as Le Geyt came spurring up to me I rode forward a few paces, on impulse, and waved my sword over my head. It was impressively bloody from having hit somebody in the scramble.

"Akbar Khan!" I roared, and on the hillside faces began to turn to look down towards me. "Akbar Khan, you forsworn, treacherous dog!" Le Geyt was babbling at my elbow, but I paid no heed.

"Come down, you infidel!" I shouted. "Come down and fight like a man!"

I was confident that he wouldn't, even if he could hear me, which was unlikely. But some of the nearer Afghans could; there was a move in my direction.

"Come away, sir, do!" cries Le Geyt. "See, they are advancing!"

They were still a safe way off. "You dirty dog!" I roared. "Have you no shame, you that call yourself Sirdar? You murder unarmed old men, but will you come and fight with Bloody Lance?" And I waved my sabre again.

"For God's sake!" cries Le Geyt. "You can't fight them all!"

"Haven't I just been doing that?" says I. "By God, I've a good mind—"

He grabbed me by the arm and pointed. The Ghazis

were advancing, straggling groups of them were crossing the bridge. I didn't see any guns among them, but they were getting uncomfortably close.

"Sending your jackals, are you?" I bawled. "It's you I want, you Afghan bastard! Well, if you won't, you won't, but there'll be another day!"

With which I wheeled about, and we made off for the cantonment gate, before the Ghazis got within charging distance; they can move fast, when they want to.

At the gate all was chaos; there were troops hastily forming up, and servants and hangers-on scattering everywhere; Shelton was wrestling into his sword-belt and bawling orders. Red in the face, he caught sight of me.

"My God, Flashman! What is this? Where is the Envoy?"

"Dead," says I. "Cut to bits, and Mackenzie with him, for all I know."

He just gaped. "Who—what?—how?"

"Akbar Khan cut 'em up, sir," says I, very cool. And I added: "We had been expecting you and the regiment, but you didn't come."

There was a crowd round us—officers and officials and even a few of the troops who had broken ranks.

"Didn't come?" says Shelton. "In God's name, sir, I was coming this moment. This was the time appointed by the General!"

This astonished me. "Well, he was late," says I. "Damned late."

There was a tremendous hubbub about us, and cries of "Massacre!" "All dead but Flashman!" "My God, look at him!" "The Envoy's murdered!" and so on. Le Geyt pushed his way through them, and we left Shelton roaring to his men to stand fast till he found what the devil was what. He spurred up beside me, demanding to know what had taken place, and when I told him all of it, damning Akbar for a treacherous villain.

"We must see the General at once," says he. "How the devil did you come off alive, Flashman?"

"You may well ask, sir," cries Le Geyt. "Look here!" And he pointed to my saddle. I remembered having felt a blow near my leg in the skirmish, and when I looked, there was a Khyber knife with its point buried in the saddle bag. One of the Ghazis must have thrown it; two inches either way and it would have disabled me or the mare. Just the thought of what that would have meant

blew all the brag I had been showing clean away. I felt ill
and weak.

Le Geyt steadied me in the saddle, and they helped me
down at Elphy's front door, while the crowd buzzed
around. I straightened up, and as Shelton and I mounted
the steps I heard Le Geyt saying:

"He cut his way through the pack of 'em, and even then
he would have ridden back in alone if I hadn't stopped
him! He would, I tell you, just to come at Akbar!"

That lifted my spirits a little, and I thought, aye, give a
dog a good name and he's everyone's pet. Then Shelton,
thrusting everyone aside, had us in Elphy's study, and was
pouring out his tale, or rather, my tale.

Elphy listened like a man who cannot believe what he
sees and hears. He sat appalled, his sick face grey and his
mouth moving, and I thought again, what in God's name
have we got for a commander? Oddly enough, it wasn't
the helpless look in the man's eyes, the droop of his shoulders, or even his evident illness that affected me—it was
the sight of his skinny ankles and feet and bedroom slip-
pers sticking out beneath his gown. They looked so ridiculous in one who was a general of an army.

When we had done, he just stared and said:

"My God, what is to be done? Oh, Sir William, Sir William, what a calamity!" After a few moments he pulled
himself together and said we must take counsel what to
do; then he looked at me and said:

"Flashman, thank God you at least are safe. You come
like Randolph Murray, the single bearer of dreadful news.
Tell my orderly to summon the senior officers, if you
please, and then have the doctors look at you."

I believe he thought I was wounded; I thought then, and
I think now, that he was sick in mind as well as in body.
He seemed, as my wife's relatives would have said, to be
"wandered."

We had proof of this in the next hour or two. The cantonment, of course, was in a hubbub, and all sorts of rumours were flying. One, believe it or not, was that Mc-
Naghten had not been killed at all, but had gone into
Kabul to continue discussions with Akbar, and in spite of
having heard my story, this was what Elphy came round
to believing. The old fool always fixed on what he wanted
to believe, rather than what common sense suggested.

However, his daydream didn't last long. Akbar released
Lawrence and Mackenzie in the afternoon, and they con-

firmed my tale. They had been locked up in Mohammed Khan's fort, and had seen McNaghten's severed limbs flourished by the Ghazis. Later the murderers hung what was left of him and Trevor on hooks in the butchers' stalls of the Kabul bazaar.

Looking back, I believe that Akbar would rather have had McNaghten alive than dead. There is still great dispute about this, but it's my belief that Akbar had deliberately lured McNaghten into a plot against the Douranis to test him; when McNaghten accepted Akbar knew he was not to be trusted. He never intended to hold power in Afghanistan in league with us; he wanted the whole show for himself, and McNaghten's bad faith gave him the opportunity to seize it. But he would rather have held McNaghten hostage than kill him.

For one thing, the Envoy's death could have cost Akbar all his hopes, and his life. A more resolute commander than Elphy—anyone, in fact—would have marched out of the cantonment to avenge it, and swept the killers out of Kabul. We could have done it, too; the troops that Elphy had said he couldn't rely on were furious over McNaghten's murder. They were itching for a fight, but of course Elphy wouldn't have it. He must shilly-shally, as usual, so we skulked all day in the cantonment, while the Afghans themselves were actually in a state of fear in case we might attack them. This I learned later; Mackenzie reckoned if we had shown face the whole lot would have cut and run.

Anyway, this is history. At the time I only knew what I had seen and heard, and I didn't like it a bit. It seemed to me that having slaughtered the Envoy the Afghans would now start on the rest of us, and having seen Elphy wringing his hands and croaking I couldn't see what was to stop them. Perhaps it was the shock of my morning escape, but I was in the shivering dumps for the rest of the day. I could feel those Khyber knives and imagine the Ghazis yelling as they cut us to bits; I even wondered if it might not be best to get a fast horse and make off from Kabul as quickly as I could, but that prospect was as dangerous as staying.

But by the next day things didn't look quite so bad. Akbar sent some of the chiefs down to express his regrets for McNaghten's death, and to resume the negotiations—as if nothing had happened. And Elphy, ready to clutch at anything, agreed to talk; he didn't see what else he could do, he said. The long and short of it was that the Afghans told us we must quit Kabul at once, leaving our guns behind, and also certain married officers and their wives as hostages!

It doesn't seem credible now, but Elphy actually accepted. He offered a cash subsidy to any married officer who would go with his family as hostages to Akbar. There was a tremendous uproar over this; men were saying they would shoot their wives sooner than put them at the mercy of the Ghazis. There was a move to get Elphy to take action for once, by marching out and occupying the Bala Hissar, where we could have defied all Afghanistan in arms, but he couldn't make up his mind, and nothing was done.

The day after McNaghten's death there was a council of officers, at which Elphy presided. He was in terribly poor shape; on top of everything else, he had had an accident that morning. He had decided to be personally armed in view of the emergency, and had sent for his pistols. His servant had dropped one while loading it, and the pistol had gone off, the ball had passed through Elphy's chair, nicking his backside but doing no other damage.

Shelton, who could not abide Elphy, made the most of this.

"The Afghans murder our people, try to make off with our wives, order us out of the country, and what does our commander do? Shoots himself in the arse—doubtless in an attempt to blow his brains out. He can't have missed by much."

Mackenzie, who had no great regard for Elphy either, but even less for Shelton, suggested he might try to be helpful instead of sneering at the old fellow. Shelton rounded on him.

"I will sneer at him, Mackenzie!" says he. "I *like* sneering at him!"

And after this, to show what he thought, he took his blankets into the council and lay on them throughout, puffing at a cheroot and sniffing loudly whenever Elphy said anything unusually foolish; he sniffed a good deal.

I was at the council, in view of my part in the negotiations, I suppose, and for pure folly it matches anything in my military career—and I was with Raglan in the Crimea, remember. It was obvious from the first that Elphy wanted to do anything that the Afghans said he must do; he desired to be convinced that nothing else was possible.

"With poor Sir William gone, we are at a nonplus here," he kept repeating, looking around dolefully for someone to agree with him. "We can serve no purpose that I can see by remaining in Afghanistan."

There were a few spoke out against this, but not many. Pottinger, a smart sort of fellow who had succeeded by default to Burnes's job, was for marching into the Bala Hissar; it was madness, he said, to attempt to retreat through the passes to India in midwinter with the army hampered by hundreds of women and children and camp followers. Anyway, he didn't trust Akbar's safe conduct; he warned Elphy that the Sirdar couldn't stop the Ghazis cutting us up in the passes, even if he wanted to.

It seemed good sense to me: I was all for the Bala Hissar myself, so long as someone else led the way and Flashy was at his post beside Elphy Bey, with the rest of the army surrounding us. But the voices were all against Pottinger; it wasn't that they agreed with Elphy, but they didn't fancy staying in Kabul through the winter under his command. They wanted rid of him, and that meant getting him and the army back to India.

"God knows what he'll do if we stay here," someone muttered. "Make Akbar Political Officer, probably."

"A quick march through the passes," says another. "They'll let us go rather than risk trouble."

They argued on, until at last they were too tired and dispirited to talk any further. Elphy sat glooming round in the silence, but not giving any decision, and finally Shelton got up, ground out his cheroot, and snaps:

"Well, I take it we go? Upon my word, we must have a clear direction. Is it your wish, sir, that I take order for the army to remove to India with all possible speed?"

Elphy sat looking miserable, his fingers twitching together in his lap.

"It will be for the best, perhaps," he said at last. "I could wish it were otherwise, and that you had a commander not incapacitated by disease. Will you be so kind, Brigadier Shelton, as to take what order you think most fitting?"

So with no proper idea of what lay ahead, or how we should go, with the army dispirited and the officers divided, and with a commander announcing hourly that he was not fit to lead us, the decision was taken. We were to quit Kabul.

It took about a week to conclude the agreement with

the Afghans, and even longer to gather up the army and all its followers and make it even half-fit for the road. As Elphy's aide I had my hands full, carrying his orders, and then other orders to countermand the first ones, and listening to his bleating and Shelton's snarling. One thing I was determined on, that Flashy at any rate was going to get back to India, whoever else did not. I had my idea about how this should be done, and it did not consist of taking my simple chance with the rest. The whole business of getting the army to pull up its roots, and provisioned and equipped for the journey, proved to be such a mess that I was confident most of them would never see Jallalabad, beyond the passes, where Sale was now holding out and we could count ourselves safe.

So I looked out Sergeant Hudson, who had been with me at Mogala, and was as reliable as he was stupid. I told him I wanted twelve picked lancers formed into a special detail under my command—*not* my Gilzais, for in the present state of the country I doubted whether they would be prepared to get their throats cut on my behalf. The twelve would make as good an escort as I could hope for, and when the time came for the army to founder, we could cut loose and make Jallalabad on our own. I didn't tell Hudson this, of course, but explained that this troop and I would be employed on the march as a special messenger corps, since orders would be forever passing up and down the column. I told Elphy the same thing, and added that we could also act as mounted scouts and general busybodies. He looked at me like a tired cow.

"This will be dangerous work, Flashman," says he. "I fear it will be a perilous journey, and this will expose you to the brunt of it."

"Never say die, sir," says I, very manful. "We'll come through, and anyway, there ain't an Afghan of the lot of them that's a match for me."

"Oh, my boy," says he, and the silly old bastard began piping his eye. "My boy! So young, so valiant! Oh, England," says he, looking out of the window, "what dost thou not owe to thy freshest plants! So be it, Flashman. God bless you."

I wanted rather more insurance than that, so I made certain that Hudson packed our saddlebags with twice as much hard-tack as we would need; supplies were obviously going to be short, and I believed in getting our blow in first. In addition to the lovely little white mare I had taken from Akbar, I picked out another Afghan pony for my own use; if one mount sank I should have the other.

These were the essentials for the journey, but I had an eye to the luxuries as well. Confined to the cantonments as we were, I had not had a woman for an age, and I was getting peckish. To make it worse, in that Christmas week a messenger had come through from India with mails; among them was a letter from Elspeth. I recognised the handwriting, and my heart gave a skip; when I opened it I got a turn, for it began, "To my most beloved Hector," and I thought, by God, she's cheating on me, and has sent me the wrong letter by mistake. But in the second line was a reference to Achilles, and another to Ajax, so I understood she was just addressing me in terms which she accounted fitting for a martial paladin; she knew no better. It was a common custom at that time, in the more romantic females, to see their soldier husbands and sweethearts as Greek heroes, instead of the whore-mongering, drunken clowns most of them were. However, the Greek heroes were probably no better, so it was not so far off the mark.

It was a commonplace enough letter, I suppose, with news that she and my father were well, and that she was Desolate without her True Love, and Counted the Hours till my Triumphant Return from the Cannon's Mouth, and so on. God knows what young women think a soldier does for a living. But there was a good deal about how she longed to clasp me in her arms, and pillow my head on her breast, and so on (Elspeth was always rather forthright, more so than an English girl would have been), and thinking about that same breast and the spirited gallops we had taken together, I began to get feverish. Closing my eyes, I could imagine her soft, white body, and Fetnab's, and Josette's, and what with dreaming to this tune I rapidly reached the point where even Lady Sale would have had to cut and run for it if she had happened to come within reach.

However, I had my eye on younger game, in the excellent shape of Mrs Parker, the merry little wife of a captain in the 5th Light Cavalry. He was a serious, doting fellow, about twenty years older than she, and as fondly in love as only a middle-aged man with a young bride can be. Betty Parker was pretty enough, in a plump way, but she had buck teeth, and if there had been Afghan women to hand I would hardly have looked at her. With Kabul

City out of all bounds there was no hope of that, so I went quickly to work in that week after Christmas.

I could see she fancied me, which was not surprising in a woman married to Parker, and I took the opportunity at one of Lady Sale's evenings—for the old dragon kept open house in those days, to show that whoever was dismayed, she was full of spirit—to play loo with Betty and some others, and press knees with her beneath the table. She didn't seem to mind by half, so I tested the ground further later on; I waited till I could find her alone, and gave her tits a squeeze when she least expected it. She jumped, and gasped, but since she didn't swoon I guessed that all was well and would be better.

The trouble was Parker. There was no hope of doing anything while we remained in Kabul, and he was sure to stick close as a mother hen on the march. But chance helped me, as she always does if you keep your wits about you, although she ran it pretty fine and it was not until a couple of days before we were due to depart that I succeeded in removing the inconvenient husband.

It was at one of those endless discussions in Elphy's office, where everything under the sun was talked about and nothing done. In between deciding that our men must not be allowed to wear rags round their legs against the snow as the Afghans did to keep off frost-bite, and giving instructions what fodder should be carried along for his fox-hounds, Elphy Bey suddenly remembered that he must send the latest instructions about our departure to Nott at Kandahar. It would be best, he said, that General Nott should have the fullest intelligence of our movements, and Mackenzie, coming as near to showing impatience as I ever knew him, agreed that it was proper that one half of the British force in Afghanistan should know what the other half was doing.

"Excellent," says Elphy, looking pleased, but not for long. "Who shall we send to Kandahar with the despatches?" he wondered, worrying again.

"Any good galloper will do," says Mac.

"No, no," says Elphy, "he must be a man in whom we can repose the most perfect trust. An officer of experience is required," and he went rambling on about maturity and judgement while Mac drummed his fingernails on his belt.

I saw a chance here; ordinarily I never intruded an opinion, being junior and not caring a damn anyway, but now I asked if I might say a word.

"Captain Parker is a steady officer," says I, "if it ain't out of place for me to say so. And he's as sure in the saddle as I am, sir."

"Didn't know that," says Mac. "But if you say he's a horseman, he must be. Let it be Parker, then," says he to Elphy.

Elphy hummed a bit. "He is married, you know, Mackenzie. His wife would be deprived of his sustaining presence on our journey to India, which I fear may be an arduous one." The old fool was always too considerate by half. "She will be a prey to anxiety for his safety. . . ."

"He'll be as safe on the road to Kandahar as anywhere," says Mac. "And he'll ride all the harder there and back. The fewer loving couples we have on this march the better."

Mac was a bachelor, of course, one of these iron men who are married to the service and have their honeymoon with a manual of infantry drill and a wet towel round their heads; if he thought sending off Parker would cut down the number of loving couples he was going to be mistaken; I reckoned it would increase it.

So Elphy agreed, shaking his head and chuntering, and I rounded off the morning's work later by saying to Mac when we were outside that I was sorry for naming Parker, and that I'd forgotten he was a married man.

"You too?" says Mac. "Has Elphy infected you with his disease of worrying over everything that don't matter and forgetting those that do? Let me tell you, Flash, we shall spend so much time wagging our heads over nonsenses like Parker and Elphy's dogs and Lady McNaghten's chest-of-drawers that we'll be lucky if we ever see Jallalabad." He stepped closer and looked at me with those uncomfortable cold eyes of his. "You know how far it is? Ninety miles. Have you any notion how long it will take, with an army fourteen thousand strong, barely a quarter of 'em fighting troops, and the rest a great rabble of Hindoo porters and servants, to say nothing of women and children? And we'll be marching through a foot of snow on the worst ground on earth, with the temperature at freezing. Why, man, with an army of Highland ghillies I doubt if it could be done in under a week. If we're lucky we might do it in two—if the Afghans let us alone, and the food and firing hold out, and Elphy doesn't shoot himself in the other buttock."

I'd never seen Mackenzie in such a taking before.

Usually he was as cool as a trout, but I suppose being a serious professional and having to work with Elphy had worn him thin.

"I wouldn't say this to anybody but you, or George Broadfoot if he were here," says he, "but if we come through it'll be by pure luck, and the efforts of one or two of us, like you and me. Aye, and Shelton. He's a surly devil, but he's a fighting soldier, and if Elphy will let him alone he might get us to Jallalabad. There, now, I've told you what I think, and it's as near to croaking as I hope I'll ever get." He gave me one of his wintry smiles. "And you're worried about Parker!"

Having heard this, I was worried only about me. I knew Mackenzie; he wasn't a croaker, and if he thought our chances were slim, then slim they were. Of course, I knew from working in Elphy's office that things weren't shaping well; the Afghans were hampering us at every turn in getting supplies together, and there were signs that the Ghazis were moving out of Kabul along the passes—Pottinger was sure they were going to lie in wait for us, and try to cut us up in the really bad defiles, like Khoord-Kabul and Jugulluk. But I had reasoned that an army fourteen thousand strong ought to be safe, even if a few fell by the way-side; Mac had put it in a different light, and I began to feel again that looseness low down in my guts and the sick sensation in my throat. I tried to tell myself that soldiers like Shelton and Mackenzie, yes, and Sergeant Hudson, weren't going to be stopped by a few swarms of Afghans, but it was no good. Burnes and Iqbal had been good soldiers, too, and that hadn't saved them; I could still hear the hideous chunk of those knives into Burnes's body, and think of McNaghten swinging dead on a hook, and Trevor screaming when the Ghazis got him. I came near to vomiting. And half an hour back I had been scheming so that I could tumble Mrs Parker in a tent on the way back to Jallalabad; that reminded me of what Afghan women do to prisoners, and it didn't bear thinking about.

I was hard put to it to keep a good face on things at Lady Sale's last gathering, two nights before we left. Betty was there, and the look she gave me cheered me up a lit-tle; her lord and master would be half way to Kandahar by now, and I toyed with the notion of dropping in at her bungalow that night, but with so many servants about the cantonment it would be too risky. Better to wait till we're on the road, thinks I, and nobody knows one tent from another in the dark.

Lady Sale spent the evening as usual, railing about Elphy and the general incompetence of the staff. "There never was such a set of yea-and-nays. The only *certain* thing is that our chiefs have no mind for two minutes on end. They seem to think of *nothing* but contradicting each other, when harmony and *order* are most needed."

She said it with satisfaction, sitting in her last chair while they fed her furniture into the stove to keep the room tolerably warm. Everything had gone except her chest-of-drawers, which was to provide fuel to cook her meals before our departure; we sat round on the luggage which was piled about the walls, or squatted on the floor, while the old harpy sat looking down her beaky nose, her mittened hands folded in front. The strange thing was that no one thought of her as a croaker, although she complained unendingly; she was so obviously confident that *she* would get to Jallalabad in spite of Elphy's bungling that it cheered people up.

"Captain Johnson informs me," says she, sniffing, "that there is food and fodder for ten days at the most, and that the Afghans have no *intention* of providing us with an escort through the passes."

"Better without 'em," says Shelton. "The fewer we see the better I'll like it."

"Indeed? And who, then, is to *guard* us from the badmashes and brigands lurking in the hills?"

"Good God, ma'am," cries Shelton, "aren't we an army? We can protect ourselves, I hope."

"You may hope so, indeed. I am not so sure that some of your *native* troops will not take the first opportunity to make themselves *scarce*. We shall be quite without friends, and food, and *firewood*."

She then went on to tell us cheerfully that the Afghans certainly meant to try to destroy our whole force, in her opinion, that they meant to get all our women into their possession, and that they would leave only one man alive, "who is to have his legs and hands cut off and is to be placed at the entrance of the Khyber pass, to deter all feringhees from entering the country again."

"My best wishes to the Afghan who gets *her*," growled Shelton as we were leaving. "If he's got any sense he'll stick *her* up in the Khyber—that'll keep the feringhees out with a vengeance."

The next day I spent making sure that my picked lancers were all in order, that our saddle-bags were full, and that every man had sufficient rounds and powder for his carbine. And then came the last night, and the chaos of last-minute preparations in the dark, for Shelton was determined to be off before first light so that we might pass Khoord-Kabul in the first day's march, which meant covering fifteen miles.

Possibly there has been a greater shambles in the history of warfare than our withdrawal from Kabul; probably there has not. Even now, after a lifetime of consideration, I am at a loss for words to describe the superhuman stupidity, the truly monumental incompetence, and the bland blindness to reason of Elphy Bey and his advisers. If you had taken the greatest military geniuses of the ages, placed them in command of our army, and asked them to ruin it utterly as speedily as possible, they could not—I mean it seriously—have done it as surely and swiftly as he did. And he believed he was doing his duty. The meanest sweeper in our train would have been a fitter commander.

Shelton was not told that we would march on the morning of the 6th January, until evening on the 5th. He laboured like a madman through the night, loading up the huge baggage train, assembling the troops within the cantonment in their order of march, and issuing orders for the conduct and disposal of the entire force. It is a few words on paper: as I remember it, there was a black night of drifting snow, with storm lanterns flickering, troops tramping unseen in the dark, a constant babble of voices, the neighing and whining of the great herd of baggage animals, the rumble of wagons, messengers dashing to and fro, great heaps of luggage piled high outside the houses, harassed officers demanding to know where such-and-such a regiment was stationed, and where so-and-so had gone, bugle calls ringing in the night wind, feet stamping, children crying, and on the lighted verandah of his office, Shelton, red-faced and dragging at his collar, with his staff scurrying about him while he tried to bring some order out of the inferno.

And as the sun came up from the Seeah Sung hills, it seemed that he had done it. The army of Afghanistan was standing ready to march—everyone was dead tired, of course—strung out through the length of the cantonment, with everything loaded (except sufficient food), and all the troops fallen in and armed (with hardly any powder and ball among them), and Shelton shouting his last orders in a voice gone hoarse, while Elphy Bey finished an unhurried breakfast of devilled ham, omelette, and a little pheasant. (I know because he invited me to join him with the other staff officers.)

And while he was making his final toilet, with his staff and servants fussing round him, and the army waiting in the cold, I rode out to the cantonment gate to see what was happening over towards Kabul. The city was alive, with crowds on the rooftops and scattered over the snowy ground from Bala Hissar to the river; they were there to watch the feringhees go, but they seemed quiet enough just now. The snow was falling gently; it was damned cold.

In the cantonments the bugles shrilled together, and "Forward!" was the command, and with a great creaking and groaning and shuffling and bellowing the march began.

First out came Mackenzie with his jezzailchis, the wild hill marksmen who were devoted to him; like me, he was wearing poshteen cloak and turban, with his pistols stuck in his belt, and he looked the genuine Afridi chief with his long moustache and his ugly rascals behind him. Then Brigadier Anquetil with the 44th, the only British infantry regiment in the army, very dapper in their shakos and red coats with white crossbelts; they looked fit to sweep away all the hordes of Afghanistan, and my spirits rose at the sight of them. They had a few fifes playing "Yankee Doodle," of all things, and stepped out smartly.

A squadron of Sikh cavalry, escorting the guns and sappers and miners, came next, and then in a little group the English women and families, all on camels or ponies, the children and older ladies travelling in camel howdahs, the younger women riding. And of course Lady Sale was to the fore, wearing an enormous turban and riding a tiny Afghan pony side-saddle. "I was saying to Lady McNaghten that I believe we *wives* would make the best troopers of all," she cries out. "What do you think, Mr Flashman?"

"I'd take your ladyship into my troop any time," says I, at which she simpered horribly—"but the other horses might be jealous," I says to myself quietly, at which the lancers set up a great laugh.

There were about thirty white women and children, from tiny babies to grandmothers, and Betty Parker gave me a knowing smile and a wave as she trotted past. Thinks I, wait till tonight, there'll be one snug blanket-roll on the Jallalabad road anyway.

Then came Shelton, blown and weary but cursing as loud as ever, on his charger, and the three Indian regiments of foot, black faces, red coats and white trousers, their naked feet churning up the slush. And behind them the herd—for that was what it was—of baggage animals, lowing and roaring with their tottering bundles and creaking carts. There were hundreds of camels, and the stench was furious; they and the mules and ponies churned the cantonment road into a sea of liquid chocolate, through which the hordes of camp followers and their families waded up to the knee, babbling and shouting. There were thousands of them, men, women, and children, with no order whatever, their few belongings carried on their backs, and all in great consternation at the thought of the march back to India; no proper provision had been made for feeding them on the way, or quartering them at night. They were apparently just to forage what they could and sleep in the drifts.

This great brown mob surged by, and then came the rearguard of Indian infantry and a few cavalry troops. The great procession was all strung out across the plain to the river, a sprawling, humming mass that stumbled slowly through the snow; steam rose from it like smoke. And then last of all Elphy Bey's entourage came out to canter up the line and take its place with the main body beside Shelton, but Elphy was already beset by doubts, and I heard him debating loudly with Grant whether it might not be better to delay setting off.

Indeed, he actually sent a messenger to stop the vanguard at the river, but Mackenzie deliberately disobeyed and pushed on; Elphy wrung his hands and cried: "He mustn't do it! Tell Mackenzie to stop, I say!" but by that time Mac was over the bridge, so Elphy had to give up and come along with the rest.

We were no sooner out of the compound than the Afghans were in. The crowds that had been watching had moved round slowly, keeping a safe distance from us, but

now they rushed into the cantonments, yelling and burning, looting what was left in the houses and even opening
fire on the rearguard. There was some rough work at the
gates, and a few Indian troopers were knocked from their
saddles and butchered before the rest got clear.

One effect of this was to cause a panic among the porters and camp-followers, many of whom flung away their
loads and ran for dear life. The snow on either side of the
road was soon dotted with bundles and sacks, and it has
been reckoned that a good quarter of our stores were lost
this way before we had even reached the river.

With the mob hanging on the heels of the column we
got across, marched past the Bala Hissar, and turned on to
the Jallalabad road. We were travelling at a snail's pace,
but already some of the Indian servants were beginning to
fall out, plumping down and wailing in the snow, while
the bolder spirits among the Afghan spectators came close
to jeer and pelt us with stones. There was some scuffling
and a shot or two, but in the main the Kabulis just seemed
glad to let us go—and so far we were glad enough to be
going. If we had even dreamed what lay ahead we would
have turned back as one, even if all Afghanistan had been
pursuing, but we did not know.

On Elphy's instructions Mackenzie and I and our troops
kept up a constant patrol along the flanks of the column,
to discourage the Afghans from coming too close and prevent straggling. Some bodies of Afghans were moving
along with us, but well out on either side of the road, and
we kept a sharp eye on them. One of these groups, drawn
up on a little knoll, took my eye; I decided to keep well
clear of them, until I heard my name called, and who
should be sitting at their head, large as life, but Akbar
Khan.

My first instinct was to turn tail for the column, but he
rode a little forward from his companions, calling to me,
and presently I edged my pony up to within a short pistol
shot of him. He was all in his steel back-and-breast, with
his spiked helmet and green turban, and smiling all over
his face.

"What the devil do you want?" says I, beckoning Sergeant Hudson up beside me.

"To bid you God speed and a good journey, old friend,"
says he, quite cheerful. "Also to give you a little advice."

"If it's the kind you gave Trevor and McNaghten, I
don't need it," says I.

"As God is my judge," says he, "that was no fault of mine. I would have spared him, as I would spare all of you, and be your friend. For this reason, Flashman huzoor, I regret to see you marching off before the escort is ready that I was assembling for your safety."

"We've seen some of your escorts before," says I. "We'll do very well on our own."

He rode closer, shaking his head. "You do not understand. I, and many of us, wish you well, but if you go off to Jallalabad before I have taken proper measures for your protection on the march, why then, it is no fault of mine if you meet disaster. I cannot control the Ghazis, or the Gilzais."

He seemed serious, and quite sincere. To this day I cannot be sure whether Akbar was a complete knave or a fairly honest man caught up in a stream of circumstances which he could not resist. But I wasn't trusting him in a hurry, after what had happened.

"What d'ye want us to do?" says I. "Sit down in the snow and wait for you to round up an escort while we freeze to death?" I wheeled my pony round. "If you have any proposals to make, send them to Elfistan Sahib, but I doubt if he'll listen to 'em. Man alive, your damned Kabulis have been sniping at our rearguard already; how's that for keeping faith?"

I was for riding off, but he suddenly spurred up closer yet. "Flashman," says he, speaking very fast and low. "Don't be a fool. Unless Elfistan Sahib lets me help him, by providing an escort in exchange for hostages, you may none of you reach Jallalabad. You can be one of those hostages; I swear on the grave of my mother you would be safe. If Elfistan Sahib will wait, it shall be arranged. Tell him this, and let him send you out again with a reply."

He was so earnest that I was half-convinced. I imagine now that what he was chiefly interested in was hostages, but it is also possible that he genuinely believed that he could not control his tribesmen, and that we should be massacred in the passes. If that happened, Afghanistan might well see another British army the following year, and it would be shooting as it came. At the time, however, I was more concerned about his interest in me.

"Why should you want to preserve my life?" says I. "What do you owe me?"

"We have been friends," says he, grinning that sudden grin of his. "Also I admired the compliments you paid me as you rode away from Mohammed Khan's fort the other day."

"They weren't meant to flatter you," says I.

"The insults of an enemy are a tribute to the brave," laughs he. "Think on what I have said, Flashman. And tell Elfistan Sahib."

He waved and rode back up the hill, and the last I saw of his troop they were following slowly on our flank, the tips of their spears winking on the snowy hillside.

All that afternoon we toiled on, and we were long short of Khoord-Kabul when night came freezing down. The Afghans hung on our flanks, and when men—aye, and women and children—dropped by the wayside, they were pounced on as soon as the column had passed and murdered. The Afghans saw that our chiefs were not prepared to fight back, so they snapped at our heels, making little sorties on the baggage train, cutting up the native drivers, and scattering into the rocks only when our cavalry approached. Already the column was falling into utter disorder; the main body gave no thought to the thousands of native camp-followers, who were bitterly affected by the cold and want of food; hundreds fell by the way, so that in our wake there was a litter not only of bundles and baggage, but of corpses. And this was within a twenty-minute gallop of Kabul.

I had taken Akbar's message to Elphy when I rejoined the column, and it sent him into a great taking. He dithered and consulted his staff, and eventually they decided to push on.

"It will be for the best," bleated Elphy, "but we should maintain our relations with the Sirdar in the meantime. You shall ride to him tomorrow, Flashman, and convey my warmest good wishes. That is the proper way of it."

The stupid old bastard seemed oblivious of the chaos around him. Already his force was beginning to wither at the edges. When we camped it was a question of the troops simply lying down on the snow, in huddled groups for warmth, while the unfortunate niggers wailed and whimpered in the dark. There were some fires, but no field kitchens or tents for the men; much of the baggage was already lost, the order of march had become confused, some regiments had food and others none, and everyone was frozen to the bone.

The only ones fairly well off were the British women

and their children. The dragon Lady Sale saw to it that their servants pitched little tents or shelters; long after dark her sharp, high voice could be heard carping on above the general moan and whimper of the camp-followers. My troopers and I were snug enough in the lee of some rocks, but I had left them at dusk to help with the ladies' tents, and in particular to see where Betty was installed. She seemed quite gay, despite the cold, and after I had made sure that Elphy was down for the night, I returned to the little group of wagons where the women were. It was now quite dark, and starting to snow, but I had marked her little tent, and found it without difficulty.

I scratched on the canvas, and when she called out who was there I asked her to send away her servant, who was in the tent with her for warmth. I wanted to talk to her, I said, keeping my voice down.

The native woman who served her came snuffling out presently, and I helped her into the dark with my boot. I was too cock-a-hoop to care whether she gossiped or not; she was probably too frightened, like the rest of the niggers, to worry about anything except her own skin that night.

I crawled under the low canvas, which was only about two feet high, and heard Betty move in the darkness. There was a pile of blankets covering the floor of the tent, and I felt her body beneath them.

"What is it, Mr Flashman?" says she.

"Just a friendly call," says I. "Sorry I couldn't send in a card."

She giggled in the dark. "You are a great tease," she whispered, "and very wrong to come in like this. But I suppose the conditions are so unusual, and it is kind of you to look after me."

"Capital," says I, and without wasting more time I dived under the blankets and took hold of her. She was still half-dressed against the cold, but gripping that young body sent the fire running through me, and in a moment I was on top of her with my mouth on hers. She gave a gasp, and then a yelp, and before I knew it she was writhing away, striking at me, and squeaking like a startled mouse.

"How dare you!" she squealed. "Oh, how dare you! Get away! Get away from me this instant!" And lunging in the dark she caught me a great crack on the eye.

"What the devil!" says I. "What's the matter?"

"Oh, you brute!" she hissed—for she had the sense to keep her voice down—"you filthy, beastly brute! Get out of my tent at once! At once, d'you hear?"

I could make nothing of this, and said so. "What have I done? I was only being friendly. What are you acting so damned missish for?"

"Oh, base!" says she. "You . . . you. . . ."

"Oh, come now," says I. "You're in very high ropes, to be sure. You weren't so proper when I squeezed you the other night."

"Squeezed me?" says she, as though I had uttered some unmentionable word.

"Aye, squeezed. Like this." And I reached over and, with a quick fumble in the dark, caught one of her breasts. To my amazement, she didn't seem to mind.

"Oh, that!" she says. "What an evil creature you are! You know that is nothing; all gentlemen do that, in affection. But you, you monstrous beast, presume on my friendship to try to. . . . Oh, oh, I could die of shame!"

If I had not heard her I shouldn't have believed it. God knows I have learned enough since of the inadequacies of education given to young Englishwomen, but this was incredible.

"Well," says I, "if you're accustomed to gentlemen doing that to you, in affection, you know some damned queer gentlemen."

"You . . . you foul person," says she, in indignation. "It is no more than shaking hands!"

"Good God!" says I. "Where on earth were you brought up?"

At this, by the sound of it, she buried her face in the blankets and began to weep.

"Mrs Parker," says I, "I beg your pardon. I have made a mistake, and I am very sorry for it." The quicker I got out of this, the better, or she might start shouting rape round the camp. I'll say this for her, ignorant and full of amazing misconceptions as she was, she had appeared angry rather than frightened, and had kept her abuse of me down to a whisper. She had her own reputation to think about, of course.

"I shall go," says I, and started crawling for the flap. "But I may tell you," I added, "that in polite society it ain't usual for gentlemen to squeeze ladies' tits, whatever you may have been told. And it ain't usual, either, for ladies to let gentlemen do it; it gives the gentlemen a wrong impression, you know. My apologies, again. Good night."

She gave one last muffled squeak, and then I was out in the snow. I had never heard anything like it in my life, but I didn't know, then, how astonishingly green young women could be, and what odd notions they could get. Anyway, I had been well set down, for certain; by the looks of it I should have to contain my enthusiasm until we reached India again. And that, as I huddled down in my blankets beside my troopers, with the cold getting keener every minute, was no consolation at all.

Looking back on it now, I suppose it is funny enough, but lying shivering there and thinking of the pains I had been at to get Captain Parker out of the way, I could have twisted Mrs Betty's pretty neck for her.

It was a bitter, biting night, and there was little sleep to be had, for if the cold was not bad enough the niggers kept up a great whining and wailing to wake the dead. And by morning not a few of the poor devils *were* dead, for they had no more than a few rags of clothing to cover them. Dawn broke on a scene that was like something from an icy hell; everywhere there were brown corpses lying stiff in the drifts, and the living crackled as they struggled up in their frozen clothes. I saw Mackenzie actually crying over the body of a tiny native child; he was holding her in his arms, and when he saw me he cried out:

"What are we to do? These people are all dying, and those that don't will be slaughtered by those wolves on the hillside yonder. But what can we do?"

"What, indeed?" says I. "Let 'em be; there's no help for it." He was remarkably concerned, it seemed to me, over a nigger. And he was such a ramrod of a man, too.

"If only I could take her with me," says he, laying the small body back in the snow.

"You couldn't take 'em all," says I. "Come on, man, let's get some breakfast." He saw this was sensible advice, and we were lucky enough to get some hot mutton at Elphy's tent.

Getting the column under way was tremendous work; half the sepoys were too frost-bitten to be able to lift their muskets, and the other half had deserted in the night, skulking back to Kabul. We had to flog them into line, which warmed everyone up, but the camp followers needed no such urging. They were crowding ahead in panic in case they should be left behind, and threw Anquetil's vanguard into tremendous confusion. At this point a great cloud of mounted Ghazis suddenly came yelling out of a nullah in the hillside, and rode into the mob, cutting down everything in their way, soldiers and civilians, and made off with a couple of Anquetil's guns before he could stop them.

He made after them, though, with a handful of cavalry, and there was a warm skirmish; he couldn't get back the guns, but he spiked them, while the 44th stood fast and did nothing. Lady Sale damned them for cowards and hang-backs—the old baggage should have been in command, instead of Elphy—but I didn't blame the 44th myself. I was farther down the column, and in no hurry to get near the action until Anquetil was riding back, when I brought my lancers up at the canter (true to life, Tom Hughes, eh?). The guns were going to be no use to us, anyway.

We blundered along the road for a mile or two, with troops of Afghans hanging on our flanks and every now and then swooping down at a weak part of the column, cutting up a few folk, snatching at the stores, and riding off again. Shelton kept roaring for everyone to hold his place and not be drawn in pursuit, and I took the opportunity to damn his eyes and demand to know what we were soldiers for, if not to fight our enemies when we saw them in front of us.

"Steady on, old Flash," says Lawrence, who was with Shelton just then. "It's no use chasing 'em and getting cut up in the hills; they'll be too many for you."

"It's too bad!" I bawled, slapping my sabre. "Are we just to wait for 'em to chew us up as they please, then? Why, Lawrence, I could clear that hillside with twenty Frenchmen, or old ladies!"

"Bravo!" cries Lady Sale, clapping her hands. "You hear, gentlemen?"

There was a knot of the staff round Elphy's palankeen, with Shelton in the middle of them, and they were none too pleased to hear the old dragon crowing at them. Shelton bristled up, and told me to hold my place and do as I was told.

"At your orders, sir," says I, mighty stiff, and Elphy joined in.

"No, no, Flashman," says he. "The Brigadier is right. We must preserve order." This, in the middle of a column that was a great sprawling mass of troops and people and animals, with no direction at all, and their baggage scattered.

Mackenzie, coming up, told me that my party and his jezzailchis must flank the column closely, watching the likely places, and driving in hard when the Afghans appeared—what the Americans call "riding herd." You can guess what I thought of this, but I agreed heartily with Mac, especially when it came to picking out the most likely spots for attack, so that I could keep well clear of them. It was simple enough, really, for the Afghans would only come where we were not, and at this time they were less interested in killing soldiers than in cutting up the unarmed niggers and pillaging the baggage animals.

They made pretty good practice at this during the morning, running in and slitting a throat and running off again. I did pretty well, halloo-ing to my lancers and thundering along the line of march, mostly near the headquarters section. Only once, when I was down by the rearguard, did I come face to face with a Ghazi; the fool must have mistook me for a nigger, in my poshteen and turban, for he came yelling down on a party of servants close by and cut up an old woman and a couple of brats. There was a troop of Shah's cavalry not far off, so I couldn't hang back; the Ghazi was on foot, so I let out a great roar and charged him, hoping he would sheer off at the sight of a mounted soldier He did, too, and like an ass I tried to ride him down, thinking it would be safe enough to have a swipe at him. But the brute whipped round and slashed at me with his Khyber knife, and only by the grace of God did I take the cut on my sabre. I drove on past him, and wheeled just in time to see one of my lancers charging in to skewer him beautifully. Still, I had a good hack at him, for luck, and was able to trot up the line presently looking stern, and with my point impressively bloody.

It had been a lesson to me, though, and I took even greater care to be out of distance whenever they made a sortie out of the hills. It was nerve-racking work, and it was all I could do to maintain a bold-looking front as the morning wore on; the brutes were getting braver all the time, and apart from their charges there was an uncomfortable amount of sniping taking place.

At last Elphy got fed up, and ordered a halt, which was the worst thing he could have done. Shelton swore and stamped, and said we must push on; it was our only hope to get through Khoord-Kabul before dark. But Elphy insisted we must stop to try and make some sort of peace with the Afghan leaders, and so stop the slow bleeding to death of the army at the hands of the harassing tribesmen. I was for this, and when Pottinger spotted a great mass of Afghans far up the slope, with Akbar at their head, he had no difficulty in persuading Elphy to send out messengers to him.

By God, I was sorry to be on hand when that happened, for of course Elphy's eye lighted on me. There was nothing I could do about it, of course; when he said I must ride to Akbar and demand to know why the safe-conduct was not being observed, I had to listen to his orders as though my guts were not dissolving inside me, and say, "Very good, sir," in a steady voice. It was no easy task, I can tell you, for the thought of riding out to meet those ruffians chilled me to the backbone. What was worse, Pottinger said I should go alone, for the Afghans might mistake a party for an attacking force.

I could have kicked Pottinger's fat backside for him; he was so damned full of self-importance, standing there looking like Jesus Christ, with his lovely brown beard and whiskers. But I just had to nod as though it was all in the day's work: there was a fair crowd round, for the womenfolk and English families naturally clung as close to Elphy's presence as they could—much to Shelton's annoyance—and half the officers in the main body had come up to see what was happening. I noticed Betty Parker, in a camel howdah, looking bewildered and mimmish until she caught my eye, when she looked quickly away.

So I made the best of it. As I wheeled my pony I shouted out to Gentleman Jim Skinner:

"If I don't come back, Jim, settle Akbar Khan for me, will you?"

Then I clapped in the spurs and went at the slope hell-for-leather; the faster I went the less chance I stood of getting picked off, and I had a feeling that the closer I got to Akbar Khan the safer I should be.

Well, it was right enough; no one came near me, and

the Ghazi parties on the hill just stared as I swept by; as I came up towards where Akbar sat his horse before his host—for there must have been five or six hundred of them—he waved to me, which was a cheering sight.

"Back again, prince of messengers," he sings out. "What news from Elfistan Sahib?"

I pulled up before him, feeling safer now that I was past the Ghazi outliers. I didn't believe Akbar would let me be harmed, if he could help it.

"No news," says I. "But he demands to know if this is how you keep faith, setting on your men to pillage our goods and murder our people."

"Did you not tell him?" says he, jovial as ever. "He himself broke faith, by leaving Kabul before the escort was ready for him. But here it is—" and he gestured at the ranks behind him "—and he may go forward in peace and safety."

If this was true, it was the best news I had heard in months. And then, glancing past him at the ranks behind, I felt as though I had been kicked in the stomach: immediately in his rear, and glaring at me with his wolf smile, was my old enemy, Gul Shah. Seeing him there was like a dash of cold water in the face; here was one Afghan who did not want to see Flashman, at least, depart in peace and safety.

Akbar saw my look, and laughed. Then he brought his horse up closer to mine, so that we were out of earshot, and said:

"Have no fear of Gul Shah. He no longer makes mistakes, such as the one which was almost so unfortunate for yourself. I assure you, Flashman, you need not mind him. Besides, his little snakes are all back in Kabul."

"You're wrong," says I. "There are a damned lot of them sitting either side of him."

Akbar threw back his head, and laughed again, flashing those white teeth.

"I thought the Gilzais were friends of yours," says he.

"Some of them," says I. "Not Gul Shah's."

"It is a pity," says Akbar, "for you know that Gul is now Khan of Mogala? No? Oh, the old man—died, as old men will. Gul has been very close to me, as you know, and as a reward for faithful service I granted him the lordship."

"And Ilderim?" I asked.

"Who is Ilderim? A friend of the British. It is not fashionable, Flashman, greatly though I deplore it, and I need friends myself—strong friends, like Gul Shah."

Well, it didn't matter to me, but I was sorry to see Gul Shah advanced, and sorrier still to see him here, watching me the way a snake watches a mouse.

"But Gul is difficult to please, you know," Akbar went on. "He and many others would gladly see your army destroyed, and it is all I can do to hold them back. Oh, my father is not yet King again in Afghanistan; my power is limited. I can guarantee you safe-conduct from the country only on conditions, and I fear that my chiefs will make those conditions harsher the longer Elfistan Sahib resists them."

"As I understand it," says I, "your word is pledged already."

"My word? Will that heal a cut throat? I talk of what is; I expect Elfistan Sahib to do the same. I can see him safe to Jallalabad if he will deliver up six hostages to me here, and promises me that Sale will leave Jallalabad before your army reaches it."

"He can't promise that," I protested. "Sale isn't under his command now; he'll hold Jallalabad till he is given orders from India to leave."

Akbar shrugged. "These are the terms. Believe me, old friend, Elfistan Sahib must accept them—he must!" And he thumped his fist against my shoulder. "And for you, Flashman; if you are wise you will be one of the six hostages. You will be safer with me than down yonder." He grinned, and reined back his pony. "Now, go with God, and come again soon with a wise answer."

Well, I knew better than to expect any such thing from Elphy Bey, and sure enough, when I carried Akbar's message to him he croaked and dithered in his best style. He must consider, he said, and in the meantime the army was so exhausted and confused that we should march no farther that day. It was only two o'clock.

Shelton flew into a great passion at this, and stormed at Elphy that we must press on. One more good march would take us through Khoord-Kabul Pass and, what was more important, out of the snow, for beyond the pass the ground dropped away. If we spent another night in the freezing cold, said Shelton, the army must die.

So they argued and wrangled, and Elphy had his way.

We stayed where we were, thousands of shivering wretches on a snow-swept road, with nearly half our food already gone, no fuel left, and some of the troops even reduced to burning their muskets and equipment to try to keep a tiny flicker of warmth in their numb bodies. The niggers died in droves that night, for the mercury was far below freezing, and the troops kept alive only by huddling together in huge groups, burrowing in among each other like animals.

I had my blankets, and enough dried meat in my saddlebags not to go hungry. The lancers and I slept in a tight ring, as the Afghans do, with our cloaks above; Hudson had seen to it that each man carried a flask of rum, and so we kept out the cold tolerably well.

In the morning we were covered with snow, and when I clambered out and saw the army, thinks I, this is as far as we'll go. Most of them were too frozen to move at first, but when the Afghans were seen gathering on the slopes in the dawn light, the camp-followers flew into a panic and blundered off down the road in a great mob. Shelton managed to heave the main body of troops up in their wake, and so we stumbled on, like a great wounded animal with no brain and no heart, while the crackle of that hellish sniping started afresh, and the first casualties of the day began to totter from the ranks to die in the drifts on either side.

From other accounts of that frightful march that I have read—mostly Mackenzie's and Lawrence's and Lady Sale's[18]—I can fit a few of my recollections into their chronicle, but in the main it is just a terrible, bloody nightmare even now, more than sixty years after. Ice and blood and groans and death and despair, and the shrieks of dying men and women and the howling of the Ghazis and Gilzais. They rushed and struck, and rushed and struck again, mostly at the camp-followers, until it seemed there was a slashed brown body every yard of the way. The only place of safety was in the heart of Shelton's main body, where the sepoys still kept some sort of order; I suggested to Elphy when we set off that I and my lancers should ride guard on the womenfolk, and he agreed at once. It was a wise move on my part, for the attacks on the flanks were now so frequent that the work we had been doing yesterday was become fatally dangerous. Mackenzie's jezzailchis were cut to ribbons stemming the sorties.

As we neared Khoord-Kabul the hills rose up on either

side, and the mouth of that awful pass looked like a gateway into hell. Its walls were so stupendous that the rocky bottom was in perpetual twilight; the dragging tread of the army, the bellowing of the beasts, the shouts and groans and the boom of shots echoed and rang from its cliffs. The Afghans were on the ledges, and when Anquetil saw them he halted the vanguard, because it seemed certain death to go on.

There was more consulting and arguing around Elphy, until Akbar and his people were seen among the rocks near the pass mouth. Then I was sent off again, and it was to tell him that at last Elphy had seen reason: we would give up six hostages, on condition that Akbar called off his killers. He agreed, clapping me on the shoulders and swearing that all should now be well; I should come as one of the hostages, he said, and a merry time we would have of it. I was torn two ways about this; the farther away I could keep from Gul Shah, the better; on the other hand, how safe would it be to remain with the army?

It was settled for me, for Elphy himself called on Mackenzie, Lawrence, and Pottinger to give themselves over to Akbar. They were among the best we had, and I suppose he thought Akbar would be the more impressed by them. Anyway, if Akbar kept his word it did not matter much who remained with the army, since it would not have to fight its way to Jallalabad. Lawrence and Pottinger agreed at once; Mac took a little longer. He had been a trifle cool with me—I suppose because my lancers had not shared the fighting that day, and his folk had been so badly mauled. But he said nothing, and when Elphy put it to him he didn't answer, but stood staring out over the snow. He was in a sad pass, with his turban gone and his hair all awry, his poshteen spattered with blood and a drying wound on the back of his hand.

Presently he drew his sword, and dropped it point first into the ground, and walked over without a word to join Pottinger and Lawrence. Watching his tall figure moving away I felt a little chill touch me; being a ruffian, perhaps I know a good man when I see one better than most, and Mac was one of the mainstays of our force. A damned prig, mind you, and given to immense airs, but as good a soldier—for what that's worth—as I've met.

Akbar wanted Shelton as well, but Shelton wouldn't have it.

"I trust that black bastard as far as I'd trust a pi-dog," says he. "Anyway, who's to look after the army if I'm gone?"

"I shall be in command still," says Elphy, taken aback.

"Aye." says Shelton, "that's what I mean."

This started another bickering match, of course, which ended with Shelton turning on his heel and stumping off, and Elphy whining about discipline. And then the order to march sounded again, and we turned our faces towards Khoord-Kabul.

At first it was well enough, and we were unmolested. It looked as though Akbar had his folk under control, and then suddenly the jezzails began to crack from the ledges, and men began to fall, and the army staggered blindly in the snow. They were pouring fire into the pass at almost point-blank range, and the niggers began to scream and run, and the troops broke their ranks, with Shelton bawling, and then in a moment everyone was running or riding full tilt through that hellish defile. It was just a great wild rush, and the devil take the hindmost; I saw a camel with two white women and two children shot, and it staggered into the snow and threw them out. An officer ran to help, and went down with a ball in his belly, and then the crowd surged over them all. I saw a Gilzai mounted warrior seize on a little girl of about six and swing her up screaming to his saddlebow and make off; she kept shrieking "Mummy! Mummy!" as he bore her away. Sepoys were throwing down their muskets and running blindly forward, and I saw an officer of the Shah's Cavalry riding in among them, belabouring them with the flat of his sword and yelling his head off. Baggage was being flung recklessly away, the drivers were abandoning their animals, no one had any thought but to rush through the pass as fast as possible, away from that withering fire.

I can't say I wasted much time myself: I put my head down to my pony's neck, dug in my heels and went like billy-be-damned, threading through the pack and praying to God I wasn't hit by a stray ball. The Afghan ponies are as sure-footed as cats, and she never stumbled once. Where my lancers were I had no idea, not that I cared; it was every man (and woman) for himself, and I wasn't too particular who I rode over in my flight. It was nip and tuck like a steeplechase, with the shots crashing and echoing and thousands of voices yelling; only once did I check

for an instant, when I saw young Lieutenant Sturt shot out
of his saddle; he rolled into a drift and lay there screaming, but it would have done no good to stop. No good to
Flashy, anyway, and that was what mattered.

How long it took to make the passage I don't know, but
when the way began to widen and the mass of fugitives
ahead and around began to slow down I reined in to take
stock. The firing had slackened and Anquetil's vanguard
were forming up to cover the flight of those still coming
behind. Presently there was a great mob streaming out of
the defile, troops and people all mixed together, and when
they reached the light of day they just collapsed in the
snow, dead beat.

Three thousand people died in Khoord-Kabul, they say,
most of them niggers, and we lost all our remaining baggage. When we made camp beyond the eastern limit of the
pass we were in the middle of a snow-storm, all order was
completely lost; stragglers kept coming in until dark, and I
remember one woman who arrived having carried her
baby on foot the whole way. Lady Sale had been shot in
the arm, and I can see her now holding her hand out to
the surgeon and shutting her eyes tight while he cut the
ball out; she never flinched, the tough old bitch. There was
a major struggling with his hysterical wife, who wanted to
go back for her lost child; he was weeping and trying to
stop the blows she was aiming wildly at his chest. "No, no,
Jenny!" he kept saying. "She's gone! Pray to Jesus to look
after her!" Another officer, I forget who, had gone snow-
blind, and kept walking about in circles until someone led
him away. Then there was a British trooper, reeling
drunk on an Afghan pony and singing a barrack-room
song; where he had got the liquor, God knows, but there
was plenty of it, apparently, for presently he fell into the
snow and lay there snoring. He was still there next morning, frozen dead.

Night was hell again, with the darkness full of crying
and groaning. There were only a handful of tents left, and
the English women and children all crowded into one of
them. I wandered about all night, for it was freezing too
bitterly to sleep, and anyway I was in a fearful funk. I
could see now that the whole army was going to be destroyed, and myself with it; being a hostage with Akbar
would be no better, for I had convinced myself by this
that when he had finished butchering the army he would
kill his prisoners too. There was only one hope that I

could see, and that was to wait with the army until we were clear of the snow, and then strike out by night on my own. If the Afghans spotted me I would ride for it.

Next day we hardly advanced at all, partly because the whole force was so frozen and starved as to be incapable of going far, but also because Akbar sent a messenger into camp saying that we should halt so that he could have provisions brought up. Elphy believed him, in spite of Shelton's protests; Shelton almost went on his knees to Elphy, urging that if we could only keep going till we were out of the snow, we might come through yet. But Elphy doubted if we could get even that far.

"Our only hope is that the Sirdar, taking pity on our plight, will succour us at this late hour," says he. "You know, Shelton, he is a gentleman; he will keep his word."

Shelton just walked away in disgust and rage. The supplies never came, of course, but the following day comes another messenger from Akbar, suggesting that since we were determined to march on, the wives and families of the British officers should be left in his care. It was just this suggestion, made back in Kabul, that had provoked such indignation, but now every married man leaped at it. Whatever anyone might say openly, however much Elphy might talk as though he still expected to march to Jallalabad, everyone knew that the force as it stood was doomed. Frost-bitten, starving, cluttered still with camp-followers like brown skeletons who refused to die, with its women and children slowing it down, with the Ghazis and Gilzais sniping and harrying, death stared the army in the face. With Akbar, at least, the women and children would stand a chance.

So Elphy agreed, and we watched the little convoy, on the last of the camels, set off into the snow, the married men going along with their wives. I remember Betty riding bareheaded, looking very pretty with the morning sun shining on her hair, and Lady Sale, her wounded arm in a sling, poking her head out of a camel howdah to rebuke the nigger who was trotting alongside carrying the last of her belongings in a bundle. But I didn't share the general satisfaction that they were leaving us; I was keeping as well out of harm's way as I could by staying next to Elphy, but even that was not going to be safe for long.

I still had dried mutton enough left in my saddle-bags, and Sergeant Hudson seemed to have a secret store of fodder for his horse and those of the lancers who survived—

there were about half a dozen left of my original party, I think, but I didn't count. But even clinging to Elphy's palankeen, on the pretext of riding bodyguard, I was in no doubt of what must happen eventually. In the next two days the column was under constant attack; in about ten miles we lost the last of the camp-followers, and in one terrible affray which I heard behind us but took good care not to see, the last of the sepoy units were fairly wiped out. To tell the truth, my memories of that period are hazy; I was too exhausted and afraid to pay much heed. Some things, though, are clear in my mind; images like coloured pictures in a magic lantern that I shall never forget.

Once, for example, Elphy had all the officers of the force line up at the rearguard, to show a "united front," [19] as he called it, to our pursuers. We stood there for a full half hour, like so many scarecrows, while they jeered at us from a distance, and one or two of us were shot down. I remember Grant, the Adjutant-General, clapping his hands over his face and shouting, "I'm hit! I'm hit!" and falling down in the snow, and the young officer next to me —a boy with yellow side-whiskers covered with frost— saying, "Oh, poor old fellow!"

I saw an Afghan boy, once, chuckling to himself as he stabbed and stabbed again at a wounded sepoy; the boy was not over ten years old. And I remember the glazed look in the eyes of dying horses, and a pair of brown feet marching in front of me that left bloody footprints on the ice. I remember Elphy's grey face, with his jowls wobbling, and the rasping sound of Shelton's voice, and the staring eyes in the dark faces of the few Indians that were left, soldiers and camp-followers—but mostly I remember the fear that cramped my stomach and seemed to turn my legs to jelly as I listened to the crackle of firing before and behind, the screams of stricken men, and the triumphant screeching of the Afghans.

I know now that when we were five days out from Kabul, and had reached Jugdulluk, the army that had been fourteen thousand strong was just over three thousand, of whom a bare five hundred were fighting troops. The rest, apart from a few hostages in the hands of the enemy, were dead. And it was here that I came to my senses, in a barn at Jugdulluk where Elphy had made his quarters.

It was as though I came out of a dream to hear him

arguing with Shelton and some of the staff over a proposal that had come from Akbar that Elphy and Shelton should go to see him under a flag of truce, to negotiate. What they were to negotiate, God knows, but Shelton was dead against it; he stood there, his red cheeks fallen in, but his moustache still bristling, swearing that he would go on for Jallalabad if he had to do it alone. But Elphy was for negotiating; he would go and see Akbar, and Shelton must come, too; he would leave Anquetil to command the army.

Aye, thought I, and somehow my brain was as clear as ice again, this is where Flashman takes independent action. They would never come back from Akbar, of course; he would never let such valuable hostages go. If I, too, let myself fall into Akbar's hands, I would be in imminent danger from his henchman, Gul Shah. If I stayed with the army, on the other hand, I would certainly die with it. One obvious course suggested itself. I left them wrangling, and slipped out in search of Sergeant Hudson.

I found him dressing his horse, which was so thin and jaded now it looked like a run-down London hack.

"Hudson," says I, "you and I are riding out."

He never blinked. "Yes, sir," says he. "Where to, sir?"

"India," says I. "Not a word to anyone; these are special orders from General Elphinstone."

"Very good, sir," says he, and I left him knowing that when I came back he would have our beasts ready, saddle-bags as full as he could manage, and everything prepared. I went back to Elphy's barn, and there he was, preparing to leave to see Akbar. He was fussing as hard as ever, over such important matters as the whereabouts of his fine silver flask, which he intended to take as a gift to the Sirdar—this while the remnants of his army were dying in the snow round Jugdulluk.

"Flashman," says he, gathering his cloak round him and pulling his woollen cap over his head, "I am leaving you for only a little time, but in these desperate days it is not wise to count too far ahead. I trust I find you well enough in a day or two, my boy. God bless you."

And God rot you, you old fool, I thought; you won't find me in a day or two, not unless you ride a damned sight faster than I think you can. He sniffed some more about his flask, and shuffled out, helped by his valet. Shelton wasn't yet ready, apparently, and the last words I heard Elphy say were: "It is really too bad." They should be his epitaph; I raged inwardly at the time when I thought of how he had brought me to this; now, in my maturer years, I have modified my view. Whereas I would have cheerfully shot him then, now I would hang. draw and quarter him for a bungling, useless, selfish old swine. No fate could be bad enough for him.

Hudson and I waited for night, and then we simply saddled up and slipped off into the dark, striking due east. It was so easy I could have laughed; no one challenged us, and when about ten minutes out we met a party of Gilzais in the dark I gave them good night in Pushtu and they left us alone. There was no moon, but light enough for us to pick our way easily enough through the snowy rocks, and after we had ridden a couple of hours I gave the order to halt, and we bedded down for the night in the lee of a little cliff. We had our blankets, and with no one to groan around us I slept the best sleep I had had in a week.

When I woke it was broad day, and Sergeant Hudson had a little fire going and was brewing coffee. It was the first hot drink I had tasted in days; he even had a little sugar for it.

"Where the devil did you come by this, Hudson?" says I, for there had been nothing but dried mutton and a few scraps of biscuit on the last few days of the march.

"Foraged, sir," says he, cool as you please, so I asked no more questions, but sipped contentedly as I lay in my blankets.

"Hold on, though," I said, as he dropped more sticks on his fire. "Suppose some damned Ghazi sees your smoke; we'll have the whole pack of 'em down on us."

"Beg pardon, sir," says he, "but this hardwood don't make no smoke worth mentioning." And neither it did, when I came to look at it.

A moment later he was begging my pardon again, and asking if I intended we should ride on shortly, or perhaps rest for that day where we were. He pointed out that the ponies were used up, what with lack of fodder, but that if they were rested and given a good feed next morning, we should be out of the snow soon and into country where we might expect to come by grazing.

I was in two minds about this, for the more distance we put between ourselves and Akbar's ruffians—and Gul Shah especially—the better I would like it. On the other hand, both the beasts and ourselves would be the better of rest and in this broken country it didn't seem likely that we would be spotted, except by sheer chance. So I agreed, and found myself considering this Sergeant Hudson for the first time, for beyond noting that he was a steady man I had given him not much notice before. After all, why should one notice one's men very much?

He was about thirty, I suppose, powerfully built, with fair hair that had a habit of falling over one eye, when he would brush it away. He had one of those square tough faces that you see on working men, with grey eyes and a cleft in his chin, and he did everything very deft and smartly. By his accent I would have said he was from somewhere in the west, but he was well spoken enough, and, although he knew his place, was not at all your ordinary trooper, half-yokel, half-guttersnipe. It seemed to me as I watched him tending the fire, and presently rubbing down the ponies, that I had made a lucky choice in him.

Next morning we were up and off before dawn, Hudson having given the beasts the last of the fodder which he confessed he had been hoarding in his bags—"just in case we was going to need one last good day's gallop." Using the sun, I set off south-east, which meant we had the main road from Kabul to India somewhere away to our right; it was my intention to follow this line until we came to the River Soorkab, which we would ford and follow along its southern bank to Jallalabad, about sixty miles away. That should keep us well clear of the road, and of any wandering bands of Afghans.

I was not greatly concerned about what tale we would tell when we got there; God knew how many folk had become separated from the main army, like Hudson and myself, or how many would eventually turn up at Jallalabad. I doubted if the main force would ever get there, and that would give everyone too much to think about to worry about a few strays like us. At need I could say we had become separated in the confusion; Hudson wasn't likely to blab my remark about being despatched on orders from Elphy—and God knew when Elphy would return to India, if he ever did.

So I was in excellent fettle as we threaded our way

through the little snowy passes, and well before noon we crossed the Soorkab and made capital speed along its southern shore. It was rocky enough, to be sure, but there were occasional places where we could raise a gallop, and it seemed to me that at this rate we should soon be out of the snows and on to easier, drier going. I pressed on hard, for this was Gilzai country, and Mogala, where Gul Shah lorded it when he was at home, was not far away. The thought of that grim stronghold, with the crucifixes at the gates, cast a shadow over my mind, and at that moment Sergeant Hudson edged his pony up beside mine.

"Sir," says he. "I think we're being followed."

"What d'ye mean?" says I, nastily startled. "Who is it?"

"Dunno," says he, "but I can feel it, if you know what I mean, sir." He looked round us; we were on a fairly clear stretch, with the river rumbling away to our left, and broken hills to our right. "Mebbe this way isn't as lonely as we thought."

I'd been long enough in the hills to know that when a seasoned soldier has that instinct, he is generally right; a less experienced and less nervous officer might have pooh-poohed his fears, but I knew better. At once we turned away from the river and up a narrow gully into the hill country; if there were Afghans behind us we would let them pass on while we took a long loop into the hills. We could still hold our course for Jallalabad, but midway between the Soorkab and the main road.

It was slower going, of course, but after an hour or so Hudson said he felt we were clear of whoever had been behind us. Still I kept well away from the river, and then another interruption came: from far away to our right, very faint on the afternoon air, came the sound of firing. It was ragged, but there was enough of it to suggest that a fair-sized force was involved.

"By God!" says Hudson. "It's the army, sir!"

The same thought struck me; it might be that the army, or what was left of it, would have got this far on the road. I guessed that Gandamack would be somewhere up ahead of us, and as I knew that the Soorkab swings south in that area, we had no choice but to ride towards the firing if we were not to risk running into our mysterious pursuers on the river.

So we pushed on, and always that damned firing came closer. I guessed it couldn't be more than a mile off now, and was just about to call to Sergeant Hudson, who had forged ahead, when he turned in his saddle and waved to me in great excitement. He had come to a place where two great rocks reared up at the mouth of a gully that ran down steeply in the direction of the Kabul road; between them we had a clear view down from the heights, and as I reined in and looked I saw a sight I shall never forget.

Beneath us, and about a mile away, lay a little cluster of huts, with smoke rising from them, that I guessed must be Gandamack village. Close by, where the road swung north again, was a gentle slope, strewn with boulders, rising to a flat summit about a hundred yards across. That whole slope was crawling with Afghans; their yells came clearly up the gully to us. On the summit of the slope was a group of men, maybe a company strong; at first, seeing their blue poshteens, I took them for Afghans, but then I noticed the shakos, and Sergeant Hudson's voice, shaking with excitement, confirmed me:

"That's the 44th! Look at 'em, sir! It's the 44th, poor devils!"

They were in a ragged square, back to back on the hill-top, and even as we watched I saw the glitter of bayonets as they levelled their pieces, and a thin volley crashed out across the valley. The Afghans yelled louder than ever, and gave back, but then they surged in again, the Khyber knives rising and falling as they tried to hack their way into the square. Another volley, and they gave back yet again, and I saw one of the figures on the summit flourishing a sword as though in defiance. He looked for all the world like a toy soldier, and then I noticed a strange thing; he seemed to be wearing a long red, white and blue weskit beneath his poshteen.

I must have said something of this to Hudson, for he shouted out:

"By God, it's the colours! Damn the black bastards, give it to 'em, 44th! Give 'em hot hell!"

"Shut up, you fool!" says I, although I needn't have worried, for we were too far away to be heard. But Hudson stopped shouting, and contented himself with swearing and whispering encouragement to the doomed men on the hilltop.

For they were doomed. Even as we watched the grey and black robed figures came charging up the slope again, from all sides, another volley cracked out, and then the wave had broken over them. It boiled and eddied on the hilltop, the knives and bayonets flashing, and then it rolled slowly back with one great, wailing yell of triumph, and on the hilltop there were no figures standing up. Of the man with the colours round his waist there was no sign; all that remained was a confusion of vague shapes scattered among the rocks, and a haze of powder smoke that presently drifted off into nothing on the frosty air.

Somehow I knew that I had just seen the end of the army of Afghanistan. Of course one would have expected the 44th to be the last remnant, as the only British regiment in the force, but even without that I would have known. This was what Elphy Bey's fine army of more than fourteen thousand had come to, in just a week. There might be a few prisoners; there would be no other survivors. I was wrong, as it turned out; one man, Dr Brydon, cut his way out and brought the news to Jallalabad, but there was no way of knowing this at the time.

There is a painting of the scene at Gandamack,[20] which I saw a few years ago, and it is like enough the real thing as I remember it. No doubt it is very fine and stirs martial thoughts in the glory-blown asses who look at it; my only thought when I saw it was, "You poor bloody fools!" and I said so, to the disgust of other viewers. But I was there, you see, shivering with horror as I watched, unlike the good Londoners, who let the roughnecks and jailbirds keep their empire for them; they are good enough for getting cut up at the Gandamacks which fools like Elphy and McNaghten bring 'em to, and no great loss to anybody.

Sergeant Hudson was staring down, with tears running over his cheeks. I believe, given a chance, he would have gone charging down to join them. All he would say was, "Bastards! Black bastards!" until I gave him the right about, pretty sharp, and we hurried away on our path, letting the rocks shut off the hellish sight behind us.

I was shaken by what we had seen, and to get as far away from Gandamack as we could was the thought that drove me on that day at a dangerous pace. We clattered along the rocky paths, and our ponies scrambled down the screes in such breakneck style that I go cold to look back on it. Only darkness stopped us, and we were well on our way next morning before I would rein in. By this time we had left the snow-line far behind us, and feeling the sun again raised my spirits once more.

It was as certain as anything could be that we were the only survivors of the army of Afghanistan still moving eastward in good order. This was a satisfactory thought. Why shouldn't I be frank about it? Now that the army was finished, there was little chance of meeting hostile tribesmen farther east than the point where it had died. So we were safe, and to come safe out of a disaster is more gratifying than to come safe out of none at all. Of course, it was a pity about the others, but wouldn't they have felt the same gratification in my place? There is great pleasure in catastrophe that doesn't touch you, and anyone who says there isn't is a liar. Haven't you seen it in the face of a bearer of bad news, and heard it in the unctuous phrases at the church gate after a funeral?

So I reflected, and felt mighty cheery, and perhaps this made me careless. At any rate, moralists will say I was well served for my thoughts, as our ponies trotted onwards, for what interrupted them was the sudden discovery that I was looking along the barrel of a jezzail into the face of one of the biggest, ugliest Afridi badmashes I have ever seen. He seemed to grow out of the rocks like a genie, and a dozen other ruffians with him, springing out to seize our bridles and sword-arms before we could say galloping Jesus.

"Khabadar, sahib!" says the big jezzailchi, grinning all over his villainous face, as though I needed telling to be careful. "Get down," he added, and his mates hauled me from the saddle and held me fast.

"What's this?" says I, trying to brave it out. "We are friends, on our way to Jallalabad. What do you want with us?"

"The British are everyone's friends," grins he, "and they are all going to Jallalabad—or were." And his crew cackled with laughter. "You will come with us," and he nodded to my captors, who had a thong round my wrists and tied to my own stirrup in a trice.

There was no chance of putting up a fight, even if all the heart had not gone out of me. For a moment I had hoped they were just broken men of the hills, who might have robbed us and let us go, but they were intent on holding us prisoner. For ransom? That was the best I could hope for. I played a desperate card.

"I am Flashman huzoor," cries I, "the friend of Akbar

Khan Sirdar. He'll have the heart and guts of anyone who harms Bloody Lance!"

"Allah protect us!" says the jezzailchi, who was a humorist in his way, like all his lousy kind. "Guard him close, Raisul, or he'll stick you on his little spear, as he did to the Gilzais at Mogala." He hopped into my saddle and grinned down at me. "You can fight, Bloody Lance. Can you walk also?" And he set the pony off at a brisk trot, making me run alongside, and shouting obscene encouragement. They had served Hudson the same way, and we had no choice but to stumble along, jeered at by our ragged conquerors.

It was too much; to have come so far, to have endured so much, to have escaped so often, to be so close to safety —and now this. I wept and swore, called my captor every filthy name I could lay tongue to, in Pushtu, Urdu, English, and Persian, pleaded with him to let us go in return for a promise of great payment, threatened him with the vengeance of Akbar Khan, beseeched him to take us to the Sirdar, struggled like a furious child to break my bonds—and he only roared so hard with laughter that he almost fell from the saddle.

"Say it again!" he cried. "How many lakhs of rupees? Ya'llah, I shall be made for life. What was that? Noseless bastard offspring of a leprous ape and a gutter-descended sow? What a description! Note it, Raisul, my brother, for I have no head for education, and I wish to remember. Continue, Flashman huzoor; share the riches of your spirit with me!"

So he mocked me, but he hardly slackened pace, and soon I could neither swear nor plead or do anything but stumble blindly on. My wrists were burning with pain, and there was a leaden fear in my stomach; I had no idea where we were going, and even after darkness fell the brutes still kept going, until Hudson and I dropped from sheer fatigue. Then we rested a few hours, but at dawn they had us up again, and we staggered on through the hot, hellish day, resting only when we were too exhausted to continue, and then being forced up and dragged onwards at the stirrups.

It was just before dusk when we halted for the last time, at one of those rock forts that are dotted on half the hillsides of Afghanistan. I had a vision of a gateway, with a rickety old gate swung back on rusty hinges, and beyond it an earth courtyard. They did not take us so far, but cut the thongs that held us and shoved us through a narrow door in the gatehouse wall. There were steps leading down, and a most fearsome stink coming up, but they pushed us headlong down and we stumbled on to a floor of mixed straw and filth and God knows what other debris. The door slammed shut, and there we were, too worn out to move.

I suppose we lay there for hours, groaning with pain and exhaustion, before they came back, bringing us a bowl of food and a chatti of water. We were famished, and fell on it like pigs, while the big jezzailchi watched us and made funny remarks. I ignored him, and presently he left us. There was just light enough from a high grating in one wall for us to make out our surroundings, so we took stock of the cellar, or dungeon, whichever it was.

I have been in a great variety of jails in my life, from Mexico (where they are truly abominable) to Australia, America, Russia, and dear old England, and I never saw a good one yet. That little Afghan hole was not too bad, all round, but it seemed dreadful at the time. There were bare walls, pretty high, and a roof lost in shadow, and in the middle of the filthy floor two very broad flat stones, like a platform, that I didn't half like the look of. For above them, swinging down from the ceiling, was a tangle of rusty chains, and at the sight of them a chill stabbed through me, and I thought of hooded black figures, and the Inquisition, and torture chambers that I had gloated over in forbidden books at school. It's very different when you are actually in one.

I told Hudson what I thought of them, and he just grunted and spat and then begged my pardon. I told him not to be such a damned fool, that we were in a frightful fix, and he could stop behaving as though we were on Horse Guards. I've never been one to stand on ceremony anywhere, and here it was just ridiculous. But it took Hudson time to get used to talking to an officer, and at first he just listened to me, nodding and saying, "Yes, sir," and "Very good, sir," until I swore with exasperation.

For I was in a funk, of course, and poured out my fears to him. I didn't know why they were holding us, although ransom seemed most likely. There was a chance Akbar might get to hear of our plight, which was what I hoped —but at the back of my mind was the awful thought that

Gul Shah might hear of us just as easily. Hudson, of course, didn't understand why I should be so horrified at this, until I told him the whole story—about Narreeman, and how Akbar had rescued me from Gul's snakes in Kabul. Heavens, how I must have talked, but when I tell you that we were in the cellar a week together, without ever so much as seeing beyond the door, and myself in a sweat of anxiety about what our fate might be, you will understand that I needed an audience. Your real coward always does, and the worse his fear the more he blabs. I babbled something sickening in that dungeon to Hudson. Of course, I didn't tell him the story as I've told it here —the Bloody Lance incident, for example, I related in a creditable light. But I convinced him at least that we had every reason to fear if Gul Shah got wind that we were in Afghan hands.

It was difficult to tell how he took it. Mostly he just listened, staring at the wall, but from time to time he would look at me very steady, as though he was weighing me up. At first I hardly noticed this, any more than one does notice a common trooper looking at one, but after a while it made me feel uncomfortable, and I told him pretty sharp to leave off. If he was scared at the fix we were in, he didn't show it, and I admit there were one or two occasions when I felt a sneaking regard for him; he didn't complain, and he was very civil in his speech, and would ask me very respectfully to translate what the Afridi guards said when they brought us our food—for he had no Pushtu or Hindustani.

This was little enough, and we had no way of telling how true it was. The big jezzailchi was the most talkative, but mostly he would only recall how badly the British had been cut up on the march from Kabul, so that not a single man had been left alive, and how there would soon be no feringhees left in Afghanistan at all. Akbar Khan was advancing on Jallalabad, he said, and would put the whole garrison to the sword, and then they would sweep down through the Khyber and drive us out of India in a great jehad that would establish the True Faith from Peshawar to the sea. And so on, all bloody wind and water, as I told Hudson, but he considered it very thoughtfully and said he didn't know how long Sale could hold out in Jallalabad if they laid proper siege to it.

I stared at this, an ordinary trooper passing opinion on a general's business.

"What do you know about it?" says I.

"Not much, sir," says he. "But with respect to General Elphinstone, I'm powerful glad it's General Sale that's laying in Jallalabad and not him."

"Is that so, and be damned to you," says I. "And what's your opinion of General Elphinstone, if you please?"

"I'd rather not say, sir," says he. And then he looked at me with those grey eyes. "He wasn't with the 44th at Gandamack, was he, sir? Nor a lot of the officers wasn't. Where were they, sir?"

"How should I know? And what concern is that of yours?"

He sat looking down for a moment. "None at all, sir," says he at last. "Beg pardon for asking."

"I should damned well think so," says I. "Anyway, whatever you think of Elphy Bey, you can rely on General Sale to give Akbar the right about turn if he shows his nose at Jallalabad. And I wish to God we were there, too, and away from this hellish hole, and these stinking Afridis. Whether it's ransom or not, they don't mean us any good, I can tell you." I didn't think much of Hudson's questions about Bandamack and Elphy at the time; if I had done I would have been as much amused as angry, for it was like a foreign language to me then. But I understand it now, although half our modern generals don't. They think their men are a different species still—fortunately a lot of 'em are, but not in the way the generals think.

Well, another week went by in that infernal cell, and both Hudson and I were pretty foul by now and well bearded, for they gave us nothing to wash or shave with. My anxieties diminished a little, as they will when nothing happens, but it was damned boring with nothing to do but talk to Hudson, for we had little in common except horses. He didn't even seem interested in women. We talked occasionally of escape, but there was little chance of that, for there was no way out except through the door, which stood at the top of a narrow flight of steps, and when the Afridis brought our food one of them always stood at the head of them covering us with a huge blunderbuss. I wasn't in any great hurry to risk a peppering from it, and when Hudson talked of trying a rush I ordered him to drop it. Where would we have got to after-wards, anyway? We didn't even know where we were, ex-cept that it couldn't be far to the Kabul road. But it wasn't worth the risk, I said—if I had known what was in store for us I'd have chanced that blunderbuss and a hundred like it, but I didn't. God, I'll never forget it. Never.

It was late one afternoon, and we were lying on the straw dozing, when we heard the clatter of hooves at the gate outside, and a jumble of voices approaching the door of the cell. Hudson jumped up, and I came up on my elbow, my heart in my mouth, wondering who it might be. It might be a messenger bringing news of ransom—for I believed the Afridis must be trying that game—and then the bolts scraped back and the door burst open, and a tall man strode in to the head of the steps. I couldn't see his face at first, but then an Afridi bustled past him with a flaring torch which he stuck in a crevice in the wall, and its light fell on the newcomer's face. If it had been the Devil in person I'd have been better pleased, for it was a face I had seen in nightmares, and I couldn't believe it was true, the face of Gul Shah.

His eye lit on me, and he shouted with joy and clapped his hands. I believe I cried out in horror, and scrambled back against the wall.

"Flashman!" he cried, and came half down the steps like a big cat, glaring at me with a hellish grin. "Now, God is very good. When I heard the news I could not be-lieve it, but it is true. And it was just by chance—aye, by the merest chance, that word reached me you were taken." He sucked in his breath, never taking his glittering eyes from me.

I couldn't speak; the man struck me dumb with cold terror. Then he laughed again, and the hairs rose on my neck at the sound of it.

"And here there is no Akbar Khan to be importunate," says he. He signed to the Afridis and pointed at Hudson. "Take that one away above and watch him." And as two of them rushed down on Hudson and dragged him strug-gling up the steps, Gul Shah came down into the room and with his whip struck the hanging shackles a blow that set them rattling. "Set him"—and he points at me—"here. We have much to talk about."

I cried out as they flung themselves on me, and strug-gled helplessly, but they got my arms over my head and set a shackle on each wrist, so that I was strung up like a rabbit on a poulterer's stall. Then Gul dismissed them and came to stand in front of me, tapping his boot with his whip and gloating over me.

"The wolf comes once to the trap," says he at last. "But you have come twice. I swear by God you will not wriggle out of it this time. You cheated me once in Kabul, by a miracle, and killed my dwarf by foul play. Not again, Flashman. And I am glad—aye, glad it fell out so, for here I have time to deal with you at my leisure, you filthy dog!" And with a snarl he struck me backhanded across the face.

The blow loosened my tongue, for I cried out:

"Don't, for God's sake! What have I done? Didn't I pay for it with your bloody snakes?"

"Pay?" sneers he. "You haven't begun to pay. Do you want to know how you will pay, Flashman?"

I didn't, so I didn't answer, and he turned and shouted something towards the door. It opened, and someone came in, standing in the shadows.

"It was my great regret, last time, that I must be so hurried in disposing of you," says Gul Shah. "I think I told you then, did I not, that I would have wished the woman you defiled to share in your departure? By great good fortune I was at Mogala when the word of your capture came, so I have been able to repair the omission. Come," says he to the figure at the top of the steps, and the woman Narreeman advanced slowly into the light.

I knew it was she, although she was cloaked from head to foot and had the lower half of her face shrouded in a flimsy veil: I remembered the eyes, like a snake's, that had glared up at me the night I took her in Mogala. They were staring at me again, and I found them more terrifying than all Gul's threats. She didn't make a sound, but glided down the steps to his side.

"You do not greet the lady?" says Gul. "You will, you will. But of course, she is a mere slut of a dancing girl, although she is the wife of a prince of the Gilzai!" He spat the words into my face.

"Wife?" I croaked. "I never knew . . . believe me, sir, I never knew. If I. . . ."

"It was not so then," says Gul. "It is so now—aye, though she has been fouled by a beast like you. She is my wife and my woman none the less. It only remains to wipe out the dishonour."

"Oh, Christ, please listen to me," says I. "I swear I meant no harm . . . how was I to know she was precious to you? I didn't mean to harm her, I swear I didn't! I'll do anything, anything you wish, pay anything you like. . . ."

Gul leered at me, nodding, while the woman's basilisk eyes stared at me. "You will pay indeed. No doubt you have heard that our Afghan women are delicately skilled in collecting payment? I see from your face that you have. Narreeman is very eager to test that skill. She has vivid recollections of a night at Mogala; vivid recollections of your pride. . . ." He leaned forward till his face was almost touching mine. "Lest she forget it, she wishes to take certain things from you, very slowly and cunningly, for a remembrance. Is it not just? You had your pleasure from her pain; she will have hers from yours. It will take much longer, and be infinitely more artistic . . . a woman's touch." He laughed. "That will be for a beginning."

I didn't believe it; it was impossible, outrageous, horrible; it was enough to strike me mad just listening to it.

"You can't!" I shrieked. "No, no, no, you can't! Please, please, don't let her touch me! It was a mistake! I didn't know, I didn't mean to hurt her!" I yelled and pleaded with him, and he crowed with delight and mocked me, while she never moved a muscle, but still stared into my face.

"This will be better than I had hoped," says he. "Afterwards, we may have you flayed, or perhaps roasted over hot embers. Or we may take out your eyes and remove your fingers and toes, and set you to some slave-work in Mogala. Yes, that will be best, for you can pray daily for death and never find it. Is the price too high for your night's pleasure, Flashman?"

I was trying to close my ears to this horror, trying not to believe it, and babbling to him to spare me. He listened, grinning, and then turned to the woman and said:

"But business before pleasure. My dove, we will let him think of the joyous reunion that you two will have—let him wait for—how long? He must wonder about that, I think. In the meantime, there is a more urgent matter." He turned back to me. "It will not abate your suffering in the slightest if you tell me what I wish to know; but I think you will tell me, anyway. Since your pathetic and cowardly army was slaughtered in the passes, the Sirdar's army has advanced towards Jallalabad. But we have no word of Nott and his troops at Kandahar. It is suggested that they have orders—to march on Kabul? On Jallalabad? We require to know. Well?"

It took a moment for me to clear my mind of the hellish pictures he had put there, and understand his question. "I don't know," I said. "I swear to God I don't know."

"Liar," said Gul Shah. "You were an aide to Elfistan; you must know."

"I don't! I swear I don't!" I shouted. "I can't tell you what I don't know, can I?"

"I am sure you can," says he, and motioning Narreeman aside he flung off his poshteen and stood in his shirt and pyjamy trousers, skull-cap on head and whip in hand. He reached out and wrenched my shirt from my back.

I screamed as he swung the whip, and leaped as it struck me. God, I never knew such pain; it was like a fiery razor. He laughed and swung again and again. It was unbearable, searing bars of burning agony across my shoulders; my head swam and I shrieked and tried to hurl myself away, but the chains held me and the whip seemed to be striking into my very vitals.

"Stop!" I remember shrieking, and over and over again. "Stop!"

He stepped back, grinning, but all I could do was mouth and mumble at him that I knew nothing. He lifted the whip again; I couldn't face it.

"No!" I screamed. "Not me! Hudson knows! The sergeant who was with me—I'm sure he knows! He told me he knew!" It was all I could think of to stop that hellish lashing.

"The havildar knows, but not the officer?" says Gul. "No, Flashman, not even in the British army. I think you are lying." And the fiend set about me again, until I must have fainted from the pain, for when I came to my senses, with my back raging like a furnace, he was picking his robe from the floor.

"You have convinced me," says he, sneering. "Such a coward as I know you to be would have told me all he knew at the first stroke. You are not brave, Flashman. But you will be even less brave soon."

He signed to Narreeman, and she followed him up the steps. At the door he paused to mock me again.

"Think on what I have promised you," says he. "I hope you will not go mad too soon after we begin."

The door slammed shut, and I was left sagging in my

chains, sobbing and retching. But the pain on my back was as nothing to the terror in my mind. It wasn't possible, I kept saying, they can't do it . . . but I knew they would. For some awful reason, which I cannot define even now, a recollection came to me of how I had tortured others—oh, puny, feeble little tortures like roasting fags at school; I babbled aloud how sorry I was for tormenting them, and prayed that I might be spared, and remembered how old Arnold had once said in a sermon: "Call on the Lord Jesus Christ, and thou shalt be saved."

God, how I called; I roared like a bull calf, and got nothing back, not even echoes. I would do it again, too, in the same position, for all that I don't believe in God and never have. But I blubbered like an infant, calling on Christ to save me, swearing to reform and crying gentle Jesus meek and mild over and over again. It's a great thing, prayer. Nobody answers, but at least it stops you from thinking.

Suddenly I was aware of people moving into the cell, and shrieked in fear, closing my eyes, but no one touched me, and when I opened them there was Hudson again, chained up beside me with his arms in the air, staring at me in horror.

"My God, sir," says he, "what have the devils done to you?"

"They're torturing me to death!" I roared. "Oh, dear saviour!" And I must have babbled on, for when I stopped he was praying, too, the Lord's Prayer, I think, very quietly to himself. We were the holiest jail in Afghanistan that night.

There was no question of sleep; even if my mind had not been full of the horrors ahead, I could not have rested with my arms fettered wide above my head. Every time I sagged the rusty manacles tore cruelly at my wrists, and I would have to right myself with my legs aching from standing. My back was smarting, and I moaned a good deal; Hudson did his best to cheer me up with the kind of drivel about not being done yet and keeping one's head up which is supposed to raise the spirits in time of trouble—it has never done a damned thing for mine. All I could think of was that woman's hating eyes coming closer, and Gul smiling savagely behind her, and the knife pricking my skin and then slicing—oh, Jesus, I couldn't bear it, I would go raving mad. I said so, at the top of my voice, and Hudson says:

"Come on, sir, we ain't dead yet."

"You bloody idiot!" I yelled at him. "What do you know, you clod? They aren't going to cut your bloody pecker off! I tell you I'll have to die first! I must!"

"They haven't done it yet, sir," says he. "Nor they won't. While I was up yonder I see that half them Afridis have gone off—to join up wi' the others at Jallalabad, I reckon—an' there ain't above half a dozen left, besides your friend and the woman. If I can just. . . ."

I didn't heed him; I was too done up to think of anything except what they would do to me—when? The night wore away, and except for one visit at noon next day, when the jezzailchi came to give us some water and food, no one came near us before evening. They left us in our chains, hanging like stuck pigs, and my legs seemed to be on fire one minute and numb the next. I heard Hudson muttering to himself from time to time, as though he was working at something, but I never minded; then, just when the light was beginning to fade, I heard him gasp with pain, and exclaim: "Done it, by God!"

I turned to look, and my heart bounded like a stag. He was standing with only his left arm still up in the shackle; the right one, bloody to the elbow, was hanging at his side.

He shook his head, fiercely, and I was silent. He worked his right hand and arm for a moment, and then reached up to the other shackle; the wrist-pieces were kept apart by a bar, but the fastening of the manacles was just a simple bolt. He worked at it for a moment, and it fell open. He was free.

He came over to me, an ear cocked towards the door.

"If I let you loose, sir, can you stand?"

I didn't know if I could, but I nodded, and two minutes later I was crouched on the floor, groaning with the pain in my shoulders and legs that had been cramped in one position so long. He massaged my joints, and swore softly over the weals that Gul Shah's whip had left.

"Filthy nigger bastard," says he. "Look'ee, sir, we've got to look sharp they don't take us unawares. When they come in we've got to be standing up, with the chains on our wrists, pretendin' we're still trussed up, like."

"What then?" says I.

"Why, sir, they'll think we're helpless, won't they? We can take 'em by surprise."

"Much good that'll do," says I. "You say there's half a dozen apart from Gul Shah."

"They won't all come," says he. "For God's sake, sir, it's our only hope."

I didn't think it was much of one, and said so. Hudson said, well, it was better than being sliced up by that Afghan tart, wasn't it, begging my pardon, sir, and I couldn't disagree. But I guessed we would only get slaughtered for our pains, at best.

"Well," says he, "we can make a bloody good fight of it. We can die like Englishmen, 'stead of like dogs."

"What difference does it make whether you die like an Englishman or like a bloody Eskimo?" says I, and he just stared at me and then went on chafing my arms. Pretty soon I could stand and move as well as ever, but we took care to stay close by the chains, and it was as well we did. Suddenly there was a shuffling at the door, and we barely had time to take our positions, hands up on the shackles, when it was thrown back.

"Leave it to me, sir," whispered Hudson, and then drooped in his fetters. I did the same, letting my head hang but watching the door out of the corner of my eye.

There were three of them, and my heart sank. First came Gul Shah, with the big jezzailchi carrying a torch, and behind was the smaller figure of Narreeman. All my terrors came rushing back as they descended the steps.

"It is time, Flashman," says Gul Shah, sticking his sneering face up to mine. "Wake up, you dog, and prepare for your last love play." And he laughed and struck me across the face. I staggered, but held tight to the chains. Hudson never moved a muscle.

"Now, my precious," says Gul to Narreeman. "He is here, and he is yours." She came forward to his side, and the big jezzailchi, having placed the torch, came on her other side, grinning like a satyr. He stood about a yard in front of Hudson, but his eyes were fixed on me.

The woman Narreeman had no veil now; she was turbanned and cloaked, and her face was like stone. Then she smiled, and it was like a tigress showing its teeth; she hissed something to Gul Shah, and held out her hand towards the dagger at his belt.

Fear had me gripped, or I would have let go the chains and rushed blindly past them. Gul put his hand on his hilt, and slowly, for my benefit, began to slide the blade from its sheath.

Hudson struck. His right hand shot down to the big jezzailchi's waist band, there was a gleam of steel, a gasp,
and then a hideous shriek as Hudson drove the man's own
dagger to the hilt in his belly. As the fellow dropped Hudson tried to spring at Gul Shah, but he struck against Narreeman and they both went sprawling. Gul leaped back,
snatching at his sabre, and I let go my chains and threw
myself out of harm's way. Gul swore and aimed a cut at
me, but he was wild and hit the swinging chains; in that
moment Hudson had scrambled to the dying jezzailchi,
grabbed the sabre from his waist, and was bounding up the
steps to the door. For a moment I thought he was desert-
ing me, but when he reached the doorway it was to slam
the door to and shoot the inside bolt. Then he turned,
sabre in hand, and Gul, who had sprung to pursue him,
halted at the foot of the steps. For a moment the four of
us were stock still, and then Gul bawls out:

"Mahmud! Shadman! Idderao, juldi!"

"Watch the woman!" sings out Hudson, and I saw Narreeman in the act of snatching up the bloody dagger he
had dropped. She was still on hands and knees, and with
one step I caught her a flying kick in the middle that flung
her breathless against the wall. Out of the tail of my eye I
saw Hudson spring down the steps, sabre whirling, and
then I had thrown myself at Narreeman, catching her a
blow on the head as she tried to rise, and grabbing her
wrists. As the steel clashed behind me, and the door re-
echoed to pounding from outside, I dragged her arms behind her back and held them, twisting for all I was worth.

"You bitch!" I roared at her, and wrenched so that she
screamed and went down, pinned beneath me. I held her
so, got my knee on the small of her back, and looked
round for Hudson.

He and Gul were going at it like Trojans in the middle
of the cell. Thank God they teach good swordsmanship in
the cavalry,[21] even to lancers, for Gul was as active as a
panther, his point and edge whirling everywhere while he
shouted oaths and threats and bawled to his rascals to
break in. The door was too stout for them, though. Hudson fought coolly, as if he was in the gymnasium, guard-
ing every thrust and sweep, then shuffling in and lunging
so that Gul had to leap back to save his skin. I stayed
where I was, for I daren't leave that hell-cat for a second,
and if I had Gul might have had an instant to take a swipe
at me.

Suddenly he rushed Hudson, slashing right and left, and the lancer broke ground; that was what Gul wanted, and he sprang for the steps, intent on getting to the door. Hudson was right on his heels, though, and Gul had to swing round halfway up the steps to avoid being run through from behind. He swerved outside Hudson's thrust, slipped on the steps, and for a moment they were locked, half-lying on the stairway. Gul was up like a rubber ball, swinging up his sabre for a cut at Hudson, who was caught all a-sprawl; the sabre flashed down, ringing on the stone and striking sparks, and the force of the blow made Gul overbalance. For a moment he was crouched over Hudson, and before he could recover I saw a glittering point rise out of the centre of his back; he gave a choked, awful cry, straightened up, his head hanging back, and crashed down the steps to the cell floor. He lay there, writhing, mouth gaping and eyes glaring; then he was still.

Hudson scrambled down the steps, his sabre red to the forte. I let out a yell of triumph.

"Bravo, Hudson! Bravo, shabash!"

He took one look at Gul, dropped his sabre, and to my amazement began to pull the dead man out of the middle of the floor to the shadowy side of the cellar. He laid him flat on his back, then hurried over to me.

"Make her fast, sir," says he, and while I trussed Narreeman's arms with the jezzailchi's belt, Hudson stuffed a gag into her mouth. We dropped her on the straw, and Hudson says:

"Only one chance, sir. Take the sabre—the clean one —and stand guard over that dead bugger. Put your point to his throat, an' when I open the door, tell 'em you'll slaughter their chief unless they do as we say. They won't see he's a corp, in this light, an' the bint's silenced. Now, sir, quick!"

There could be no argument; the door was creaking under the Afridis' hammering. I ran to Gul's side, snatching up his sabre on the way, and stood astride him, the point on his breast. Hudson took one look round, leaped up the steps, whipped back the bolt, and regained the cell floor in a bound. The door swung open, and in surged the lads of the village.

"Halt!" roars I. "Another move, and I'll send Gul Shah to make his peace with Shaitan! Back, you sons of owls and pigs!"

They bore up sharp, five or six of them, hairy brutes, at

the head of the steps. When they saw Gul apparently helpless beneath me one lets out an oath and another a wail.

"Not another inch!" I shouted. "Or I'll have his life!"

They stayed where they were, gaping, but for the life of
me I didn't know what to do next. Hudson spoke up, ur-
gently.

"Horses, sir. We're right by the gate; tell 'em to bring
two—no, three ponies to the door, and then all get back to
the other side o' the yard."

I bawled the order at them, sweating in case they didn't
do it, but they did. I suppose I looked desperate enough
for anything, stripped to the waist, matted and bearded,
and glaring like a lunatic. It was fear, not rage, but they
weren't to know that. There was a great jabbering among
them, and then they scrambled back through the doorway;
I heard them yelling and swearing out in the dark, and
then a sound that was like music—the clatter of ponies'
hooves.

"Tell 'em to keep outside, sir, an' well away," says Hudson, and I roared it out with a will. Hudson ran to Narreeman, swung her up into his arms with an effort, and set
her feet on the steps.

"Walk, damn you," says he, and grabbing up his own
sabre he pushed her up the steps, the point at her back.
He disappeared through the doorway, there was a pause,
and then he shouts:

"Right, sir. Come out quick, like, an' bolt the door."

I never obeyed an order more gladly. I left Gul Shah
staring up sightlessly, and raced up the steps, pulling the
door to behind me. It was only as I looked round the
courtyard, at Hudson astride one pony, with Narreeman
bound and writhing across the other, at the little group of
Afghans across the yard, fingering their knives and muttering—only then did I realise that we had left our hostage.
But Hudson was there, as usual.

"Tell 'em I'll spill the bint's guts all over the yard if
they stir a finger. Ask 'em how their master'll like that
—an' what he'll do to 'em afterwards!" And he dropped his
point over Narreeman's body.

It held them, even without my repetition of the threat,
and I was able to scramble aboard the third pony. The
gate was before us; Hudson grabbed the bridle of Narreeman's mount, we drove in our heels, and in a clatter of
hooves we were out and away, under a glittering moon,

down the path that wound from the fort's little hill to the open plain.

When we reached the level I glanced back; Hudson was not far behind, although he was having difficulty with Narreeman, for he had to hold her across the saddle of the third beast. Behind, the ugly shape of the fort was outlined against the sky, but there was no sign of pursuit.

When he came up with me he said:

"I reckon down yonder we'll strike the Kabul road, sir. We crossed it on the way in. Think we can chance it, sir?"

I was so trembling with reaction and excitement that I didn't care. Of course we should have stayed off the road, but I was for anything that would get that damned cellar far behind us, so I nodded and we rode on. With luck there would be no one moving on the road at night, and anyway, only on the road could we hope to get our bearings.

We reached it before very long, and the stars showed us the eastern way. We were a good three miles from the fort now, and it seemed, if the Afridis had come out in pursuit, that they had lost us. Hudson asked me what we should do with Narreeman.

At this I came to my senses again; as I thought back to what she had been preparing to do my gorge rose, and all I wanted to do was tear her apart.

"Give her to me," says I, dropping my reins and taking a grip on the sabre hilt.

He had one hand on her, sliding her out of the saddle; she slipped down on to the ground and wriggled up on her knees, her hands tied behind her, the gag across her mouth. She was glaring like a mad thing.

As I moved my pony round, Hudson suddenly reined into my way.

"Hold on, sir," says he. "What are you about?"

"I'm going to cut that bitch to pieces," says I. "Out of my way."

"Here, now, sir," says he. "You can't do that."

"Can't I, by God?"

"Not while I'm here, sir," says he, very quiet.

I didn't credit my ears at first.

"It won't do, sir," says he. "She's a woman. You're not yourself, sir, what wi' the floggin' they gave you, an' all. We'll let her be, sir; cut her hands free an' let her go."

I started to rage at him, for a mutinous dog, but he just sat there, not to be moved, shaking his head. So in the end I gave in—it occurred to me that what he could do to Gul Shah he might easily do to me—and he jumped down and loosed her hands. She flew at him, but he tripped her up and remounted.

"Sorry, miss," says he, "but you don't deserve better, you know."

She lay there, gasping and staring hate at us, a proper handsome hell-cat. It was a pity there wasn't time and leisure, or I'd have served her as I had once before, for I was feeling more my old self again. But to linger would have been madness, so I contented myself with a few slashes at her with my long bridle, and had the satisfaction of catching her a ringing cut over the backside that sent her scurrying for the rocks. Then we turned east and drove on down the road towards India.

It was bitter cold, and I was half-naked, but there was a poshteen over the saddle, and I wrapped up in it. Hudson had another, and covered his tunic and breeches with it; between us we looked a proper pair of Bashi-Bazouks, but for Hudson's fair hair and beard.

We camped before dawn, in a little gully, but not for long, for when the sun came up I recognised that we were in the country just west of Futtehabad, which is a bare twenty miles from Jallalabad itself. I wouldn't feel safe till we had its walls around us, so we pushed on hard, only leaving the road when we saw dust-clouds ahead of us that indicated other travellers.

We took to the hills for the rest of the day, skirting Futtehabad, and lay up by night, for we were both all in. In the morning we pressed on, but kept away from the road, for when we took a peep down at it, there were Afghans thick on it, all travelling east. There was more movement in the hills now, but no one minded a pair of riders, for Hudson shrouded his head in a rag to cover his blond hair, and I always looked like a Khyberi badmash anyway. But as we drew nearer to Jallalabad I got more and more anxious, for by what we had seen on the road, and the camps we saw dotted about in the gullies, I knew we must be moving along with an army. This was Akbar's host, pushing on to Jallalabad, and presently in the distance we heard the rattle of musketry, and knew that the siege must be already under way.

Well, this was a pretty fix; only in Jallalabad was there

safety, but there was an Afghan army between us and it. With what we had been through I was desperate; for a moment I thought of bypassing Jallalabad and making for India, but that meant going through the Khyber, and with Hudson looking as much like an Afghan as a Berkshire hog we could never have made it. I cursed myself for having picked a companion with fair hair and Somerset complexion, but how could I have foreseen this? There was nothing for it but to push on and see what the chances were of getting into Jallalabad and of avoiding detection on the way.

It was a damned risky go, for soon we came into proper encampments, with Afghans as thick as fleas everywhere, and Hudson nearly suffocating inside the turban rag which hooded his whole head. Once we were hailed by a party of Pathans, and I answered with my heart in my mouth; they seemed interested in us, and in my panic all I could think to do was start singing—that old Pathan song that goes:

> There's a girl across the river
> With a bottom like a peach—
> And alas, I cannot swim.

They laughed and let us alone, but I thanked God they weren't nearer than twenty yards, or they might have realised that I wasn't as Afghan as I looked at a distance.

It couldn't have lasted long. I was sure that in another minute someone would have seen through our disguise, but then the ground fell away before us, and we were sitting our ponies at the top of a slope running down to the level, and on the far side of it, maybe two miles away, was Jallalabad, with the Kabul river at its back.

It was a scene to remember. On the long ridge on either side of us there were Afghans lining the rocks and singing out to each other, or squatting round their fires; down in the plain there were thousands of them, grouped any old way except near Jallalabad, where they formed a great half-moon line facing the city. There were troops of cavalry milling about, and I saw guns and wagons among the besiegers. From the front of the half-moon you could see little prickles of fire and hear the pop-pop of musketry, and farther forward, almost up to the defences, there were scores of little sangars dotted about, with white-robed figures lying behind them. It was a real siege, no question, and as I looked at that tremendous host between us and safety my heart sank: we could never get through it.

Mind you, the siege didn't seem to be troubling Jallalabad unduly. Even as we watched the popping increased, and we saw a swarm of figures running hell-for-leather back from before the earthworks—Jallalabad isn't a big place, and had no proper walls, but the sappers had got some good-looking ramparts out before the town. At this the Afghans on the heights on either side of us set up a great jeering yell, as though to say they could have done better than their retreating fellows. From the scatter of figures lying in front of the earthworks it looked as though the besiegers had been taking a pounding.

Much good that was to us, but then Hudson sidled his pony up to mine, and says, "There's our way in, sir." I followed his glance, and saw below and to our right, about a mile from the foot of the slope and maybe as far from the city, a little fort on an eminence, with the Union Jack fluttering over its gate, and flashes of musketry from its walls. Some of the Afghans were paying attention to it, but not many; it was cut off from the main fortifications by Afghan outposts on the plain, but they obviously weren't caring much about it just now. We watched as a little cloud of Afghan horsemen swooped down towards it and then sheered off again from the firing on its walls.

"If we ride down slow, sir," says Hudson, "to where them niggers are lying round sniping, we could make a dash for it."

And get shot from our saddles for our pains, thinks I; no thank 'ee. But I had barely had the thought when someone hails us from the rocks on our left, and without a word we put our ponies down the slope. He bawled after us, but we kept going, and then we hit the level and were riding forward through the Afghans who were lying spread out among the rocks watching the little fort. The horsemen who had been attacking were wheeling about to our left, yelling and cursing, and one or two of the snipers shouted to us as we passed them by, but we kept on, and then there was just the last line of snipers and beyond it the little fort, three-quarters of a mile off, on top of its little hill, with its flag flying.

"Now, sir," snaps Hudson, and we dug in our heels and went like fury, flying past the last sangars. The Afghans there yelled out in surprise, wondering what the devil we were at, and we just put our heads down and made for the fort gate. I heard more shouting behind us, and thundering hooves, and then shots were whistling above us—from the fort, dammit. Oh Jesus, thinks I, they'll shoot us for Afghans, and we can't stop now with the horsemen behind us!

Hudson flung off his poshteen, and yelled, rising in his stirrups. At the sight of the blue lancer tunic and breeches there was a tremendous yelling behind, but the firing from the fort stopped, and now it was just a race between us and the Afghans. Our ponies were about used up, but we put them to the hill at top speed, and as the walls drew near I saw the gate open. I whooped and rode for it, with Hudson at my heels, and then we were through, and I was slipping off the saddle into the arms of a man with enormous ginger whiskers and a sergeant's stripes on his arm.

"Damme!" roars he. "Who the hell are ye?"

"Lieutenant Flashman," says I, "of General Elphinstone's army," and his mouth opened like a cod's. "Where's your commanding officer?"

"Blow me!" says he. "I'm the commanding officer, so far's there is one. Sergeant Wells, Bombay Grenadiers, sir. But we thought you was all dead. . . ."

It took us a little time to convince him, and to learn what was happening. While his sepoys cracked away from the parapet overhead at the disappointed Afghans, he took us into the little tower, sat us on a bench, gave us pancakes and water—which was all they had—and told us how the Afghans had been besieging Jallalabad three days now, in ever-increasing force, and his own little detachment had been cut off in this outlying fort for that time.

"It's a main good place for them to mount guns, d'ye see, sir, if they could run us out," says he. "So Cap'n Little —'e's back o' the tower 'ere, wi' 'is 'ead stove in by a bullet, sir—said as we 'ad to 'old out no matter what. 'To the last man, sergeant,' 'e sez, an' then 'e died—that was yesterday evenin', sir. They'd bin 'ittin' us pretty 'ard, sir, an' 'ave bin since. I dunno as we can last out much longer, 'cos the water's runnin' low, an' they damn near got over the wall last night, sir."

"But can't they relieve you from Jallalabad, for God's sake?" says I.

"I reckon they got their 'ands full, sir," says he, shaking his head. "They can 'old out there long enough; ol' Bob Sale—Gen'l Sale, I should say—ain't worried about that. But makin' a sortie to relieve us 'ud be another matter."

"Oh, Christ," says I, "out of the frying pan into the fire!"

He stared at me, but I was past caring. There seemed no end to it; there was some evil genie pursuing me through Afghanistan, and he meant to get me in the end. To have come so far, yet again, and to be dragged down within sight of safety! There was a palliasse in the corner of the tower, and I just went and threw myself down on it; my back was still burning, I was half-dead with fatigue, I was trapped in this hellish fort—I swore and wept with my face in the straw, careless of what they thought.

I heard them muttering, Hudson and the sergeant, and the latter's voice saying: "Well, strike me, 'e's a rum one!" and they must have gone outside, for I heard them no more. I lay there, and must have fallen asleep out of sheer exhaustion, for when I opened my eyes again it was dark in the room. I could hear the sepoys outside, talking; but I didn't go out; I got a drink from the pannikin on the table and lay down again and slept until morning.

Some of you will hold up your hands in horror that a Queen's officer could behave like this, and before his soldiers, too. To which I would reply that I do not claim, as I've said already, to be anything but a coward and a scoundrel, and I've never play-acted when it seemed pointless. It seemed pointless now. Possibly I was a little delirious in those days, from shock—Afghanistan, you'll admit, hadn't been exactly a Bank Holiday outing for me—but as I lay in that tower, listening to the occasional crackle of firing outside, and the yelling of the besiegers, I ceased to care at all for appearances. Let them think what they would; we were all surely going to be cut up, and what do good opinions matter to a corpse?

However, appearances still mattered to Sergeant Hudson. It was he who woke me after that first night. He looked pouch-eyed and filthy as he leaned over me, his tunic all torn and his hair tumbling into his eyes.

"How are you, sir?" says he.

"Damnable," says I. "My back's on fire. I ain't going to be much use for a while, I fear, Hudson."

"Well, sir," says he, "let's have a look at your back." I turned over, groaning, and he looked at it.

"Not too bad," says he. "Skin's only broke here an' there, and not mortifying. For the rest, it's just welts." He was silent a moment. "Thing is, sir, we need every musket we can raise. The sangars are closer this morning, an' the niggers are massing. Looks like a proper battle, sir."

"Sorry, Hudson," says I, rather weak. "I would if I could, you know. But whatever my back looks like, I can't do much just yet. I think there's something broken inside."

He stood looking down at me. "Yes, sir," says he at length, "I think there is." And then he just turned and walked out.

I felt myself go hot all over as I realised what he meant by that; for a moment I almost jumped off the palliasse and ran after him. But I didn't, for at that moment there was a sudden yelling on the parapets, and the musketry crashed out, and Sergeant Wells was bawling orders; but above all I heard the blood-curdling shrieks of the Ghazis, and I knew they were rushing the wall. It was all too much for me; I lay shuddering on the straw while the sounds of fighting raged outside. It seemed to go on forever, and every moment I expected to hear the Afghan war-cries in the yard, hear the rush of feet, and see the bearded horrors dashing in the door with their Khyber knives. I could only hope to God that they would finish me off quickly.

As I say, I may genuinely have had a shock, or even a fever, at this time, although I doubt it; I believe it was just simple fear that was almost sending me out of my mind. At all events, I have no particular idea of how long that fight lasted, or when it stopped and the next assault began, or even how many days and nights passed by. I don't recall eating and drinking, although I suppose I must have, or even answering the calls of nature. That, incidentally, is one effect that fear does not have on me; I do not wet or foul myself. It has been a near thing once or twice, I admit. At Balaclava, for example, when I rode with the Light Brigade—you know how George Paget smoked a cigar all the way to the guns? Well, my bowels moved all the way to the guns, but there was nothing inside me but wind, since I hadn't eaten for days.

But in that fort, at the very end of my tether, I seemed to lose my sense of time; *delirium funkens* had me in its grip. I know Hudson came in to me, I know he talked, but I can't remember what he said, except for a few isolated passages, and those I think were mostly towards the end. I do remember him telling me Wells had been killed, and myself replying, "That's bad luck, by God, is he much hurt?" For the rest, my waking moments were less clear than my dreams, and those were vivid enough. I was back in the cell, with Gul Shah and Narreeman, and Gul was laughing at me, and changing into Bernier with his pistol raised, and then into Elphy Bey saying, "We shall have to cut off all your essentials, Flashman, I'm afraid there is no help for it. I shall send a note to Sir William." And Narreeman's eyes grew greater and greater, until I saw them in Elspeth's face—Elspeth smiling and very beautiful, but fading in her turn to become Arnold, who was threatening to flog me for not knowing my construe. "Unhappy boy, I wash my hands of you; you must leave my pit of snakes and dwarves this very day." And he reached out and took me by the shoulder; his eyes were burning like coals and his fingers bit into my shoulder so that I cried out and tried to pull them free, and found myself scrabbling at Hudson's fingers as he knelt beside my couch.

"Sir," says he, "you've got to get up."

"What time is it?" says I. "And what d'ye want? Leave me, can't you, leave me be—I'm ill, damn you."

"It's no go, sir. You can't stay here any longer. You must stand up and come outside with me."

I told him to go to the devil, and he suddenly lunged forward and seized me by the shoulders.

"Get up!" he snarled at me, and I realised his face was far more haggard than I'd ever seen it, drawn and fierce like an animal's. "Get up! You're a Queen's officer, by God, an' you'll behave like one! You're not ill, Mr Precious Flashman, you're plain white-livered! That's all your sickness! But you'll get up an' look like a man, even if you aren't one!" And he started to drag me from the straw.

I struck out at him, calling him a mutinous dog, and telling him I'd have him flogged through the army for his insolence, but he stuck his face into mine and hissed:

"Oh, no, you won't! Not now nor never. Because you an' me ain't going back where there's drum-heads an' floggings or anything, d'ye see? We're stuck here, an' we'll die here, because there's no way out! We're done for, lieutenant; this garrison is finished! We haven't got nothing to do, except die!"

"Damn you, then, what d'ye want me for? Go and die in your own way, and leave me to die in mine." I tried to push him away.

"Oh, no sir. It ain't as easy as that. I'm all that's left to fight this fort, me and a score of broken-down sepoys—

and you. And we're going to fight it, Mr Flashman. To the last inch, d'ye hear?"

"You bloody fight it!" I shouted at him. "You're so confounded brave! You're a bloody soldier! All right, I'm not! I'm afraid, damn you, and I can't fight any more—I don't care if the Afghans take the fort and Jallalabad and the whole of India!" The tears were running down my cheeks as I said it. "Now go to hell and let me alone!"

He knelt there, staring at me, and pushed the hair out of his eyes. "I know it," he said. "I half-knew it from the minute we left Kabul, an' I was near sure back in that cellar, the way you carried on. But I was double certain sure when you wanted to kill that poor Afghan bitch—*men* don't do that. But I couldn't ever say so. You're an officer and a gentleman, as they say. But it doesn't matter now, sir, does it? We're both going, so I can speak my mind."

"Well, I hope you enjoy doing it," says I. "You'll kill a lot of Afghans that way."

"Maybe I will, sir," says he. "But I need you to help. And you *will* help, for I'm going to stick out here as long as I can."

"You poor ninny," says I. "What good'll that do, if they kill you in the end?"

"This much good, that I'll stop those niggers mounting guns on this hill. They'll never take Jallalabad while *we* hold out—and every hour gives General Sale a better chance. That's what I'm going to do, sir."

One meets them, of course. I've known hundreds. Give them a chance to do what they call their duty, let them see a hope of martyrdom—they'll fight their way on to the cross and bawl for the man with the hammer and nails.

"My best wishes," says I. "I'm not stopping you."

"Yes, you will, sir, if I let you. I need you—there's twenty sepoys out there who'll fight all the better if there's an officer to sick 'em on. They don't know what you are —not yet." He stood up. "Anyway, I'm not arguing, sir. You'll get up—now. Or I'll drag you out and I'll cut you to bits with a sabre, a piece at a time." His face was dreadful to see just then, those grey eyes in that drawn, worn skin. He meant it; not a doubt of it. "So just get up, sir, will you?"

I got up, of course. I was well enough in body; my sickness was purely moral. I went outside with him, into a courtyard with half a dozen or so sepoy bodies laid in a row with blankets over them near the gate; the living ones

were up on the parapet. They looked round as Hudson
and I went up the rickety ladder to the roof, their black
faces tired and listless under their shakos, their skinny
black hands and feet ridiculous protuding from red uniform jackets and white trousers.

The roof of the tower was no more than ten feet
square, and just a little higher than the walls surrounding
it; they were no more than twenty yards long—the place
was less a fort than a toy castle. From the tower roof I
could see Jallalabad, a mile away, apparently unchanged,
except that the Afghan lines seemed to be closer. On our
own front they were certainly nearer than they had been,
and Hudson hustled me quickly under cover before the
Afghans could get a bead on us.

We were watching them, a great crowd of horsemen
and hillmen on foot, milling about out of musket shot,
when Hudson pointed out to me a couple of cannon that
had been rolled up on their right flank. They had been
there since dawn, he said, and he expected they would
start up as soon as powder and shot had been assembled.
We were just speculating when this might be—or rather,
Hudson was, for I wasn't talking to him—when there was
a great roar from the horsemen, and they started to roll
forward towards our fort. Hudson thrust me down the ladder, across the yard, and up to the parapet; a musket was
shoved into my hands, and I was staring through an
embrasure at the whole mob surging at us. I saw then that
the ground outside the walls was thick with dead; before
the gate they were piled up like fish on a slab.

The sight was sickening, no doubt, but not so sickening
as the spectacle of those devils whooping in towards the
fort. I reckoned there were about forty of them, with footmen trailing along behind, all waving their knives and yelling. Hudson shouted to hold fire, and the sepoys behaved
as though they'd been through this before—as they had.
When the chargers were within fifty yards, and not showing any great enthusiasm, it seemed to me, Hudson bawled
"Fire!" the volley crashed out, and about four went down,
which was good shooting. At this they wavered, but still
came on, and the sepoys grabbed up their spare muskets,
rolling their eyes at Hudson. He roars "Fire!" again, and
another half dozen were toppled, at which the whole lot
sheered off.

"There they go!" yells Hudson. "Reload, handily now!

By God," says he, "if they had the bottom for one good charge they could bowl us over like ninepins!"

This had occurred to me. There were hundreds of Afghans out yonder, and barely twenty men in the fort; with a determined rush they could have carried the walls, and once inside they would have chewed us up in five minutes. But I gathered that this had been their style all along—half-hearted charges that had been beaten off, and only one or two that had reached the fort itself. They had lost heavily; I believe that they didn't care much about our little place, really, but would rather have been with their friends attacking Jallalabad, where the loot was. Sensible fellows.

But it was not going to last; I could see that. For all that our casualties had not been heavy, the sepoys were about done; there was only a little flour left for food, and barely a pannikin of water a man in the big butt down by the gate; Hudson watched it like a hawk.

There were three more charges that day, or maybe four, and none more successful than the first. We banged away and they cleared out, and my mind began to go dizzy again. I slumped beside my embrasure, with a poshteen draped over me to try to keep off the hellish heat; flies buzzed everywhere, and the sepoy on my right moaning to himself incessantly. By night it was as bad; the cold came, so bitter that I sobbed to myself at the pain of it; there was a huge moon, lighting everything in brilliant silver, but even when it set the dark wasn't sufficient to enable the Afghans to creep up on us, thank God. There were a few alarms and shots, but that was all. Dawn came, and the snipers began to crack away at us; we kept down beneath the parapet, and the shots chipped flakes off the tower behind us.

I must have been dozing, for I was shaken awake by an almighty crash and a thunderous explosion; there was a great cloud of dust swirling about, and as it cleared I saw that a corner of the tower had gone, and a heap of rubble was lying in the courtyard.

"The cannon!" shouts Hudson. "They're using the cannon!"

Out across the plain, there it was, sure enough—one of their big guns, directed at the fort, with a mob of Afghans jostling round it. Five minutes it took them to reload, and then the place shook as if an earthquake had hit it, and there was a gaping hole in the wall beside the gate. The sepoys began to wail, and Hudson roared at them to stand fast; there was another terrific crash, and then another; the air was full of flying dust and stones; a section of the parapet along from me gave way, and a screaming sepoy went down with it. I launched myself for the ladder, slipped, and rolled off into the debris, and something must have struck my head, for the next thing I knew I was standing up, not knowing where I was, looking at a ruined wall beyond which there was an empty plain with figures running towards me.

They were a long way away, and it took me a moment to realise that they were Afghans; they were charging, sure enough, and then I heard a musket crack, and there at the ruined wall was Hudson, fumbling with a ramrod and swearing, the side of his face caked with blood. He saw me, and bawled:

"Come on! Come on! Lend a hand, man!"

I walked towards him, my feet weighing a ton apiece; a red-coated figure was moving in the shadow of the wall, beside the gate; it was one of the sepoys. Curiously, the wall had been shot in on either side, but the gate was still standing, with the flag trailing at its staff on top, and the cords hanging down. As the shrieks of the Ghazis drew nearer, a thought entered my head, and I stumbled over towards the gate and laid hold of the cords.

"Give in," I said, and tugged at the cords. "Give in, and make 'em stop!" I pulled at the cords again, and then there was another appalling crash, the gates opened as though a giant hand had whirled them inwards, the arch above them fell, and the flagstaff with it; the choking dust swirled up, and I blundered through it, my hands out to grab the colours that were now within reach.

I knew quite clearly what I wanted to do; I would gather up the flag and surrender it to the Afghans, and then they would let us alone; Hudson, even in that hellish din and horror, must have guessed somehow what was in my mind, for I saw him crawling towards the colours, too. Or perhaps he was trying to save them, I don't know. But he didn't manage it; another round shot ploughed into the rubble before me, and the dirty, blue-clad figure was suddenly swept away like a rag doll into an engulfing cloud of dust and masonry. I staggered forward over the stones, touched the flagstaff and fell on my knees; the cloth of the flag was within reach, and I caught hold of it and pulled it up from the rubbish. From somewhere there came a volley of musketry, and I thought, well, this is the finish, and not half as bad as I thought it would be, but bad enough for all that, and God, I don't want to die yet.

There was a thunder like a waterfall, and things were falling on me; a horrible pain went through my right leg, and I heard the shriek of a Ghazi almost in my ear. I was lying face down, clutching at the flag, mumbling, "Here, take the bloody thing; I don't want it. Please take it; I give in." The musketry crashed again, the roaring noise grew louder, and then sight and hearing died.

There are a few wakenings in your life that you would wish to last forever, they are so blissful. Too often you wake in a bewilderment, and then remember the bad news you went to sleep on, but now and then you open your eyes in the knowledge that all is well and safe and right, and there is nothing to do but lie there with eyes gently shut, enjoying every delicious moment.

I knew it was all fine when I felt the touch of sheets beneath my chin, and a soft pillow beneath my head. I was in a British bed, somewhere, and the rustling sound above me was a punkah fan. Even when I moved, and a sudden anguish stabbed through my right leg, I wasn't dismayed, for I guessed at once that it was only broken, and there was still a foot to waggle at the end of it.

How I had got there I didn't care. Obviously I had been rescued at the last minute from the fort, wounded but otherwise whole, and brought to safety. Far away I could hear the tiny popping of muskets, but here there was peace, and I lay marvelling at my own luck, revelling in my present situation, and not even bothering to open my eyes, I was so contented.

When I did, it was to find myself in a pleasant, white-washed room, with the sun slanting through wooden shutters, and a punkah wallah dozing against the wall, automatically twitching the string of his big fan. I turned my head, and found it was heavily bandaged; I was conscious that it throbbed at the back, but even that didn't discourage me. I had got clear away, from pursuing Afghans and relentless enemies and beastly-minded women and idiot commanders—I was snug in bed, and anyone who expected any more from Flashy—well, let him wish he might get it!

I stirred again, and my leg hurt, and I swore, at which the punkah wallah jumps up, squeaking, and ran from the room crying that I was awake. Presently there was a bustling, and in came a little spectacled man with a bald head and a large canvas jacket, followed by two or three Indian attendants.

"Awake at last!" says he. "Well, well, this is gratifying. Don't move, sir. Still, still. You've a broken leg here and a broken head there, let's have peace between 'em, what?" He beamed at me, took my pulse, looked at my tongue, told me his name was Bucket, pulled his nose, and said I was very well, considering. "Fractured femur, sir—thigh bone; nasty, but uncomplicated. Few months and you'll be bounding over the jumps again. But not yet—no; had a nasty time of it, eh? Ugly cuts about your back—ne'er mind, we'll hear about that later. Now Abdul," says he, "run and tell Major Havelock the patient's awake, juldi jao. Pray don't move, sir. What's that?—yes, a little drink. Better? Head still, that's right—nothing to do for the present but lie properly still."

He prattled on, but I wasn't heeding him. Oddly enough, it was the sight of the blue coat beneath the canvas jacket that put me in mind of Hudson—what had become of him? My last recollection was of seeing him hit and probably killed. But *was* he dead? He had better be, for my sake—for the memory of our latter relations was all too vivid in my mind, and it suddenly rushed in on me that if Hudson was alive, and talked, I was done for. He could swear to my cowardice, if he wanted to—would he dare? Would he be believed? He could prove nothing, but if he was known as a steady man—and I was sure he would be—he might well be listened to. It would mean my ruin, my disgrace—and while I hadn't cared a button for these things when I believed death was closing in on me and everyone else in that fort, well, I cared most damnably for them now that I was safe again.

Oh, God, says I to myself, let him be dead; the sepoys, if any survived, don't know, and wouldn't talk if they did, or be believed. But Hudson—he *must* be dead!

Charitable thoughts, you'll say. Aye, it's a hard world, and while bastards like Hudson have their uses, they can be most inconvenient, too. I wanted him to be dead, then, as much as I ever wanted anything.

My suspense must have been written on my face, for the little doctor began to babble soothingly to me, and then the door opened and in walked Sale, his big, kind, stupid face all beaming as red as his coat, and behind him a tall, flinty-faced, pulpit-looking man; there were others peeping round the lintel as Sale strode forward and plumped down into a chair beside the bed, leaning forward to take my hand in his own. He held it gently in his big paw and gazed at me like a cow in milk.

"My boy!" says he, almost in a whisper. "My brave boy!"

Hullo, thinks I, this don't sound too bad at all. But I had to find out, and quickly.

"Sir," says I—and to my astonishment my voice came out in a hoarse quaver, it had been so long unused, I suppose—"sir, how is Sergeant Hudson?"

Sale gave a grunt as though he had been kicked, bowed his head, and then looked at the doctor and the gravedigger fellow with him. They both looked damned solemn.

"His first words," says the little doctor, hauling out a handkerchief and snorting into it.

Sale shook his head sadly, and looked back at me.

"My boy," says he, "it grieves me deeply to tell you that your comrade—Sergeant Hudson—is dead. He did not survive the last onslaught on Piper's Fort." He paused, staring at me compassionately, and then says: "He died—like a true soldier."

" 'And Nicanor lay dead in his harness' ", says the gravedigger chap, taking a look at the ceiling. "He died in the fullness of his duty, and was not found wanting."

"Thank God," says I. "God help him, I' mean—God rest him, that is." Luckily my voice was so weak that they couldn't hear more than a mumble. I looked downcast, and Sale squeezed my hand.

"I think I know," says he, "what his comradeship must have meant to you. We understand, you see, that you must have come together from the ruins of General Elphinstone's army, and we can guess at the hardships—oh, my boy, they are written all too plainly on your body—that you must have endured together. I would have spared you this news until you were stronger. . . ." He made a gesture and brushed his eye.

"No, sir," says I, speaking a little stronger, "I wanted to know now."

"It is what I would have expected of you," says he, wringing my hand. "My boy, what can I say? It is a soldier's lot. We must console ourselves with the thought that we would as gladly sacrifice ourselves for our comrades as they do for us. And we do not forget them."

" 'Non omnis moriar'," says the gravedigger. "Such men do not wholly die."

"Amen," says the little doctor, sniffing. Really, all they needed was an organ and a church choir.

"But we must not disturb you too soon," says Sale. "You need rest." He got up. "Take it in the knowledge that your troubles are over, and that you have done your duty as few men would have done it. Aye, or could have done it. I shall come again as soon as I may; in the meantime, let me say what I came to tell you: that I rejoice from my heart to see you so far recovered, for your delivery is the finest thing that has come to us in all this dark catalogue of disasters. God bless you, my boy. Come, gentlemen."

He stumped out, with the others following; the gravedigger bowed solemnly and the little doctor ducked his head and shooed the nigger attendants before him. And I was left not only relieved but amazed by what Sale had said—oh, the everyday compliments of people like Elphy Bey are one thing, but this was Sale, after all, the renowned Fighting Bob, whose courage was a byword. And *he* had said my deliverance was "the finest thing," and that I had done my duty as few could have done it—why, he had talked as though I was a hero, to be reverenced with that astonishing pussy-footing worship which, for some reason, my century extended to its idols. They treated us (I can say "us") as though we were too delicate to handle normally, like old Chinese pots.

Well, I had thought, when I woke up, that I was safe and in credit, but Sale's visit made me realise that there was more to it than I had imagined. I didn't find out what, though, until the following day, when Sale came back again with the gravedigger at his elbow—he was Major Havelock, by the way, a Bible-moth of the deepest dye, and a great name now.[22] Old Bob was in great spirits, and entertained me with the latest news, which was that Jallalabad was holding out splendidly, that a relief force under Pollock was on its way, and that it didn't matter anyway, because we had the measure of the Afghans and would probably sally out and break the siege whenever we felt like it. Havelock looked a bit sour at all this; I gathered he didn't hold a high opinion of Sale—nobody did, apart from admiring his bravery—and was none too sure of his capabilities when it came to raising sieges.

"And this," says Bob, beaming with enthusiasm, "this

we owe to you. Aye, and to the gallant band who held that little fort against an army. My word, Havelock, did I not say to you at the time that there never was a grander thing? It may not pay for all, to be sure; the catastrophe of Afghanistan will call forth universal horror in England, but at least we have redeemed something. We hold Jallalabad, and we'll drive this rabble of Akbar's from our gates —aye, and be back in Kabul before the year is out. And when we do—" and he swung round on me again "—it will be because a handful of sepoys, led by an English gentleman, defied a great army alone, and to the bitter end."

He was so worked up by his own eloquence that he had to go into the corner and gulp for a little, white Havelock nodded solemnly, regarding me.

"It had the flavour of heroism," says he, "and heaven knows there has been little enough of that to date. They will make much of it at home."

Well, I'm not often at a nonplus (except when there is physical danger of course), but this left me speechless. Heroism? Well, if they cared to think so, let 'em; I wouldn't contradict them—and it struck me that if I did, if I were idiot enough to let them know the truth, as I am writing it now, they would simply have thought me crazy as a result of my wounds. God alone knew what I was supposed to have done that was so brave, but doubtless I should learn in time. All I could see was that somehow appearances were heavily on my side—and who needs more than that? Give me the shadow every time, and you can keep the substance—it's a principle I've followed all my life, and it works, if you know how to act on it.

What was obvious was that nothing must now happen to spoil Sale's lovely dream for him; it would have been cruel to the old fellow. So I addressed myself to the task at once.

"We did our duty, sir," says I, looking uncomfortable, and Havelock nodded again, while old Bob came back to the bed.

"And I have done mine," says he, fumbling in his pocket. "For I conceived it no less, in sending my latest despatch to Lord Ellenborough—who now commands in Delhi—to include an account of your action. I'll read it," says he, "because it speaks more clearly than I can at present, and will enable you to see how others judged your conduct."

He cleared his throat, and began.

"Humph—let's see—Afghans in strength—demands that I surrender—aye, aye—sharp engagement by Dennie —ah, here we have it. 'I had despatched a strong guard under Captain Little to Piper's Fort, commanding an eminence some way from the city, where I feared the enemy might establish gun positions. When the siege began, Piper's Fort was totally cut off from us, and received the full force of the enemy's assault. In what manner it resisted I cannot say in detail, for of its garrison only five now survive, four of them being sepoys, and the other an English officer who is yet unconscious with his wounds, but will, as I trust, soon recover. How he came in the fort I know not, for he was not of the original garrison, but on the staff of General Elphinstone. His name is Flashman, and it is probable that he and Dr Brydon are the only survivors of the army so cruelly destroyed at Jugdulluk and Gandamack. I can only assume that he escaped the final massacre, and so reached Piper's Fort after the siege began."

He looked at me. "You shall correct me, my boy, if I go wrong, but it is right you should know what I have told his excellency."

"You're very kind sir," says I, humbly. Too kind by a damned sight, if you only knew.

"'The siege continued slowly on our own front, as I have already informed you,'" says Sale, reading on, "'but the violence of the assaults on Piper's Fort was unabated. Captain Little was slain, with his sergeant, but the garrison fought on with the utmost resolution. Lieutenant Flashman, as I learn from one of the sepoys, was in a case more suited to a hospital than to a battlefield, for he had evidently been prisoner of the Afghans, who had flogged him most shockingly, so that he was unable to stand, and must lie in the fort tower. His companion, Sergeant Hudson, assisted most gallantly in the defence, until Lieutenant Flashman, despite his wounds, returned to the action.

"'Charge after charge was resisted, and the enemy most bloodily repulsed. To us in Jallalabad, this unexpected check to the Sirdar's advance was an advantage beyond price. It may well have been decisive.'"

Well, Hudson, thinks I, that was what you wanted, and you got it, for all the good it did you. Meanwhile, Sale laid off for a minute, took a wipe at his eye, and started in again, trying not to quaver. I suspect he was enjoying his emotion.

" 'But there was no way in which we could succour Piper's Fort at this time, and, the enemy bringing forward cannon, the walls were breached in several places. I had now resolved on a sortie, to do what could be done for our comrades, and Colonel Dennie advanced to their relief. In a sharp engagement over the very ruins of the fort —for it had been pounded almost to pieces by the guns —the Afghans were entirely routed, and we were able to make good the position and withdraw the survivors of the garrison which had held it so faithfully and well.' "

I thought the old fool was going to weep, but he took a great pull at himself and proceeded:

" 'With what grief do I write that of these there remained only five? The gallant Hudson was slain, and at first it seemed that no European was left alive. Then Lieutenant Flashman was found, wounded and unconscious, by the ruins of the gate, where he had taken his final stand in defence not only of the fort, but of his country's honour. For he was found, in the last extremity, with the colours clutched to his broken body, his face to the foemen, defiant even unto death.' "

Hallelujah and good-night, sweet prince, says I to myself, what a shame I hadn't a broken sword and a ring of my slain around me. But I thought too soon.

" 'The bodies of his enemies lay before him,' " says old Bob, " 'At first it was thought he was dead, but to our great joy it was discovered that the flame of life still flickered. I cannot think that there was ever a nobler deed than this, and I only wish that our countrymen at home might have seen it, and learned with what selfless devotion their honour is protected even at the ends of the earth. It was *heroic!* and I trust that Lieutenant Flashman's name will be remembered in every home in England. Whatever may be said of the disasters that have befallen us here, his valour is testimony that the spirit of our young manhood is no whit less ardent than that of their predecessors who, in Pitt's words, saved Europe by their example.' "

Well, thinks I, if that's how we won the battle of Waterloo, thank God the French don't know or we shall have them at us again. Who ever heard such humbug? But it was glorious to listen to, mind you, and I glowed at the thought of it. This was fame! I didn't understand, then, how the news of Kabul and Gandamack would make England shudder, and how that vastly conceited and indignant public would clutch at any straw that might heal their national pride and enable them to repeat the old and nonsensical lie that one Englishman is worth twenty foreigners. But I could still guess what effect Sale's report would have on a new Governor-General, and through him on the government and country, especially by contrast with the accounts of the inglorious shambles by Elphy and McNaghten that must now be on their way home.

All I must do was be modest and manly and wait for the laurel wreaths.

Sale had shoved his copy of the letter back in his pocket, and was looking at me all moist and admiring. Havelock was stern; I guessed he thought Sale was laying it on a deal too thick, but he couldn't say so. (I gathered later that the defence of Piper's Fort wasn't quite so important to Jallalabad as Fighting Bob imagined; it was his own hesitation that made him hold off so long attacking Akbar, and in fact he might have relieved us sooner.)

It was up to me, so I looked Sale in the eye, man to man.

"You've done us great credit, sir," says I. "Thank'ee. For the garrison, it's no less than they deserve, but for myself, well, you make it sound . . . a bit too much like St George and the Dragon, if you don't mind my saying so. I just . . . well, pitched in with the rest, sir, that was all."

Even Havelock smiled at this plain, manly talk, and Sale nearly burst with pride and said it was the grandest thing, by heaven, and the whole garrison was full of it. Then he sobered down, and asked me to tell him how I had come to Piper's Fort, and what had happened to separate Hudson and me from the army. Elphy was still in Akbar's hands, along with Shelton and Mackenzie and the married folk, but for the rest they had thought them all wiped out except Brydon, who had come galloping in alone with a broken sabre trailing from his wrist.

With Havelock's eye on me I kept it brief and truthful. We had come adrift from the army in the fighting about Jugdulluk, I said, had escaped by inches through the gullies with Ghazis pursuing us, and had tried to rejoin the army at Gandamack, but had only been in time to see it slaughtered. I described the scene accurately, with old Bob groaning and damning and Havelock frowning like a stone idol, and then told how we had been captured and imprisoned by Afridis. They had flogged me to make me give information about the Kandahar force and other matters, but thank God I had told them nothing ("bravo!" says old

Bob), and had managed to slip my fetters the same night. I had released Hudson and together we had cut our way past our captors and escaped.

I said nothing of Narreeman—least said soonest mended—but concluded with an account of how we had skulked through the Afghan army, and then ridden into the fort hell-for-leather.

There I left it, and old Bob exclaimed again about courage and endurance, but what reassured me most was that Havelock, without a word, shook my right hand in both of his. I can say that I told it well—off-hand, but not over-modest; just a blunt soldier reporting to his seniors. It calls for nice judgement, this art of bragging; you must be plain, but not too plain, and you must smile only rarely. Letting them guess more than you say is the kernel of it, and looking uncomfortable when they compliment you.

They spread the tale, of course, and in the next few days I don't suppose there was an officer of the garrison who didn't come in to shake hands and congratulate me on coming through safe. George Broadfoot was among the first, all red whiskers and spectacles, beaming and telling me what a devil of a fellow I was—and this from Broadfoot, mind you, whom the Afghans called a brave among braves. To have people like him and Mayne and Fighting Bob making much of me—well, it was first-rate, I can tell you, and my conscience didn't trouble me a bit. Why should it? I didn't ask for their golden opinions; I just didn't contradict 'em. Who would?

It was altogether a splendid few weeks. While I lay nursing my leg, the siege of Jallalabad petered out, and Sale finally made another sortie that scattered the Afghan army to the winds. A few days after that Pollock arrived with the relief force from Peshawar, and the garrison band piped them in amongst universal cheering. Of course, I was on hand; they carried me out on to the verandah, and I saw Pollock march in. Later that evening Sale brought him to see me, and expounded my gallantries once again, to my great embarrassment, of course. Pollock swore it was tremendous, and vowed to avenge me when he marched on to Kabul; Sale was going with him to clear the passes, bring Akbar to book, if possible, and release the prisoners—who included Lady Sale—should they still be alive.

"You can stay here and take your well-earned repose

while your leg mends," says Fighting Bob, at which I decided a scowl and a mutter might be appropriate.

"I'd rather come along," says I. "Damn this infernal leg."

"Why, hold on," laughs Sale, "we'd have to carry you in a palankeen. Haven't you had enough of Afghanistan?"

"Not while Akbar Khan's above ground," says I. "I'd like to take these splints and make him eat 'em."

They laughed at this, and Broadfoot, who was there, cries out:

"He's an old war-horse already, our Flashy. Ye want tae be in at the death, don't ye, ye great carl? Aye, well, ye can leave Akbar tae us; forbye, I doubt if the action we'll find about Kabul will be lively enough for your taste."

They went off, and I heard Broadfoot telling Pollock what a madman I was when it came to a fight—"when we were fighting in the passes, it was Flashman every time that was sent out as galloper to us with messages; ye would see him fleein' over the sangars like a daft Ghazi, and aye wi' a pack o' hostiles howling at his heels. He minded them no more than flies."

That was what he made out of the one inglorious occasion when I had been chased for my life into his encampment. But you will have noticed, no doubt, that when a man has a reputation good or bad, folk will always delight in adding to it; there wasn't a man in Afghanistan who knew me but who wanted to recall having seen me doing something desperate, and Broadfoot, quite sincerely, was like all the rest.

Pollock and Sale didn't catch Akbar, as it turned out, but they did release the prisoners he had taken, and the army's arrival in Kabul quieted the country. There was no question of serious reprisals; having been once bitten, we were not looking for trouble a second time. The one prisoner they didn't release, though, was old Elphy Bey; he had died in captivity, worn out and despairing, and there was a general grief in which I, for one, didn't share. No doubt he was a kindly old stick, but he was a damned disaster as a commander. He, above all others, murdered the army of Afghanistan, and when I reckon up the odds against my own survival in that mess—well, it wasn't Elphy's fault that I came through.

But while all these stirring things were happening, while the Afghans were skulking back into their hills, and Sale and Pollock and Nott were showing the flag and blowing

up Kabul bazaar for spite; while the news of the catalogue
of disasters was breaking on a horrified England; while the
old Duke of Wellington was damning Auckland's folly for
sending an army to occupy "rocks, sands, deserts, ice and
snow"; while the general public and Palmerston were
crying out for vengeance, and the Prime Minister was re-
torting that he wasn't going to make another war for the
sake of spreading the study of Adam Smith among the Pathans—while all this was happening I was enjoying a
triumphal progress back to India. With my leg still
splinted, I was being borne south as the hero—or, at least,
the most convenient of a few heroes—of the hour.

It is obvious now that the Delhi administration regarded
me as something of a godsend. As Greville said later of
the Afghan war, there wasn't much cause for triumph in
it, but Ellenborough in Delhi was shrewd enough to see
that the best way to put a good gloss on the whole horrible
nonsense was to play up its few creditable aspects—and I
was the first handy one.

So while he was trumpeting in orders of the day about
"the illustrious garrison" who had held Jallalabad under
the noble Sale, he found room to beat the drum about
"gallant Flashman," and India took its cue from him.
While they drank my health they could pretend that Gandamack hadn't happened.

I got my first taste of this when I left Jallalabad in a
palankeen, to go down the Khyber with a convoy, and the
whole garrison turned out to hurrah me off. Then at Peshawar there was old Avitabile, the Italian rascal, who welcomed me with a guard of honour, kissed me on both
cheeks, and made me and himself riotously drunk in cele-
bration of my return. That night was memorable for one
thing—I had my first woman for months, for Avitabile
had in a couple of lively Afghan wenches, and we made
splendid beasts of ourselves. It isn't easy, I may say, handling a woman when your leg is broken, but where there's
a will there's a way, and in spite of the fact that Avitabile
was almost sick laughing at the spectacle of me getting my
wench buckled to, I managed most satisfactorily.

From there it was the same all the way—at every town
and camp there were garlands and congratulations and
smiling faces and cheering, until I could almost believe I
was a hero. The men gripped my hand, full of emotion,
and the women kissed me and sniffled; colonels had my
health drunk in their messes, Company men slapped me

on the shoulder, an Irish subaltern and his young wife got me to stand godfather to their new son, who was launched into life with the appalling name of Flashman O'Toole, and the ladies of the Church Guild at Lahore presented me with a silk scarf in red, white, and blue with a scroll embroidered "Steadfast." At Ludhiana a clergyman preached a tremendous sermon on the text, "Greater love hath no man than this that a man lay down his life for his friends"—he admitted, in a roundabout way, that I hadn't actually laid down mine, but it hadn't been for want of trying, and had been a damned near thing altogether. Better luck next time was about his view of it, and meanwhile hosannah and hurrah for Flashy, and let us now sing "Who would true valour see."

All this was nothing to Delhi, where they actually had a band playing "Hail the conquering hero comes", and Ellenborough himself helped me out of the palankeen and supported me up the steps. There was a tremendous crowd, all cheering like billy-o, and a guard of honour, and an address read out by a fat chap in a red coat, and a slap-up dinner afterwards at which Ellenborough made a great speech which lasted over an hour. It was dreadful rubbish, about Thermopylae and the Spanish Armada, and how I had clutched the colours to my bleeding breast, gazing proudly with serene and noble brow o'er the engorged barbarian host, like Christian before Apollyon or Roland at Roncesvalles, I forget which, but I believe it was both. He was a fearful orator, full of bombast from Shakespeare and the classics, and I had no difficulty in feeling like a fool long before he was finished. But I sat it out, staring down the long white table with all Delhi society gaping at me and drinking in Ellenborough's nonsense; I had just sense enough not to get drunk in public, and by keeping a straight face and frowning I contrived to look noble; I heard the women say as much behind their fans, peeping at me and no doubt wondering what kind of a mount I would make, while their husbands thumped the table and shouted "bravo!" whenever Ellenborough said something especially foolish.

Then at the end, damned if he didn't start croaking out "For he's a jolly good fellow!" at which the whole crowd rose and roared their heads off, and I sat red-faced and trying not to laugh as I thought of what Hudson would have said if he could have seen me. It was too bad, of course, but they would never have made such a fuss about a sergeant, and even if they had, he couldn't have carried it off as I did, insisting on hobbling up to reply, and having Ellenborough say that if I must stand, it should be his shoulder I should lean on, and by God, he would boast about it ever after.

At this they roared again, and with his red face puffing claret beside me I said that this was all too much for one who was only a simple English gentleman ("amen to that," cries Ellenborough, "and never was proud title more proudly borne") and that what I had done was my duty, no more or less, as I hoped became a soldier. And while I didn't believe there was any great credit to me in it (cries of "No! No!"), well, if they said there was, it wasn't due to me but to the country that bore me, and to the old school where I was brought up as a Christian, I hoped, by my masters. (What possessed me to say this I shall never understand, unless it was sheer delight in lying, but they raised the roof.) And while they were so kind to me they must not forget those others who had carried the flag, and were carrying it still ("hear! hear!"), and who would beat the Afghans back to where they came from, and prove what everyone knew, that Englishmen never would be slaves (thunderous applause). And, well, what I had done hadn't been much, but it had been my best, and I hoped I would always do it. (More cheering, but not quite as loud, I thought, and I decided to shut up.) So God bless them all, and let them drink with me to the health of our gallant comrades still in the field.

"Your simple honesty, no less than your manly aspect and your glorious sentiments, won the admiration and love of all who heard you," Ellenborough told me afterwards. "Flashman, I salute you. Furthermore," says he, "I intend that England shall salute you also. When he returns from his victorious campaign, Sir Robert Sale will be despatched to England, where I doubt not he will receive those marks of honour which become a hero." [23] (He talked like this most of the time, like a bad actor.[24] Many people did, sixty years ago.) "As is fitting, a worthy herald shall precede him, and share his glory. I mean, of course, yourself. Your work here is done, and nobly done, for the time being. I shall send you to Calcutta with all the speed that your disability allows, there to take ship for England."

I just stared at the man; I had never thought of this. To get out of this hellish country—for if, as I've said, I can now consider that India was kind to me, I was still overjoyed at the thought of leaving it—to see England again, and home, and London, and the clubs and messes and civilised people, to be fêted there as I had been assured I would be, to return in triumph when I had set out under a cloud, to be safe beyond the reach of black savages, and heat, and filth, and disease, and danger, to see white women again, and live soft, and take life easy, and sleep secure at nights, to devour the softness of Elspeth, to stroll in the park and be pointed out as the hero of Piper's Fort, to come back to life again—why, it was like waking from a nightmare. The thought of it all set me shaking.

"There are further reports to be made on affairs in Afghanistan," says Ellenborough, "and I can think of no more fitting messenger."

"Well, sir," says I. "I'm at your orders. If you insist, I'll go."

It took four months to sail home, just as it had taken four months to sail out, but I'm bound to say I didn't mind this time. Then I had been going into exile; now I was coming home a hero. If I'd had any doubts of that the voyage dispelled them. The captain and his officers and the passengers were as civil as butter, and treated me as if I were the Duke himself; when they found I was a cheery sort who liked his bottle and talk we got along famously, for they never seemed to tire of hearing me tell of my engagements with Afghans—male and female—and we got drunk most nights together. One or two of the older chaps were a bit leery of me, and one even hinted that I talked a deal too much, but I didn't care for this, and said so. They were just sour old package-rats, anyway, or jealous civilians.

I wonder, now, looking back, that the defence of Jallalabad made such a stir, for it was a very ordinary business, really. But it did, and since I was the first out of India who had been there, and borne a distinguished part, I got the lion's share of admiration. It was so on the ship, and was to prove so in England.

During the voyage my broken leg recovered almost entirely, but there was not much activity on shipboard anyway, and no women, and, boozing with the boys apart, I had a good deal of time to myself. This, and the absence of females, naturally turned me to thoughts of Elspeth; it was strange and delightful to think of going home to a wife, and I got that queasy feeling deep in my bowels whenever I found myself dreaming about her. It wasn't all lust, either, not more than about nine-tenths—after all, she wasn't going to be the only woman in England—but when I conjured up a picture of that lovely, placid face and blonde hair I got a tightness in my throat and a trembling in my hands that was quite apart from what the clergy call carnal appetites. It was the feeling I had experienced that first night I rattled her beside the Clyde—a kind of hunger for her presence and the sound of her voice and the dreamy stupidity of her blue eyes. I wondered if I was falling in love with her, and decided that I was, and that I didn't care, anyway—which is a sure sign.

So in this moonstruck state I whiled away the long voyage, and by the time we docked among the forest of shipping in London pool I was in a fine sweat, romantic and horny all at once. I made great haste for my father's house, full of excitement at the thought of surprising her —for of course she had no idea that I was coming—and banged the knocker so hard that passers-by turned to stare at the big, brown-faced fellow who was in such a devilish hurry.

Old Oswald opened, just as he always did, and gaped like a sheep as I strode past him, shouting. The hall was empty, and both strange and familiar at once, as things are after a long absence.

"Elspeth!" I roared. "Halloo! Elspeth! I'm home!"

Oswald was gabbling at my elbow that my father was out, and I clapped him on the back and pulled his whiskers.

"Good for him," says I, "I hope they have to carry him home tonight. Where's your mistress? Elspeth! Hallo!"

He just went on clucking at me, between delight and amazement, and then I heard a door open behind me, and looked round, and who should be standing there but Judy. That took me aback a bit; I hadn't thought she would still be here.

"Hallo," says I, not too well pleased, although she was looking as handsome as ever. "Hasn't the guv'nor got a new whore yet?"

She was about to say something, but at that moment there was a step on the staircase, and Elspeth was standing there, staring down at me. God, what a picture she was: corn-gold hair, red lips parted, blue eyes wide, breast heaving—no doubt she was wearing something, but I couldn't for the life of me remember what it was. She looked like a startled nymph, and then the old satyr Flashy was bounding up the stairs, grabbing her, and crying:

"I'm home! I'm home! Elspeth! I'm home!"

"Oh, Harry!" says she, and then her arms were round my neck and her lips were on mine.

If the Brigade of Guards had marched into the hall just

then to command me to the Tower I'd not have heard them. I picked her up bodily, tingling at the feel of her, and without a word spoken carried her into the bedroom, and tumbled her there and then. It was superb, for I was half-drunk with excitement and longing, and when it was over I simply lay there, listening to her prattle a thousand questions, clasping her to me, kissing every inch of her, and answering God knows what. How long we spent there I can't imagine, but it was a long, golden afternoon, and ended only when the maid tapped on the door to say that my father was home again, and demanding to see me.

So we must get dressed, and straighten ourselves, giggling like naughty children, and when Elspeth had herself in order the maid came tapping again to say that my father was growing impatient. Just to show that heroes weren't to be hurried, I caught my darling up again, and in spite of her muffled squeals of protest, mounted her once more, without the formality of undressing. *Then* we went down.

It should have been a splendid evening, with the family welcoming the prodigal Achilles, but it wasn't. My father had aged in two years; his face was redder and his belly bigger, and his hair was quite white at the temples. He was civil enough, damned me for a young rascal, and said he was proud of me: the whole town had been talking over the reports from India, and Ellenborough's eulogies of myself and Sale and Havelock were all over the place. But his jollity soon wore off, and he drank a good deal too much at dinner, and fell into a silence at last. I could see then there was something wrong, although I didn't pay him much heed.

Judy dined with us, and I gathered she was now entirely one of the household, which was bad news. I didn't care for her any better now than I had two years before, after our quarrel, and I made it pretty plain. It seemed rather steep of my father to keep his dolly at home with my wife there, and treat them as equals, and I decided to speak to him about it. But Judy was cool and civil, too, and I gathered she was ready to keep the peace if I did.

Not that I minded her or my father much. I was all over Elspeth, revelling in the dreamy way she listened to my talk—I had forgotten what a ninny she was, but it had its compensations. She sat wide-eyed at my adventures, and I don't suppose anyone else got a word in edgeways all through the meal. I just bathed myself in that simple, dazzling smile of hers and persuaded her of what a wonderful husband she had. And later, when we went to bed, I persuaded her more so.

It was then, though, that the first little hint of something odd in her behaviour crossed my mind. She had dropped off to sleep, and I was lying there exhausted, listening to her breathing, and feeling somehow dissatisfied —which was strange, considering. Then it came to me, this little doubt, and I dismissed it, and then it came back.

I had had plenty of experience with women, as you know, and can judge them in bed as well as anyone, I reckon. And it seemed to me, however hard I pushed the thought away, that Elspeth was not as she had been before I went away. I've often said that she only came to life when she was at grips with a man—well, she had been willing enough in the few hours of my homecoming, I couldn't deny, but there hadn't been any of the rapturous passion on her part that I remembered. These are fine things, and difficult to explain—oh, she was active enough at the time, and content enough afterwards, but she was easier about it all, somehow. If it had been Fetnab or Josette, I wouldn't have noticed, I dare say; it was their work as well as their play. But I had a different emotion about Elspeth, and it told me there was something missing. It was just a shadow, and when I woke next morning I had forgotten it.

If I hadn't, the morning's events would have driven it from my mind. I came down late, and cornered my father in his study before he could slip out to his club. He was sitting with his feet along the couch, preparing for the rigours of the day with a glass of brandy, and looking liverish, but I plunged right in, and told him my thoughts about Judy.

"Things have changed," says I, "and we can't have her seen about the place nowadays." You'll gather that two years among the Afghans had changed my attitude to parental discipline; I wasn't so easy to cow as I had been.

"Oh, aye," says he, "and how have things changed?"

"You'll find," I told him, "that I'm known about the town henceforth. What with India and so on. We'll be more in the public eye now, and folk will talk. It won't do for Elspeth, for one thing."

"Elspeth likes her," says he.

"Does she, though? Well, that's no matter. It ain't what Elspeth likes that counts, but what the town likes. And they won't like us if we keep this . . . this pet pussy in the house."

"My, we're grown very nice." He sneered and took a good pull at his brandy. I could see the flush of temper on his face, and wondered why he hadn't lost it yet. "I didn't know India bred such fine sensibilities," he went on. "Quite the reverse, I'd have thought."

"Oh, look, father, it won't do and you know it. Send her up to Leicestershire if you want, or give her a maison of her own—but she can't stay here."

He looked at me a long while. "By God, maybe I've been wrong about you all along. I know you're a wastrel, but I never thought you had the stuff to be brave—in spite of all the tales from India. Perhaps you have, or perhaps it's just insolence. Anyway, you're on the wrong scent, boy. As I said, Elspeth likes her—and if she don't want her away, then she stays."

"In God's name, what does it matter what Elspeth likes? She'll do as I tell her."

"I doubt it," says he.

"What's that?"

He put down his glass, wiped his lips, and said:

"You won't like it, Harry, but here it is. Who pays the piper calls the tune. And your Elspeth and her damned family have been calling the tune this year past. Hold on, now. Let me finish. You'll have plenty to say, no doubt, but it'll wait."

I could only stare at him, not understanding.

"We're in Queer Street, Harry. I hardly know how, myself, but there it is. I suppose I've been running pretty fast, all my life, and not taking much account of how the money went—what are lawyers for, eh? I took some bad tumbles on the turf, never heeded the expenses of this place, or Leicestershire, didn't stint any way at all—but it was the damned railway shares that really did the trick. Oh, there are fortunes being made out of 'em—the right ones. I picked the wrong ones. A year ago I was a ruined man, up to my neck with the Jews, ready to be sold up. I didn't write to you about it—what was the point? This house ain't mine, nor our place in Leicestershire; it's hers —or it will be, when old Morrison goes. God rot and damn him, it can't be too soon."

He jumped up and walked about, finally stopping before the fireplace.

"*He* met the bill, for his daughter's sake. Oh, you

should have seen it! More canting, head-wagging hypocrisy than I've seen in years in Parliament, even! He had the effrontery to stand in my own hall, by God, and tell me it was a judgement on him for letting his daughter marry beneath herself! Beneath herself, d'ye hear? And I had to listen to him, and keep myself from flooring the old swine! What could I do? I was the poor relation; I still am. He's still paying the bills—through the simpering nitwit you married. He lets her have what she wants, and there you are!"

"But if he's settled an allowance on her. . . ."

"He's settled nothing! She asks him, and he provides. Damned if I would if I was him—but, there, perhaps he thinks it worth while. He seems to dote on her, and I'll say this for the chit, she's not stingy. But she's the pay-mistress, Harry, my son, and you'd best not forget it. You're a kept man, d'you see, so it don't become you, or me, to say who'll come and who'll go. And since your Elspeth is astonishingly liberal-minded—why, Miss Judy can stay, and be damned to you!"

I heard him out, flabbergasted at first, but perhaps because I was a more practical man than the guv'nor, or had fewer notions of gentility, through having an aristocratic mother, I took a different view of the matter. While he splashed more brandy into his glass, I asked:

"How much does he let her have?"

"Eh? I told you, whatever she wants. The old bastard seems to be warm enough for ten. But you can't get your hands on it, I tell you."

"Well, I don't mind," says I. "As long as the money's there, it don't signify who draws the orders."

He gaped at me. "Jesus," he said, in a choked voice, "have you no pride?"

"Probably as much as you have," says I, very cool. "You're still here, ain't you?"

He took on the old familiar apoplectic look, so I slid out before he threw a bottle at me, and went upstairs to think. It wasn't good news, of course, but I didn't doubt I could come to a good understanding with Elspeth, which was all that mattered. The truth was, I didn't have his pride; it wasn't as if I should have to sponge off old Morrison, after all. No doubt I should have been upset at the thought of not inheriting my father's fortune—or what had been his fortune—but when old Morrison ceased to trouble the world I'd have Elspeth's share of the will, which would quite probably make up for all that.

In the meantime, I tackled her on the subject at the first opportunity, and found her all brainless agreement, which was highly satisfactory.

"What I have is yours, my love," says she, with that melting look. "You know you have only to ask me for anything—anything at all."

"Much obliged," says I. "But it might be a little inconvenient, sometimes. I was thinking, if there was a regular payment, say, it would save all the tiresome business for you."

"My father would not allow that, I'm afraid. He has been quite clear, you see."

I saw, all right, and worked away at her, but it was no use. A fool she might be, but she did what Papa told her, and the old miser knew better than to leave a loophole for the Flashman family to crawl in and lighten him. It's a wise man that knows his own son-in-law. So it was going to have to be cash on demand—which was better than no cash at all. And she was ready enough with fifty guineas when I made my first application—it was all cut and dried, with a lawyer in Johnson's Court, who advanced her whatever she asked for, in reason.

However, apart from these sordid matters there was quite enough to engage me in those first days at home. No one at the Horse Guards knew quite what to do with me, so I was round the clubs a good deal, and it was surprising how many people knew me all of a sudden. They would hail me in the Park, or shake hands in the street, and there was a steady stream of callers at home; friends of my father's whom he hadn't seen for years popped up to meet me and greet him; invitations were showered on us; letters of congratulation piled up on the hall table and spilled on to the floor; there were paragraphs in the press about "the first of the returned heroes from Cabool and Jellulabad," and the new comic paper *Punch* had a cartoon in its series of "Pencillings" [25] which showed a heroic figure, something like me, wielding an enormous scimitar like a pantomime bandit, with hordes of blackamoors (they looked no more like Afghans than Eskimos) trying to wrest the Union Jack from me in vain. Underneath there was the caption: "A Flash(ing) Blade," which gives you some idea of the standard of humour in that journal.

However, Elspeth was enchanted with it, and bought a

dozen copies; she was in a whirl of delight at being the centre of so much attention—for the hero's wife gets as many of the garlands as he does, especially if she's a beauty. There was one night at the theatre when the manager insisted on taking us out of our seats to a box, and the whole audience cheered and stamped and clapped. Elspeth was radiant and stood there squeaking and clasping her hands with not the least trace of embarrassment, while I waved, very good-natured, to the mob.

"Oh, Harry!" says she, sparkling. "I'm so happy I could die! Why, you are *famous*, Harry, and I. . . ."

She didn't finish, but I know she was thinking that she was famous too. At that moment I loved her all the more for thinking it.

The parties in that first week were too many to count, and always we were the centre of attraction. They had a military flavour, for thanks to the news from Afghanistan, and China—where we had also been doing well [26]—the army was in fashion more than usual. The more senior officers and the mamas claimed me, which left Elspeth to the young blades. This delighted her, of course, and pleased me—*I* wasn't jealous, and indeed took satisfaction in seeing them clustering like flies round a jampot which they could watch but couldn't taste. She knew a good many of them, and I learned that during my absence in India quite a few of the young sparks had squired her in the Park or ridden in the Row with her—which was natural enough, she being an army wife. But I just kept an eye open, all the same, and cold-shouldered one or two when they came too close—there was one in particular, a young Life Guards captain called Watney, who was often at the house, and was her riding partner twice in the week; he was a tall, curly-lipped exquisite with a lazy eye, who made himself very easy at home until I gave him the about-turn.

"I can attend Mrs Flashman very well, thank'ee," says I.

"None better," says he, "I'm sure. I had only hoped that you might relinquish her for a half-hour or so."

"Not for a minute," says I.

"Oh, come now," says he, patronising me, "this is very selfish. I am sure Mrs Flashman wouldn't agree."

"I'm sure she would."

"Would you care to test it?" says he, with an infuriating smile. I could have boxed his ears, but I kept my temper very well.

"Go to the devil, you mincing pimp," I told him, and left him standing in the hall. I went straight to Elspeth's room, told her what had happened, and cautioned her against seeing Watney again.

"Which one is he?" she asked, admiring her hair in the mirror.

"Fellow with a face like a horse and a haw-how voice."

"There are so many like that," says she. "I can't tell one from the other. Harry, darling, would I look well with ringlets, do you think?"

This pleased me, as you can guess, and I forgot the incident at once. I remember it now, for it was that same day that everything happened all at once. There are days like that; a chapter in your life ends and another one begins, and nothing is the same afterwards.

I was to call at the Horse Guards to see my Uncle Bindley, and I told Elspeth I would not be home until the afternoon, when we were to go out to tea at someone-or-others. But when I got to Horse Guards my uncle bundled me straight into a carriage and bore me off to meet—of all people—the Duke of Wellington. I'd never seen him closer than a distance, and it made me fairly nervous to stand in his ante-room after Bindley had been ushered in to him, and hear their voices murmuring behind the closed door. Then it opened, and the Duke came out; he was white-haired and pretty wrinkled at this time, but that damned hooked nose would have marked him anywhere, and his eyes were like gimlets.

"Ah, this is the young man," says he, shaking hands. For all his years he walked with the spring of a jockey, and was very spruce in his grey coat.

"The town is full of you just now," says he, looking me in the eyes. "It is as it should be. It was a damned good bit of work—about the only good thing in the whole business, by God, whatever Ellenborough and Palmerston may say."

Hudson, thinks I, you should see me now; short of the heavens opening, there was nothing to be added.

The Duke asked me a few sharp questions, about Akbar Khan, and the Afghans generally, and how the troops had behaved on the retreat, which I answered as well as I could. He listened with his head back, and said "Hum," and nodded, and then said briskly:

"It is a thorough shame that it has been so shockingly managed. But it is always the way with these damned politicals; then is no telling them. If I had had someone like McNaghten with me in Spain, Bindley, I'd still be at Lisbon, I dare say. And what is to happen to Mr Flashman? Have you spoken to Hardinge?"

Bindley said they would have to find a regiment for me, and the Duke nodded.

"Yes, he is a regimental man. You were in the 11th Hussars, as I remember? Well, you won't want to go back *there*," and he gave me a shrewd look. "His lordship is no better disposed to Indian officers now than he ever was, the more fool he. I have thought of telling him, more than once, that I'm an Indian officer myself, but he would probably just have given me a setdown. Well, Mr Flashman, I am to take you to Her Majesty this afternoon, so you must be here at one o'clock." And with that he turned back to his room, said a word to Bindley, and shut the door.

Well, you can guess how all this dazzled me; to have the great Duke chatting to me, to learn that I was to be presented to the Queen—all this had me walking on the clouds. I went home in a rosy dream, hugging myself at the way Elspeth would take the news; *this* would make her damned father sit up and take notice, all right, and it would be odd if I couldn't squeeze something out of him in consequence, if I played my cards well.

I hurried upstairs, but she wasn't in her room; I called, and eventually old Oswald appeared and said she had gone out.

"Where away?" says I.

"Well, sir," says he, looking mighty sour, "I don't rightly know."

"With Miss Judy?"

"No, sir," says he, "not with Miss Judy. Miss Judy is downstairs, sir."

There was something damned queer about his manner, but there was nothing more to be got from him, so I went downstairs and found Judy playing with a kitten in the morning room.

"Where's my wife?" says I.

"Out with Captain Watney," says she, cool as you please. "Riding. Here, kitty-kitty. In the Park, I dare say."

For a minute I didn't understand.

"You're wrong," says I. "I sent him packing two hours ago."

"Well, they went riding half an hour ago, so he must

have unpacked." She picked up the kitten and began to stroke it.

"What the devil d'you mean?"

"I mean they've gone out together. What else?"

"Dammit," says I, furious. "I told her not to."

She went on stroking, and looked at me with her crooked little smile.

"She can't have understood you, then," says she. "Or she would not have gone, would she?"

I stood staring at her, feeling a chill suddenly settle on my insides.

"What are you hinting, damn you?" I said.

"Nothing at all. It is you who are imagining. Do you know, I believe you're jealous."

"Jealous, by God! And what have I to be jealous about?"

"You should know best, surely."

I stood looking thunder at her, torn between anger and fear of what she seemed to be implying.

"Now, look'ee here," I said, "I want to know what the blazes you're at. If you have anything to say about my wife, by God, you'd best be careful. . . ."

My father came stumping into the hall at that minute, curse him, and calling for Judy She got up and walked past me, the kitten in her arms. She stopped at the door, gave me a crooked, spiteful smile, and says:

"What were *you* doing in India? Reading? Singing hymns? Or did *you* occasionally go riding in the Park?"

And with that she slammed the door, leaving me shot to bits, with horrible thoughts growing in my mind Suspicion doesn't come gradually; it springs up suddenly and grows with every breath it takes. If you have a foul mind, as I have, you think foul thoughts readier than clean ones, so that even as I told myself that Judy was a lying bitch trying to frighten me with implications, and that Elspeth was incapable of being false—at the same time I had a vision of her rolling naked in a bed with her arms round Watney's neck God, it wasn't possible! Elspeth was an innocent, a completely honest fool, who hadn't even known what "fornication" meant when I first met her. . . . *That* hadn't stopped her bounding into the bushes with me, though, at the first invitation. Oh, but it was still unthinkable! She was my wife, and as amiable and proper as a girl could be; she was utterly different from swine like me, she *had* to be. I couldn't be as wrong in my judgement as that, could I?

I was standing torturing myself with these happy notions, and then common sense came to the rescue. Good God, all she had done was go riding with Watney—why, she hadn't even known who he was when I warned her against him that morning. And she was the most scatter-brained thing in petticoats; besides, she wasn't of the mettle that trollops are made of. Too meek and gentle and submissive by half—she wouldn't have dared. The mere thought of what I'd do would have terrified . . . what would I do? Disown her? Divorce her? Throw her out? By God, I couldn't! I didn't have the means; my father was right!

For a moment I was appalled. If Elspeth *was* making a mistress for Watney, or anyone else, there was nothing I could do about it. I could cut her to ribbons, oh, aye, and what then? Take to the streets? I couldn't stay in the army, or in town even, without means. . . .

Oh, but to the devil with this. It was pure moonshine, aye, and deliberately put into my mind to make me jealous by that brown-headed slut of my father's. This was her making mischief to get her own back for the hammering I'd given her three years ago. That was it. Why, I didn't have the least reason to think ill of Elspeth; everything about her denied Judy's imputations—and, by God, I'd pay that cow out for her lies and sneers. I'd find a way, all right, and God help her when I did.

With my thoughts back in more genial channels, I remembered the news I'd been coming home to tell Elspeth —well, she would have to wait for it until after I'd been to the Palace. Serve her right for going out with Watney, damn him. In the meantime, I spent the next hour looking out my best clothes, arranging my hair, which was grown pretty long and romantic, and cursing Oswald as he helped me with my cravat—I'd have been happier in uniform, but I didn't have a decent one to my name, having spent my time in mufti since I came home. I was so excited that I didn't bother to lunch, but dandied myself up to the nines, and then hurried off to meet His Nose-ship.

There was a brougham at his door when I arrived, and I didn't have to wait two minutes before he came down, all dressed and damning the secretary and valet who were stalking along behind him.

"There probably isn't a damned warming-pan in the

place," he was barking. "And it is necessary that everything should be in the finest order. Find out if Her Majesty takes her own bed-linen when she travels. I imagine she does, but don't for God's sake go inquiring indiscreetly. Ask Arbuthnot; he'll know. You may be sure that something will be amiss, in the end, but it can't be helped. Ah, Flashman," and he ran his eye over me like a drill sergeant. "Come along, then."

There was a little knot of urchins and people to raise a cheer as he came out, and someone shouted: "There's the Flash cove! Hurrah!" by which they meant me. There was a little wait after we got in, because the coachman had some trouble with his reins, and a little crowd gathered while the Duke fretted and swore.

"Dammit, Johnson," growls he, "hurry up or we shall have all London here."

The crowd cheered and we rolled off in the pleasant autumn sunshine, with the guttersnipes running behind whooping and people turning on the pavements to lift their hats as the Great Duke passed by.

"If I knew how news travelled I'd be a wiser man," says he. "Can you imagine it? I'll lay odds they know in Dover by this time that I am taking you to Her Majesty. You've never had any dealings with royalty, I take it?"

"Only in Afghanistan, my lord," says I, and he barked a little short laugh.

"They probably have less ceremonial than we do," he says. "It is a most confounded bore. Let me tell you, sir, never become a field-marshal and commander-in-chief. It is very fine, but it means your sovereign will honour you by coming to stay, and not a bed in the place worth a damn. I have more anxiety over the furnishing of Walmer, Mr Flashman, than I did over the works at Torres Vedras." [27]

"If you are as successful this time as you were then, my lord" says I, buttering him, "you have no cause for alarm."

"Huh!" says he, and gave me a sharp look. But he was silent for a minute or two, and then asked me if I felt nervous.

"There is no need why you should be," says he. "Her Majesty is most gracious, although it is never as easy, of course, as it was with her predecessors. King William was very easy, very kind, and made people entirely at home. It is altogether more formal now, and pretty stiff, but if you stay by me and keep your mouth shut, you'll do."

I ventured to say that I'd felt happier at the prospect of charging into a band of Ghazis than I did at going to the palace, which was rubbish, of course, but I thought was probably the thing to say.

"Damned nonsense," says he, sharply. "You wouldn't rather anything of the sort. But I know that the feeling is much the same, for I've experienced both myself. The important thing is never to show it, as I am never tired of telling young men. Now tell me about these Ghazis, who I understand are the best soldiers the Afghans can show."

He was on my home ground there, and I told him about the Ghazis and Gilzais and Pathans and Douranis, to which he listened very carefully until I realised that we were rolling through the palace gates, and there were the Guards presenting arms, and a flunkey running to hold the door and set the steps, and officers clicking to attention, and a swarm of people about us.

"Come on," says the Duke, and led the way through a small doorway, and I have a hazy recollection of stairs and liveried footmen, and long carpeted corridors, and great chandeliers, and soft-footed officials escorting us—but my chief memory is of the slight, grey-coated figure in front of me, striding along and people getting out of his way.

We brought up outside two great double doors with a flunkey in a wig at either side, and a small fat man in a black tail coat bobbed in front of us, and darted forward muttering to twitch at my collar and smooth my lapel.

"Apologies," he twittered. "A brush here." And he snapped his fingers. A brush appeared and he flicked at my coat, very deftly, and shot a glance in the Duke's direction.

"Take that damned thing away," says the Duke, "and stop fussing. We know how to dress without your assistance."

The little fat man looked reproachful and stood aside, motioning to the flunkeys. They opened the door, and with my heart thumping against my ribs I heard a rich, strong voice announce:

"His Grace the Duke of Wellington. Mr Flashman."

It was a large, magnificently furnished drawing room, with a carpet stretching away between mirrored walls and a huge chandelier overhead. There were a few people at

the other end, two men standing near the fireplace, a girl
sitting on a couch with an older woman standing behind,
and I think another man and a couple of women near by.
We walked forward towards them, the Duke a little in advance, and he stopped short of the couch and bowed.

"Your Majesty," says he, "may I have the honour to
present Mr Flashman."

And only then did I realise who the girl was. We are
accustomed to think of her as the old queen, but she was
just a child then, rather plump, and pretty enough beneath
the neck. Her eyes were large and popped a little, and her
teeth stuck out too much, but she smiled and murmured in
reply—by this time I was bowing my backside off, naturally.

When I straightened up she was looking at me, and
Wellington was reciting briskly about Kabul and
Jallalabad—"distinguished defence," "Mr Flashman's
notable behaviour" are the only phrases that stay in my
mind. When he stopped she inclined her head at him, and
then said to me:

"You are the *first* we have seen of those who served so
bravely in Afghanistan, Mr Flashman. It is *really* a great
joy to see you returned safe and well. We have heard the
most *glowing* reports of your gallantry, and it is most *gratifying* to be able to express our thanks and admiration for
such *brave* and loyal service."

Well, she couldn't have said fairer than that, I suppose,
even if she did recite it like a parrot. I just made a rumbling sound in my throat and ducked my head again. She
had a thin, oddly-accented voice, and came down heavy
on her words every now and then, nodding as she did so.

"Are you *entirely* recovered from your wounds?" she
asked.

"Very well, thank'ee, your majesty," says I.

"You are exceedingly brown," says one of the men, and
the heavy German accent startled me. I'd noticed him out
of the tail of my eye, leaning against the mantel, with one
leg crossed over the other. So this is Prince Albert, I
thought; what hellish-looking whiskers.

"You must be as brown as an Aff-ghan," says he, and
they laughed politely.

I told him I had passed for one, and he opened his eyes
and said did I speak the language, and would I say something in it. So without thinking I said the first words that
came into my head: "Hamare ghali ana, achha din,"

which is what the harlots chant at passers-by, and means "Good day, come into our street." He seemed very interested, but the man beside him stiffened and stared hard at me.

"What does it *mean*, Mr Flashman?" says the Queen.

"It is a Hindu greeting, marm," says the Duke, and my guts turned over as I recalled that he had served in India.

"Why, of course," says she, "we are quite an *Indian* gathering, with Mr Macaulay here." The name meant nothing to me then; he was looking at me damned hard, though, with his pretty little mouth set hard. I later learned that he had spent several years in government out there, so my fat-headed remark had not been lost on him, either.

"Mr Macaulay has been reading us his new poems," [28] says the Queen. "They are *quite* stirring and fine. I think his Horatius must have been your model, Mr Flashman, for you know he defied great odds in defence of Rome. It is a *splendid* ballad, and very inspiring. Do you know the story, Duke?"

He said he did, which put him one up on me, and added that he didn't believe it, at which she cried out and demanded to know why.

"Three men can't stop an army, marm," says he. "Livy was no soldier, or he would hardly have suggested they could."

"Oh, come now," says Mr Macaulay. "They were on a narrow bridge, and could not be outnumbered."

"You see, Duke?" says the Queen. "How *could* they be overcome?"

"Bows and arrows, marm," says he. "Slings. Shoot 'em down. That's what I'd have done."

At this she said that the Tuscans were more chivalrous than he was, and he agreed that very likely they were.

"Which is perhaps why there are no Tuscan empires today, but an extensive British one," says the Prince quietly. And then he leaned forward and murmured something to the Queen, and she nodded wisely, and stood up —she was very small—and signed to me to come forward in front of her. I went, wondering, and the Duke came to my elbow, and the Prince watched me with his head on one side. The lady who had been behind the couch came forward, and handed something to the Queen, and she looked up at me, from not a foot away.

"Our brave soldiers in Afghanistan are to have *four*

medals from the Governor-General," she said. "You will
wear them in course of time, but there is also a medal
from their *Queen,* and it is fitting that you should wear it
first of all."

She pinned it on my coat, and she had to reach up to
do it, she was so small. Then she smiled at me, and I felt
so overcome I didn't know what to say. Seeing this, she
went all soulful about the eyes.

"You are a very gallant gentleman," says she. "God
bless you."

Oh, lor', I thought, if only you knew, you romantic little
woman, thinking I'm a modern Horatius. (I made a point
of studying Macaulay's 'Lays' later, and she wasn't too far
off, really; only the chap I resembled was False Sextus, a
man after my own heart).

However, I had to say something, so I mumbled about
her majesty's service.

"England's service," said she, looking intense.

"The same thing, ma'am," says I, flown with inspiration,
and she cast her eyes down wistfully. The Duke gave what
sounded like a little groan.

There was a pause, and then she asked if I was married.
I told her I was, but that I and my wife had been parted
for the past two years.

"What a cruel separation," says she, as one might say
"What delicious strawberry jam." But she was sure, she
said, that our reunion must be all the sweeter for that
parting.

"I know what it means to be a *devoted* wife, with the
dearest of husbands," she went on, glancing at Albert, and
he looked fond and noble. God, I thought, what a honeymoon that must have been.

Then the Duke chimed in, making his farewells, and I
realised that this was my cue. We both bowed, and backed
away, and she sat looking dumpy on the couch, and then
we were in the corridor again, and the Duke was striding
off through the hovering attendants.

"Well," says he, "you've got a medal no one else will
ever have. Only a few of 'em struck, you see, and then
Ellenborough announced that he was giving four of his
own, which did not please her majesty at all. So her medal
is to be stopped." [29]

He was right as it turned out; no one else ever received
the medal, with its pink and green ribbon (I suspect Albert chose the colours), and I wear it on ceremonial days

along with my Victoria Cross, my American Medal of
Honour (for which the republic graciously pays me ten
dollars a month), my San Serafino Order of Purity and
Truth (richly deserved), and all the other assorted tinware
which serves to disguise a cowardly scoundrel as a heroic
veteran.

We passed through the covey of saluting Guardsmen,
bowing officials, and rigid flunkeys to our coach, but there
was no getting through the gates at first for the crowd
which had collected and was cheering its head off.

"Good old Flashy! Hurrah for Flash Harry! Hip! hip!
hooray!"

They clamoured at the railings, waving and throwing up
their hats, jostling the sentries, surging in a great press
round the gateway, until at last the gates were pushed
open and the brougham moved slowly through the struggling mass, all the faces grinning and shouting and the
handkerchiefs waving.

"Take off your hat, man," snaps the Duke, so I did, and
they roared again, pressing forward against the sides of
the coach, reaching in to clasp my hand, beating on the
panels, and making a tremendous racket.

"He's got a medal!" roars someone. "God save the
Queen!"

At that they woke the echoes, and I thought the coach
must overturn. I was laughing and waving to them, but
what to you suppose I was thinking? This was real glory!
Here was I, the hero of the Afghan war, with the Queen's
medal on my coat, the world's greatest soldier at my side,
and the people of the world's greatest city cheering me to
the echo—me! while the Duke sat poker-faced snapping:
"Johnson, can't you get us out of this damned mess?"

What was I thinking? About the chance that had sent
me to India? About Elphy Bey? About the horror of the
passes on the retreat, or the escape at Mogala when Iqbal
died? Of the nightmare of Piper's Fort or that dreadful
dwarf in the snake-pit? About Sekundar Burnes? Or Bernier? Or the women—Josette, Narreeman, Fetnab and the
rest? About Elspeth? About the Queen?

None of these things. Strange, but as the coach won
clear and we rattled off down the Mall with the cheers
dying behind us. I could hear Arnold's voice saying,
"There *is* good in you, Flashman," and I could imagine
how he would have supposed himself vindicated at this
moment, and preach on "Courage" in chapel, and pretend

to rejoice in the redeemed prodigal—but all the time he would know in his hypocrite heart that I was a rotter still.[30] But neither he nor anyone else would have dared to say so. This myth called bravery, which is half-panic, half-lunacy (in my case, *all* panic), pays for all; in England you *can't* be a hero *and* bad. There's practically a law against it.

Wellington was muttering sharply about the growing insolence of the mob, but he left off to tell me he would set me down at the Horse Guards. When we arrived and I was getting out and thanking him for his kindness, he looks sharply at me, and says:

"I wish you every good fortune, Flashman. You should go far. I don't imagine you're a second Marlborough, mind, but you appear to be brave and you're certainly damned lucky. With the first quality you may easily gain command of an army or two, and lead 'em both to ruin, but with your luck you'll probably lead 'em back again. You have made a good beginning, at all events, and received today the highest honour you can hope for, which is your monarch's mark of favour. Goodbye to you."

We shook hands, and he drove off. I never spoke to him again. Years later, though, I told the American general, Robert Lee, of the incident, and he said Wellington was right—I *had* received the highest honour any soldier could hope for. But it wasn't the medal; for Lee's money it was Wellington's hand.

Neither, I may point out, had any intrinsic value.

I was the object of general admiration at the Horse Guards, of course, and at the club, and finally I took myself home in excellent fettle. It had been raining cats and dogs, but had stopped, and the sun was shining as I ran up the steps. Oswald informed me that Elspeth was above stairs; oho! thinks I, wait till she hears where I've been and who I've seen. She'll be *rather* more attentive to her lord and master now, perhaps, and less to sprigs of Guardees; I was smiling as I went upstairs, for the events of the afternoon had made my earlier jealousy seem silly, and simply the work of the little bitch Judy.

I walked into the bedroom keeping my left hand over the medal, to surprise her. She was sitting before her glass, as usual, with her maid dressing her hair.

"Harry!" she cries out, "where *have* you been? Have you forgot we are to take tea with Lady Chalmers at four-thirty?"

"The devil with Lady Chalmers, and all Chalmerses," says I. "Let 'em wait."

"Oh, how can you say so?" she laughed at me in the mirror. "But *where* have you been, looking so splendid?"

"Oh, visiting friends, you know. Young couple, Bert and Vicky. You wouldn't know 'em."

"Bert and Vicky!" If Elspeth had developed a fault in my long absence, it was that she had become a complete snob—not uncommon among people of her class. "Whoever are they?"

I stood behind her, looking at her reflection, and exposed the medal. I saw her eyes light on it, and widen, and then she swung round.

"Harry! What . . .?"

"I've been to the palace. With the Duke of Wellington. I had this from the Queen—after we had chatted a little, you know, about poetry and . . ."

"The Queen!" she squeals. "The Duke! The palace!"

And she leaped up, clapping her hands, throwing her arms round my neck, while her maid clucked and fussed and I, laughing, swung her round and kissed her. There was no shutting her up, of course; she rained questions on me, her eyes shining, demanding to know who was there, and what they said, and what the Queen wore, and how the Queen spoke to me, and what I replied, and every mortal thing. Finally I pushed her into a chair, sent the maid packing, and sat down on the bed, reciting the whole thing from start to finish.

Elspeth sat, round-eyed and lovely, listening breathlessly, and squealing with excitement every now and then. When I told her the Queen had asked about her, she gasped and turned to look at herself in the mirror, I imagine to see if there was a smut on her nose. Then she demanded that I go through it all again, and I did, but not before I had stripped off her gown and pulled her on top of me on the bed, so that between gasps and sighs the breath-taking tale was re-told. I lost track of it several times, I admit.

Even then she was still marvelling at it all, until I pointed out that it was after four o'clock, and what would Lady Chalmers say? She giggled, and said we had better go, and chattered incessantly while she dressed and I lazily put myself in order.

"Oh, it is the most wonderful thing!" she kept saying. "The Queen! The Duke! Oh, Harry!"

"Aye," says I, "and where were you, eh? Sparking in the Row all afternoon with one of your admirers."

"Oh, he is the greatest bore," says she laughing. "Nothing to talk of but his horses. We spent the *entire* afternoon riding in the Park, and he spoke of nothing else for two *hours* on end!"

"Did he, begad," says I. "Why, you must have been soaked."

She was in a cupboard by now, among her dresses, and didn't hear, and idly I reached out, not thinking, and touched the bottle-green riding coat that lay across the end of the bed. I felt it, and my heart suddenly turned to stone. The coat was bone-dry. I twisted round to look at the boots standing by a chair; they shone glossy, with not a mark or a splash on them.

I sat, feeling sick, listening to my heart thumping, while she chattered away. It had rained steadily from the time I had left Wellington at the Horse Guards until I had left the club more than an hour later and come home. She could not have been riding in the Park in that downpour. Well, where the devil had she and Watney been, then, and what . . .?

I felt rage mounting inside me, rage and spite, but I held myself in, telling myself I might be wrong. She was patting her face with a rabbit's foot before the glass, never minding me, so I said, very easy like:

"Whereabouts did you go for your ride?"

"Oh, in the Park, as I said. Nowhere at all in particular."

Now that's a lie for certain, thinks I, and yet I couldn't believe it. She looked so damned innocent and open, so feather-headed and full of nonsense as she went on and on about my wonderful, wonderful hour at the palace; why, only ten minutes ago she had been coupling with me on the bed, letting me . . . aye, *letting* me. Suddenly the ugly thought of the first night home came rushing back to me —how I had fancied she was less ardent than I remembered her. Perhaps I had been right; perhaps she had been less passionate. Well she might be, if in my absence she had found some jockey who was more to her fancy over the jumps than I was. By God, if that were true I would . . .

I sat there shaking, my head turned away so that she would not see me in the mirror. Had that slut Judy been hinting at the truth, then? Was Watney cuckolding me—

and heaven knew who else besides him? I was fairly boiling with shame and anger at the thought. But it couldn't be true! No, not Elspeth. And yet there was Judy's sneer, and those boots winking their wickedness at me—they hadn't been near the Park this afternoon, by God!

While the maid came back and attended to Elspeth's hair again, and I tried to close my ears to the shrill feminine trilling of her talk, I tried to take hold of myself. Maybe I was wrong—oh, God, I hoped so. It wasn't just that strange yearning that I had about Elspeth, it was my . . . well, my honour, if you like. Oh, I didn't give a damn about what the world calls honour, but the thought of another man, or men, frollicking in the hay with *my* wife, who should have been unable to imagine a more masterful or heroic lover than the great Flashman—the hero whose name was on everyone's lips, God help us—the thought of that! . . .

Pride is a hellish thing; without it there isn't any jealousy or ambition. And I was proud of the figure I cut—in bed and in barracks. And here was I, the lion of the hour, medal and all, the Duke's handshake and the Queen's regard still fresh—and I was gnawing my innards out about a gold-headed filly without a brain to her name. And I must bite my lip and not say a word, for fear of the row there would be if I let slip a breath of my suspicions—right or wrong, the fat would be in the fire, and I couldn't afford that.

"Well, how do I look?" says she, coming to stand in front of me in her gown and bonnet. "Why, Harry, you have gone quite pale! I know, it is the excitement of this day! My poor dear!" And she tilted up my head and kissed me. No, I couldn't believe it, looking into those baby-blue eyes. Aye, and what about those baby-black boots?

"We shall go out to Lady Chalmers's," said she, "and she will be quite over the moon when she hears about this. I expect there will be quite a company there, too. I shall be so proud, Harry—so proud! Now, let me straighten your cravat; bring a brush, Susan—what an excellent coat it is. You must always go to that tailor—which is he again? There now; oh, Harry, how handsome you look! See yourself in the glass!"

I looked, and seeing myself so damned dashing, and her radiant and fair beside me, I fought down the wretchedness and rage. No, it couldn't be true. . . .

"Susan, you have not put away my coat, silly girl. Take it at once, before it creases."

By God, though, I knew it was. Or I thought I knew. To the devil with the consequences, no little ninny in petticoats was going to do this to me.

"Elspeth," says I, turning.

"Hang it carefully, now, when you've brushed it. There. Yes, my love?"

"Elspeth. . . ."

"Oh, Harry, you look so strong and fierce, on my word. I don't think I shall feel easy in my mind when I see all these fancy London ladies making eyes at you." And she pouted very pretty and touched her finger on my lips.

"Elspeth, I—"

"Oh, I had nearly forgot—you had better take some money with you. Susan, bring me my purse. In case of any need that may arise, you know. Twenty guineas, my love."

"Much obliged," says I.

What the devil, you have to make do as best you can; if the tide's there, swim with it and catch on to whatever offers. You only go by once.

"Will twenty be sufficient, do you think?"

"Better make it forty."

(*At this point the first packet of the Flashman Papers ends abruptly*).

Notes

1. Lord Brougham's speech in May, 1839, "lashed the Queen . . . with unsparing severity" (Greville) and caused great controversy.

2. Lady Flora Hastings, Maid of Honour to the Duchess of Kent, was believed to be pregnant, until medical examination proved that she was not. She won great popular sympathy, but the young Queen, who had been bitterly hostile towards her, suffered dramatically in public esteem.

3. Captain John Reynolds, a particular butt of Cardigan's, was the centre of the notorious Black Bottle affair, in which his resignation was demanded because he was believed to have ordered a bottle of porter in the mess on guest night.

4. Cardigan had, in fact, served in India, when he went out to take command of the 11th at Cawnpore in 1837, but had spent only a few weeks with the regiment.

5. Cardigan was a favourite target of the newspapers, and especially of the *Morning Chronicle* (not the *Post*, as Flashman says). The quarrel referred to here is probably the one in which Cardigan, in response to a press attack, threatened to assault the editor. For details of this and other incidents, and of Lord Cardigan's military career, see Cecil Woodham-Smith's *The Reason Why*.

6. Choice of weapons. In fact this did not necessarily rest with the injured party, but was normally settled by mutual agreement.

7. Mr. Attwood, M.P., presented the Chartists' first petition for political reform to the Commons in July 1839. In that year there were outbreaks of Chartist violence; on November 24 people were killed at Newport.

8. Mr. Abercrombie's use of the word "chief" is inexplicable, since Sir Colin Campbell's command of the 93rd came much later. Of course, Abercrombie may have served with him in Spain.

9. Military service with the East India Company's regiments was considered socially inferior to service in the army proper, and Flashman must have been conscious of this, which possibly accounts for his casual reference to it. The Company at this time drew its artillery, engineer, and infantry officers from the Addiscombe training establishment; cavalry officers, however, could be appointed direct by the Company's Directors. Cardigan, who seems to have had a liking for Flashman (his judgement of men, when he condescended to use it, was deplorable) may well have had influence with the Board.

10. The Company did not believe in maintaining houses for transients and visitors; they were expected to find hospitality with British residents or pay their own lodgings.

11. Avitabile. Flashman's description of this extraordinary soldier of fortune is accurate; the Italian was noted as a stern, just administrator and intrepid soldier.

12. Cotton was the ringleader of the great Rugby School mutiny of 1797, in which the door of the headmaster, Dr Ingles, was blown in with gunpowder.

13. Poor army swords. The sabres issued to British cavalry at this time were notorious for their greasy brass hilts, which turned in the hand.

14. Flashman's account of Burnes's murder clears up a point which has troubled historians. Previous versions suggest that the Burnes brothers left the Residency in

disguise, accompanied by a mysterious third party who has been described as a Kashmiri Musselman. It has been alleged that this third man actually denounced them to the Ghazis. But Flashman could hardly have betrayed them without considerable risk to himself, so his account is probably the true one.

15. The actual names of these two Afghans remain a mystery. Other accounts call them Muhammed Sadeq and Surwar Khan, but Lady Sale seems to suggest that one of them was Sultan Jan.

16. Lieutenant-General Colin Mackenzie has left one of the most vivid accounts of the First Afghan War in *Storms and Sunshine of a Soldier's Life* (1884).

17. Flashman, like many other European writers, uses the word "Ghazi" as though it referred to a tribe, although he certainly knew better. In Arabic "ghazi" is literally a conqueror, but may be accurately translated as hero or champion. Europeans usually render it as "fanatic", in which connection it is interesting to note the parallel between the Moslem Ghazis and the Christian medieval ideal of knighthood. The Ghazi sect were dedicated to the militant expansion of Islam.

18. Flashman's account of the retreat tallies substantially with those of such contemporaries as Mackenzie, Lady Sale, and Lieutenant Eyre. This is also true of his version of affairs in Afghanistan generally. His description of McNaghten's murder, for example, is the fullest and most personal to survive. There are omissions and discrepancies here and there—he does not mention "Gentleman Jim" Skinner's part in the liaison work with Akbar Khan, for instance—but on the whole he can be regarded as highly reliable within his self-centred limits. Readers seeking wider and more authoritative accounts are recommended to the standard works, which include Kaye's *History of the War in Afghanistan*, vol. ii, Fortescue's *History of the British Army*, vol. xii, and Patrick Macrory's admirably clear account, *Signal Catastrophe*.

19. The "united front" of officers took place at Jugdulluk on January 11, 1842.

20. In fact some prisoners were taken by the Afghans at Gandamack, including Captain Souter of the 44th Regiment, one of two men who wrapped the battalion colours round their bodies (the other man was killed). The picture to which Flashman refers is by W. B. Wollen, R.A., hung at the Royal Academy in 1898.

21. Flashman may be excused an overstatement here. Possibly Sergeant Hudson was a fine swordsman, but this was not usual in the British cavalry; Fortescue in his passage on the Charge of the Heavy Brigade at Balaclava refers to the troopers' habit of using their sabres as bludgeons. It was not uncommon for a man to use his saber-hilt as a knuckle-duster instead of cutting or thrusting.

22. Major Henry Havelock. Later famous as the hero of Lucknow, the "stern Cromwellian soldier" became one of the great figures of the Indian Empire.

23. Sale was indeed hailed as a celebrity, but returned to India and was killed at Mudki in 1845, fighting the Sikhs. Shelton's adventurous career ended when he fell from his horse on parade at Dublin and was killed. Lawrence and Mackenzie both achieved general rank.

24. Flashman saw Ellenborough at his worst. Arrogant, theatrical, and given to flights of rhetoric, the Governor-General went to extravagant lengths to honour the "heroes of Afghanistan", and was widely ridiculed. But in the main he was an able and energetic administrator.

25. *Punch* began publication in 1841; the "Pencillings" were its first full-page cartoons.

26. The "Opium War" in China had ended with a treaty whereby Hong Kong was ceded to Britain.

27. The Duke's reference to the Queen's impending visit to Walmer Castle fixes the date of Flashman's appear-

ance at Buckingham Palace very closely. Wellington wrote to Sir Robert Peel on October 26, 1842, assuring him that Walmer was at the Queen's disposal, and she visited it in the following month.

28. Macaulay's *Lays of Ancient Rome* was first published on October 28, 1842.

29. The Queen's Medal. That Her Majesty was piqued at Lord Ellenborough's decision to issue medals is evident from her letter to Peel on November 29, 1842.

30. Dr Thomas Arnold, father of Matthew Arnold and headmaster of Rugby School, had died on June 12, 1842, aged 47.

Glossary

badmash a scoundrel
feringhee European, possibly a corruption of "Frankish" or "English"
Ghazi a fanatic
havildar sergeant
hubshi negro (literally "woolly-head")
huzoor lord, master, in the sense of "sir" (Pushtu equivalent of "sahib")
idderao come here (imp.)
jao go, get away (imp.)
jawan soldier
jezzail long rifle of the Afghans
juldi quickly, hurry up
khabadar be careful (imp.)
maidan plain, exercise ground
munshi teacher, usually of language
puggarree turban cloth
rissaldar native officer commanding cavalry troop
sangar small stone breastwork like grouse butt
shabash bravo
sowar trooper

HANDY FILES AND CASES FOR STORING MAGAZINES, CASSETTES, & 8-TRACK CARTRIDGES

CASSETTE STORAGE CASES

Decorative cases, custom-made of heavy bookbinder's board, bound in Kid-Grain Leatherette, a gold-embossed design. Individual storage slots slightly tilted back to prevent handling spillage. Choice of: Black, brown, green.

#JC-30—30 unit size (13½x5½x6½") $11.95 ea.
3 for $33.00
#JC-60—60 unit size (13½x5½x12⅝") $16.95 ea.
3 for $48.00

MAGAZINE VOLUME FILES

Keep your favorite magazines in mint condition. Heavy bookbinder's board is covered with scuff-resistant Kivar. Specify the title of the magazine and we'll send the right size case. If the title is well-known it will appear on the spine in gold letters. For society journals, a brass-rimmed window is attached and gold foil included—you type the title.

#J-MV—Magazine Volume Files $4.95 ea.
3 for $14.00
6 for $24.00

8-TRACK CARTRIDGE STORAGE CASE

This attractive unit measures 13¾ inches high, 6½ inches deep, 4½ inches wide, has individual storage slots for 12 cartridges and is of the same sturdy construction and decorative appearance as the Cassette Case.

#J-8T12—4½" wide (holds 12 cartridges)
$8.50 ea.
3 for $23.50
#J-8T24—8½" wide (holds 24 cartridges)
$10.95 ea.
3 for $28.00
#J-8T36—12¾" wide (holds 36 cartridges)
$14.25 ea.
3 for $37.00